BEHIND FRENEMY LINES

BEHIND FRENEMY LINES

LAUREN PRICE

INK ROAD

First published in the UK in 2022 by Ink Road

INK ROAD is an imprint and trademark of
Black & White Publishing Ltd
Nautical House, 104 Commercial Street, Edinburgh EH6 6NF

A division of Bonnier Books UK
4th Floor, Victoria House, Bloomsbury Square, London, WC1B 4DA
Owned by Bonnier Books
Sveavägen 56, Stockholm, Sweden

Copyright © Lauren Price 2022

All rights reserved.
No part of this publication may be reproduced,
stored or transmitted in any form by any means, electronic,
mechanical, photocopying or otherwise, without the
prior written permission of the publisher.

The right of Lauren Price to be identified as Author of this
work has been asserted by her in accordance with the
Copyright, Designs and Patents Act, 1988.

This is a work of fiction. Names, places, events and
incidents are either the products of the author's
imagination or used fictitiously. Any resemblance to
actual persons, living or dead, or actual
events is purely coincidental.

A CIP catalogue record for this book is available from the British Library.

ISBN: 978 1 78530 378 4

1 3 5 7 9 10 8 6 4 2

Typeset by Iolaire Typesetting, Newtonmore
Printed and bound in Great Britain by Clays Ltd, Elcograf S.p.A.

www.blackandwhitepublishing.com

To my mum – the world's greatest teacher. Thank you for introducing me to the joy of storytelling, and for being an endless source of inspiration and encouragement.

1

The Answer

The ring of the intercom is almost inaudible amid the noise.

"Eric Monroe, please make your way to the principal's office immediately."

Students swarm through the school hallway, buzzing like flies, and the air is thick with the stench of perfume and puberty. The first day back at school after spring break is always exhausting: freshman kids with new class schedules, gossip about tan lines and vacation romances, and the hyperbolic reunions between people who barely remember each other outside of these walls. I pause mid-step at the mention of my name and, almost instantly, a freshman boy stumbles into my back, eager for his next class.

Eric Monroe?

A sigh of disbelief hisses through my teeth. I've had three and a half years at this school and the secretary still struggles with that pivotal extra *a*.

Casting a parting glance towards my locker, I turn abruptly on my heel and battle back through the clusters of students towards the school entrance.

I'm pretty certain that everybody and their hamster has heard about the arrival of our new school principal. Lindale is a small town, and the loss of a large presence like Mr. Boston quickly made headlines in the local newsletter. It hasn't fully dawned on me that I won't be seeing my favorite, four-chinned principal stalking the hallways anymore. According to our secretary's tale-bearing Twitter, Boston took a vacation to France this spring and decided not to come back. I can't say I blame the guy. If I had the option between Lindale High and Lyon, I'd choose to sit in the sunshine and drink wine too.

His gain is our loss. Supposedly, Principal Blythe is a stickler for discipline and obedience. Anya Dombrowski told me that Blythe's previous school boasted an impeccable behavioral record ... alongside iron-barred windows. I wonder what I could possibly have done to get on her radar within the first hour of the new semester. I'm outspoken and cheeky in class sometimes, but never enough to land me in any real trouble.

People greet me on the way to her office, but my apprehension doesn't allow me to stop and chat. The school reception is small, boxy, and unsurprisingly vacant—aside from the secretary sitting behind a pale birch desk. Brian offers me a thumbs up as he spots me.

"Come on Brian, I'm Erika. *Erika*," I enunciate. "You've got to stop missing the a—my whole identity is at stake here."

"Oops, sorry kid," Brian says, stretching. Our school secretary is in his mid-twenties, wearing an un-ironed polo shirt and a goofy grin. Brian is somewhat of a legend for being so down to earth and friendly, and he tweets under his desk more than any student.

"No worries," I say, rolling my eyes. "Principal wants to see me?"

"Sure does. Go straight in, Eric my man."

"Thanks *Brianne*."

The large wooden door looms on my right, and I wonder if it was intended to be this intimidating. My knock is tentative. The principal's office is daunting in itself, but especially so when you have no idea why you've been summoned. A sharp female voice beckons me to enter and, after a brief hesitation, I obey.

Immediately across from me, Mrs. Blythe is standing behind an impressive mahogany desk with a binder outspread on her arm. She registers my presence only momentarily—with a flash of her gray eyes and a flick of her free hand—before she turns back to the document.

"Take a seat, take a seat," she ushers. "I'll be with you in a second."

I sink into one of the empty chairs in front of me, dropping my bag to the floor with a thud. The principal's occupation with the binder in her arm provides a perfect opportunity for snooping. This office, once plush with potted ferns and threadbare velvet cushions, is now bare aside from a ceramic espresso mug and some framed diplomas. The scattered papers and photo frames that used to clutter the desk are nowhere to be seen, and the only personal touch is a mouse mat featuring the picture of a tabby cat.

"Miss Monroe," Principal Blythe greets, closing the ring binder with a snap. Her hair is auburn and hangs in loose waves around her shoulders, and her smile is thin. She appears to be in her early fifties, perhaps a little older than our previous principal. "My name is Mrs. Blythe. It's a pleasure to meet one of our liveliest seniors."

"Ah, thank you. It's nice to meet you too."

"I trust you're having a nice first day back?"

"So far I am, thank you." I have only been in school for an hour, after all.

"I'm happy to hear it." She slides into the intimidating leather chair positioned across from me, depositing her binder in the top drawer of the desk. It shuts with the click of a lock.

I cut to the chase. "You wanted to see me?"

"Yes, I did." She settles back in the chair with her shoulders straight and her chin high; the effortlessly confident posture of someone with natural—and conferred—authority. "Tell me, Erika, what are your hopes and plans when you finish your senior year?"

My goals can be summed up in one word.

"Stanford."

Blythe purses her lips. I recognize from the expression that my answer hasn't surprised her, in fact, she may even have anticipated it. I hurriedly expand my description.

"I want to study chemistry and run track. Stanford has a great reputation for both."

"Chemistry?"

I nod. "I really love the sciences. Chemistry is my best subject."

"Good," she compliments. "It's very reassuring to know what you want and be willing to work for it. What do your parents think about your ambitions?"

"They support me completely."

"That's fantastic news, Erika." Her hands clasp together

on the desk in that patronizing way adults have when they address you about something important. "So, I take it that you and your parents have discussed how to fund your tuition and living costs? You must be aware how expensive it is to attend a school as prestigious as Stanford."

I squirm uncomfortably in my hard-backed seat. It is unclear whether the concern coloring Blythe's tone is authentic, or if she's aware that she's touching a nerve.

It was only a matter of days ago that I walked into the kitchen to see my dad, hunched over his laptop and scrutinizing a spreadsheet of my estimated school costs. His fist was in his mouth, and his expression was grave. Although the rows of black numbers were only pixels on a screen, it dawned on me how tangible they could really become. Physical enough to form a roadblock. A wall.

"Um, well..."

Although my parents have never addressed me with the financial realities of Stanford, I understand my situation only too well. My parents can only support me so much. If I get a scholarship, I can move to California. Study at my dream college, run track, get a weekend job to help with living costs and meet a host of intelligent and diverse people.

If not ... Well, I'm trying not to contemplate that possibility.

I'm conscious that Blythe is waiting for my response. My fingers are laced in the material of my skirt, tugging anxiously at the hem. Instead of describing the full extent of my monetary concerns, I settle for a short and considerably sweeter summary.

"I'm hoping to get a scholarship or grant to help with the expenses."

"I see."

My hands move to grip my knees, squeezing in a way that should be comforting but fails to be. Deep down, I know that I am not an outstanding candidate for either academic or sport scholarships. My grades are good, but not great. I'm fast, but not the fastest. I just have to hope that someone can recognize my potential and how hard I'm willing to work.

"Erika, I've invited you to the office today because I have an opportunity for you," Principal Blythe says. Her clasped hands fall apart, and her palms face upwards. "A way that can help you financially secure a position at Stanford this fall."

"Secure?"

Did I hear her correctly?

"I know," she says with a coy smile. "I thought you might like the sound of that."

"Like?" I can hear the disbelief in my tone. My elbows are now pressing into the tops of my knees as I lean forward excitedly. "What the—that's amazing."

"It's great that you're so enthusiastic."

"What's the opportunity?"

"I'm happy you ask." Settling back into the leather chair, she picks up the fountain pen on the desk and begins to twist it between her manicured fingers. "You would be working with me directly to complete a private assignment. In return, I can help you obtain a partial scholarship at Stanford. It would make that transition to college so much easier for both you and your family."

One word stands out.

"Private?" My voice sounds noticeably lower. Skepticism has bled through my rosy visions of student life. This doesn't sound like an official route.

"Yes." She lowers the pen. Her words are slow and carefully selected. "We both have something to gain from each other, Erika. I'm suggesting a deal of sorts."

At this point, my enthusiasm has dissipated entirely. Rather, my mind is clouded by caution and confusion. This woman doesn't know me—what could she possibly think I can offer her? I'm not the smartest student in school. I'm not the strongest public speaker. I'm not captain of a sports team, or a cheerleader or a technology genius. Why me?

"What is it?" I ask finally.

Placing the pen back down on the desk as a demonstration of her undivided attention, Principal Blythe studies my face with intensity. Her lips purse for a moment's hesitation before she speaks.

"I want you to help me expel a student, Erika."

My remaining hope plummets like a stone in my chest.

"You want me to snitch." A fact, not a question.

"That's not the phrasing I'd prefer, but put bluntly, yes."

"One student?"

"Just one."

"You're bribing me," I say quietly. "That's why you've chosen me. You know I need money to get into Stanford, and you can offer me that—or so you say. How did you know?"

I'm not entirely sure where my confidence is coming from, but when I look up at Principal Blythe, it's through narrowed eyes. I realize that the emotion stirring within my chest is anger: anger at the abuse of power, the manipulation, and the hope I was made to feel. Largely, I'm mad that a part of me is tempted to take her up on this shady deal.

"Your careers interview at the end of Junior Year is on

record. You mentioned that you were hoping for financial assistance from your college."

"Right."

"You're not a target, Erika, but this is a transaction." Her eyes are softened with something akin to pity. "I picked you because I can genuinely offer you something in return. Please don't question that."

"Which student do you want to expel?"

"Chase Thatcher. He's a senior, you may know him already."

"Know of him," I correct with a frown. Chase and I exist in similar social circles, and although I've never met the guy, his reputation makes it clear that he has no reason to challenge the school system. It exists purely to his advantage. He's popular, has a number of people drooling over him and miles of confidence. Why would he rebel?

As if reading my mind, Mrs. Blythe releases an exasperated sigh. "Chase is suspected of vandalism, violence, and drug possession. All on school grounds. Add this to an unsatisfactory attendance record this year and his aggressive reactions to authority, and the school board believe that we have a problem. *I* believe that we have a problem."

Well, that's a plot twist.

"What makes you think he won't be different this semester?" I challenge. For some reason, I feel tugged towards this guy's defense. He doesn't seem like the type of student to be expelled, let alone targeted for this exact reason. "Why are you pouncing on him?"

"Your optimism is admirable, Erika," Blythe says with a light laugh, clasping her hands together again. "His grades are below average, he's insolent, and he has attracted attention from local authorities. Now, listen."

She leans forwards across the desk with a patient, thin smile. "You don't know me yet, and I can't expect you to understand my methods, so let me be clear. I am not keen on giving hundredth chances. My primary concern is the school's reputation, and he is a scar upon it."

I resist the urge to surrender under the weight of her intense gaze, but with difficulty. I have to challenge her again. At least one more time.

"I have a question."

"Go ahead."

"Have you even tried to get through to him?" I ask quietly. "You've been here for five minutes and already you want him expelled. That seems a little extreme—I mean, I thought schools use expulsion as a last resort. Isn't *that* a scar on the school's reputation?"

"Chase has made absolutely no indication to any of the cops, or teachers, he's spoken to that he's improving." Her head cocks to the side slightly, but she doesn't sound frustrated. "This is not a decision I take lightly, Erika. We need evidence, not opinions. Proof, not possibility. That's where you come in."

"Right." I sigh. My fingers are clenched around the lip of the desk.

This is an answer to my financial problems, but not the one I wanted.

"I appreciate your compassion Erika, it's lovely to see." Mrs. Blythe smiles and reaches across the remaining distance to squeeze the top of my fist. "Despite your commitment to Stanford, I'm sensing that you might not be the person for this job. I thought you might value this opportunity most, but I have other people to ask if you prefer."

My stomach clenches automatically. The picturesque Stanford campus, shining sports facilities and indisputable college reputation run through my mind. Then, my mother's face as I open my acceptance letter. I look down at my lap. "Can I please have some time to decide?"

"Okay," Blythe responds after a moment of deliberation. "You have until the end of the day to get back to me, or I will ask someone else."

"Thank you." I rise from my seat, scooping my backpack up from the floor. Then, as quickly as I can manage on shaky legs, I dart towards my escape.

"It was lovely to meet you Erika," Mrs. Blythe calls after me as the door closes.

The cool air of the reception is a welcome respite from the intensity of the principal's office. I lean back against the wall with my eyes closed, focusing on my breathing. *How* am I going to make this decision? I don't know how I feel about throwing another student under the bus to get everything I want. If I help Blythe, though, Stanford would be within reach for the first time. What are the chances that I would get a scholarship by talent alone? Blythe picked me because she knew they were slim.

The unofficial Ivy League of the west coast. My parents would be so proud of me.

Before I can get too lost in the fantasy of my mom's expression, I force myself to consider the downsides of this decision. It's selfish, for one. He might not be a decent person, but kicking him out of school would mark his record irreparably. People would be mad at me; I'd be mad at myself. I would feel like a fraud. It could ruin Chase's life.

Then again—surely, it's his own fault for doing bad

things. Is it only inevitable that he's going to get caught? Maybe hurrying it along isn't *that* awful of me. Shouldn't he see some consequences if the choices are his own?

"Um." A throat clears, and my eyes open instantly. "Eric, are you alive?"

I frown at the secretary, who's clearly teasing me. "Yes Brian, I think Eric is alive. However, you might want to ask him yourself."

Brian chuckles. "Back to class, kid."

I nod and drag my body away from the wall and out the door. I need longer than a day to make this decision. I need advice, and research, and time to think things through.

Research.

I need to see for myself what Chase is like. I need to see what I'd be getting myself into. Determination slowly dissolves the knot of unease in my stomach as I walk through the empty hallway towards my first class.

Yes. *I'll see what Chase is like. Then I'll decide.*

"No way, that is scandalous!"

Miko matches her pace with mine as we head towards my locker. She has one of those strides that only models can achieve; she always looks so damn graceful. That is, until you're her best friend and you've seen her with noodles hanging from her mouth or attempting to follow TikTok dance routines.

"I can't believe she's trying to recruit you for this, on her first day. That's outrageous."

"Beyond outrageous," I agree. "This woman is a machine."

Kumiko Tamura has been my best friend for over a year

now, and she never fails to entertain me with her eccentricity. Her name is Japanese, and it sounds like poetry, but she shortens it to Mickey, or Miko. I maintain that she *should* have poems written about her—one of those fiery feminist ones with a kick-ass female protagonist. Not only is Miko completely beautiful, with enviable skin and black hair that drips through her braids like ink, but she's hilarious and stubborn as a mule. That girl could be my muse any day.

"What are you going to do?" she asks, adjusting a pink scrunchie on her braid.

"I guess I'm going to talk to him, see what he's like."

"And if he's an asshole?"

I laugh lightly. "Then I'll do it."

"What if he's not?"

"Well, ideally he will be."

Her nose crinkles. "I think this plan is a little flawed, honey."

"I'd prefer if you didn't point it out."

"Look, he's right over there!" Miko's voice falls to a frantic whisper. She grabs my forearm and pulls us to my locker at the side. "That's him, right?"

Sure enough, Chase Thatcher is standing a little further down the hallway with Uma Khatri—my friend from the school track team. Immediately, I open my locker and pretend to fumble for something in an attempt to look inconspicuous. I feel all kinds of creepy as I notice her place a hand on his forearm. I'm not quite sure what I'm hoping for—watching them flirt is not going to provide me with any answers.

"I think she's upset," Miko whispers.

She's right. Upon closer inspection, Uma's face is creased with anguish. The hand on his arm suddenly looks less like flirtatiousness and more like desperation. I watch Chase in shock as he plucks her hand from his forearm and flings it aside. Uma, perhaps the sweetest girl I've ever met, bursts into tears and hurries away down the corridor.

Chase turns to face his locker again, his expression blank.

"What an ass," Miko comments from behind me.

"Tell me about it," I mutter.

"Oh no, I meant his actual ass. It's divine."

I roll my eyes and shut my locker door. "It looks like it needs some kicking."

With a refreshed sense of determination, I push myself away from the wall of lockers and approach Chase. It isn't until I'm a few steps away that his eyes meet mine. I feel a rush of guilt, but I refrain from letting any of my feelings seep into the emotionless mask that is my face. Calmly and confidently, I come to a stop and lean on the locker beside him.

There's no doubt about it, Chase Thatcher is possibly *the* most attractive heartthrob at our school. His eyes are a rich pecan brown, his hair is tousled, and his skin is beautifully freckled over his tall, fit frame. I try not to let the accumulation of those things intimidate me as I smile and release a slightly forced and uncomfortable "hi."

Standing this close to him, it's hard not to notice minor details that explain why the female population at Lindale High is so attracted to him. Chiseled jawline and cheekbones, full lips and sparkling eyes—I can understand why people turn brain dead in his presence.

"Do I know you?" he asks cautiously. "If I met you on

Saturday night, I'm sorry but I was drunk out of my mind. I don't do second dates."

And just as quickly as it arrived, the attraction disappears.

"Good for you," I reply curtly. Does he really forget what girls look like so often that he uses it in his introductory line? "No, you don't know me, actually. I'm not an ex of yours."

"Oh, okay." Chase seems relieved, but the emotion only lingers on his expression for a fleeting second. His eyes roll over my body, lingering on the bare leg showing below the hem of my denim skirt. "In which case, we can go out. I can make a dinner reservation if you want but give me a call so I can make the arrangements."

He slides something from his back pocket into my hand and finishes with a winning smile that lasts for half a second. Then, his gaze flutters around the hallway, distracted.

"I—what?" I say blankly.

"I said yes, we can go on a date."

"Well, that's mighty lucky for me, but I didn't ask to go on a date." Truly, I was expecting him to be charming and overly flirtatious, but a decent guy. This guy is an egotistical and assumptive asshat.

"You didn't?"

Is that genuine surprise I hear?

"No, you just assumed." My nose scrunches as I inspect the crumpled sticky note in my palm. "I didn't come to profess my love, or beg for a second date, or give you my number or anything like that."

Chase frowns. His shoulders adjust to face me fully for the first time since I began talking. "What is it exactly that you want then?"

"A conversation, maybe?" I let some of the irritation seep into my tone. My hands shoot up in a sarcastic display of surrender. The note is tucked underneath my thumb. "Maybe to discuss why you just hurt Uma like that? She's a really sweet person, you know."

Chase crosses his arms over his chest. I don't allow myself to do more than glance at the vein running over his left bicep. "Is that really any of your business?"

"Uma is my friend."

"So, no, then."

He's already annoying.

"I'm just saying, why date girls if you're just going to ditch them right afterwards? Surely that's an incredibly lonely way to live."

His dark eyes widen minutely—enough that despite his best efforts at masking, I can tell I struck a chord. The proximity increases as his shoulders square over me, and a minty breath fans across my nose. He scowls.

"I don't do second dates—that's my right. Not your business. Another thing I don't do is pointless chit-chat with judgmental girls like you."

Chase steps away from me, shoves his hands in the back pockets of his skinny jeans, and stalks down the hallway away from me. I watch him leave in stunned silence, glued to the spot beside his closed locker. As I think back to the list of things that Principal Blythe told me he has done, I try to connect his description with our encounter. *Drug possession. Violence. Vandalism. Insolence. Aggression.* He was pretty moody, so I suppose it makes sense. Maybe this guy really does deserve to be expelled.

Ultimately, am I wrong for catching him in the act?

No one should shoot the messenger, after all.

Impulsively, I grab my phone from my back pocket and enter the number written on Chase's note into a new text. I type with shaking hands, and without hesitation press send.

> It must be hard to see how you hurt people, with your head so far up your ass. You seemed pretty desperate for a date, so I'll make sure to give this number to someone in need. I'm sure you'll find someone who sticks around ☺

Chase Thatcher will be doing all of the incriminating work for me.

I can't be blamed for simply holding the camera.

2

Mocha Me Crazy

Maintaining a watchful eye on my sister the entire time, I lift my right leg gradually over the arm of the second upholstered chair facing her desk. My foot practically floats down upon the pink crochet cushion, and I mentally award myself for achieving such crisp silence. My breath stifles as my left leg follows suit. Slowly, painfully, my ankle comes to rest on top of my right foot. Like a ninja, I—

"You know I don't like it when you put your feet up," Chloe interrupts. The scribbling of her biro on the page doesn't even slow; her focus remains fixed on her work.

I release a rumbled sigh and my foot collapses down on the seat. "These chairs are uncomfortable. My feet have to go someplace—would you prefer your desk?"

"My cushions are always dirty because of you."

"A small price to pay for your sister's comfort, I'm sure."

She doesn't bother to rebuke my statement.

"Do you happen to know anything about Chase Thatcher?" I ask casually.

I'm now sprawled comfortably across both chairs facing

her desk, my back is straight, and my voice is hopeful. Chloe looks up from her paperwork and frowns.

"Why do you ask?"

Frowning has always looked very odd on my sister. Mom used to say that Chloe's face was made for smiling, and I think she's lived by that. Watching her frown is unfamiliar and bordering upon unnatural. She's far too pretty. Mom also said that my face was made for complaining, but I never really saw the logic behind that theory.

"I'm just curious," I say, shrugging loosely and squinting at Chloe's sunshine features. Unlike my slightly darker hair, Chloe has the endearing combination of Mom's frizzy blond curls and hazel eyes. She works as our school guidance counselor, which makes for some moments of pure awkwardness. Not to mention, I hear a near-constant commentary from the boys in my year about how hot she is. Gross.

"So, do you know anything?"

She turns back to her work. "I wouldn't discuss anything with you even if I *was* allowed to."

Chloe's purple biro dances across the paper in front of her. Her hair is milkmaid braided today and pinned down neatly with daisy clips. My hair hangs itself pin straight on my head, with emphasis on *hangs itself*.

"It's not like I'd tell anyone," I whine, kicking the base of Chloe's desk with my sneakers. My frustration wobbles the potted succulent sitting on the edge of her desk, and a couple of her colored gel pens roll across the paper she's working on. Chloe stares pointedly at me with one eyebrow raised. Her pen is poised an inch above her notebook.

"Erika, I could get fired, you idiot."

"Never mind that." I wave my hand dismissively. "It's for the greater good."

I never truly expected that Chloe would tell me anything; I know how seriously she takes her job here. She's twenty-four and, after studying at Oregon State in Portland, returned home to be a part-time counselor at two local district schools. For as long as I can remember, Chloe wanted to help people. She worked her ass off for it, but no one around her ever doubted that she'd be successful. Chloe never fails.

"Erika, why are you asking this? Is there something wrong?"

I glance up briefly to see her hazel eyes watching my face with concern. The pen that was in her hand is now laid flat on the paper, cushioned with lines of curly violet letters. Chloe is a fixer; a problem solver with an insatiable desire to save the world.

"Nothing wrong," I say, shaking my head. "Don't worry about it."

Her eyes narrow. "You like him?"

"My middle finger likes him, if that's what you're implying."

Chloe sighs and picks up her pen again. "He's complicated, okay? I'm not going to say any more but don't go too hard on him with all of your . . ." She waves the pen around in the air, gesturing to me. ". . . sass."

I release an exaggerated gasp. "Sass? Me? I am *supremely shocked* that you would accuse me of such a trait."

"Very clever."

I grin. Chloe glances at the clock mounted on the wall. The pink gel fingernails on her free hand tap rhythmically on the desk. "Isn't this your lunch break? Have you not got anything better to do than pestering me?"

"I have," I say sweetly. "I just popped by again to steal some of your—"

"No."

"Just one cup, come on," I plead, leaning forward in my seat. "Your coffee machine is way better than the filter stuff they give us in the cafeteria."

"You're a nightmare."

"A cup of coffee might help me wake up then."

Chloe releases a frustrated groan. "Fine. Am I driving you home tonight?"

I'm out of my seat like a shot, grabbing one of Chloe's paper cups and pressing the buttons on the coffee machine for some liquid love. Chloe's office is small and homely, warm with colored trinkets, cacti, and paintings. It's supposed to feel comforting to students, I guess. The coffee machine is my favorite feature.

"Nope, don't worry, Miko is coming over after practice."

Chloe glares at my hands as I seal the cup of coffee with a flimsy plastic lid. "I'm going to start charging you for those coffee pods."

"I pay you in the light I bring to your life," I declare cheerily, scooping up my things and sauntering to the door. "See you later, have a good day!"

"Enjoy practice. Oh, and bite that tongue before it cuts someone."

Her office door clicks shut behind me and I emerge back into the quiet hallway.

It's the beginning of lunch and Miko will be waiting for

me in the cafeteria. It's officially been a whole day since I agreed to help Principal Blythe expel Chase, and I haven't told a soul aside from her. I'm not sure I ever will. The concept of deliberately snitching on somebody for my own gain is still enough to bring a queasy feeling to my stomach. That's without mentioning the anxiety of how exactly I plan to *achieve* this feat.

Maybe I should ask Blythe if I can assemble a team. We could form a group chat, share ideas. Call ourselves *The Anti-Delinquent Squad* or—

"I am not desperate."

I almost jump out of my skin as a person appears in my path, cutting me off and sending me reeling backwards in shock. I hiss as the hot mocha I'm holding splashes onto my forearm, spots of pain igniting on my skin. I mourn the spillage briefly before I look up to meet the brown eyes glaring down at me. Chase Thatcher is standing defiantly in front of me, his arm pressed against the locker and jaw set in irritation.

I quickly assemble a smile. "I see you got my message, then."

Chase grimaces and pulls his arm away from the lockers to cross it over his chest. Today he's wearing a black-and-white baseball T-shirt with the sleeves rolled up to his elbows, exposing toned forearms. "What do you want from me?"

I pause to assess. "I want a new coffee, now that half of mine is gone."

He has no patience for my nonchalant façade. "Why did you approach me yesterday?"

"Told you: I wanted a conversation."

Chase laughs incredulously. "We've never met before, but you somehow felt justified enough to march over and judge me for things you know nothing about. So, tell me honestly, what do you want from me? Unless you just want to annoy me."

"You owe me a new coffee," I repeat. "And I genuinely did just come over for a conversation. You *made* me judge you when you were an assumptive ass."

I check the invisible watch on my wrist. "Now look, I need to go meet my friends, so if you have anything remotely interesting to say, I suggest you hurry. This cup of coffee is now pretty much empty, as is my cup of care."

I know it's probably not my best move to push his buttons, but I can't help it. I still don't know how I'm going to get him caught. I need to bide my time.

"Is this some weird, creepy way of getting my attention?"

"I honestly don't believe this." I slap my free hand to my forehead. "You still think I'm hitting on you?"

"Well, I don't believe that you came up to me just for a conversation," he replies, leaning closer to me. His tone is sharp, skeptical. I'm suddenly intensely grateful that this hallway is quiet. "We don't know each other, and we've never spoken, so don't pretend like it's normal to approach me for a conversation for absolutely no reason."

He's right, of course. It is unusual that I'd approach and start chatting with a random stranger for no purpose, but what am I supposed to tell him? *I wanted to do some research on you, to know who I'd be trying to expel from school?* That would go down well, I'm sure.

What I need is a way to get footage of him doing something bad, as soon as possible. No emotional attachment, no friendliness, never getting close enough for it to feel like betrayal. I can't stalk him and I'm pretty sure I can't catch him on CCTV, or he'd have already been caught. The most cunning thing to do is to be there with him, but how can I do that without trying to befriend him?

I blink at Chase for a couple of awkward seconds as I strain my mind-muscles for ideas, before I finally think back to the movie I was watching last night. *Wild Child*. Suddenly, the solution appears clearly in my brain.

"I want you to help me be bad."

I regret the words as soon as they exit my mouth, realizing immediately quite how many flaws there might be with this plan, but I can't turn back now. Chase's mouth slackens in surprise.

"What?" he asks stupidly.

"I want to act out," I say, with more determination than I feel. "I want to rough up my reputation, stop everyone thinking I'm so squeaky clean. I want to push myself."

"You approached me at random in the corridor because you want to *push* yourself?"

Incredulity is apparent in his tone. Even I can recognize how ridiculous I sound.

Abort mission. Abort.

"You know what? Never mind," I say, flushing with embarrassment and backing away. "Forget about it. Just continue with your day."

A hand grabs my arm as I turn in the other direction. Chase's grip is warm, and he pulls me back towards him with easy strength. I look at him warily as he releases my arm, but his expression is no longer confused. His features are slightly pinched, yet unreadable.

"Why are you doing this?"

Improvise, Erika. Don't they say that the best lies are the ones closest to the truth?

"I want to ... catch my parents' attention," I say softly, and swallow down my discomfort. I hope that my hesitation comes across as a dramatic pause for effect. "My sister, she's perfect in every sense of the word, the model daughter. I can never hope to compare to that. It's like all they ever see is her ... I want them to see me, notice me for once."

I almost wince. *That ended up a little close to home.*

Chase's expression seems to have softened, and his eyes are flickering over my face to read my expression. I try to look as sincere as possible. "What exactly do you want *me* to do? What is it that you're asking me for?"

"Just a little guidance," I hedge, my confidence restoring. He's not flat out laughing or rejecting me, so my cards are still on the table. "I don't want to get caught."

I want to get you *caught instead.*

Chase leans back against the lockers, staring blankly at the other side of the hallway. He hesitates for a few seconds, before looking back at me. "Why would I help you?"

"I don't know," I say coolly. "But you're going to, aren't you?"

Chase chuckles, a low sound in the back of his throat. "Now who's assumptive?"

"Look. Let's just say I'll owe you, okay?"

A small smirk curves his lips as he looks at me. "What's your name?"

"Erika Monroe," I say. I watch the name register in his expression—he has heard of me. With my snarky mouth, track team record, and pretty sister, I'm far from invisible at this school. Chase nods almost knowingly before his expression flattens into nonchalance.

"Meet me at Sophie Houghton's party tonight." He stands up from his position against the lockers, running a hand through his hair. "Eight p.m. Be there, or I'm not helping you. And this better not be some long-winded flirtation. I have a low tolerance for mind games."

"What about my coffee?" I lift the mostly empty cup and wiggle it.

Chase raises an irritated eyebrow. "What about it?"

"You owe me one," I accuse. "I will collect."

"We'll see about that."

"We will." I begin to back away. "Oh, and seriously, *please* stop thinking that I'm trying to hit on you. I like my coffee how I like myself ... dark, bitter, and way too hot for you." My face bursts into a grin and I spin on my heel to walk away.

Now walk away quickly. It only works if you have the last word.

I'm now heading in the wrong direction.

Despite that, I can't help but feel a little bounce in my step. I'm meeting Chase at Sophie's party tonight, and phase one of the plan begins.

The sooner I get this boy kicked out of school, the better.

"I have come to the realization that push-up bras only work if there is something to push up," Miko says sadly, cupping her chest through her sunshine yellow crop top and angling herself in front of the full-length mirror. "Yet I am president of the itty-bitty-titty committee."

I smile over at her from my position, sitting cross-legged

on the stool in front of my desk. "They need you to lead them, Miko. Your work is integral."

"You're right." She sighs dramatically. Her hands fall from her chest, and she turns around to prance over to me. "Me and my teeny tiny breasts are going to own this party."

I hum with approval, turning back to face the mirror in front of me and smearing a layer of charcoal-gray mud mask over my nose. No mask I've ever encountered has actually made a difference to the size of my pores, but I think it's nice to feel like you're taking care of yourself regardless.

"You should definitely borrow that top."

Miko plucks an eyebrow pencil from the assortment of cosmetics cluttering my desk and rolls it between her fingers absentmindedly. "I've worn this top more than you have."

"That's because you look hot in yellow. Don't get clay on it," I warn as I finish coating my forehead. I attempt to keep my face as expressionless as possible, but I can already feel the characteristic tightness of the mask tugging on my skin. I push the tub in Miko's direction using my elbow, before rising to go and wash my hands in the bathroom.

As soon as I told Miko about the party tonight, our planned preparation for the history pop quiz transformed into party preparation. Miko *loves* parties. Alongside the fact that she thrives in a social scene, she is also completely addicted to the drama and gossip provided by the catalyst of alcohol. Sometimes, I'll catch her with an ear to the door as a couple argue in a bedroom, or completely engrossed watching as a guy talks to his best friend about who sent him a nude. In most scenarios, I'm there and able to drag her away by her ear, but one of these days her shameless nosiness is going to backfire.

When I return to my bedroom, Miko is sprawled back on my bed with her legs directly in the air, examining her feet.

"What are you doing?"

She glances over at me briefly before resuming her analysis. "Oh, just trying to figure out if one of my legs is longer than the other."

"You'd walk a bit funny if they were," I say with a laugh, sitting back down on my desk stool. "And you'd probably be in pain."

Miko's milky legs lower to the blankets again, and she props herself up on one elbow. "I'm pretty sure one of my feet is bigger than the other. I might also have one boob bigger than the other. Is it really that much of a stretch that it applies to legs too?"

I bite my lip to contain my laugh. "Did you see Kai today?"

Instantly the amusement dies from Miko's face. Kaito is Miko's sixteen-year-old brother, and in her own words, the biggest thorn in her ass. Since the divorce was finalized and their father moved out, he's become increasingly troubled and isolated himself from the family. He was hardly at home over spring break, always occupied with a group of unruly older boys, and Miko said that he was snappy and insolent when she did see him. She's worried that his relationship with Sada has broken down almost entirely. Their mother has always had a low tolerance for bad behavior, and Kai seems to be testing it more every day.

Miko is hoping that Kai starting back at school again will help him to recover his sense of routine and peace. I hope it works. I know Miko is struggling a lot with the fractures in her family life. Back when he spent all of his free time playing

World of Warcraft or Fortnite, they used to be really close.

"No, I haven't seen him," she reports. "But I asked his homeroom teacher to tell me if he doesn't show up."

"So that means he showed up, right?"

Miko attempts a smile. "Probably."

Just as I'm about to ask her if she's planning to go to the debate team meeting tomorrow, Miko yelps and springs upwards from the bed, scrambling up against the pillows.

"My butt just vibrated. I *knew* there was something wrong with me."

Rolling my eyes, I heave myself up from my seat and move to my bed. My phone is lying face up on the covers, screen lit and buzzing periodically.

"No, you idiot, somebody is calling me."

Unknown number. *Strange*.

I slide the button to answer the call and lift it to my ear. "Hello?"

"Erika," a baritone voice speaks. "I need to cash in that favor."

3

Delinquent in Distress

Despite our limited interaction, his voice is unmistakable.

"Chase." I slump back against the nearest wall and the back of my scalp makes a dull thudding noise. I stare up at the ceiling. "How did you get my number?"

"You texted him, dumb beetle," Miko answers from across the room. She's sat upright on the bed now, eating the bowl of salted popcorn that I cooked for her earlier. I hate salted popcorn, but Miko loves it, so my dad always ensures to stock up. Miko's eyes are wide as she watches the phone in my hand, crunching through handfuls of the snack.

"Never mind," I groan before Chase can answer my question. I step away from the wall and walk over to the desk, reaching for a pen to twist idly around my fingers. "You're better off calling somebody else. You haven't agreed to help me, so the chances of me helping you are equivalent to the note A0 on a piano. You know—*really quite low.*"

"I need a lift." I hear Chase sigh. "If you want my help, you'll come and collect me from Redwood Avenue as soon as you can and take me to my friend Joe's house. I'll meet you at the party at eight, as planned, and we can talk about my end of the bargain then."

I catch a glimpse of myself in the mirror and jump a little, dropping my pen to the floor. I had completely forgotten that my face was covered in gray mud. "Look, hypothetically I would come and collect you, but I actually have plans."

"Are they plans you can get out of?" Chase asks, clearing his throat. His voice softens a little. "You'd be doing me a solid. I need to get out of here and get my lift bailed."

"Cab? Bus? There are options." In my peripheral vision, I see Miko shaking her head adamantly. She outstretches her hand towards me, knocking the popcorn bowl off balance so that fluffy kernels spread across my bedsheets. I scowl. "Miko wants to talk to you."

"Wait, who's—"

Before I can answer him, Miko has snatched my phone away and is pressing it to her ear with a bright smile. "Hi, I'm Miko, Erika's best friend. I heard about your conundrum, and I just wanted to let you know that I'm happy to let you borrow Erika for half an hour."

My mouth falls open. *That traitor.*

"So, Redwood Avenue. That's the other side of town, right?" Miko asks, chucking a piece of popcorn towards my mouth. It bounces from my cheek. She pauses to hear his response. "Yeah, Erika will know where that is. She'll be there as soon as she can. Please don't keep her too long, I need her to wax my legs before the party."

I perch on the edge of my desk, arms crossed as I frown at my so-called best friend.

Miko crosses her ankles. "No, nobody has the same

technique as Erika. She's very gentle. Tender, really. I'm sure that she'd make an excellent lover—"

"Hey!" My arm swipes through the air to snatch the phone, but Miko dodges easily.

"Aw!" Miko coos to Chase, angling her body away to block my attacks. "Erika, he offered to help wax my legs!"

"I think that's enough," I grumble as I finally manage to pluck my phone from her grasp. I lean back against the desk again and press the warm screen to my ear. "You're not going anywhere near her legs. That's not your jurisdiction, Thatcher."

Miko throws another kernel of popcorn at me, hitting me squarely in the forehead.

"I just wanted to prove that I could be way gentler than you," Chase replies smoothly. "At both waxing and love maki—"

I interrupt with a short burst of sarcastic laughter. "I would *love* ... *making* you stop."

"Are you coming then?"

I groan and shoot a glare at Miko. "Hang tight. I'll be there as soon as I can."

When I finally hang up, Miko is sitting cross-legged on my bed, smiling angelically. Ignoring her, I reach for my car keys from the little hook beside my desk and sit down to slide my sneakers on. I always order sneakers a touch too big because I hate the inconvenience of shoelaces. It's one of my mom's pet peeves.

"Hey, Miko?" I say, finally looking up as I stand.

Her smile twitches. "Yes, beautiful best friend?"

"I'm going to let the wax harden a little *too* much."

Miko's smile drops, and her eyes narrow. "You wouldn't."

I smile and wiggle my fingers in farewell as I head out of my bedroom door towards the bathroom, to wash this stupid mud mask away. "Maybe consider jeans?"

I drive slowly down the narrow road, my hands cemented to the steering wheel. Around me, dusk has settled, and the streetlights have only recently flickered into activity, unfurling an eerie glow across the roadside. The buildings are blemished and scarred, bottles litter the sidewalk, and the trees are the color of nicotine stains. I search for a glimpse of Chase Thatcher, and with every second of failure, I become increasingly uneasy. I've never been to this part of town before.

A dog barks at my car and I flinch.

I miss the warmth of my bedroom and the smell of salted popcorn.

I've almost reached the end of Redwood Avenue now, and my options are limited to crawling around the block another time or pulling over. Just as I'm about to flick my indicator on, movements on the left catch my eye. At the opening of a shaded street corner, there are shadows dancing across the tarmac: a fluctuating silhouette of a group of people.

Should I get out and look for him?

Bad idea. Very bad idea. Call first.

"You're an idiot for agreeing to this," I mutter as I swing my car into an available space on the right-hand side of the road. As soon as the motor has died, I fumble for my phone to fill the uncomfortable silence which has fallen. I can't press the redial button fast enough. However, the reassuring ring of the dial tone never comes. Instead, my phone beeps in protest and the call ends before it has even begun. I have no signal.

Of course.

My anger at Chase's no-show is the necessary fuel to propel me out of the car and into the cool evening air. As the door shuts and the lock clicks behind me, the breeze nips lightly at my bare arms as a warning sign. I stride towards the moving shadows, at the mouth of the neighboring street. I'm able to suppress my fear for an impressive twenty seconds. That is, until I'm standing at the corner and listening to the intimidating sounds and shrieks of the people ahead. Cold anxiety seeps through my chest and clutches at my throat.

Two minutes, I resolve. *If I don't find him in two minutes, I'm out of here.*

With a sharp inhale, I emerge onto the street corner.

Immediately, I sense my mistake. The Admiral Bar stands ahead of me on the left, a derelict hub for the aggregation of people overspilling into the street. Nearest to me, four men are sitting on a picnic bench and watching me approach. Their gazes are meaner than the motorcycles behind them and I find myself stumbling on my feet. The bar building itself seems almost lopsided, sagging into the concrete below as if longing to disappear. Its parking lot, small and lined with bushes, is crammed with humming drag cars.

I've heard of this place. The old bar on the far side of town, where the housing dies off into junkyards and neglected business parks.

This is where you find the people your parents warn you about.

Muttering curses under my breath, I force myself to continue walking into the heart of the bar's parking lot. I'm receiving too many curious looks to turn back now. The air is thick and sour with the scent of gasoline and smoke, and I'm breathing hard and fast. The parking lot around me is thrumming with lively chatter and the vibration of engines that reverberates through the soles of my sneakers. I try to focus on the sensation.

"Excuse me," I say breathlessly to a woman on my right. She's strangely tall with dark hair and a tattoo curling around her throat. "Do you know where Chase Thatcher is?"

"He's over there with Seth, sweet." She gestures towards the back of the lot, but her expression is pinched with concern. "Are you here with somebody? It's not safe for a girl to wander around these things on her own."

"I'm just picking him up." I attempt to smile. "Thank you, though. I'll be careful."

Her expression remains skeptical. "I'll walk with you."

Flinging a dirty oilskin to the side, she abandons the polished engine exposed in the open indigo hood of her car and begins to clear a route through the gathering. Gratefully, I step into her shadow and follow closely as she divides the crowd. So close that when she stops, my body narrowly avoids ploughing into her back.

"Look after this one," I hear her say. "Make sure she's safe."

She turns around and squeezes my shoulder briefly. I barely have time to thank her before she's melted back into the commotion.

"Erika?" a voice sounds in front of me. I twist around to find Chase staring at me with an expression of disbelief. His usually immaculate face and clothes are stained with grease, his hair is sticking up in odd directions and he's wearing a dark shirt that adorns his torso like a second skin. "What are you doing here? Why didn't you stay in the car?"

"I couldn't find you!"

"Why didn't you call?"

"No signal."

I instinctively reach for my phone and pull it from my back pocket, to check my bars again. Sure enough, I now have four bars of signal and a message from my mother asking why on earth I'm not studying with Miko. I swiftly return my phone to my pocket.

Chase frowns. "You should've stayed in the car."

"I don't have all day, buddy. Are you nearly done or what?"

Despite my irritation, I can't help but relax a little now that he's with me. While he might not be my preferred candidate, there is always safety in numbers. If any creep dares approach, I will have no problem letting Chase fight them off. My eyes flit over his lean, muscular arms. Yep. He's a big boy, I'm sure he can take it.

"Yeah." Chase sighs with exasperation. "Hold on."

Turning around, Chase leads me to a stop in front of a guy in a tight black hoodie, bending over the hood of a neon green drag car. I can't see his face, but his tanned forearms are exposed from his rolled sleeves, patterned with bright tattoos and smudges of oil.

"Seth, my ride's here. I've got to go now."

In one fluid movement, Seth withdraws from the underside of the car hood and twists around to face us. He stretches to his full towering height, wiping his forehead clean with a rag. Under a mess of raven curls, pecan-colored eyes register our appearance.

"Your ride?" Seth repeats, flicking the snake bite piercing in the corner of his mouth. After a questioning glance at Chase, his eyes finally move to mine and the confusion melts away from his forehead. He is clearly older but not by much, with a stocky physique and overtly handsome, angular features. A small smile blooms on his lips. "Oh. I didn't realize you'd called someone."

"This is Erika," Chase introduces me. "Erika, Seth Bautista."

"I'd shake your hand but..." Seth raises his oil-smudged palms and gives me a slow wave.

"I won't take offence, don't worry." I glance sideways at the equally grubby Chase and frown. "Any chance you have some trash bags lying around? If Chase gets oil on my interiors, he won't be making it to his friend's house."

Chase scoffs.

"Sure." Seth leans over to snatch a roll of trash bags from the messy, collapsible worktable beside the car hood. He tosses it upwards in his hands, grinning wickedly. Then, without warning, he launches the roll underarm towards me. It shoots through the air straight for my stomach, but lands neatly in my awaiting hands.

"Nice catch," Chase mutters, folding his arms.

"Thanks," I answer a little smugly, toying with the loose plastic in my hand. The roll has loosened considerably with the momentum of the pass. I unwind it further to reveal a full bag, then hold it up vertically in front of Chase's body and squint my eyes. "Think if I cut a head hole at the top of one of these, it would fit you?"

"No." His scowl peeks out above the black plastic in my vision.

"Worth a shot," Seth says, bumping his shoulder. "You are—"

"Trash, I know. Ha-ha," Chase interrupts sarcastically. He reaches his hand out and pulls the trash bag down. "So inventive. Erika, can we go now?"

With potent timing, the rumble of engines around us rises to a roaring crescendo. I'm startled back into the reality of my surroundings outside of our little bubble, and anxiety squeezes in my chest. I look at the drag cars scattered through the parking lot; metal beasts sleek with the vibrant colors of danger. The drivers themselves are no less intimidating, ripping their motors fiercely to the glee of their hungry audience.

"Of course," I say swiftly. I tear a trash bag free for my car seat and throw the remaining roll to Seth. "It was nice to meet you."

He catches it perfectly, grinning. "You too."

Nodding my goodbye to Seth, I follow Chase closely as he leads me past the crumbling wall of the Admiral Bar and through its bustling parking lot. Although I barely know him, his back provides a welcome shield from the swarms of intimidating strangers and flashes of neon. Even when we're back on Redwood Avenue and the clamor of man and machine has faded into background noise, neither one of us attempts to speak.

It isn't until I'm driving the safe, familiar roads leading home that our surprisingly comfortable silence breaks. Chase is sitting on his trash bag, staring out of the window. I am finally able to breathe out the lingering, stubborn remnants of my anxiety.

"So, where am I going?"

Before I can get a response, Chase has pressed on my

center console to open all four of the windows. Swells of wind enter the car as I speed along the roads, whipping my hair around my face and killing all potential for conversation. He glances sideways at me, his arm rested casually on the passenger side. Scowling as a strand of my hair smacks me on the nose, I reach out and press the button to close the windows again. The car becomes quieter and quieter again, before finally the windows seal with a dull squeak.

"I'm not Edward Cullen, you idiot. I need you to tell me where I'm driving."

Chase reopens his window. "Joe lives on Mayson Road, number 23. First left when you hit the main street. I can guide you from there."

The distance between streetlights seems to increase dramatically as I turn onto the country lane leading towards Lindale. My shoulders lower as I relax.

"Okay, good," I say, keeping my tone breezy and casual. "Now why did you ask me to pick you up from that place?"

"Well, I—"

Chase hardly gets to open his mouth before I interrupt him again. "You know—the kind of place where a crack dealer runs the local hair salon, or a murderer in an apron sells you gummy bears in the store, or you think you're getting into a cab but *bam,* it actually turns out to be a drag car? You know—that place?"

Chase lazily rolls his head sideways to look at me. "Has anyone ever told you that you have a tendency to overdo the drama? It's really not that bad."

I loosen my grip on the wheel. "I try not to listen to other people's opinions. You're welcome to write it down, put it in an envelope, and shove it up your own ass, though."

Chase faces out of his open window again. "Whatever you're into, Erika."

"Ew."

He laughs lightly, shifting his tanned forearm. "I didn't have another way back."

"What were you doing there? Do you race?"

At first, I don't think he's going to reply, but he speaks after a few seconds of hesitation. "No, I'm just there by association. Does that answer all of your questions?"

His gaze feels warm on the side of my face.

"For now," I say simply.

The difference in light from Lindale's main street hits me the moment we exit the shadowed forest road. Unlike Redwood Avenue, dusk blankets Lindale with a warm, happy glow and the string lights that decorate the trees make it even more enchanting. I may be biased, but I'm happy to be home. Sighing in contentment, I obey Chase's instructions and take the first left, towards the cliffs overlooking Lindale's beach.

Chase leans forwards and presses the aux button on my center console.

Taylor Swift blasts through the speakers very suddenly, declaring that she knew Harry Styles was trouble when he walked in. The sheer volume of the music is enough to startle even me. With a sound almost resembling a hiss, Chase switches it off again.

"I want that on," I protest.

"Are you kidding?"

"No."

He scoffs. "Remind me to teach you good taste in music one day."

I avert my eyes from the road to show him my scowl. "I'll do that if you remind me to teach you some manners."

Chase stares at me with bright eyes, contrasting with the dark smudges of oil on his cheekbones. I can't help but blink stupidly for a second. Fortunately, my moment of madness is disrupted quickly when he drags a finger down his greasy cheek and then leans over to wipe it clean on my own.

"Hey!" I screech, attempting and failing to dodge while my eyes focus back on the road ahead. "Driving over here!"

Chase leans back into his seat. His smile is smug. "I thought you could use some oil; you seem a little *stiff*."

I huff out a breath. The grease from his finger feels oddly warm, a tingling trail from the skin just beside my eye to the top of my cheekbone. I itch to rub it clean, but I can't, which is immensely irritating. I scan the street with narrowed eyes.

"This is Mayson Road. Tell me which house is Joe's before I boot you out of that open window."

"Just on the right here."

I slow the car to a crawl and, with a quick glance over my shoulder to survey the road, pull into the empty space. I'm parked in front of a detached white house, with a birch front door and some pretty, well-tended flower beds. The boy I recognize as Joe Travis is leaning out of the front window, waving excitedly when he spots Chase in the car. I barely hear the seat belt unclick. I'm too busy staring at Joe's shirtless torso.

"Thanks for the ride," Chase says, catching my attention again. I turn around to see him watching me with amusement in his features, his muscled arm stretched across to reach for the door handle. "You might want to wash your face before the party."

"You might want to wash your attitude," I retort as he gets out of the car. I catch the faint trace of a grin on his lips before the door slams behind him, and he's walking in front of my car towards Joe's house. Joe is now waiting on the doorstep.

"Honey, I'm home!" I hear Chase call in a sugary voice.

I bite my lip to restrain my smile and start the car ignition again. I'll see Chase again at Sophie's party, in less than two hours.

That's enough time to come up with a strategy, right?

4

Let the Evening Be-Gin

"What do you think?"

I turn around from my closet mirror to show Miko the new boyfriend jeans that I've been changing into. They're black denim with distressed knees and they create the excellent illusion that I actually *have* some junk in my trunk. My usual style consists of anything sporty or oversized, so it's nice to wear something flattering for a change.

Lying on my bed, she lifts her eyes from her phone screen and lazily looks me up and down. "They make your butt look fantastic."

"Don't they?" I twist my hips to admire the curve of my rear in the mirror. Once I'm satisfied with my outfit, I reach for my perfume and spritz myself down with enough scent to withstand the musky odor of a party. My hair is tamed today, my eyebrows are shaped neatly, and my skin is miraculously clear. I feel good.

"What exactly is your plan tonight?" Miko asks through a yawn. Her elbows dig into my bedcovers as she props her chin up with her hands. "Distract him with your new jeans and charm him with your smile, and hope that he doesn't notice you're lying through your teeth?"

I pause. "Kinda."

"Venturing behind frenemy lines," Miko considers. "I like it."

I'm just placing my perfume back on my dressing table when three light knocks sound at my bedroom door, and it is gently pushed open. Even before she's stepped into the room, I can tell that it's my mom. While Dad actually waits for me to invite him inside after he knocks, my mom has little concern for my privacy when she wants something.

"Sorry to interrupt," she lies sweetly, peeking around the edge of the door. Her blond hair is piled up loosely into a crocodile clip and she's wearing the fluffy robe I bought her last Christmas. "Dad and I couldn't remember if Miko is vegetarian at the moment. He's making his parmigiana."

"No, no, that sounds perfect!" Miko rushes out. "I'm only strictly vegetarian on weekends currently, and I would break that vow for Eli's chicken parmigiana."

I can't help but smile. Dad's parmigiana is Miko's kryptonite—she genuinely raves about it.

"Fantastic," Mom says, leaning against the doorframe and folding her arms across her chest. "Whose party is it that you're going to tonight? Do they live nearby?"

"Her name's Sophie," I pipe up, stuffing my house keys into a black purse. "She lives in one of those new houses by that Italian restaurant you like."

"Oh, the ones by Marco's? Her parents must have good jobs then." Mom tightens her robe. "Are they going to be there for the party?"

"I think they're out of town," Miko contributes. "Sophie's a sensible girl, though."

"I don't understand you kids and your parties on school nights." Mom shakes her head, sighing deeply. A few frizzy tendrils of hair fall from behind her ear. "Erika, remember you have track tomorrow, and that history pop quiz. I've left some White Claws on the table for you. You don't need to drink anything stronger."

"Okay, thank you."

"You're old enough now that I expect you to remember what's important."

I zip my purse. "Of course, Mom. I'll be careful. Good *and* careful."

She nods, tucks the tendrils back into place. "And how are you getting home?"

"Chloe's offered to pick us up. I said Miko can stay here if that's okay."

"Of course, she can." She smiles affectionately at Miko before returning her stern focus to me. "Don't stay at the party too late then. You know Chloe has work tomorrow too."

"We agreed on midnight. I'm getting her a jar of peanut butter as her cab fare."

"Okay, good." Mom nods and withdraws from the doorframe. "I'll leave you girls to get ready. Dinner is in ten."

A moment of silence. Then—

"Oh, and remember, Erika, you need to be sensible. Think of Stanford."

The door closes softly behind her. I turn back to the mirror and realize that I'm grimacing. If only my mom realized just how much I actually think about Stanford, or the lengths I will go to in order to secure that place of my dreams.

There is a chance she might grimace too.

A pair of warm hands covers my eyes, and the dimly lit room becomes entirely dark. The fast-paced music swells around me like liquid and I stiffen in alarm, until I hear the low, familiar chuckle behind my ear. "Guess who?"

I bite the inside of my lip, tugging my smile back into a neutral expression. My voice strains over the ambient noise. "Do you happen to be tall, blond, and terrible at football?"

The hands are removed instantly, and I hear a scoffing noise behind me.

Unable to restrain my grin this time, I twist around on my heels to stare up into the accusatory eyes of Dylan Merrick. Dylan has been one of my closest friends since I first joined Lindale High. We bonded in the freshman track team, started running together and never really stopped. He's achingly attractive, with cool gray eyes, tan skin, and messy blond hair. To everyone else at school, that is.

Unfortunately for me, I think any possibility of a romantic connection between us died the minute we started doing yoga together after practice. I can't unsee any of Dylan's wobbly "tree" poses or his attempt at the "crow." That's not to mention the time that he pulled faces at me through his legs while in the "downward dog" position. Definitely just friends.

"I'm many things, Erika, but terrible at football?" Dylan repeats, shaking his head. He leans down to collect his beer from the coffee table beside us. "Bull. You must have heard that we won the game. You're winding me up."

I survey his navy football jersey and damp hair. "I didn't hear it, I just smelled you across the room. The stench of sweat was so strong that I figured you *must* have won."

Dylan's eyes spark with amusement. "I showered."

"Oh." I widen my eyes. "Is that not a regular occurrence?"

Dylan pushes my arm teasingly and takes a swig from his beer. "Very funny, Ricky."

We're at Sophie's party, in a cozy detached house on the nice side of Lindale. It's too small for the number of people that were invited, and everyone has spilled into the yard. The glass doors are open, and outside is a deck strung with string lights. I'm situated in what must be the living room, judging by the couches that people are gathered on. The beat of the music dances in the soles of my shoes, and the room is warm and smells sickly sweet, like the artificial bubble-gum scent from vapes.

"Erika!" another voice in the crowd greets me.

A pair of slender, dark brown arms loop around my neck and a familiar voice coos in my ear. Kebe from cheerleading. Miko is hanging around somewhere with the other cheerleaders, but I lost her ten minutes ago. Kebe begins to swing her body behind mine, singing badly. After ten or so seconds, she kisses my cheek and disappears into the crowd. Another fleeting greeting.

I take a sip from my plastic cup, containing a weak mix of gin and pink lemonade that tastes like candy. The alcohol is already beginning to take effect: I can feel the lulling weight in my head, note the tiniest lack of focus in my vision. That means I'm ready.

I check my phone. *7.58 p.m.*

"Dylan?" I clear my throat and quickly slide the phone

back into my pocket. Dylan, who has been greeting one of the other football team members, quickly turns back towards me. "Do you happen to know where Chase is? Chase Thatcher?"

His gray eyes instantly narrow. "How do you know Chase?"

I wave a hand dismissively. "Just from around school."

"Please tell me you aren't about to make a drunken mistake with one of my friends."

"Hey!" I protest, prodding a sharp fingernail into his chest. "You know I never make mistakes. It's one of the symptoms of always being right, remember?"

Dylan raises his eyebrows.

"I'm not interested in him," I state simply. "Now, do you know where he is or not?"

With his expression still accusatory, Dylan points towards the open glass doors on our right. I thank him with a smile before turning and stumbling my way through the crowd towards the exit. A guy tries to grab my hips as I walk past, laughing raucously in front of his friends. I silence him promptly with a heel on his foot, and the hands release.

When I finally step outside into the cool evening air, it's hard not to breathe a sigh of relief. I love parties, but out here ... the music is dulled, the heat diminishes into the evening air, and everything is so much more peaceful. Nearby, a crowd of boys are gathered around a ping pong table, whooping. Clusters of people are scattered across the deck.

"Looking for me?"

The skin on my bare neck tingles, and I spin on my heel to see Chase. He's sitting on a low brick wall at the side of the house, raising a green bottle to his lips. He maintains eye contact briefly as he takes a swig, but as the bottle lowers again, his gaze rolls over my exposed skin. I'm showing more than usual, in a bandeau top and my best jeans. My skin is faintly tanned, textured with eczema in the bend of my arms, and I'm wearing it proudly. That doesn't mean I want Chase to ogle it.

"Has nobody ever told you where you can find a person's eyes?" I ask dryly, taking a sip from my cup. The gin warms my mouth and throat, even diluted.

Chase rolls the cap of his beer between his fingers, the corner of his lips tugging into an infuriating smile. "I wasn't trying to look at your eyes."

"Careful." I twist and lower myself onto the wall beside him. "Joe might get jealous."

Chase takes a swig of beer. "Shut up."

"What about that talk we need to have, Mister *come at eight and don't be late*?" I tease innocently. "You did want to discuss my proposal, didn't you?"

"Of course." Chase leans down, resting his elbows on his knees and ruffling the back of his dark hair with one hand. I watch with strange fascination as his lips falter for a second before he starts talking, as if he's struggling to find the words. "What exactly is it that you want me to do, Erika?"

"Something bad." I hesitate. "I want you to show me what you do to attract attention."

He shifts on the wall. "How bad are we talking?"

"Noticeably bad."

His head cocks slightly as he examines me. "You're really serious about this."

"Deadly serious." I cradle the cup of gin and lemonade in

my hands and maintain my steady expression, masking the hammering of my heart. "Box jellyfish serious. King Cobra serious."

Chase rolls his eyes, but it seems well-humored. Straightening up, he angles his body to face me and rests his palms on the bricks behind him. "Why me?"

Blink. Take a drink. Answer.

"What do you mean, why you?"

Chase lifts his hand, beer bottle and all, and gestures around the small yard. "You know a lot of people; you could have asked anyone."

Before I can even open my mouth, he's talking again. "In fact—why do you need help at all? You're clearly confident and smart-mouthed, it doesn't seem like you need me for anything. So, what am I here for?"

He's got you stumped there, Monroe.

I take another long sip of sticky alcopop, then tug at the back of my lip with my teeth. "Okay, if you want to play that game then what are your reasons for helping *me*?"

He frowns.

"I'm not your friend, you don't owe me anything," I continue. The cup makes a plasticky cracking noise under my hand, and I realize how tightly I'm gripping it. "You say you don't like to waste your time, so it seems to me that you must have a reason for saying yes. Especially considering you're such a busy guy already."

A lingering second passes before he responds. "Okay. You win, gorgeous."

"I win?"

He nods. "I won't ask if you don't."

"Deal." I nod, focusing my gaze back on our surroundings

and ignoring the tickle in my stomach from his half-hearted compliment. "So, what exactly is your plan for me?"

Chase chuckles dryly. "You're at a party. If you want to ruin your reputation, this is the perfect place to start. Get drunk off your ass, make out with a random guy, and come home with a tattoo. I wouldn't object to being the guy if you're running low on material."

Ew.

"Do you often do that?" I wonder aloud, rolling my near-empty cup between my fingers and watching him curiously. "Flirt with everyone without meaning it?"

The remark startles him. He blinks a few times before he's able to maintain his brooding stare. "Why? You want to know if I really think that you're gorgeous?"

"Hakuna your tatas," I say with a light laugh. "I don't care what you think. I'm just curious if this whole empty-flirtation thing actually works for you."

"You tell me, gorgeous."

"Stop calling me that."

Chase's smile emerges slowly. "Bother you?"

Before I can put him in his place, his gaze shifts to something beyond me. I turn and follow his line of vision, and for the first time I notice Chase's friends approaching us. I recognize Alec Ryder and his girlfriend Riley at the head of the group, his arm casually slung over her shoulder. Joe Travis is walking slightly behind them, focused on his phone like a classic third wheel. I realize the proximity between Chase and me, and hastily shuffle farther along the wall.

"Hi," Riley greets, her blue eyes flitting between the two of us as if suggesting something. Her features are soft with kindness, framed with auburn curls. "I'm Riley, one of Chase's friends. This is Alec and Joe."

Alec, her boyfriend, is dark-haired and tanned, considerably taller than her. They look like complete opposites, somehow, yet they go so well together. I don't fail to notice the way his arm tightens around her shoulders. "Hi, I'm Alec. Who are you?"

Before I can respond, Riley has elbowed her boyfriend in the ribs. "Hey, grasshole, you can't just ask someone who they are! It's rude."

Alec smirks down at her. "Would you prefer I introduce myself in another way?"

"No!"

Joe pushes past them both and comes to a stop directly in front of Chase and me. His bright, mischievous blue eyes are trained exclusively on me. "You're the girl from the car."

"Erika," I respond charmingly. "At your cab-service."

"Anyone who drives my best buddy home is already in my good books." Joe gives me a beaming smile and leans on Chase's shoulder. Chase, scowling, shrugs him off, but Joe isn't deterred. His voice lowers to a whisper, and he leans towards me, gesturing back at his Chase with his thumb. "He doesn't like me friendzoning him."

"Shut up, you," Chase groans, smacking Joe on the back. Everyone in our year is aware of the bromance between the pair: they've been friends since they were preschoolers, but they act more like brothers. It's easy to tell which of the two is more approachable.

Joe, seemingly reading my mind, adds, "He thinks he's very intimidating. Don't worry, he's a big ol' teddy bear when you get to know him."

Chase glares menacingly, and I can't help but laugh.

"This is Erika," he introduces with a sigh. "Erika, everyone."

"Didn't I hear you call her gorgeous before we came over, Thatcher?" Alec asks, his cobalt eyes glinting with amusement as they flit between us.

"I did it to annoy her," Chase says quickly. "She doesn't like it."

"I just don't like you," I chime.

"Feeling's mutual."

Riley is grinning. "Is Chase being rude to you, Erika? If so, I can kick his ass."

Chase snorts. "You're five foot three. I could sit on you, and you would die."

"I am small but mighty. Like a bullet."

Alec makes a scoffing sound, rubbing her hair. "Okay, Greene."

It's weird to watch Alec Ryder being so sentimental. Last year, Alec had a bit of a bad reputation, and everyone is still adjusting to his changed ways. He and Riley have become the new "it" couple of Lindale High: all of Alec's previous jealousy-ridden admirers have now transformed into hardcore fangirls. I never got involved with that whole debacle, but it's strange how much things have changed.

"Where's Violet?" Chase grumbles.

"She's just grabbing a drink," Joe replies.

"You'd like Violet." Chase tugs at the label on his beer bottle before evaluating me with dark eyes. "And Riley's the same too, actually. You all share the same annoying sarcasm and sharp tongue. It's exhausting."

Riley winks at me and I smile.

"Here I was, thinking that you were a player, Chase,"

Alec says. "And here *you* are, proving exactly how to get girls *not* to like you."

"Like you can talk, Alec," Joe drawls. He twists and leans on the brick wall beside me, his tanned arm only inches away. "You did the same tactic with Riley: winding her up to get a reaction. Leave Chase's strategy alone."

Chase groans, places his empty glass bottle on the wall, and stands up. His eyes flicker to mine. "We mutually irritate each other."

I nod. "That's accurate."

"Remember when we were like that?" Riley whispers not-so-softly to Alec, looking up at him from her position nestled under his arm.

Chase makes another grumbling sound. I watch him as he scratches the back of his neck, nodding a quick goodbye before disappearing into the crowd on his way indoors.

"It was fun meeting you all," I say with a smile. "I should probably go check if my friend is okay. I'll see you around?"

My voice ends on a hopeful note. They seem like nice people.

"Definitely," Joe affirms.

Smiling, I hop down from the wall and walk back to the house. I can feel the bass in the floor already, the rise of chatter and the heat. Despite the increasing noise levels, I somehow manage to hear another of Riley's murmurs to Alec.

"I think that's the first girl that Chase has ever actually introduced us to."

That girl really doesn't know how to whisper.

Miko smells like coconut rum and floral body spray. Holding a mostly empty plastic cup in one hand and swaying slightly, she looks at me with hopeful expectation.

"Want another—" Hiccup. "Drink?"

"I'm all good!" I reply, holding up my newly filled cup. "Are you drunk, Mi-Miko?"

"Nah, I'm fine." She grins sheepishly. "Are you?"

"Sobriety is not in my vodka-bulary."

Miko erupts into giggles, bending over her knees, and even I can't seem to stop my laughter spilling over. I'm so *funny*. As my eyes wander around my surroundings, I sip more and more of the candy-tasting poison called gin. Mom warned me not to have more than the cans I brought with me, but I couldn't help myself. Someone clearly took some of the drinks from my bag because they disappeared so quickly. Miko's mom wouldn't condone her drinking at all, which is why she needs to be especially careful. Not that she is.

She exhales sharply beside me, recapturing my attention. Despite my blurring vision, I can see that her eyebrows are furrowed and she's glaring at something outside. I follow her gaze, and instantly I realize exactly why she's so tense. Kai, Miko's younger brother, is standing on the deck with a green can in his hand. He's relaxed, his free hand tucked loosely into his pocket, and laughing at something with a group of older guys, from our year group. A sophomore amongst seniors.

"What is he doing here?"

"I don't know," Miko responds. She's stopped swaying. The role of responsible older sister has sobered her up almost instantly. "Okan would kill him if she knew he was here."

Saying that aloud seems to switch something on in her brain, and Miko grabs my hand and tugs me towards the glass doors. We step into the colder air. The music is quite muted out here, but the conversations are louder.

Several raucous boys cheer and crow at each other from opposite ends of the ping pong table. There are lines of cups filled with amber-colored liquid on the green surface. Beer pong. Kai is under the string lights. His hair is too long for his face, and his smile is controlled enough to hide the braces on his teeth. When his eyes finally fix upon us, they instantly roll. I'm pretty sure that Kaito Tamura rolls his eyes more than he breathes.

"What are you doing here?" Miko hisses, storming to a halt in front of him. "You're a sophomore! You're underage."

"And? So are you."

"I'll keep this from Okan if you leave *now*."

"I don't want to leave, Miko."

The four senior guys exchange looks and step away, sensing the shift in atmosphere. I offer them a little nod in thanks. My hand is still in Miko's and she's squeezing it tightly. I know how much she hates doing this. Fights with her brother never work out well.

"This isn't fair, Kaito. You can't keep doing this, you know what could happen."

"She doesn't need to know about this. I can look after myself."

"You're sixteen!" I can hear the pain and frustration in Miko's voice. "Please, Kai. We've lost Dad already; our whole family is falling apart. I can't lose you too."

Kai's chin drops to his chest, and his cheeks burn pink. The dispute is catching quite a bit of surrounding attention. The beer pong game has quietened.

I tug on Miko's hand to draw her attention and mutter softly. "You may want to go somewhere a bit more private."

Miko glances around instantly, and her cheeks flush too

as she notices the attention she's gathered. She nods and drops my hand to grab Kai's forearm instead. Any contact with her brother seems to cause her immense stress currently. Her voice is strained, a complete contrast from her happy giggles only three minutes earlier.

"I'll see you in a bit," she says to me, tugging Kai back into the house.

I take a sip of my drink and sigh. Miko only wants to keep the peace, but any intervention she attempts is met with defensiveness, shouting, and the slamming of doors. It can be really aggravating to see how upset she gets. Sometimes I want to shake Kai and show him what his actions are doing to her. Other times, I feel like the boy needs a hug and someone to reassure him that it's going to be okay. It's a constant coin toss.

"Quite a scene."

I look over my shoulder with a smile. "Spying on me, Thatcher?"

Chase smirks slightly and leans back against the brick wall behind him. "Only if there's drama involved. Who was the kid?"

"Miko's brother, Kai," I murmur. I step back and lean against the wall beside him, angling my head back against the rough brick and admiring how everything is out of focus, slightly fuzzy when I've been drinking. Colors seem brighter, and everything feels warm and inviting and funny. "He's been acting out a bit recently."

"Maybe you should be asking him for guidance instead."

I shrug. "You're right. He wouldn't constantly assume I was hitting on him."

Chase does something I didn't expect, then. He laughs.

"Chasey-boo," says Joe, leaning out from the open glass doors and peering at us. "I've been looking for you everywhere, man. Don't suppose you two would be interested in some drinking games?"

Joe smiles merrily, his eyes glittering as they bounce from Chase to me.

"I definitely am," says Chase, pushing himself away from the wall to follow his friend inside. He halts at the door and both boys look to me for my answer. Miko won't be back for a while, so I guess it could be fun. Drinking with new people is always fun.

"Go on then," I say, throwing my free hand up. "You've coerced me."

And I follow them inside.

5

Heartbreaker, Nose-breaker

Alec's gaze flits dangerously around the table.

"Most likely to..." Dramatic pause. "Get arrested."

There is no pause for deliberation because we all know where to look. Chase and Joe, who are sitting opposite me at the table, instantly glance towards each other. Joe smiles his signature cheeky grin—the one that breaks hearts from afar.

"Together?"

Chase nods. "Together."

The two boys tap their cups together and lift them to their mouths simultaneously. A few seconds of respectful, hushed silence pass as we watch them drain the remainder of alcohol from their cups. I've lost count of how many drinks they've had during this game, but I can recognize the hazy, unfocused glimmer in their eyes. It's the same one that's in my eyes. The same one that everyone at this table has adopted. Regardless of who has consumed how much, we're all absolutely, unquestionably *hammered*.

I glance sheepishly at the other people around the table, my vision blurring with alcohol. I'm sitting between Riley and Miko, who joined in as soon as she'd managed to persuade Kai to go home. While there are only eight people playing the game, we've been surrounded by a crowd of interested onlookers, commenting and cheering as they gather around us. I suppose it's entertaining to watch people destroy their livers.

Joe hums loudly, his head rolling to the side. "Most likely to have a hangover."

With a resounding noise of complaint, every person at the table lifts their cups.

As the last of the drink runs down my throat, I squeeze my eyes shut in relief. My throat is burning, physically rejecting the flow of liquor, and I slam my empty cup down to the table with watering eyes.

"That was awful," I complain. "Who poured more gin into my drink?"

"You did," Riley replies, grinning.

"Oh." I clear my throat. "Oops."

I stretch my fingers out for my gin bottle and refill my cup with a shaking hand. I'm pretty sure each of my drinks has grown progressively stronger as my ability to measure has degraded. As I add in the lemonade, I glance up and through my foggy vision, then distinguish Chase watching me. I stick my tongue out at him.

"Most likely to steal a bra," Dylan pipes up.

Rolling his eyes, Alec drinks from his bottle.

"Maybe you should slow down a little bit," Riley says teasingly to her boyfriend.

Alec smiles at her, grabbing her hand and squeezing it tightly. "I'm not drunk, Greene, just intoxicated by your effect on me."

The boys cheer, and Joe slaps Alec on the shoulder. Riley pulls her hand away from his but there's a smile on her face. There seems to be some sort of inside joke when it comes to Alec's pick-up lines. The ones that I've witnessed have been very creative.

"Most likely to break someone's heart," Violet drawls, her elbow on the table, her hand cupping her chin.

Joe leans closer to Chase, his voice apologetic. "Don't worry, Chasey, I'll get that oak casket you like for the funeral."

"Hey!" Miko protests as Chase reaches for his cup, edging forwards in her chair. "I think this one needs a discussion."

"A discussion?" Violet repeats incredulously. She points a finger at Chase. "You do realize that this guy singlehandedly keeps Kleenex in business, don't you?"

Miko props up her swaying head with her hand. "Everyone knows that Chase does *one date* before he loses interest in a girl. How can someone truly be heartbroken if they've only had one date with the guy?"

I notice a hushed murmur of agreement from the onlookers surrounding us.

Alec frowns. "She raises a good point."

"Who would you say needs to drink, Miko?" Violet asks curiously.

"I nominate Erika," Miko says, pointing at me with a shaky finger. Her face is lit up with wicked humor, dark eyes sparkling. "She breaks hearts, and she doesn't even try. She becomes their *friend*, ensnares them with her killer personality, and then they break their own hearts crushing on her. It's like magic."

I shake my head, blushing under the weight of people's attention. "That's not true!"

Dylan, sitting at the top of the table, scoffs. "Oh, come on, enough members of the football team have thought about shooting their shot with you and cowered out."

"That doesn't make me a heartbreaker!"

"You're right," Riley chimes in, grinning mercilessly. "It makes you competition."

I follow the meaning of her words and, instantly, my gaze flits over to Chase. Our stares lock and a tingle dances downwards from the nape of my neck. His eyes are practically buttery with playfulness, the small upward quirk of his lips somehow simultaneously irritating and captivating.

"Bit of a heartbreaker, are you, gorgeous?"

I lean back in my seat, my arms crossed over my chest. "No, but I will happily break your bones if you keep calling me that."

"I vote they both take a drink," Dylan says smoothly. "Chase for being a one-date-wonder and Erika for being painfully unattainable."

"All in favor say aye!" Joe calls.

A multitude of voices, both sitting around the table and surrounding it, chime in with an assortment of *aye*s. Muttering low complaints, I reach over for my cup again. Just as I've lifted it from the table, I feel something bounce against the rim. I glance up to see Chase, leaning forwards with his own cup outstretched, only inches from mine.

"Drink up."

Frowning, I lift the drink to my lips again, wincing as the familiar burn of alcohol sears my throat. After a few seconds, I finish, wiping my mouth dry with the back of my hand.

The world is rolling and lulling around me as I glance around the table.

"I'm going to go and get some water," I announce, standing up from my chair and wobbling with the sudden shift in balance. "I'll be back in a mo—minute."

I don't wait to hear responses and drunkenly wind myself through the people in the living room towards the hallway. I've sunk into my usual routine at parties: to drink too much, dance too much, cry a bit, and then call my sister for a messy ride home. My mom is going to kill me if she finds out. I push my way out into the hallway and blink at the change in pace. Everybody seems to be moving into the dining room. They're playing different music in there, and the two beats are overlapping hideously in this hall. Curious, I follow a group into the smaller room.

The dining room is at full capacity, and I struggle to squeeze in. The music is louder, an upbeat number by The Killers that ricochets through my legs and into my chest. A guy I know from track is dancing goofily on the table, cheered on by his friends. I can't remember what his name is. I'm not sure what it is in my alcohol-soaked brain that tells me to join him. Unfortunately, I listen to it.

Wobbling precariously on my heels, I place one foot on a leather dining room chair and giggle to myself.

"I used to do ballet classes," I tell nobody in particular, and climb onto the seat.

Cheered on by the hoots and wolf whistles of people around me, I take one unsteady step onto the table and push myself up next to my friend. Nicolas—that's his name. He greets me enthusiastically, hugging me tightly before grabbing my hands and pulling them in odd directions. A little squeal of excitement exits my mouth as I look down and see that I'm taller than everybody else in the room, and they're all looking at me.

"I used to take ballet classes," I repeat loudly, and they cheer once more.

"Let's see your moves, sweetheart!" someone shouts.

"Erika!" I hear another shout from my left.

I turn towards the source of the voice, but it's difficult to make out faces in the crowd below. I spot someone, a boy, pushing through crowds of people and headed towards me. His hair is dark, but other than that, I can't see anything. I shake my head to clear some of the fluff from my brain so that I can concentrate. The song changes to a fast-paced dance track, and I begin to bump my hips against Nic's, to the delighted cheers of our many fans.

Suddenly, someone grabs my leg.

I gasp in surprise, looking down to see a smug blond guy called Max, his hand on my calf. Frowning, I quickly shake off his hold.

Beside him, Chase appears, standing in front of the table. He's staring up at me in disbelief and I can't help but laugh loudly at his expression.

"Are you insane?" Chase shouts over the music.

I continue swaying, ignoring him, until Max grabs my leg again. *This boy needs to be careful before I shove his grabbing hand so far up his ass he has to sit on his elbow.* I try to shake him off but this time he's more persistent. I shriek a little in anger, straining to pull myself away from his grip without losing balance. Chase finally notices the tool bag standing next to him and, even through my drunken vision, I can see his eyes narrow.

"Get the hell off of her."

Max, oblivious, lifts his hands up to my knee.

Thinking quickly, I pull back my leg sharply, before sailing it through the air. I intend to kick him lightly in the shoulder, but the room is swaying. The toe of my ankle boot hits Max right on the nose with too much force behind it. He yells out in pain as he stumbles backwards into the mass of dancing bodies, knocking people over behind him and falling to the floor amongst them. He was being a pest, but still. *Oops*.

Dropping to my knees on the table, I slide off the edge and ignore the grumbling complaints around me. "Um, I didn't mean to kick you *that* hard."

Max silences me with a heated glare, a hand covering his nose. When he lifts it away, I stiffen at the sight of the blood seeping from his nostrils.

"Well crap," I mutter, kneeling in front of him. I reach out and grab his chin firmly, tilting it back to stop the blood flow. Max seems so surprised that he doesn't even resist. Then, I lift his hand back up and force him to pinch his nose, arranging his fingers with my own. "Hold it up here, like this. Keep your head back."

"You're getting blood on your hands," a voice comments from behind me. I look to my side to see that Chase has appeared beside me, his unimpressed frown trained on Max.

"I might've broken the guy's nose, Chase! I don't care!"

Chase shrugs. "He deserved it."

"That's not the point."

Chase leans down beside me, his jaw taut with irritation as he examines the boy in front of me as if he were something slimy. Max, even with his head tilted back, manages to glare back.

"What the hell is your problem?"

"You are," Chase says simply. He cocks his head slowly, watching as a drop of blood dances its way down Max's neck until it stains the collar of his white T-shirt. "Strange. I always thought Maxi-pads were supposed to soak up blood, and here you are gushing it out."

"This bitch kicked me in the face," Max hisses.

My bloody hands fall from his chin, and I scowl. "I only meant to tap you."

"Trust me, Erika, you can tap far better than this guy," Chase says bluntly. "Come on, you need to get that blood off."

Nodding, I stumble up to my feet, the gin-rush returning in full force. Chase loops a hand around my wrist and pulls me back through the crowd towards the quieter hallway. I think how it's quite funny how quickly a crowd parts when they notice a girl with blood all over her fingers. We make it through the hallway and up the stairs without a problem, but we're finally forced to stop by the closed bathroom door. Chase leans against the wall, releasing my wrist and sighing as he notices the blood on his own hand.

Two girls stumble past us, staring at my hands with wide eyes. I wiggle my fingers, a taunting smile on my face.

"Don't worry," I call. "I'm just on my period and I sneezed!"

The girls drop their gazes to the floor and quicken their pace.

Grinning with self-satisfaction, I glace back at Chase. He's watching me with a faintly amused expression, his cheekbones highlighted in the low lighting of the corridor. I lean a little closer, squinting to focus my vision on his face.

"So, you're helping me."

Chase glowers down at me. "Not really."

"You are," I insist. "Very uncharacteristic behavior. Are you feeling alright?"

Without warning, I press a bloody hand to his forehead, miming concern. I watch as the action dawns on him: the way that his eyes light up with horrified realization, the way he stumbles away so quickly that his legs almost tangle together. He looks at me in shock, but the sight is made infinitely more amusing by the dark red handprint stamped on his forehead.

A guy from our chemistry class wanders past, whining the words to an old James Blunt song. This is an opportunity too good to waste.

I gesture a frantic thumb towards Chase, widen my eyes and whisper, "Big vampire kink."

He stops singing.

"You're going to pay for that, gorgeous," Chase mutters darkly, stepping towards me. He reaches for one of my wrists, and the very second that he pins it against the wall is the second that the bathroom door unlocks beside us. With a loud click, Violet emerges, ruffling her hair until she spots us. Her eyebrows shoot upwards as she registers our compromising position. Then, her gaze falls to my bloodied hands and her mouth pops open in horror.

"Oh God, you didn't *actually* rip someone's heart out, did you?"

Chase ignores her. "She got into a fight with Max Tennyson. Spread the word."

Before Violet or I can protest, he utilizes his grip on my wrist to pull me sharply into the bathroom behind him. When he releases my wrist, I stumble a few steps towards the bath. The door clicks shut behind me and I spin just in time to watch Chase lock it.

"Spread the word?" I echo incredulously.

"You want to ruin your reputation, don't you?" he asks, heading for the basin. The music is muted in here, and it's suddenly a lot easier to hear him speak. "If people think you've been in a fight, that instantly tarnishes your shiny halo. Max has the bloody nose to prove it."

"Right." I nod uncertainly. "Of course."

Only I don't actually want to tarnish my reputation.

Chase turns the faucet on. He waits a few seconds for the water to heat up before plunging his hands into the stream, tinting the water a rusty red color as Max's blood washes away. Then he soaps his palms, cups the water in them, and stoops down to wash his face clear of my mark. After a minute, he turns to look at me again. The front of his chocolate-colored hair is darkened with moisture, and droplets dance through the hollows of his face and cling to his angular cheekbones and jaw, highlighting his features perfectly.

He swipes a towel from the rack and begins to dry himself.

"Are you going to keep staring at me or are you going to get clean?" he asks, his voice muffled by the thick cotton.

"I was staring at you because I was concerned," I say coolly, gliding over to the running faucet and submerging my hands in the water. I lather them with bar of scented soap. It all feels extraordinarily good. "You have no idea what people have done with that towel, and you're rubbing it all over your face."

Chase stiffens, before promptly throwing the towel down to the white tiles like it's on fire. His hair is messy—damp spikes sticking in odd directions—and he'd look cute if it wasn't for the scowl.

Before I can react, he leans over to the faucet and places his finger over the lip of the opening, angling the water stream directly at me. I squeak as water sprays over my face and chest, stumbling back a few steps. My eyes fly open in disbelief, and my gaze lands on the laughing idiot standing beside the basin. "I can't believe you just did that!"

"Now, now," he says teasingly. "What will people think of you when you emerge soaking wet from the bathroom with a *boy*, I wonder?"

Without hesitating, I cup my hands under the faucet to fill them with water and fling it directly at his face. As soon as the splash hits, Chase dives towards me with a wicked grin, seizing my wrists and pushing me backwards until my calves hit the bathtub.

"You wanted to ruin your reputation, didn't you?" He tilts his head to the side and droplets flick from his wet hair over my face.

I push my wrists forward as hard as I can, bumping his chest. "You're infuriating."

"So are you."

I scowl up at him, my makeup undoubtedly running down my wet face. Slowly, he detaches his fingers from my wrists and leans down to turn off the running faucet. The floor tiles are slick with water, and the towel that he has abandoned is lying in a crumpled pile.

"Are you—" Chase murmurs, interrupting the flow of my thoughts. My eyes snap up to his and he clears his throat. "Are you sure about this?"

I stare up at the boy with the wet hair and the sparkling dark eyes, and I feel a sudden rush through my body. The liquor in my system nods my head before I give it permission to.

"I'm sure," I say, with a dry mouth.

"Okay, I just want to double-check," Chase states, lifting his hand to his mouth. "What do you want to do first?"

"I don't know—steal something? Vandalize school property? I thought you were supposed to lead the way with this."

Slowly, almost tentatively, he bites down on his left knuckle as he thinks. It takes him a few seconds to speak again, and his hand falls. "We can do some graffiti on the principal's car tomorrow. Meet me at the bike sheds at noon, middle of third class."

"The middle of third class?" I echo. "I have sprints practice then. How?"

"I'm sure you can figure something out."

Then, without a backwards glance, he unclicks the bathroom door and saunters away into the party. The one that I had almost forgotten about entirely.

6

No Paint, No Gain

"Erika, are you listening?"

I hurriedly avert my gaze from the fitness watch on my wrist and offer Dylan an apologetic smile. We're standing in the first and second lanes of Lindale High's athletic track, practicing our interval sprints. The late morning sun has made the surface of the tarmac sticky underfoot; there are few clouds around to filter its glare. I'm unsure if the sweat gathering in my hairline is because of the weather, the exercise, or if I'm simply burning away the stubborn remnants of my hangover from last night.

Interval sprints are tough at the best of times, but they seem particularly torturous today. Dylan is attempting to discuss my next set, but I can't seem to remain focused. Instead, I'm occupied with watching every minute of time tick by on my watch.

"I'm so sorry, Dyl," I murmur, wiping my forehead dry. "I'm a bit out of it today."

"Hungover?"

"I don't know. Maybe."

"You don't look it," he comments, crossing his arm over his torso to stretch his shoulder. "Did your mom catch on to your excessive consumption last night?"

"I wouldn't be standing in front of you, alive and well, if she had." I gesture down at my body, begrudgingly squeezed into a sports bra and running clothes.

"Fair point."

Before I can stop it, my gaze flits back down to the digital numbers glowing on my watch. It's five minutes to noon now, and I need to leave to meet Chase. Nevertheless, my body is refusing to cooperate, and I haven't moved an inch. Why am I not moving?

Around me, the ambient noise of the sports field suddenly feels louder. Every shout from the coach, every squeal of a whistle, every sprinter slicing through the air beside us is triggering. This is the part where I meet Chase and catch him in the act of vandalizing Principal Blythe's car. This is the end of my troubles—so why don't I want to do it?

"Monroe?" Coach yells, jogging the final twenty paces towards us. She's a stout woman, with the strongest calf muscles I've ever seen. Her eyebrow is raised. "Is everything okay there? Why aren't you doing your next set?"

"Uh." I clear my throat and force myself into action after several seconds of staring aimlessly at the track. "Sorry, Coach, I'm just not feeling very well."

For added effect, I place a hand on my stomach. I can see Dylan's questioning expression in my peripheral vision, but I stare forward determinedly.

Coach Taylor comes to a stop beside us, breathing heavily. Her nose is scrunched with confusion at my lack of sassy comment. She glances at Dylan.

He shrugs.

"Maybe you should head to the medical office," she suggests finally.

"Yeah, I think so. Thanks."

Clutching my stomach in fake pain, I begin to jog in the direction of the girls' changing rooms. Behind me, I can hear Coach organizing for Dylan to join with another pair of sprinters. I would wave goodbye to him, but I can't allow myself to stop for long enough to be able to question my decision. Instead, I quicken my pace. My breathing doesn't slow until I'm standing in the cool changing rooms, scooping the last of my belongings into my rucksack.

Stop feeling so nervous. Let's get this over with.

I force myself back out into the sunshine, flinching as the brightness of the sky contradicts the dull anticipation stirring in my stomach. I focus my mind on the crunch of the gravel beneath my sneakers to try and distract myself. My phone feels hot in the pocket of my shorts, like a weapon that I'm trying to conceal.

The walk to the parking lot, along the perimeter of the school grounds, isn't a long one. I arrive at the bike shed much quicker than I'd like. Hidden from the view of windows, the shed is notorious for smokers at lunchtime and couples that want to make out. The structure itself is old and rotting, with a padlock on the door and a window meshed with spiderwebs. I grit my teeth as I sneak around the exterior.

Where the hell is Chase?

"You came, then."

I jump at the voice behind me and the warm breath tickling my ear. After a few seconds of cold surprise, my expression morphs into a scowl, and I whirl around to face the dark-haired idiot snickering unashamedly at my reaction.

"That's funny," I snap, pressing a hand over my thumping heart. "I thought it was only spiders that hang out near this shed, but clearly there are snakes too."

Chase snickers again, leaning against the shed and crossing his ankles casually. "If I'm a snake, then you're the bunny. Who knew you could jump so high?"

My frown deepens at his amusement, and the sickly feeling of guilt ebbs a little with my irritation. I cross my arms over my chest. "I'm here, I managed to get out of practice—now can you tell me what the plan is? How are we supposed to spray paint the principal's car in the middle of the day without being seen?"

"Well, Joe gave me the spray paint." Chase gestures to a black holdall sitting on the ground to our left. "We just have to choose the right moment and be speedy about it."

"Are you sure you know what you're doing?"

My voice is unmistakably wary. After all, if I get caught doing this, what is Blythe going to think? As if to reassure myself, my hand hovers over my phone in my pocket, the camera facing outwards. When we get caught, it's going to be on my terms. I don't owe Chase anything. Repeat. Repeat. Repeat.

"In precisely ..." Chase lifts his phone and checks the time. "... two minutes, the secretary will be on his coffee break. He has a fifteen-minute break. Blythe has parked in the same space every day so far: directly outside of her office. No other window has a view of us, and the camera above the reception door hasn't worked since before last summer. We have a fifteen-minute gap to get in, do some damage and leave."

"Wow," I mutter. "You're smarter than you look, Thatcher."

Chase kneels to rifle through the contents of the black bag. I watch nervously as he draws out four silver spray cans and places them on the ground beside him. He seems to sense my apprehension, because he smirks at me as he holds up two cans for me to take. That smirk only grows when I hesitate for a few seconds before taking them.

"Why are you doing this?" I ask, my lip sliding between my teeth.

Chase quirks an eyebrow up, rolling a can between his hands. "Why not?"

"I could give you lots of reasons," I murmur, glancing down at the spray paint in my hands. I decide to move the conversation on. "So, how come I'm stuck with pink and purple?"

"Because blue and green are mine," Chase says simply. "Now after we do this, we need to throw the cans away. We can't leave any traces so be careful not to get any onto your clothes. Have you ever used spray paint before?"

"No," I admit honestly. "Haven't really needed to before now."

Chase stands up from the floor in one fluid movement, kicking the bag under a bush and turning to face me. His fingers switch onto the buttons of the two cans, and I automatically wince and shy away, thinking he's going to spray me.

"You're an idiot," Chase says with a sigh. "Did I not just tell you we can't have paint on our clothes? I'm not going to spray you. I'm just showing you how to use the cans."

"I'm not an imbecile. I know how to use one." I glower at Chase. "I have this amazing thing called hairspray at home; looks just like it."

"Stop being a smart-ass. It's irritating."

"I'm sorry if my intelligence insults your ego," I snap back. "It's been two minutes now, I'm pretty sure we can go. Unless you've forgotten the fifteen-minutes-and-no-more window we're operating in?"

As if to prove my point, I roll the cans between my hands and put my pointer fingers on the activating buttons. All I'd have to do would be to apply a little pressure, and Chase would be covered in a hot pink spray. *Hey, that's a way I could get him caught.* I consider my idea for a second, but it's probably not going to happen. If Chase saw any of my paint on him, he'd just spray me back. The video is my plan—I'll stick to it.

I follow Chase's lead as we creep to the side of the shed and he scours the parking lot for any sign of activity. My pulse begins to quicken, until I can almost hear the thrumming in my ears. Just this one recording, and then it's over. Tucking a paint can under my arm, I reach for my phone and begin to navigate the screen to turn on my video recorder.

But before I can even unlock the damn thing, Chase darts away from our hiding place and out across the parking lot. I curse, fumbling to shove my phone back into my pocket before I sprint across the tarmac after him. It's only a short sprint, but I collapse breathless beside him at the side of Mrs. Blythe's car: a brand new and undoubtedly expensive Mercedes.

Which you are about to vandalize.

We're positioned by the hood of the car, and the reception window is situated on our left. Where I'm chewing my lip at the sight of the camera above the door, Chase is attempting to peer into the window to check for signs of the office faculty.

"I don't think anyone is in there," he says quietly. "Let's do this."

My mouth drops open as he stands up, in full view, and shakes one of the cans. It makes clicking noises in quick succession, and I almost wince at the sound.

"My heart is beating so fast," I mutter. "How are you doing this?"

Chase grins down at me. "Gorgeous, anything that gets your blood racing is probably worth doing."

I stare at him in surprise for a few seconds, before hesitantly rising to my feet. I feel very exposed, standing up in the lot with the evidence in my red, red hands, but I bite back the feeling. Chase is watching me, a smirk playing on his lips. My cue.

Before I can overthink my actions, I press my fingers down on both spray cans, watching as jets of hot pink and purple begin to coat the shiny graphite exterior of the car. It dawns on me that I haven't even considered what I want to paint. My hands seize up in panic and I release the buttons, leaving a stripe of each color on the side of the car. Chase, beside me, is in the process of drawing male genitalia on the hood. Immature, I admit, but a bit of a classic.

My hands are shaking with nerves. Excitement. Adrenaline. Something.

"Are you just going to stand there or are you actually going to paint?"

Chase's voice snaps me out of my daze, and I force myself to continue. I try to dispel my anxieties, my morals, my excitement and focus on each vibrant line of color. I write four wobbly letters in hot pink, matching Chase's vulgar drawing perfectly. It's only as I finish going over the K with purple shadow that the worries catch up with me.

I need to record this; I need to get it over with.

Glancing warily at Chase on the other side of the car, I place the spray cans down and reach into my pocket for my phone. The screen is hot and hard to see in the sunlight. Scooping a hand over it to dim the light, I almost curse aloud at the sight I'm greeted with. The apple logo, and a thin loading bar.

My phone is doing its scheduled updates.

"Crap," I mutter, sliding the useless thing back into my pocket. I need to stop this spray painting before someone sees me; especially now that I can't get the proof. Yet when I glance down at the can on the floor, I feel a twinge of excitement in my chest. Some self-sabotaging, adrenaline-junkie part of my brain is enjoying this danger.

So, with my heart pounding and a grin threatening to break out on my face, I pick up the cans from the floor and resume painting. Every nerve in my chest is fizzing with anticipation, the logical side of my brain is screaming at me in protest, and is it all worth it for a couple of wobbly purple daisies? Oddly, yes. A bubble of laughter escapes my chest.

Chase is grinning too. "You like?"

"I love."

I bite my lip and watch as the last of the pink paint sputters out onto the car. I could mark Chase with paint, I could get him expelled without a camera ... but as I look over at him, I know I can't. He's just a boy. He's having a good time. He doesn't deserve this.

Damn you, Erika, for feeling guilty.

The warm feeling dies the second I hear the shrill ring of a phone from somewhere nearby. An icy shiver runs down my spine and I look at Chase in unmasked horror. It's getting louder, someone is approaching. Chase ducks down on his side of the car, and I follow suit, before crawling around to meet him in the middle. The cans suddenly feel like branding irons in my hands.

Well, this is it. You're both being expelled now, Erika, well done.

The ringtone cuts off suddenly—has the person seen us?

"We need to go," Chase hisses. "We need to go, now."

"How are we going to do that without being seen?"

The corner of Chase's mouth lifts into an awkward smile, and the panic ebbs away from my expression. He's done this before, I realize. He can get us out of this.

"Follow me," he whispers. Before I can even nod, he darts away from the car, dodging across the tarmac, leaning over to keep out of sight. Cursing under my breath, I follow him, running from shadow to shadow and not daring to look up for the fear of being seen. The sun on my back burns down on me like a spotlight, and my breathing is ragged. Chase and I race from car to car, and that's when I notice where he is leading us.

"We're headed for the exit?" I whisper incredulously. "Is that not the most obvious thing in the world? If we're missing in action, absent for half of the day, and Blythe's car is freshly decorated?"

Chase comes to a stop by a red car, less than five yards

from the exit gates. He presses his back against the passenger door, and I flop down beside him, breathless.

"I thought you wanted to catch attention?"

I give him a flat look.

"Relax, gorgeous," he mutters, rolling his eyes. "Everybody sneaks out at this time because Brian isn't on duty. Nobody is going to see or know for certain that it was us."

I continue to stare at him doubtfully, and he goes on.

"I know at least five other people who are skipping today," he says, his voice adopting a calm, reasoning tone. I'm almost surprised by how reassuring he's being. That is, until that lofty grin appears. "I must say, it's cute that you're getting so paranoid. I almost forgot that you're a newbie at all of this."

"We left our bags behind the shed," I point out, ignoring his latter comment.

"We'll collect them at the end of the day."

"What are we doing with the paints?"

"We'll ditch them in a random trash can. Stop worrying."

I huff out a loud breath. "Then stop worrying me."

"Gorgeous, just—" Chase's stops his sentence abruptly as his attention is captured by something across the lot. I watch with concern as his jaw turns to the left and his eyes follow a hasty movement towards the school gates. Instinctively, I scour the lot to decipher the root of his distraction. I register the figure in black just as Chase says, "See? I told you. Someone else is sneaking out now too."

The figure doesn't appear to have noticed us. With one hand rooted deep into the pocket of their jeans, and a dark hood pulled down over their face, they stride with intent toward the exit gate. A phone is pressed tightly to their ear, and their mutter is so low that the only indication they're talking at all is the indistinct motion of their lips. This person must be the source of the ringtone that startled us.

As if sensing that they are being observed, their head lifts to survey their surroundings. At the exact moment that we catch a glimpse of furrowed dark eyebrows and anxious eyes, the boy notices us in our position by the car. His hoodie is slightly too small, decorated with the faded yellow Nirvana logo on the front.

Although it barely fits anymore, he won't throw it away because it's his favorite.

"Hey," Chase mumbles as my realization dawns. "Isn't that Miko's kid brother?"

The question hardly seems worth responding to. Kai stares at me in surprise for a cold second before his features twist into the familiar expression of annoyance. Then he's darting away, the soles of his sneakers slapping against the tarmac.

I instinctively move to follow him, but Chase touches my arm lightly.

"You won't catch him. Even if you did, what would you say to him?"

"I would tell him to get his butt back to school before his sister decapitates him."

Chase shakes his head. "He wouldn't listen."

My sigh hisses through my teeth. I know that Chase is right, but frustration is still bubbling inside my chest. I watch, helpless, as Kai darts through the school gate. He glances back to check if he's being pursued, before finally disappearing into the street.

"You okay?" Chase asks.

"Yeah, yeah." I shake my head. "We should go too, before we get caught."

"Are you ready to make a run for it?" Chase bumps my shoulder with his own, his expression wicked with mischief. A thrill of excitement races through my chest.

Surprising even myself, I nod and turn my gaze towards the school gates.

"Let's do this."

7

The Great Escape

Twenty minutes later, Chase and I stride into a local diner casually, as if we aren't supposed to be in school and we haven't just vandalized the principal's freshly acquired personal property. The spray paints are in a random trash can and now the only thing connecting us to our crime is the dazed expression on my face and the fact that we're missing from our chemistry laboratory stools. My mind is buzzing with anxiety. I know I've been oddly quiet for the whole walk here.

I think about what my mom would say if she knew I had done this. I can picture the fierce expression on her face, the cold disappointment in her eyes. Then I see her turn away, look at Chloe and smile. The image my mind conjures is enough to make me feel sick.

"What do you want?" Chase asks, pulling his wallet from his back pocket as we approach the counter. Neon signs are hung around the room, and the one beside the food display board has painted Chase with an eerie pink glow. It doesn't distract from his brooding features, unfortunately, which are enough to catch the waitress's attention. She tucks a strand of hair behind her ear and watches us with hopeful eyes.

"I can pay for myself," I respond finally, moving my gaze to the menu.

Chase looks at me doubtfully.

"Seriously, don't worry about it."

Chase turns to face the girl behind the counter. She looks fresh out of high school, with red hair and a toothy smile. The signature Chase Thatcher charm seeps from every part of him as he returns it.

"Ignore her," he says brazenly, placing his hand on the counter and leaning towards the poor girl. "I do it all the time. We'll have two cheeseburger meals with Pepsi, please."

I raise an eyebrow. So, this is the flirty player personality that I've been missing out on: the one that scores him all the attention. While I'm sure Prince Chase the Charming would get annoying quickly, he's probably more tolerable than the moody alter ego I've been putting up with.

I step forward into the spot beside him and quickly intervene. "Make that a vanilla milkshake for me. And hold the ice for him—he's not hot enough to need it."

Chase looks at me with disbelief.

The girl giggles. "You two are a cute couple."

I open my mouth to clarify that we are *not* a couple, but before I can, Chase has looped an arm around my shoulders and tugged me into the side of his muscled torso.

"Thanks, Gemma," he says, reading her nametag. Then, squeezing my shoulders tightly, he looks down at me with adoration. "Isn't she just gorgeous? Sometimes I wonder how I was lucky enough to catch this little fish in that turbulent, cold sea of girls out there."

He thinks he's funny. Well, this little fish has got a bite.

"I was attracted to your tiny worm," I say sweetly. "What can I say? I have a low standard for bait."

The air practically sparks as he registers my comment. His eyes are narrowed with frustration, but his tone is wickedly, deceptively sweet. "Is that right, gorgeous? I don't remember you calling it tiny last night."

I pat his arm fondly. "That's because I didn't know it was there, silly!"

I turn away before I can see his glare. A waiter approaches from behind the counter, bearing a red tray filled with food and sliding it onto the counter ahead of us. He's biting back a smile.

Gemma releases an uncertain laugh and adjusts her hair. "So . . . um, *cute*. Let us know if you want anything else."

"Aw, thank you!" I say in my angelic tone. "We've had a few setbacks recently; this stupid erectile dysfunction has been taking its toll on our fledgling relationship. But they say you've got to work through problems like this. We're taking a firm approach, aren't we, Squidge? Well . . . as firm as we can manage."

I shift my gaze poignantly to Chase's crotch for a second. Gemma stares at me in outright horror.

Chase's fingers are digging into my shoulder now, and he releases a bitter laugh. "You're funny, babe."

"Oh hey!" I pluck a fry from the tray in front of us, examining it with pursed lips. It's crumpled, soft, and bending under its own weight. "Squidge, doesn't this remind you—"

"That's enough backchat for today!" Chase interrupts me, slapping my hand down. The fry falls to the floor. Chase removes his arm from around my shoulder and grabs the tray from the counter as quickly as he can manage. "Thank you for your help, Gemma."

"Yes." Gemma clears her throat uncomfortably, wiping down her shirt. "Yes, that. Droop by any time if you want refills . . . oh shit, I meant drop. Drop!"

That's my limit. The laughter explodes out of my chest, in unrestrained, musical giggles. I am faintly aware of Chase pushing me towards the back of the diner, as far as possible from the counter, but that only makes it funnier. My eyes close in exaltation, and I only have a blurry view of the patterned floor tiles. Eventually, we stop. I hear the smack of the tray on the tabletop and Chase tugs me into a red booth.

"*Squidge?*" he repeats in a hiss, sliding into the seat opposite me. "*Worm? Erectile Dysfunction?*"

"Now, now," I say, sobering up from my laughter. "You can't judge a craftsman by his tools."

"You're lucky we're in a public place," he mutters darkly, leaning over the small table between us. His features are pinched with frustration, jaw rigid and catching the light like a chiseled archangel. The freckles scattered across his nose soften his intimidation. "I only met you a few days ago and you are already the most irritating person I know."

"Here, have a peace offering." I slide my bag of fries towards him, a smile playing on my lips.

The tension melts from his face. He looks down at them questioningly. "You don't want them?"

"Never really been a big fan of fries," I say, lifting the cheeseburger up to my lips and taking a massive bite. The familiar comfort food instantly satiates the cavity of anxiety in my stomach, and I make a noise of appreciation before I swallow. "Thanks for this, Squidge. I didn't think people tended to buy burgers for the most irritating person they know."

Chase scowls, his fry lingering mid-air. "Stop calling me that."

I pretend to deliberate, then reach for my drink. "No."

"The nickname doesn't fit," he states confidently. "Trust me, gorgeous."

I bring the milkshake straw to my mouth and let it run over my bottom lip. Before he can help it, Chase's gaze drops to catch the movement. He quickly recovers and forces his gaze upwards again. This time his eyes are narrowed. I grin. I'm quite enjoying this game we seem to be playing—flirting enough to make the other person uncomfortable. If he insists on calling me gorgeous, I can do one better.

"Okay, Squidge."

He grunts with annoyance and turns back to the food. After cramming a suitable number of fries in his mouth, he swallows and his unfazed smirk returns. "So, newbie. You successfully pulled your first prank on the principal. Are you proud of yourself?"

"It was fun," I admit, pulling at a piece of lettuce. "I had a good time, surprisingly."

Chase's eyebrows rise. "Are you sticking around for more lessons?"

I know that I intend to make the next prank our last. My pulse quickens uncomfortably as I reply, "I suppose so."

We sit in comfortable silence for a couple of minutes as we eat. There's not much to talk about, and I'm enjoying my burger way too much to distract myself from it. Faint chatter lulls in the air from the scatter of customers, and the peace of it all settles over me, disintegrating most of my worry. I find myself smiling slightly and hurriedly take a sip of my milkshake to cover it. "Do you want to play a game?"

Chase doesn't even hesitate. "If it's something kinky then yes."

"Tell me, Squidge. Did your mother drop you as a baby?"

"Yup." Chase flashes a dimple. "Into a pool of sexy."

"Odd. I thought it was a chasm of jackass."

"Enough about where *I* came from." Chase leans forward, mischief tugging away his cool façade. "Did breaking through the earth's crust hurt when you ascended from hell?"

I find myself leaning forwards too. "Why? Curious about where you're headed?"

After a second, our palpable tension breaks and Chase laughs. He leans back in his chair, pushing the heft of his shoulders back and stretching his shirt tightly across his lean chest. "What game, gorgeous?"

"Never have I ever?"

Chase looks a little surprised by my idea, but he recovers quickly. He takes a long sip from his glass before banging it down on the table. The liquid inside slaps against its prison walls in frustration. "Never have I ever played this game without alcohol but sure. You can go first."

I take a bite from my burger, thinking as I chew. "Never have I ever . . . stood someone up."

Chase scowls. "I'm not that much of an asshole, Erika."

"I guess you're just so desperate for dates that you have to go," I tease.

His expression flinches the tiniest amount—it would be

unnoticeable if I wasn't watching out for it. I make a mental note not to touch the dating topic again. Clearly, it's something he's sensitive about. As much as I enjoy irritating Chase, I would be a hypocrite if I called him out for toying with girls' emotions. Some of my friends do the same thing with guys, and I bite my tongue.

Chase's expression is neutral again. "Never have I ever bullied someone."

I take a short sip from my milkshake. "I bullied a bully. He was picking on this little boy in elementary school, so I pushed him against a wall. He stopped after that."

"I don't think it counts as bullying if they enjoy it, Erika."

"Really?" I ask leisurely. "I'm not so sure he enjoyed the part where I spilled my orange juice all over his crotch. His friends called him 'Wet Willy' for the rest of the day."

Chase's lip twitches. "Touché."

I twist my straw around "Never have I ever got a tattoo."

Chase sips at his Pepsi, his eyes refocusing on the table in front of him as if the surface is suddenly very interesting. He doesn't explain why or when he was inked, although I'm dying to ask more questions.

"Never have I ever had a bad date."

I cringe at this one and take a long gulp. "He asked if I wanted to meet him after school, and we arranged to have coffee nearby. The entire time he was talking about his problems; he didn't ask me anything about myself whatsoever. I realized when he offered me money at the end that it wasn't a date. He thought I was my sister and he had been trying to organize a *counseling appointment*."

"I hope you took the money."

"I never corrected him," I say sheepishly. "I didn't want him to go and tell everyone that I mistook it for a date. We still meet every month to discuss his progress."

Chase laughs. The sound is husky, deep, and intensely addictive. I find myself smiling before I can help it.

"Never have I ever been mistaken for my sister. Oh wait," I say pointedly, tilting my cup to the ceiling before drinking.

"I don't get that," Chase comments, leaning back and squinting at my face. "I see some similarity, but not enough to mistake you."

"It doesn't happen very often. Most people agree that she's the hot one."

Chase's head tilts. "I don't call you gorgeous for no reason, Erika."

I bite my lip to fight back my smile. "Thanks, Squidge."

Chase rolls his eyes and props his feet up on the seat beside me. Lounging back with his arms across the back of the seat, he looks the picture of buff carelessness. "Never have I ever . . . *Shit*."

As the cuss word leaves his mouth, Chase's insouciant posture snaps to attention. His feet disappear from the booth beside me, he slumps over the table, and his wide eyes are trained on something behind me, where the entrance to the diner is located. Startled by his reaction, I crane around in my seat to see the object of his fear. But before I can get a glimpse, Chase grabs my wrist and tugs me towards him. We're both slumped over the diner table, with the empty tray of food underneath us, our faces inches apart.

"We need to leave now."

"Why?" I hiss.

"Principal Blythe is here."

"What?" I whisper-screech. I can feel the blood draining from my face.

"She's about to walk past. Quick—look like you're tying your shoelace."

In a smooth motion, I duck underneath the table and clasp my foot. I wrinkle my nose in disgust at a soggy fry on the floor, coated in thick dust, before noticing that I'm not alone. Chase has stooped underneath the table too; I can feel his warm breath on my forehead. He's staring down at the very same fry.

"Why are we *both* tying my shoelace?" I whisper incredulously. "That looks suspicious!"

"Well." Chase is glaring down at my sneakers. "What might look more suspicious is the fact that you don't even have shoelaces."

"Brilliant cover!" I exclaim, throwing my hands up as far as I can without hitting the gum stuck to the underside of the table. "So discreet we might as well be wearing fluorescent vests and sunglasses and directing Mrs. Blythe to the culprits of her recently vandalized car!"

Chase glares at me. "We need to slip out. She's on my right so we need to duck out of this booth on my *left* and for heaven's sake, keep *low*. I know that might be difficult for you, Miss High and Mighty."

I ignore his jab. "What about paying for the food?"

Chase winces. "Looks like we're getting a freebie. Get ready to run."

Cold horror washes over my body. "But they know what we look li—"

Before I can even finish my sentence, Chase is tugging me

out of the booth away from Principal Blythe. I fall to the floor with a faint thud, and we scoot around the back of my red leather seat to hide from the counter. The earlier adrenaline from the graffiti seems diluted and weak now. This rush is thick and hot as it courses through my veins, and my pulse is accelerating so much I can't help but worry briefly about my health.

"She's at the counter," Chase whispers, peering around the edge of the seat. "She's just ordered a coffee. It won't take long. We need to go now."

He must see the fear in my face. Eyes softening, he reaches for the hood at the back of my neck and pulls it up over my hair. He tucks those stubborn shorter pieces at the front behind my ear and gives me a small nod. *We can do this.* Before I can overthink or panic, we're up and racing out of the diner. The soles of our shoes slap against the patterned linoleum, instantly drawing attention to us. I can just hear Gemma's indignant cry as the glass door slams shut behind us, and we're in the parking lot.

The cool air swells around me as we sprint towards the road, but the realization of my situation feels even colder. *We just stole. You, Erika. You just stole!*

Chase leads us through side streets, alleyways, and footpaths so expertly that I'm forced to suspect that he's done this before. My chest is burning from lack of oxygen and my legs are aching, but I don't stop. I imagine the panic pouring after me like lava, I imagine Blythe following us like the inspector in *Subway Surfers*, and it spurs me on.

I thank my mother for forcing me to do track on Tuesday nights. I thank Dylan for being such a good runner that I've pushed myself to keep up with him on every "casual jog." I thank the heavens that I'm still wearing my running sneakers from practice earlier.

Inevitably, our steps slow. We're in a neighborhood I don't recognize, with small white houses and neatly trimmed yards. Chase grabs my hand and tugs me to the left, behind a bush. I stumble into the empty driveway, panting like I've just run a marathon, and my legs are so unsteady that I fall straight into Chase's chest.

He's panting for breath too, hands on my shoulders to steady me. We stay like that for a few seconds as we recover, listening for the noise of approaching footsteps or police vehicles, before finally we can relax. He dampens his lips enough to speak again.

"I think we got away with that."

"Where on earth did you learn to run like that?" I ask breathlessly.

"I do a lot of jogging. Helps with basketball practice."

He does basketball. Why didn't I know that?

My voice becomes wary. "Have you run away from that diner before?"

"What? No. Of course not."

He seems so taken aback by the suggestion that I can't help but believe him.

"Never." I smack his chest. "Ever, ever, ever do that to me again. Ever."

Chase laughs lightly. "I promise. Never again."

"Stop laughing! This is not funny; we could be arrested."

"We won't be." His grin is infectious, and I try my hardest to ignore the slow churn of guilt in my stomach when I consider the idea that it's *me* he's smiling at. The biggest threat is standing in front of him.

"I can't believe that just happened," I say weakly. Adrenaline is making me woozy.

"Me neither." Chase squeezes my shoulders. "How alive do you feel right now?"

The answer is *very*, but the sour taste of guilt makes it impossible to force the word beyond my lips.

8

Build a Badass

I'm ambling towards the food court, shopping bags digging uncomfortably into the crook of my arm and debit card warm in my back pocket, when Dylan decides to rudely interrupt my peaceful, thoughtless Saturday afternoon.

"Did you hear about the juniors' locker inspection yesterday?" he asks conversationally, throwing an empty bottle into the nearest trash can. "This Blythe lady is not messing around, is she? Less than a week and she's already suspending students."

The casual interjection of reality feels like a splash of ice-cold water, and I almost stop walking entirely. "What?"

"I know," he continues, his expression solemn. "She's super strict. Priya Morton had vodka stashed in her locker, and she's been suspended and kicked off the soccer team."

"I didn't think Blythe would be this bad," Miko says faintly from my left. Dylan nods.

"Usually rumors are exaggerated, but this woman is legitimately terrifying."

Miko must sense my immediate discomfort because her

hand finds mine and squeezes tightly. I glance at her as inconspicuously as I can with Dylan present, attempting to translate my panic. If Blythe is in such a rush to discipline students, I can't have much time left before she loses patience. Anxiety collects in the pit of my stomach and sits heavily.

"I just wanted to tell you because I know you've been up to some questionable stuff with Chase," Dylan says softly, re-capturing my attention. "It might not be the best time to start living out your rebel fantasies, especially if you have your heart set on Stanford."

My reply is weak. "Thanks for the warning, Dyl."

He bumps my shoulder teasingly, but his gray eyes betray his concern. "Just don't be *too* dumb. Chase told me about what happened at the diner on Wednesday."

I almost wince. "Ah. Don't worry, I took care of that."

"Took care of it?"

I nod, squeezing Miko's hand tighter. "Don't tell Chase about this, but I sent money to the diner after hours, plus a little apology for not paying before we left. I figured that they won't bother reporting the incident to the cops if they get the money."

"That was probably a good idea," Dylan says with a smile. "Look at you, you've known Chase for less than a week and you're already a criminal."

"I would like to make it known that Erika Monroe has been a bad bitch for far longer than a week," Miko pipes up. "She's just experimenting a little. Spreading her wings."

"I don't feel like a bad bitch," I mutter. "I feel like a sad bitch."

"Better let me carry some of that baggage then," Dylan teases, snatching my bags away from my arm and looping them over his instead. The gesture brings a smile back to my face despite my unease. It's hard not to smile when I'm seeing the captain of the football team strutting around with a Forever 21 shopping bag.

"What?" Dylan follows my gaze and grins. "Am I looking fabulous right now?"

"Hella fabulous," I tease. "Work it, baby. Work it."

Miko and I laugh as he messes up his hair to bedhead-chic and pouts exaggeratedly. The atmosphere suddenly feels less constricting and warm, and my steps get lighter and lighter until my unease lifts entirely. Left behind, as usual, is the familiar churn of hunger.

"Where do you both want to eat?" I ask absentmindedly, already scanning the food court for options. I ignore the crowded seating area in the center and focus on the brightly lit restaurants and takeouts around the perimeter. As I'm examining a pizza takeout with interest, I unexpectedly recognize the group standing in front of it.

"Look who's over there," Miko chimes, beating me to it. The pom-pom earrings she's wearing bounce happily as she nods in the direction of the pizzeria.

They've noticed us too. Riley waves, then beckons us over.

"Let's go and say hi." I grab Dylan's arm and tug us both into action.

When we reach the opposite side of the food court, my greeting is slightly breathless. "Well, fancy seeing you here."

"Small town life," Riley says animatedly. She's standing at the front of their little group, swinging Alec's hand in hers between their waists. Chase and Violet are standing beside them, and Joe is ordering at the pizza counter. He salutes us.

"Are you guys hungry?" Alec smirks, glancing sideways

at Chase. "We're about to order some pizza if you'd like to join us."

"Like we'd say no to pizza," Miko scoffs. She releases my hand and dances forwards a few steps to situate herself next to Violet, effectively melding the two groups.

"Do you want me to order for you?" Dylan asks me. I nod and gently slide our shopping bags free from his arm. I trust that he knows my taste by now.

"You're an angel. I'll give you the money later."

"Yeah, yeah."

Grinning, I follow Miko's footsteps and approach the girl with dark purple hair and a wicked grin. Riley joins us a second later, our shopping bags bumping clumsily.

"How was the hangover, Erika?" Violet teases, raising her eyebrow. "You were covered in blood the last time I saw you, so I'm guessing painful."

"Meh." I shrug. "Probably not as painful as Max's nose."

Before I can help it, my gaze flits over to Chase. He's talking to Alec, a few steps out of hearing range, running his hand through his messy hair.

"People haven't stopped talking about that kick. I wish I could have seen it."

"He's deserved a kick in the face for a while," Miko adds.

"I really love your earrings," Riley says randomly, leaning forward to admire the pink pom-poms dangling from Miko's ear lobes. "Did you make them yourself?"

Miko smiles, tucking an inky braid behind her ear. "Yeah, I dabble in accessories in my free time. Erika has had to try on some questionable creations over the years."

"The spider hairclips you made me for Halloween were the worst. Far too realistic."

"No way, I *love* spiders," Violet says with wide eyes. "Can you make me some? I won't even save them for Halloween, I'll wear them every day."

Miko snickers. "I can, but I warn you, they deter people."

I wince at the memory. "I was flirting with a guy, and I tucked my hair behind my ear. He screamed so loud that he scored us both detentions."

My story does not have the anticipated effect on Violet. Instead, she's looking at me with *awe*. "They'll look cute *and* keep people away from me? Where can I buy them?"

Just as Miko is about to reply, a voice interrupts from behind my shoulder.

"Erika doesn't need the help of hairclips to deter guys."

I smirk and spin around on my heel, coming face to face with none other than the intensely irritating Chase Thatcher. He's remarkably close, my face inches from his toned chest, and he's staring down at me with those decadent brown eyes glinting with amusement.

"And yet," I say. "I need something even more potent than hairclips to deter you."

One corner of his mouth tugs up into a half-smile, and his teeth slide out to catch it and hold it there. He doesn't give me any response as his eyes lazily scan over my face.

"You don't seem very deterred right now," I mutter.

"It's called fascination with the grotesque," he quips, wrinkling his nose. "People can't look away from gross things."

"Strange," Violet says, appearing beside me and bumping my shoulder. "Everyone else at school thinks she's gorgeous. Oh wait... so do you."

Before he can muster a response, Violet is sliding past me

towards the pizzeria counter, followed quickly by Miko and Riley. Riley winks at me as she brushes by. "Why don't you two go and grab some ketchup for the fries? Just be careful that things don't get *too* saucy, we are in a public place after all."

My mouth falls open. Those devious little—

"Machiavellians," Chase mutters.

"Bad mood?"

"A bit," he admits. He grabs me by the crook of the elbow and leads me towards a side counter, containing paper straws, sauces, and salt. "What's your mood like today?"

I grab a handful of salt sachets, humming under my breath. "Today's forecast is bitchy with a ninety-five percent chance of 'too tired to function.' Scattered sass and partial aggression should also be expected later in the afternoon."

Chase's shoulder brushes mine, his chuckle sending the hairs on the back of my neck into an electrifying paralysis. He begins to select ketchup sachets agonizingly slowly. "You seemed like you were in a pretty good mood earlier."

I glance over at Dylan, who's standing at the pizzeria counter and laughing with Joe and Miko. "Yeah, Dyl looks after me."

"I thought you didn't want to be looked after."

"What's that supposed to mean?"

He shrugs.

"Squidge," I say sharply, plucking a paper straw from the glass container and pressing it into his chest firmly. "If you're going to be cryptic, you should just take one of these straws and go and suck the fun out of somebody else's day."

I try to ignore the muscle under my fingertips, but I can't. I whisk my hand away like I've burned it, and in some ways I have. I hate to admit it, but Chase Thatcher is hot. Smoking hot. Surface of the sun hot. I hurriedly begin to gather ketchup sachets, avoiding his gaze. The sooner I get to the table, the better.

"Ouch," I hear him say. "I just mean for someone who wants to catch attention from their parents so badly, you still seem to be playing everything very... safe."

I look up from the sachets squashed in my fist. "What's your point?"

"Well, I didn't think that squeaky clean track star was the image you wanted."

My mood turns sour. "Oh, just go and stick your dick in a Venus flytrap, would you?"

"A Venus flytrap?"

"They eat bugs, and you, Chase Thatcher, are *bugging me.*"

Just as I'm turning away, his hand latches onto my arm and pulls me back. A couple of straws and sachets fall to the floor, and I huff with irritation. Chase's warm hand releases my arm, and we kneel simultaneously to collect the fallen items. He's about five inches away from me but I refuse to look up and make eye contact.

"I'm not trying to piss you off."

"Well, then I guess you're just effortlessly good at it," I say, standing up.

"You want to change your reputation, don't you?" Chase has the audacity to block me from walking again. I peer in frustration over his shoulder, watching Dylan sit down with the others. If this lump would move, I could be sitting down too. "Bad girls don't run track for their school team and buy stationery at the weekend. How are you expecting to alarm your parents with that behavior, exactly?"

He gestures loosely at one of the bags hanging on my arm.

"What would a bad girl do then, Chase?" I ask, throwing my hands up scornfully. "Steal the straws? Graffiti the tabletop with ketchup?"

"That's not what this is all about. It's about not caring about people's expectations."

"You're such a hypocrite," I hiss, shoving past him. "Changing my sneakers for biker leathers or my friends for drag-racing gang members is just succumbing to a different kind of expectation."

The group look up as I head over, and I drop a heap of sachets onto the table. A lanky adolescent waiter is currently serving the pizzas. I long to join them but Chase grabs me again before I can. He really needs to stop doing that, before I kick that dough, passata, and melted mozzarella as far up his ass as it can go. That'll give him a pizza my mind.

"Okay, you've got a point," Chase says simply.

I scowl. "Damn right."

Holding my arm loosely, he pulls me more gently back towards the quieter area in front of the counter. "Can we talk about this?"

"There's nothing to talk about. I will live my life with who I want, when I want, and however the hell I want. No discussion."

He raises his palms in surrender. "Okay, like I said, I'm sorry."

The tension in my chest fizzles away, and my glare softens. "Good."

His smile returns and he reaches out an arm to hook over my shoulders, squeezing in a way that I can only interpret as affectionate as we walk back to the table. "I think we just had our first fight, gorgeous."

"Call me gorgeous one more time and I will use my fists." I slip out from under his arm and take a seat at the end of the table, beside Violet. Chase ducks into the seat opposite me, and before even pausing to look at his own pizza, reaches across the table to grab my hand. I've never met a boy who is such an effortless, and exasperating, flirt.

"These tiny things?" He makes a scoffing sound and releases it.

"Small hands make other items look bigger, Chase," Joe says.

"Like pizza," Violet finishes. "The ones in front of you."

For the first time, I notice the thin-crust pizza on my plate. Dylan knows how much I love ham and pineapple pizza, even though he thinks it's the worst flavor combo in the world. We fight about it every time we get takeout. I smile at him, and he pulls a face.

"Pineapple doesn't belong on pizza," Alec informs me. "It belongs in hell."

"We have that in common," I say, lifting a slice to my mouth.

"Does anyone have a milkshake that I can dip my fries into?" Miko asks from the other end of the table, resting her elbow on the table. "I don't like ketchup."

"Milkshake?" Joe repeats incredulously. "For fries?"

"Yeah, can I borrow yours?"

Hesitantly, Joe reaches out and pushes his vanilla milkshake towards her. He watches with disgust as Miko dips two fries into his drink and then pops them into her mouth whole. She makes a sweet humming noise, then gives a thumbs up.

"You two have weird tastes," Riley says simply.

I shake my head. "Riley, you're the one putting ketchup on your pizza."

"I don't see how that's weird in any way. It's literally extra tomato sauce."

"You're just wrong, Greene." Alec wrinkles his nose. "It's gross."

"You're gross," she fires back.

As the group launches into a discussion about eating habits, I find myself gazing out around the restaurant as I chew. The pizzeria is small, with only a few workers behind the cherry red counter. Ivy hangs from the wall lights and there's a sign above the counter that reads *Tasty* in sparking blue LEDs. I smile when I notice that all the workers have the phrase stitched into their baseball caps. What a company uniform.

"What are you smiling at?" Chase asks me through a mouthful of pizza.

"Their caps." I point at our waiter, a boy with a spotty complexion and an adorable smile. "Look how *tasty* they are. I want one."

"Go and get one."

I turn back to Chase, frowning. "What?"

He's got that cheeky half-smile on his face. "Go and grab it."

I laugh scathingly. "I think I've had enough stealing for one week, thanks."

Chase bites his lip. Then, without warning, he twists in his seat and calls the boy over. The teenager looks up in surprise, his eyes widening and the spray bottle he's using to clean the tables faltering in mid-air. He stumbles around the tables towards us.

"What can I help you with?" he asks when he reaches us, his gaze flitting nervously around our large table. I get the sense he's feeling intimidated.

"I'll give you twenty bucks if you give me your cap."

My mouth falls open. Conversation around the table has ceased now and we're all staring at Chase in surprise. The boy blinks a few times in quick succession.

"My cap?"

"Your tasty cap," Chase clarifies. "The one on your head."

"Twenty bucks?" The boy laughs in disbelief. "Deal!"

He can't get it off quickly enough. In a matter of seconds, the cherry red baseball cap with blue stitching is in Chase's hand and the boy is skipping off smugly with a twenty-dollar bill tucked into his back pocket. I can scarcely believe what's just happened. Nobody at the table is talking; they're all watching Chase with equal surprise.

He seems unfazed by the attention. Casually, he leans over the table to hook the baseball cap over my head. The momentum of the action pulls me forwards a few inches towards him, and he utilizes our proximity to straighten the peak over my eyes.

"Consider it an apology gift."

For once in my life, I am utterly and completely speechless.

Then I hear the angry shriek of the woman behind the counter. "Remy, you better not be selling that *gear* of yours in my restaurant again!"

"It's okay, Mom! It was just my cap!"

"Your cap?" A large red-haired woman appears from beside the counter, her hands on her hips and a ferocious expression on her face. "Do you mean to tell me you just sold your *company uniform*, Remigius St. James?!"

Her gaze lands on me. Her fierce eyebrows furrow.

"Ready to run?" Chase asks me.

My hand tightens around the strap of my purse.

I barely have time to laugh before we're out of our seats, sprinting away from the second restaurant this week with a terrified Remy at our heels.

"We have to go to Build-a-Bear."

"We are *not* going to Build-a-Bear."

"Come on," I whine, pointing towards the colorful fronting, where lines of nostalgic teddy bears are positioned in bright, funky outfits. I look at Chase pleadingly, but he's purposefully avoiding my eye. He groans and stares down at the floor in exasperation.

"I don't even want a bear," I promise. "I just want to use my new Polaroid to get a photo of you holding one, so that I can humiliate you. Then we can leave."

"Choose someplace else." Chase shakes his head and laughs slightly, meeting my eyes at last. "I have never entered that store and I am *not* ever planning to."

"Chase Evan Thatcher," I threaten, grabbing his arm. I manage to pull him a good few steps towards the store before his arm escapes my grip.

"Erika whatever-your-middle-name-is Monroe," he mimics.

"I dare you." I tug at his sleeve again.

He blinks at my challenge, hesitates a few seconds, and finally releases an exasperated sigh. Mumbling something under his breath, he allows me to pull him towards the store.

I can't help but smile. The one thing an arrogant guy like him cannot shy away from is a challenge. The window is filled with gorgeous teddy bears, alongside a slightly crumpled paper sign which reads *Vacancies Available*. Chase lingers stubbornly at the display, but with one final tug, I lead us into the bright interior.

The onslaught of rainbow decoration makes him shudder. Everybody in here is either below the age of eight or a parent, and the woman behind the checkout frowns at us.

"Right," I say, pulling my new Polaroid camera from my purse and directing it at Chase, "grab a bear of your choice and pose with it."

Chase stares at me for a second with a dubious expression. He doesn't think I'm serious. I'll show him serious.

"Go," I order, shooing him towards a rack of beautiful bears that I would have killed for as a child. I was one of those unfortunates who never received a Build-a-Bear or had the luck to be invited to a Build-a-Bear party. Time to right that wrong.

Chase stares at the rack in front of him, before turning back to me. "Are you serious?"

"Deadly."

He clicks his tongue on the back of his teeth, turning towards the rack. Glass eyes stare back at him as he browses, and I watch him reach for a small bear on a lower shelf. The bear is wearing a leather jacket and a white Build-a-Bear T-shirt, with Converse-style shoes and a pair of dark sunglasses. The fur on the top of its head is styled into a quiff.

"Build-a-Badass," he says with a grin, holding it out to me.

"Perfect. Strike a pose," I order, pulling the camera to my

eye and watching him through the lens. He grits his teeth in a very sarcastic smile and holds the bear awkwardly in front of him.

"No, no, no. You need to show me the love, Chase."

"Erika," he says, his voice low.

"Give me some passion! I want to see how much you love that bear."

Chase rolls his eyes at me. Then, for a split second, he pulls the bear into his neck and hugs it tightly with a dazed smile on his face. I snap the picture just before his silly joke ends, and he shoves the teddy back into its position on the shelf. I hiss in excitement as the gloss paper rolls from the bottom of the camera, grabbing the edge and flapping the picture in the air as the colors begin to show.

Wiping his hands on his shirt, he grabs me by the elbow and drags me out of the store, while I'm still flapping the Polaroid around for the photo to load.

"Erika! Chase!" Riley's voice sounds the moment we step out. She and the others are making their way towards us. They all look incredibly confused.

"Dude, did you just come out of the 'Build-a-Bear' store?" Alec asks Chase in an incredulous tone.

"No," Chase retorts defensively, but the smirk on Joe's face indicates that they can see through his lie as if it's glass.

"I have proof," I sing happily, shoving the Polaroid into Joe's hands. The three boys lean over to see the picture, snickering at their thoroughly embarrassed Chase-shaped friend.

Chase is glaring at the ground.

Violet grabs the photo from the boys and shows it to Miko and Riley. Soon, all of them are chuckling at Chase, ribbing him mercilessly. Dylan hands me my shopping bags.

"Thanks for leaving these with me," he says, rolling his eyes. "Come on, we need to get going. My dad needs me home."

"Okay." I can't help feeling slightly disappointed. I've had a lot of fun. I turn back to the others with a weak smile. "I guess I'll see you guys at school."

Miko and I share hugs with Riley and Violet, and awkwardly wave goodbye to the guys. Together, the three of us begin walking away from the group, towards the exit to the parking lot. I can't help but register a sinking feeling in my stomach.

"Wait, you forgot this!" Violet calls after us. A few seconds later, her hand wraps over my shoulder to pull me to a stop. She pushes the Polaroid into my bag. "Keep that, it's a piece of art. Never, ever lose it. Oh, and send me a picture of it on Snapchat."

"Deal," I say with a laugh.

Violet's hand falls and she smiles breathlessly. "Oh, and also, Chase has a message for you."

"What?"

"He said, and I quote: 'Bye, gorgeous.'" Violet's eyes twinkle with amusement. "He's over there getting teased by the others right now. Anyway, I should go. Talk to you soon, okay?" She takes off running, leaving me standing there like an idiot.

I touch my *Tasty* baseball cap and fight to keep the smile from my lips.

Bye, Squidge.

9

Hot-Headed

The kitchen blinds are already closed when I arrive home, concealing the dusky evening sky.

"You're late," Mom says, looking up from her magazine.

She is sitting at the breakfast bar, with damp blond hair coiled into a cotton hair wrap and the magazine spread on the marble surface. Her face is bare of makeup, exposing the freckles that dapple her cheeks like sunlight on a woodland floor. Her eyes, hazel like Chloe's, scrutinize my bags as I place them on the empty counter in front of her.

"It was fun," I say simply. I pad barefoot to the fridge and help myself to a can of lemonade. The speaker is playing an old eighties song in the corner of the room, and Chloe is standing beside the stove, wiggling her hips and stirring what looks to be a large pan of chili. I flick her French braid teasingly as I pass, before settling on the bar stool across from Mom. The can of lemonade hisses as I push down on the tag.

Mom purses her lips and glares down at the glossy image of Jennifer Aniston in front of her. "You know you should ask before you help yourself to something, Erika."

"Sorry, Mom."

The flick of her page slices through the air. "Did you have a good time?"

"Yeah." I bite my lip a little to restrain my smile.

"We didn't know if you'd be hungry. I told Chloe to wait for dinner."

The urge to smile disappears. "Ah, I actually had pizza while I was out."

"Ah right," Mom says.

"Sorry, I should have said."

Mom frowns. "Chloe made veggie chili. She knows you like it."

This time, I look at my sister. She's wearing fluffy socks and sliding around on the white kitchen tiles, her lips moving in synchrony with the cheesy pop hit playing out of the speakers. She doesn't seem too bothered by my lack of hunger. "Sorry, Chlo."

Chloe waves a wooden spoon. "It's fine, don't worry. We can always save leftovers."

"What did you buy?" Mom asks, unhooking her hair towel and releasing damp curls over her shoulders. She looks at my bags with interest. "Anything nice?"

I pull out a white, cropped tee from one of the Abercrombie bags and hold it in front of my body to show Mom the fit. "Isn't it cute?"

A dimple forms between Mom's eyebrows. "Isn't it a bit ... small?"

"I've worn smaller," Chloe calls from the other side of the kitchen.

Mom still seems skeptical.

"I was thinking with a pair of high-waisted jeans," I say

with feigned brightness. "Maybe a cropped sweater. Style it so it's not too revealing."

Mom looks back at the magazine. The squeeze of hope in my chest sinks down until it reaches the pit of my stomach and stays there, aching. I take a sip of lemonade, but my taste for it has disappeared in the bitterness on my tongue.

The kitchen door opens and Dad strolls in, his olive skin golden and his hands dirty from the building site. He's the head of a development company, and he comes home with burns, scars, and dirt under his fingernails every day. As he passes by me in the direction of the faucet, he reaches across to ruffle my hair—he's only about my height but he's been doing this since I was tiny—and I squeak.

"Hey, kiddo. Nice top. Is that new?"

"I bought it today," I reply, grinning at him. "I'll get you one next time."

Dad makes a scoffing noise, rubbing soap over his hands and lathering it all the way up his exposed forearms. "Not sure it's my color. The yellow of a hard-hat is more my thing."

"Are you having chili, Dad?" Chloe asks, placing a stack of plates on the smooth granite counter. "Do you want meat or veggie? Any toppings?"

"All of the above," Dad says.

Mom turns around on her barstool to face Chloe. "Need any help, sweetheart?"

Chloe shakes her head and tucks her hair behind her ear, unaware of the sour cream decorating her cheek. "It's all under control. I'm handling it."

"Do you want to tell everyone your news, now that we're all together?"

Chloe slips, her hand almost hitting the hot stove top. "Oh, sure."

"News?" I question.

Dad is drying his hands with a dish towel, equally confused.

"I spoke to one of my friends from college this morning," Chloe explains, frantically grating cheese over the hot plates of chili. "She's an executive lead at this big non-profit organization, supporting kids from financially unstable households."

I can sense where this is going, and before I can help it, my gaze flits to Mom.

"They provide these kids with ambition training, counseling, and financial grants to support them as they adjust to working life and help them to get employed. Anyway, they're looking for a new Team Lead and my friend wants to put my name in."

Mom's smile is radiant as she looks between Dad and me. "Isn't that fantastic?"

"It's a big step up in workload, but there's a raise too."

"That's amazing, Chloe," I say, as brightly as I can. I barely hear Dad's compliments because my gaze is centered solely on my mom. She's looking at Chloe with glowing pride, her eyes warm and her smile genuine. I can't remember the last time she looked at me like that. Then she reaches out to squeeze Chloe's hand and delivers the final blow.

"We're so proud of you, sweetheart."

Ouch. That pit in my stomach grows until I feel like it'll swallow the rest of my body whole. I stare at the countertop and concentrate on my smile, until I'm sure that it's frozen on my face and cannot waver. *I am happy for Chloe.* I repeat the sentence in my brain until it begins to throb. Then I clear my dry throat, blink a few times to rid the emotion from my eyes, and try my hardest to feel pleased for my sister.

If I get into Stanford, maybe my mom will look at me like that.

When I finally look up, my smile is fixed in place. I pour as much pride as I can into my expression and dip my shaking hands below the lip of the counter, out of sight.

"You deserve this so much, Chloe. I can't tell you how proud I am of you."

My eyes flit to my mom; her smile, her hand squeezing Chloe's.

I'll make her proud of me, too.

The freshman boy stares at us in disbelief. "You're offering me fifty bucks to *what?*"

"Get beaten up," Miko articulates clearly, throwing her hands up in frustration. The cute space buns in her hair seem more like devil's horns when paired with the determined expression on her face. "Honestly, what is so difficult to understand about that?"

"But I don't want to get beaten up," the poor kid says, frowning.

"Do you want fifty dollars?"

He nods.

Miko pats his arm. "Well, honey, you've got to stand in the dark to see the stars."

"What?"

A sigh hisses through her teeth. "Let me rephrase that in teenage-boy terms. Sometimes, you've got to get through a bit of zombie goo to survive the apocalypse."

He continues to stare blankly at her. Miko groans.

"I suppose that's a bad example. Zombies eat brains, and you clearly don't have any."

"Hey!"

"What's your name?" I interrupt, pressing a hand on Miko's shoulder to stop her from strangling the poor kid. He seems grateful for the interruption and smiles at me.

"Lewis," he says confidently, adjusting his rucksack strap. He's a short, wiry freshman, with a mop of blond hair and a pale complexion. Despite his appearance, Miko said that this kid supposedly has a bit of a reputation for picking fights with the other freshman boys, which makes him the perfect recruit for my plan.

"Well, Lewis, I need you to go up to Chase Thatcher," I say, pointing discreetly around the corner. "And pick a fight with him. For fifty bucks."

Lewis considers my proposal, adjusting the collar of his polo shirt. "What about?"

"Anything. Be creative but make it a scene. He needs to land a punch on you."

"Why?"

"Part of the fifty bucks is not asking questions, kid," Miko snaps.

Lewis scowls, then looks back at me. "Can I fight her instead?"

"As funny as that would be, I'm going to answer no."

"Shame," Lewis says sourly. Then he lifts his hand to his mouth to chew on his thumbnail. After a few seconds of deliberation, he stops. "Okay, I'll do it."

"You'll do it?" Miko repeats.

Lewis raises an eyebrow. "Did I stutter?"

Miko crosses her arms. "No, but I'm sure you will when Chase is done with you."

"She's just teasing," I say hurriedly, grabbing Lewis's arm. "He's just around the corner, in the next hallway. He's with Alec Ryder, you can't miss him."

Miko and I watch, leaning against the lockers, as Lewis grips his rucksack and sidles off with exaggerated confidence. My fingers latch together in my pocket and my stomach gurgles with guilt and unease. If Chase attacks a younger student in the hallway, he'll be expelled. No question. My mission will be complete, and Blythe will pull whatever strings she needs to obtain my scholarship at Stanford. And Chase... well, I swallow the painful lump rising in my throat.

"Let's hope Chase's temper is as hot as his bod," Miko mutters, grabbing my hand. We turn around the corner together and into the hallway where we anticipate that hell is going to be raised.

Only the sight we're greeted with isn't exactly what we expected.

Lewis barely scrapes the height of Chase's shoulders, but still he's standing in front of him, his chin raised defiantly.

"You're fat!" he barks.

Chase stares at him in confusion.

Lewis bristles, squaring his shoulders. "You—you're such a pig! An ugly pig!"

"Oh no," Miko says quietly beside me. I barely register her comment, I'm too busy staring in horror as Lewis presses a finger into Chase's solid stomach.

"You big—big, um, fuckboi!"

"Who is this kid, Chase?" Alec asks, scratching the back of his head.

Chase looks totally bewildered. "Dude, I have no idea."

"I hate you!" Lewis is shouting, but the sound is more whiny than aggressive. "You—you, um, slept with ... my mom!"

"I'm worried about him," Alec says. "Do you think he needs some help?"

"She said you were more disappointing than a raisin in a chocolate chip cookie!" Lewis tries again. "You were about as satisfying as the Percy Jackson movies!"

"I'm so confused," Chase says to Alec, and he does seem genuinely dumbfounded. "Is he criticizing me for hypothetically not giving his mom enough pleasure?"

Lewis is flushed bright red now. "She took you out because she knows you're trash!"

"I like this narrative he's spinning," Miko comments from beside me. "I mean, you told him to be creative. He's definitely following your instructions."

Chase tentatively pokes Lewis's shoulder. "Um, child, go away."

"No!" Lewis shouts, batting Chase's finger away and glowering up at him, enraged. "Fight me like a man, you big coward!"

"You want me to fight you?" Chase echoes incredulously. "Who are you?"

"I'm your worst nightmare!"

"Okay, kid. Be like E.T. and go the hell home."

Well, this isn't working out very well.

"Do you think it's possible that you recruited the wrong Lewis?" I whisper to Miko, gazing worriedly around the hallway, which has steadily become more and more crowded. People are nudging each other, phones are raised. Oh Lewis.

"I suppose it's possible that there's more than one Lewis in freshman year." Miko smiles sheepishly. "It's possible I chose one of the less intimidating candidates."

I glare at her. She quickly raises her palms in surrender.

"Kumiko, what is going on?" Kai asks, appearing at her side. Despite being two years younger, Miko's brother is already taller than her. His sharp jaw and narrowed dark eyes give his appearance a maturity that Miko often downplays with her butterfly clips and space buns, and strangers would easily assume that he's the elder sibling. He scowls as he notices the people recording. "Are they humiliating Lewis?"

"Wait, Kaito—"

Before Miko can grab his arm, Kai is storming through the crowd towards Chase and Alec. He pushes the fumbling Lewis aside, and in seconds he's inches away from Chase with his shoulders squared, chest inflated. Chase's eyes flare at the sudden intrusion. He straightens up until his body returns the threat, paralleling Kai's motions with primitive instinct.

"So that's how you start a fight," I mumble. "Lewis should take notes."

"Erika!" Miko hisses. "Kai is in enough trouble as it is!"

"I know, let's stop it before it gets any further," I say. With my hands on her shoulders, I propel us through the scattered crowds of teenagers until we're standing at the side of the action, beside the two idiots. I can't tell if Chase has even noticed our arrival—his stare is locked unwaveringly on his opponent. Kai's eyes are burning like coal, and his tone is equally scalding.

"Do you think it's funny to pick on someone smaller than you?"

"Funnily enough, I think *he* was trying to pick on *me*." Chase tosses a brief look of skepticism towards Lewis. "So maybe get your facts right before you get up in my face."

"Kai." Miko reaches out for her brother. "Stop this. We're leaving."

Kai releases a guttural noise of indignation, before turning sharply and barging his way through our audience. Miko throws me a helpless expression before she chases after him, her ballet pumps pattering on the linoleum flooring like rain on a rooftop.

Alec bumps my shoulder as he moves to stand beside me. "Well, that was more dramatic than a season finale of *Dance Moms*."

"Hey gorgeous," Chase murmurs, appearing at my other side. His face is dark with a frown as he watches Kaito's retreating figure. "I don't know what the hell just happened."

"No," I lie weakly, watching Lewis follow his friend. "Me neither."

"Erika," a voice croons behind me.

I purse my lips. Then I hear a sigh and a shuffle as Joe Travis tucks his chair closer.

"Erika," he coos again. "We're sorry!"

"Don't be grumpy with us." Chase leans forward over his desk to join the conversation. Something brushes the back of my arm and, glancing down at it, I realize that he's outstretching his hand to touch me. I bat it away quickly and refocus my attention to the front of the class, where the teacher is explaining the practice paper we're tackling.

Mrs. Lopez is Lindale High's youngest, and easily most

intimidating, teacher. She has a notoriously thin patience; she can't stand inattention and she has never forgotten a student's name. She happens to be my chemistry teacher—making her the person I need to impress most if I want a glowing reference for my college applications.

"If you talk to us, we'll stop pestering you." I hear Joe tapping that darned pencil again, trying to irritate me into turning around. I hold firm, staring forwards at the whiteboard until my eyes start to burn. I refuse to give them the satisfaction. They will *not* get me into trouble in this lesson. No.

"Erika," whines Chase. "Don't shun me, gorgeous."

"Concentrate," I hiss. I scold myself in my head for replying to them. The silent treatment is always more effective. *Don't bite the bait, Erika.*

"Chase wants to ask you a question." Joe's voice is closer to my ear this time; he must be leaning over his desk. "He wants to take you on a date."

I scowl. Joe and Chase have taken the let's-make-Erika-uncomfortable-by-flirting-with-her game to the extreme today. The rivalry between Chase and me has become more apparent with every interaction, but with Joe's catalytic encouragement, it has reached new heights in our chemistry lessons. They've vowed to persevere until I blush, fumble or break. Their game is strong, admittedly, but I have yet to lose.

"Stop lying."

"Not a lie." Joe's voice is sing-song in his giddiness. "He really does want to take you someplace after school. Turn around!"

I eye the teacher skeptically, but she seems concentrated

in her explanations to Frankie at the front of the class. she won't notice if I turn around *quickly*, plus I've already learned about the chlorofluorocarbons question from the textbook anyway.

Unable to resist the temptation, I twist in my seat to talk to the two smug idiots sitting behind me. Chase opens his mouth to speak, but I cut him off before he has the chance.

"If you want to take me on a date, you can join the waiting list."

I turn back around to face the front of the classroom, folding my arms.

I sense Joe lean across to Chase in my peripheral vision, exaggerating his whisper so that I can hear. "She's very high maintenance, bro, are you sure you even want to date her?"

I reach a hand back to smack him.

Joe whimpers. "She's violent too!"

I tuck my hair behind my ear as I whisper, "Squidge, if you somehow want to con me into believing that you are more charming than I am, you need to try harder."

"Okay. What's my challenge?"

I scan the paper in front of me for inspiration. "If you can tell me which type of alcohol is oxidized to a ketone, without looking at your textbook, I'll come with you."

Satisfied with my choice of challenge, I fold my arms over my chest and wait. After a few seconds of telling silence, I decide to answer the question myself.

"Too slow. It's the oxidation of a primary alcohol—"

"You're wrong," Chase interrupts.

"What?" Surprised, I crane around in my seat to look at him.

He looks up at me and his smile is slightly smug. "It's a

compound containing a carbonyl group formed by the oxidation of a *secondary* alcohol."

"Oh." I hesitate. "Damn."

"If it's effort you want, gorgeous," Chase mutters cryptically, "it's effort you'll get."

Without another word, he leans over his notebook and begins to write furiously. Joe gives me a mourning expression from his seat beside Chase, pouting and widening his blue eyes in a way that I won't ever admit is adorable. "Roses are red," he whines dramatically. "Violets are blue, you two should bang . . . and invite me too!"

That earns him another smack.

"Jeez, even my poem wasn't charming enough for her, bro. We're so going to lose."

I turn back to face the whiteboard, a smile tugging at my lips. That's when I notice Mrs. Lopez approaching from my left. Her face is creased with disdain, and her eyebrows have disappeared upwards into a heavy fringe. *No, no, no.*

"How many times do I have to tell you three?"

She comes to a halt at the side of Chase's desk, releasing a rattled sigh and plucking the paper out from under his arm. The class around us hushes as they take notice of what's happening. Chase's spats with Mrs. Lopez can be quite entertaining.

Our teacher sighs again as she unfolds the note.

"Come with me somewhere after school, gorgeous," she reads, frowning.

"Oh, Miss," Joe replies, dramatically clasping a hand to his forehead. "I'm sure you're a lovely person, but I really think people would frown on us dating."

The class erupts into laughter, and Joe grins like a cat with a saucerful of cream as he assesses the effect of his humor. I can practically see his ego inflating from here. I shake my head, but I can't bite back my smile. He'll regret his witticisms when he's bored in detention after school.

"Very funny, Mr. Travis," Mrs. Lopez comments dryly, positioning her hands on her hips in a subtle display of authority. "Now, Mr. Thatcher, would you like to explain why you think it's acceptable to talk and pass notes in my class when you should be listening?"

Chase smiles. "I thought it was romantic to make a spontaneous effort."

Mrs. Lopez does not seem endeared by this information. "And who might this spontaneous romantic effort be for?"

Please no. My heart pounds a little harder in my chest.

"Bro." Chase turns to Joe, his eyebrows creasing in mock-emotion. "I love you."

"Oh, *bro.*" Joe slaps a melodramatic hand to his mouth. "I love you too!"

Laughter fills the room again, and I roll my eyes, glad to have escaped. That's two detentions, then.

Chase reaches out for Joe's hand. "I was gonna buy you a bouquet of broses from the supermarket, but they ran out, bro."

"*Bro.*" Joe's voice cracks. "You're the real-life Bromeo to my Juliet."

Chase leans towards Joe, their noses almost touching. "Bro, your eyes are as beautiful as the brocean."

"I can't believe you're so bromantic, bro." Suddenly, they're clasping hands in front of their chests.

"I didn't know the true meaning of bromosexual until I met you, bro."

The whole class is in hysterics, and even I'm laughing when Joe leans in and pecks Chase lovingly on the nose. "I wish I had a brotograph to commemorate this broment."

Mrs. Lopez's hands fall from her hips. "Very funny, boys. You can both commemorate this moment with a thousand-word essay on why causing disruption in class is unacceptable, in detention tonight. Think of it as a first date, perhaps."

Just as I dare to think I might be off the hook, she turns to me.

"You too, Erika," she adds, frowning. The smile on my face quickly disappears. "This is the third lesson in a row that you've talked through. It's disappointing that you've taken to following their example. We both know you're better than that."

As she sweeps back to the front of the classroom, announcing the homework assignment, Joe and Chase release hands. I sigh deeply and rest my chin in my palms.

Chase clears his throat and stretches his arms out across the desk. "Well ... we can go after detention instead?"

I answer him with my iciest glare.

"I think you should come. It will help with the plan."

Despite my better instincts, I consider his offer momentarily. If I go with him, that means I won't have to tell my sister that I got detention. I could tell her that I'm hanging out with a friend after school, and that's why I don't need a lift home at the usual time. That means my mom won't necessarily find out about this.

Chase's smug smile grows with every second of deliberation.

"So, you'll come then?"

10

Delusional

Chase Thatcher drives *fast*.

Pin you back in your seat while you struggle for air kind of fast. Miko when she hears the microwave timer go off kind of fast. Or when she spots something polka dotted.

It's probably a combination of the speed at which we flew down those country lanes and the sheer volume of Nirvana blasting from the speakers that makes me so unsteady as I leave the car. My legs wobble, my head feels oddly airy, and it takes all my effort to click the door in place before I lean against it. *Yikes*. Next time I'm in a car with Chase, I'll remember *not to be*. I close my eyes, but even blind, I can sense his warmth as he ambles around the hood to examine me.

"Well," he says smoothly. "It seems I finally broke Erika Monroe."

"Of course, you didn't," I say with a sigh, keeping my eyes closed and tilting my head back for ample comfort against the cold window. "I'm just trying to diagnose your problem."

His voice is closer this time. "My problem?"

"Yeah, whatever made you like . . ." I wave a hand around blindly. "This."

"My hotness isn't due to a fever, gorgeous."

I finally open my eyes to see that Chase is standing directly in front of me. "Well, delusions are clearly a symptom. Useful to know."

Chuckling, he places a hand on the glass above my head and leans in closer, his chest tauntingly close. He smells fresh, clean, and masculine—like limes and coconut with woody undertones. From under his unkempt, messy hair, his honey eyes glow with playfulness.

"Well, I must be a little mad to hang out with you."

Lovely.

I raise my eyebrows and stand up properly, stretching my arms behind my back to expand my shoulders. Once I'm certain that I won't topple over, I utilize my proximity with Chase's hard chest to reach my hand up and lazily trace a finger over his collarbone. The cotton of his T-shirt is soft under my fingertip. I hear the noticeable hitch in Chase's breathing and smile at my small victory.

"Or maybe," I say, rolling my head back to look at him coyly, "I just drive you insane."

His lips part, but his retort is stolen by surprise.

"Now, come on," I say brightly, slipping out from under his arm and dancing away. "You're not a dog, so it's not considered socially appropriate to drool."

A second passes before Chase responds, but I finally hear his sigh of amusement. He removes his hand from the car window and strolls over to me with a neutral expression. "My bad. I must have been confused by the bitch in my presence."

"What an original insult."

"Don't slam the classics, gorgeous."

I turn my attention to our surroundings: an inconspicuous industrial road lined with intimidating metal fencing and fir trees. I lost all sense of direction about halfway through our journey, but this place seems disconcertingly familiar. It's only as we begin to walk that I recognize the claustrophobic infrastructure and scraggy greenery. Even in the yellow hues of daylight, Redwood Avenue is no more charming than the last time I was here.

"This bitch wants to know why we're here," I demand, halting my steps abruptly.

"I need to see Seth about something; I figured I'd bring you along."

"And you figured that *why?*"

"You want to be bad," he says with a shrug. "This is where bad comes to drink."

Before I can protest, he's tugging me by the wrist back through the alleyway and into the parking lot of the Admiral Bar. Against my will and better judgment, I am pulled back into the exotic and terrifying world that he seems so easily accustomed to.

I am able to find some consolation in the absence of drag cars, but my relief is short-lived. While on my last visit, I was forced to battle my way through a throng of men and machinery to find Chase, the parking lot is quieter this time. The crowds were bustling and unruly; however, there is much to be said for the protection of invisibility. In that way, this environment is far less forgiving in the daytime. We wind our way through an assortment of weathered picnic tables, populated by grim-faced onlookers and their amber drinks.

I tilt my face downwards.

"Don't be scared," Chase says quietly, running his thumb over my wrist. "You'll see."

Despite the wisps of anxiety curling around my windpipe, I flatten my features into nonchalance. My best chances of leaving this place unscathed are if I act like I fit in.

Chase leads me to the far-left corner of the bar's parking lot, in an area partially secluded from everybody else by an unruly hedge. The doorway to the Admiral itself is on our right. The proud lettering seems like it was once gold but has now cracked and rusted into a crusty copper. As I slide onto the picnic bench opposite its wide steps, I hear deep peals of laughter and soft jazz music. Then a smile appears in the doorway.

"I was wondering when you two would show up," Seth greets, approaching the bench. He holds a frosty bottle of beer in one hand, and ducks down onto the seat beside me.

"I got detention," Chase says, grinning. "Sorry to be late."

"And now you're at a bar." Seth rests his strong inked forearms on the table, the beer resting loosely between his fingers. He looks at me with a devastatingly handsome smirk. "Is he corrupting you, Erika?"

"He wishes he had that much influence over me."

Chase snickers. "I'm turning you into a bad girl, aren't I, gorgeous?"

"Ah," Seth says, clicking his fingers. "*You're* gorgeous. Well, that makes sense."

Before I can cover them, my cheeks warm. Usually, I'm quite good at restricting that inner giggly girl, but this older, rugged man is something else. Before I can respond with something mildly dignified, or indifferently flirty, Chase reaches across the table to flick Seth's knuckles. I note that there's a small crescent moon shape on his finger.

"Yeah, yeah, Bautista charm. Can we skip past the flirting part, please?"

"Who's flirting?" Seth asks, leaning back and rolling the beer between his hands absentmindedly. His grin is wicked. "I'm courting a lady, sir."

"The lady has a name," I chime. "And it's Erika, not *gorgeous*."

Seth's gaze returns to me. "Shame. The nickname seemed so fitting."

Oh, he's good.

"Just wait," Chase says, glancing sideways at the bleak, gray wall of the Admiral building. "You'll find she's more Beast than Beauty."

I make a scoffing noise. "Then you're like Gaston, Squidge, because I'd quite happily throw you to your death."

Chase averts his eyes from the bar to stare back at me with that vexingly impassive expression. His eyes don't leave mine for a second, even while he addresses his friend. "See what I mean?"

"I see alright." Seth chuckles. "She's good, she keeps you in check."

"About time somebody did," I say with a shrug.

A woman approaches our table, with a bar tray held tight under her arm. She must be in her late forties, wearing a low-cut black top and carmine lipstick. She smiles as she notices Chase, and it looks sticky. Her voice is deeper than expected, with a Southern twang. "Can I get you kids any drinks?"

"No thanks," Chase says, scratching the back of his neck. "I'm driving."

"And for you, doll?" She looks at me expectantly.

"Um," I say shakily. "No, I'm good thanks."

"Gimme a shout if you change your mind." She nods, then saunters away to serve the next table, coiling her finger through her belt loop.

"You get served here?" I hiss, the second she's out of earshot. My heart is hammering and, no doubt, my cheeks are flushed. I look outrageously and obviously underaged. I can't believe she would have served me.

"Chill, we don't bite," Chase says smoothly. "Well... not hard."

My response is irritatingly breathy, betraying my nerves. "Shut up."

"It's been great to see you again, Erika," Seth says, standing up from the bench with his eyes directed on the doorway. "I hope you come around more. Is it okay if I steal Chase from you for a moment? We have something to talk about."

He turns to look at Chase, his gaze lingering potently. Chase nods.

They're going to leave me alone.

"Sure," I say, as confidently as I can manage. I don't allow my gaze to stray to my surroundings, to the men and women who look like they could devour me whole. I keep my chin lifted and my expression steady despite the cold feeling seeping over me like mist.

Chase glances at me. "I'll only be two minutes. Stay here."

Then I watch as my only safety blanket in this daunting

place disappears into the Admiral with his older friend and I am left utterly and chillingly alone.

He lied.

Two minutes became ten. Ten became fifteen. At this point, a man with platinum blond hair tied back in an impressive ponytail asked if he could have the table. Naturally, I said yes. Now it's been eighteen minutes since the boys left, and I'm still leaning against this brick wall, sending angry texts to Chase and scrolling through Twitter to avoid any further possibility of social contact.

My face is warm with anger, and thus far I've pictured one hundred and three different ways to punish Chase for abandoning me here, with no way to get home or anyone to stick by. I don't need someone to protect me, I'm a big girl, but *anyone* to talk to would be better than standing here so isolated and vulnerable. He brought me here and it was his responsibility to stay by my side; he shouldn't have left me like this.

I hope I can slap him before karma does.

The sky is beginning to spit with rain. Water droplets on my screen. Brilliant.

I slip my phone into my back pocket and I'm just pulling my hood up to cover my hair when I notice the whispering from my right. Under the soft music and the rush of wind, there's the unmistakable murmuring of people in the bushes. I inch forwards and crane my neck to peer around the corner. Ahead of me, tucked into a small gap in the bushes, are two men standing closely together.

The one facing towards me only takes a second to detect me peering at him. He stiffens and ducks away quickly, but

I have time enough to register the five o'clock shadow on his jaw. He's older. Noticing the reaction of his friend, the other guy twists to look over his shoulder. I see an expression of annoyance, and then a little bag falls to the floor.

I've never looked away from something so quickly. My blood is hot in my veins, and I stare pointedly at the ground with my pulse thrumming in my ears. There's no mistaking what I just saw—there was weed in that little plastic bag. If I look like a threat to their exchange ... well, I could be in danger. *Keep your head down, Erika.*

I stare adamantly at the dusty ground until the voices disappear and the bush is no longer rustling with activity. Even then, I can't summon the courage to look up properly.

What kind of place is this? To take me to this rough bar across town is one thing, but to leave me alone is another. I briefly wonder if Chase and Seth have disappeared to conduct their own shady dealings. If that idiot has abandoned me here to go and buy some bud, then hell is going to look like a luxury spa when I'm done with him.

Screw this. I'm not waiting around any longer.

I've just pressed send on the text to my sister when a girl appears in front of me.

Her hair is vibrant orange, piled on top of her head haphazardly. The hollowness of her cheeks is instantly apparent, and there's a darkness under her gaunt eyes that has nothing to do with the smudged kohl eyeliner. Despite being thinner and smaller than me in every conceivable way, she seems viciously intimidating. I meet her gaze with feigned self-assurance, side-step and attempt to walk past her back into the parking lot.

"Hey, hey, not so fast."

She blocks my path easily. The scent of stale liquor fans over my face and I stumble backwards into the craggy bushes, uncomfortable with her proximity.

"You're a pretty thing, aren't you?" she comments. Her glazed eyes scan over my body with a hunger that lifts the hairs on the back of my neck. "Such pretty, pretty hair."

"Thank you," I mumble. Suffocating panic is rising up my throat, and my breathing has deteriorated into shallow, desperate pants. I reach for my pockets protectively.

She notices.

"Your clothes look fancy. Did Daddy buy them?" Even through the drizzling rain, I can see the sparks of greed in her eyes. Her lips pull back from her teeth in a primal, menacing sneer. "Did you bring Daddy's credit card with you, pretty girl?"

She steps towards me, and I move backwards instinctively. The sharp twigs behind me snag on the cotton of my top and pierce into the skin of my neck.

"Felicity!" a voice snaps.

Suddenly, the demon in front of me is being pulled away by her carrot-colored ponytail, yowling in protest. Seth towers behind her like an avenging angel, his fist still wrapped securely around her scrunchie. He stoops down to address her.

"Scram," he snarls into her pale ear, releasing his grip. Felicity glares at him before ducking out of his way, tendrils escaping down her neck from her now loosened ponytail.

"Jesus," I say stupidly, rubbing my stinging neck.

"I prefer the name Seth." He grimaces. "You okay?"

"Just peachy. Can't you tell?"

"Erika." A low rumble. Chase steps up beside Seth. The apprehensive expression on his face tells me that he knows this is his fault, but I pointedly look away. I don't care if he's sorry.

"I'll give you two a minute." Seth pushes his hands into his pockets and strolls away.

One second passes.

"Erika—"

"I really don't want to hear it," I say, my voice brittle. My hand remains curled over my neck protectively, but my voice is as strong and sharp as steel. "You are an idiot for bringing me somewhere like this. You are an asshole for leaving me completely alone. For messing around with your drugs and your alcohol while I was almost mugged."

"Drugs? What?"

"I'm not an idiot, Chase, I know the kind of guy you are—remember."

This time his response is fast, and his tone is as acidic as mine. His eyes, previously softened with apology, are now analytical. "And what kind of guy is that?"

"Reckless and unreliable," I say, gesturing widely at the parking lot around us. "The kind that hangs around with drug dealers, drag racers, and wannabe thieves."

"I knew I shouldn't have brought you here," Chase snaps, running a hand through his hair raggedly. "I thought this was what you wanted from me."

"To be mugged?"

"No! To be around this kind of stuff." He hisses a breath through his teeth. "I just needed to speak to Seth. It was only supposed to be two minutes—I got caught up."

"I don't care what you were doing with Seth."

Chase's jaw clenches. "I don't like the accusation in your tone."

"Is it really that misplaced?"

"Where on earth have you got this idea that I'm some kind of criminal?" Chase demands incredulously. "If you must know, I was in the bar applying for a *job*. Not dealing or shooting or fighting or scoring, or whatever it is you think I do. If you could get off your high horse for a goddamn second, you might see the world around you a little bit clearer."

"Don't you dare tell me that I'm judgmental for not wanting to be a part of all of this," I cry. My eyes burn with the threat of tears, and I realize how much that encounter with Felicity has shaken me. "I'm an idiot for trusting that you would look out for me."

Chase's gaze instantly softens. He outstretches a hand.

"No," I interrupt, before he can try to explain himself or touch me. "I guess we figured out who's really delusional, after all. I'm going home."

When I walk away, he doesn't protest.

A grainy, radio version of Lana Del Rey is humming through the speakers. My passenger side window is partially open, and rain bleeds down both sides of the pane of glass and puddles on the plastic setting. Damp, fresh air rushes through the gap, and if I focus on it, Lana's wailing dissolves into background noise. I've never really been a fan of those beautiful, haunting voices, but my sister never tires of them.

"Are you going to tell me why you were there?" Chloe asks hesitantly, breaking the silence for the first time in the journey. She's just turned the car onto our road, so I suppose I should be grateful that she held out this long.

"Chase took me there while he applied for a job. But it's so sketchy." I sigh. "I just wanted to go home." My head is resting against the wet glass, rain droplets on my forehead, and I don't look over at her.

"Okay," she agrees, in a tone that tells me she won't push for more detail. "Mom was notified about your detention, by the way. She wants to know what happened."

The cherry on top of the cake.

"Thanks for the heads-up."

With a sigh, Chloe swings the car to the right and crawls up our long driveway to park in her usual position behind Dad's estate. I lift my cheek away from the glass as the window rolls back up, sealing the elements outside again. The purring motor splutters to a stop and violently interrupts Lana's second verse. Keys jingle in Chloe's hand.

"Do you need to talk about it?"

"I'll be okay, thanks, Chloe." I glance over at her for the first time in fifteen minutes and manage to pull together a small smile. "Thank you for rescuing me, too."

"Anytime." I can tell she means it.

Together, we exit her small blue car and walk up the steps to the front door. It's evening now, and yellow light glows behind the cream drapes in the living room window. Chloe unlocks the front door and ushers me into the warm house. I barely have time to kick off my sneakers in the hallway before Mom has padded out of the kitchen to greet us.

"Where have you been?" she demands. "Detention finished over an hour ago."

"I went somewhere with a friend," I reply tiredly.

"Was that friend something to do with your detention?" Mom leans against the wall to her left, her expression both expectant and somehow already disappointed. "When I asked your teacher what had happened, she said you were disrupting the class!"

"She thought we were talking too loudly, that's all."

"Erika." She drags a hand over her face. "You know better than to talk in class."

"I guess not," I say curtly.

"Did you say thank you to your sister for picking you up? She was busy, y'know."

"Of course, I didn't, Mom." Irritation dribbles openly into my tone and I lift my shoulders to intensify my sarcasm. "That would require me doing something right for once."

"What are you talking about?"

"I don't know." Scooping my sneakers up from the floor, I sigh loudly. "Don't worry, you don't have to send me to my room for my attitude—I'm already going."

I storm up the carpeted stairs, making sure that each step thuds louder than the last, and leave my angelic older sister and my disappointed mother to stare after me, wondering how I could turn out so differently from them.

11

Nacho Business

"Cheese."

"Huh?" I mumble, tugging out my blaring earphones to focus my attention on my sister, standing beside me at the kitchen countertop. Chloe's expression is flat and unimpressed, and she points a baby pink fingernail at the bowl in front of me.

"Those pathetic excuses for nachos need more cheese."

"Oh." I blink, then turn my attention to the hot bowl of nachos in front of me, my salsa spoon lingering tauntingly in the air. I lower a satisfying dollop of tomato directly in the center. "Well, what I lack in cheese, I make up for in guacamole and salsa."

"Erika." Chloe sighs and twists around to rest her lower back against the countertop beside me, rendering it impossible for me to ignore those concerned eyes. "What's wrong?"

"Why would anything be wrong?" I ask casually, placing a heaping spoonful of guacamole onto my already towering stack of nachos. After half a second of deliberation, I add a second spoon. The tower wobbles uncertainly. "Everything is fine."

"You look about as stable as those nachos."

Scowling, I collect my bowl of food and twist away from her, padding towards the living room in my fluffy socks. "Well, it's *nacho* concern, Chloe. Day job, remember?"

"Counseling is my day job," Chloe agrees, following closely behind to my annoyance. "But caring for my sister is a 24/7 occupation. I'm on call permanently."

I collapse onto the couch, slinging my fluffy purple feet over the armrest with the bowl nestled into my lap. I take a cheesy triangle and scoop up as much avocado as I can possibly manage. "I hope you're getting paid well, then."

As I pop the nacho into my mouth and begin to fumble for the remote, Chloe positions herself directly in front of me with her hands on her hips, blocking my view of the television. She glowers down at me, and the Pikachu pajama T-shirt she's wearing does nothing to detract from her powers of intimidation. "You've been moping around for days, eating nachos. You've been through *three packs* of tortilla chips, Erika."

"That wasn't just *me*," I retort. "Miko had some."

"Miko hasn't been here."

"FedEx. They'll be delivered to her in two to three working days."

Chloe's frown intensifies. "Erika, be serious, please."

I sigh and sink further into the cushions. I would be lying if I said I'd been in a good mood for the past three days. Since that argument with Chase about whatever it was that went down in the Admiral parking lot, everything else seems to have gone downhill.

I haven't spoken to him, and I'm catching myself missing him more than I should. I got a bad grade back from my history pop quiz, and my chances for even an offer of a place at Stanford seem to be slipping through my fingers with every failure I make; educational, emotional, and moral. And to top things off, my period has started, triggering my excessive nacho intake and some serious back aches.

But avocado is healthy, right? Nachos are a balanced meal.

Just as I'm about to reward Chloe with another deflective quip, I hear a distinct *tap* from the window. Chloe's head snaps to look towards the cream drapes.

"As I was saying," I continue, turning back to Chloe. "A girl does not need an excuse to eat nachos to her heart's content, so stop shami—"

Tap.

"What is that?" Chloe mumbles, clearly not paying attention to me. She strides over to the window and peels back the heavy, pleated material to reveal the dark driveway outside.

"It's probably nothing," I say, licking guacamole from my fingertips.

"It's not nothing."

There's something eerie in the way that Chloe says it that catches my attention. I twist around slowly to examine further. She's grinning, holding the curtains close to block my view. "It seems you have a gentleman caller, Miss Erika Monroe."

"Ha," I say, crunching on another nacho. "Funny."

"I'm serious."

Tap.

Tugged to my feet by curiosity, I slide across the floor in my socks towards the window. But as soon as I get close, Chloe places a firm hand on my shoulder to keep me away.

She shakes her head so adamantly that her wild messy bun wiggles on top of her head, and the printed face of Pikachu on her T-shirt seems to disagree along with her.

"Get your shoes on and go outside."

Muttering complaints under my breath, I head out into the hallway and slide my sneakers on. The cool breeze washes over me as I step outside, ruffling my loose curls. This is my favorite time: just past dusk, when the world is drained of most light, but the air is still faintly warm. Like bath water that has cooled exactly the right amount.

"Hello?" I murmur, feeling stupid.

Tap.

Following the source of the noise, I cautiously step down from the porch and walk over the yard to the side of my house. A figure clothed in a tight, dark hoodie is standing beside the large fir tree, throwing what appears to be pebbles at the living room window. He blends into the night, but it can only be Chase Thatcher. Despite my white Bowie sweatshirt, he hasn't seen me.

"Chase," I call softly. "What the hell are you doing?"

He glances at me in shock, just as he releases another pebble. "Erika—"

Clunk.

My gaze flits to the window. I stare, chilled to the spot, as the glass reverberates in anger. While it doesn't fracture, the noise will be loud enough to catch my mother's attention. This thought is scary enough to spur me into action.

Chase, meanwhile, curses low. "Oh shit."

I clamp down hard on his hand and tug him towards the bushes lining the side of our front yard. I can already hear my mom exclaiming at the noise from inside the house.

"What are you doing?" Chase whispers, as I push him into the largest shrub I can find. Tugging hard on his hand, I pull us both down to a crouching position. Our backs are exposed to the road behind us, but this leafy camouflage should be enough to protect us from Mom's wrath.

"I'm praying to the Gods of Glass that they'll forgive your sins."

"Really?"

"No, you dumbass, I'm hiding us!"

I adjust my feet, close my eyes and wait for the drama to ensue.

"Listen, Erika—"

"Shush, I'm trying to listen."

I can hear Mom shouting inside the house. Although her words are indistinct, the sheer volume of her voice is enough for my knees to clamp. Chase is adjusting his position in the shrub beside me, and that's when I realize that I haven't let go of his hand. His fingers are slim and cool, and somehow, in the last thirty seconds of us sitting here in silence, they've managed to intertwine themselves with mine.

Chase catches me staring, and I promptly pull my hand away.

"Gorgeous—"

"Don't call me that. I don't want to hear it."

Chase looks at me, exasperated. There's a faint tinge of pink in his cheeks, like the inside of a rose petal. "I'm trying to apologize to you. Please, can you just listen?"

I glare. "Apologize then."

"I—" Chase hesitates. "Let me take you somewhere."

I pretend to ponder, lifting one of my tingling fingers to scratch my chin. "That's a funny-sounding apology. If

I thought it possible, I might even interpret it as a *request*."

Chase leans out and takes my hand again, squeezing it firmly. Under the dark locks of hair scattered in a haphazard fringe across his forehead, his eyes hold an intensity that somehow denies me the power of leaning away. "Erika. Trust me."

"What is it?" Despite myself, my voice sounds drained and weak. "Are we going to rob a bank? Plot to steal the Declaration of Independence, or better yet, the Moon?"

"You've been watching too many kids' movies."

Chase rolls his eyes and, utilizing his grip on my hand, pulls me back up to a standing position. It's only when we've emerged from the sanctuary of the branches that we notice the dark figure standing in the grass ahead of us. My dad is watching us with raised eyebrows, a pink baseball bat held loosely in both hands. In the darkness, I can't see much of his expression, but the way his eyes drop to our linked hands is completely unmistakable.

"Dad." I tug my hand free from Chase.

Dad groans, and I can see the crinkles of his forehead even in the dim light. "Please tell me you're the ones who threw the pebble."

"Please?" I repeat stupidly. "You want us to have done it?"

Dad's hands clamp tighter around the floral baseball bat. "Well yes, because the alternative is that you were in that bush for an entirely different reason, and I really would rather not have a conversation about—"

"No," I say sharply, cutting him off. I clear my throat, all too aware of the catch in my voice. "There was nothing like um—*that* going on. I threw the pebble."

In my peripheral vision, I see Chase glance at me.

"You threw it?" Dad echoes. He lets the bat fall from one of his hands and it swings in front of his body, before resting at his side. "Why?"

"I want to take up rock-skimming. I was practicing my aim."

"Of course." Dad makes a disgruntled noise, his suspicious gaze flitting between the two of us. "Why are you out here, Erika? And who is this?"

I can feel Chase's body tense under the spotlight of my father's scrutiny.

"He's my chemistry partner," I lie. "We have a homework assignment to work on."

"Now?" Dad doesn't seem convinced. "It's already dark."

"It's due tomorrow. We forgot about it."

Without removing his stare from Chase, my dad addresses me with a velvet soft mumble. "Okay. Are you coming inside to work on it, then?"

I shake my head slowly.

"I don't want Mom to find out about this. She's still mad about that detention."

Dad sighs.

"Fine," he agrees begrudgingly. "Be back before eleven o'clock. It's a school night."

"Thanks, Dad," I say, cracking a tentative smile.

"And no funny business in the bushes."

"Never, sir," Chase agrees hastily.

"Also, no more rock-skimming. It clearly isn't the sport for you, Erika."

"I begrudgingly accept that. I really thought it was my thing, y'know?"

"Shut up," my dad grunts, eyeing Chase. He lifts the baseball bat tauntingly, smacking it down in his other palm. "Remember this bat, boy. Keep it imprinted in your mind, because if you lay your hands on my daughter, you'll have to explain to the doctors the last thing you saw before it all went black. And it will be this fashionable pink floral design."

"Um—yes, sir."

Dad nods at both of us in turn, before turning and marching back up the yard.

"Is that your dad's bat or yours?" Chase mumbles under his breath.

"His," I say with a proud smile. "He really likes the color pink."

"I genuinely thought we were plotting to burn down the Houses of Parliament," I say, examining the iron fence in front of me. "Like, in London. I didn't think you'd take me to *school*."

Chase brushes his fingers over the heavy padlock. "Do you trust me?"

"In theory."

"Then get that cute ass of yours over the gate."

"Guy Fawkes has nothing on your recklessness," I mutter. Nevertheless, with a firm exhale, I wedge my foot into a gap between the bars and begin to climb the horizontal supports of the school gate. My phone feels heavy in my back pocket. I try to convince myself that the weight is reassuring as I pull myself up higher.

After thirty seconds, I am sitting uneasily at the top of the school gate, squinting into the darkness on the other side and wondering *how in the hell* I plan to get down.

"Well, that was a nice view," Chase says as he clambers up beside me.

"Not as nice as my dad's pretty baseball bat," I remind Chase.

"Touché."

My eyes focus on a recycling container, slightly further along the fence. I begin edging carefully over the thin metal, silently cursing the untied laces on my white sneakers. "I've been doing squats so that my ass matches my sass. I'm glad it paid off."

Before Chase can summon a response, I launch myself from the fence and land squarely on the large green trash can, bending my knees to absorb the impact and praying the lid is strong enough to withstand my weight. Then, in a fluid movement, I slide down and land firmly on the grass. I brush my knees off and can't restrain my sigh of relief at the comfort of solid ground.

"Impressive," Chase comments, jumping down to the spot beside me.

He takes his sweet time, brushing his jeans down and ruffling his hair to check it's intact, but when he turns to me with a glint in his eye, I can't help but forget the insult I was going to quip. I'm going to miss this, I realize—when I've engineered his departure from school. I'm going to miss the adrenaline, the confidence, the excitement of being around him.

"Coming, gorgeous?" he calls, strolling ahead.

"Yeah." I quicken my pace to catch up, trying to make sense of my surroundings when they're blurred with darkness. Finally, I realize that we're approaching the bicycle sheds. The telltale triangular roofs rise in the darkness ahead of us like the crest of ships in the mist. When we're fifteen yards or so away, Chase touches my arm, and I stop walking.

"Sit," he commands softly.

"Here?" I ask, kicking the patch of grass. "What are we doing?"

Swiftly, he twists until his foot connects with the back of my knee. My legs crumple beneath my weight and I fall to the grass with a thud, scowling and rubbing my backside.

"I meant it when I said sit."

"What the hell are you doing?"

"I'm checking the coast is clear. This parking lot has been busy recently."

I watch as he disappears behind the trimmed hedgerows: the perfect lookout angle for someone who wants to survey the parking lot without being seen. When he returns a minute or so later, he's brushing twigs from his hair. Then he gives me a thumbs-up.

"What do you mean it's been busy lately?" I ask.

"I come here quite often at night," Chase says, adjusting his T-shirt. "Most nights I've been here, the parking lot fills up at around ten. Must be some kind of meet-up."

"You come to school at night?"

"Don't look at me like that; it's just someplace to spend time."

"No, no judgment here," I tease, raising my palms in surrender. The pressure of my weight on the grass has imprinted crosshatch patterns on my skin. "Just didn't realize you enjoyed school so much. We'll be gone by then, though, right?"

"Yeah, I'll make sure we are."

"This is not how you say sorry to someone, you know," I call, watching him amble towards the bike sheds with disconcerting grace. He glances back at me, and I can see the glimpse of a smirk in the darkness. Then, suddenly, a warm yellow light erupts in front of him. He's holding a match. In the light of an ebbing flame, he looks strangely beautiful.

"Are you sure?" he asks.

I rub my hands free of dirt on my leggings. "That depends on why we're here."

"You were quite close with the Guy Fawkes idea," he calls back. Then, before I can respond or question further, he's running towards the sheds and underneath the fuzzy halo of a security lamp. I lean forward, slipping my phone out of my pocket. There are boxes stacked on the roof of the shed, decorated in patterned, bloody colors. Chase places a foot on the small windowsill, pushing himself up. The match glows in his hands.

Then I realize.

The excitement abruptly disappears when it dawns on me what I need to do.

Under the light of the lamp, his face is unmistakable. Before I can overthink, I lift my phone up and swipe the video record on. I watch, my heartrate accelerating to a deafening frenzy, as the tiny, pixelated Chase on my screen bunches the fuses together. The flash of a match in the dim light, and the fizzing of a rope, burning into cinder.

"I hope you like fireworks!" he calls, climbing down quickly.

I end the video. Then, as fast as it appeared, I slide my phone back into my pocket. It feels hot and incriminating. I swallow the sour lump of guilt in my throat as Chase jogs towards me. He collapses beside me in a breathless slump, and I pray that his adrenaline will distract him from my own discomfort.

I am a terrible, selfish person. I can never forgive myself.

"Just wait," Chase murmurs, leaning back to rest on his elbows in a lounging position. He watches the sky with childlike eagerness, his teeth bright.

He will never forgive you.

And then the colors appear. I watch his face, transfixed, as spots of color cascade over his smooth, freckled complexion and shoot from his forehead down to his lips. Like somebody up there has broken apart a rainbow and decided to shower him with light.

Around us, the sky explodes into kaleidoscopic shards, but nothing can rival how broken I feel. The explosions thunder so hard I can feel them reverberate through the ground into my palms, but they aren't enough to drown out my hammering heartbeat. I look away, blinking back tears at the sight of a luminescent beauty I don't deserve.

He did this for me. He set up a firework display for me.

"Gorgeous," I hear him whisper. A cool finger touches the top of my hand, and I finally dare to look back at him. His eyebrows are furrowed into a faint frown, and it almost triggers more tears. My teeth are digging into my lip hard enough to hurt, hard enough to bleed, but it's the only thing holding back the floodgates.

"Now, now," I say weakly, moving my hand away. "No funny business."

"Erika. I really am sorry for leaving you alone in that place."

"I'm sorry too, for judging you so quickly," I say softly. The murmur is quiet enough that he probably can't hear. I turn back to the explosions of luminance in the sky. In every deafening crack, where it seems as though the heavens themselves are fighting off an attack, color rains down. Sparks of brilliance dance in the air.

I slip my phone out from my pocket, slide it unlocked. My finger lingers over the red *delete* button. Behind me, Chase drops from his elbows and lies fully in the grass.

I hear him ask. "Are you cold?"

And that's it.

Enough to break my resolve. Enough to finish this, forever. Any plan I had about trying to kick this idiotic, arrogant, reckless, smart, brilliant, *gorgeous* wonder of a boy out of school explodes—yes, like a firework—into vibrant rain. My thumb presses down on the button with startling ferocity, and the video disappears. The evidence disappears.

And, for the first time since the fireworks began, I smile.

12

Hoe-down Throwdown

I can feel the painful gravity of my decision across my shoulders as I enter the office.

"Erika Monroe," Principal Blythe greets, without looking up. I watch with aching apprehension as she lifts her thumb slowly to the corner of her painted mouth before sliding another page across her ring binder. Her gray eyes finally snap up to meet mine. "Take a seat. I'll be just a moment."

Without hesitation, I stumble forwards and collapse into the leather seat in front of her desk. The room hasn't changed much from my last visit. It's still stark and strangely cold, denied the luxury of plush furnishing or trinkets. There is, however, the addition of a small potted cactus. Somehow, the plant covered in long spines seems to be the less intimidating of the two living creatures facing me.

Seemingly unaffected by my presence, Blythe continues leisurely reading through immaculate lines of serif font. Only after half a minute of perusal does she close the purple binder and place a protective, perfectly manicured hand over the cover. She smiles.

"What can I help you with, Erika?"

After so many days of guilty sickness and self-doubt, the words tumble out of me like vomit: fast, messy, and yet ultimately relieving.

"I can't do this anymore." I listen to my shaky voice say the words I've been screaming internally for two weeks. "I can't help you with evidence. He's my friend, and as much as I want this ... I can't do it to him. To Chase, I mean. I'm sorry for wasting your time."

The words float uncomfortably in the air for a few seconds, then sink into acceptance, like a feather fluttering down to a motionless resting place.

Mrs. Blythe makes a humming noise and leans back further into her chair with unexpected nonchalance. Her fingers are already re-opening the binder on her desk, her eyes scattering across the paperwork distractedly.

"Okay, Erika. Thank you for letting me know."

A few moments pass, but my confusion doesn't dissipate. That was ... anti-climactic. I was expecting her to protest or complain or at least berate me for making promises that I don't intend to keep. Somehow, her understanding has unsettled me more than blame would.

"Was there something else?" She looks up at me. Her reading glasses are now balanced on her nose. Delicate and rimmed with gold, they look expensive.

"No, no," I rush. "I'm sorry, I'm just confused."

"You look so worried. Bless you." Her eyes return to her binder, and she seems anything but fazed. She lifts her fountain pen into the air and flicks it dismissively. "Don't worry. I can find a replacement easily enough."

My mouth dries.

"A replacement?"

Her eyes rise from the page. "Well, yes. Plenty of students in this school want a scholarship for Stanford, Erika. I'll just ask somebody else if they'd prefer to take the position."

Why hasn't that ever occurred to me?

Principal Blythe continues scouring the book in front of her. When she reaches the end of the page, she hums under her breath. "Stanford University attracts bright, business-savvy young students who know what they want and how they'll get it."

My defensiveness flares. I find myself leaning forward slightly with my fists clenched around the weathered armrests of the chair. "I know how I'll get it. I'll work hard."

I sound impressively determined out loud. I pray it hides my insecurity.

"Of course, you will," Blythe responds sweetly, with the air of someone telling a child that *of course the tooth fairy is real*. I watch in angered silence as she runs her fingers along the length of her fountain pen. "With or without you, however, the job will be done."

"I don't want to be any part of it. I don't agree with it."

Mrs. Blythe nods, as if she'd expected this. "Getting into Stanford is going to be a challenge with your current grades, Erika. Your recent evaluations are ... not promising."

"I'll rise up to that challenge."

"Yes." She purses her dark lips briefly, then strikes for the kill. "I can't say that I'm not a little disappointed, Erika. I had such high hopes for you, but your passion clearly doesn't manifest beyond paper. I pray for your sake that Stanford doesn't recognize your lack of drive."

The threat is as evident as the fangs of a Gaboon viper. I

suck in a breath that stings my throat. My voice shakes with anger or anxiety, maybe a combination.

"I'm a good student."

When I open my eyes, Mrs. Blythe is watching me with sympathy. She offers a Kleenex in her outstretched hand. "Sometimes, Erika, good isn't *good enough*. Colleges like Stanford look for the individual ready to go that extra mile. The thing that makes you stand out."

I have lost all sensation beyond the burning in my eyes.

"What are you saying?"

Mrs. Blythe leans back and drops her gaze to her pen, nestled between the pockets of her folder. She seems satisfied at the weakness of the victim in her clutches. "With your grades, and your extra curriculars ... I don't like to say this, but you are nothing special, Erika."

My coiled fists, once so determined, fall to my lap.

"I am 'nothing special,'" I repeat, not-at-all bitterly, tearing the crust from the first of my triangular quartered sandwiches. "From now on, I will not answer to Erika, Ricky, gorgeous or any other of my previous titles. From now on, I answer only to *Nothing Special*."

Miko places a hand on my arm sympathetically. "Erika—"

"No, no," I cut her off, brushing her arm aside and waving the sandwich angrily. "It's *Nothing Special*, remember? I'll even let you call me *Not Special* as a nickname if you're feeling flirtatious."

"Stop!" Miko orders, batting my sandwich aside. A drop of mayo falls to the surface of our lunch table, but the *slop* sound is lost within the chaotic noise of the school cafeteria. "You're making a dad joke into a *sad joke* and I can't take it anymore! Where was this attitude when that Prick-cipal threatened and manipulated you?"

"This attitude—" I continue mournfully, through a mouthful of brown bread "—was in a hospital bed, suffering from extensive injuries. Right beside my fatally bruised ego."

"What are you doing?" Miko says with a fierce glare. "Where is my fiery Erika? The one that would have told this asshole where to stick it?"

"She's buried underneath a pile of *Nothing Special*."

Miko shakes her head, and the cherry-soda earrings she's wearing shake as fiercely as if they were pointed fingers. "Why did you agree to this, Erika?"

"I don't know," I mumble, physically deflating. "She literally told me I didn't have a shot at Stanford without her. If she writes a bad character reflection ... that undoes everything I've been working towards. Every one of my stupid extra-curriculars, every study night."

Miko must sense that the tears are threatening me again because her hand returns to my forearm. "It's okay. It's okay, Erika."

"It's not okay," I murmur despairingly. "I hate that I caved."

Miko loops her arm around my shoulder and squeezes me to her side tightly. She smells like floral perfume and strawberry bubble gum, and it's one of the most comforting smells in the world to me. I hope she never loses it. "You move mountains on your best day, Erika Monroe. Everybody is allowed to cave sometimes."

I chew on another dissatisfying mouthful of sandwich and lean my head against Miko's for support, as if she could transmit me strength via osmosis. "I need to get this over with. The longer I draw this out, the more pain I'll cause him."

"Maybe he'll never find out," Miko says, unsure.

"I couldn't be his friend after I did that to him."

"Yeah." She sighs.

"I need to do this. Tonight. I need your help."

A moment passes.

"Okay," she agrees softly. "We'll get you out of this, honey."

"Are we breaking up a cuddle?" a voice calls from behind us.

Before Miko or I have even had chance to turn at the greeting, our lunch table is being surrounded. Joe flashes us a cheeky grin as he slides into the seat opposite, followed by Dylan and Alec. Violet chucks a mango juice box at the side of his head, and it hits his cranium with a thump before smacking to the table surface. She and Riley collapse into the seats beside Miko, with full trays of cafeteria food.

"If I weren't already concerned about your brain capacity," Joe grunts, rubbing his head and scowling at Violet, "I would throw this right back at you."

Violet scoffs and takes a sip from her water bottle. "Joey, you have your own brain problems to worry about before you concern yourself with mine."

Miko gives my shoulders one final comforting squeeze before we detach from our embrace. Clearing her throat and playing absentmindedly with the tennis charm on her bracelet, she asks the others the question I've been wondering about myself. "Where's Chase?"

A tangible pause. Riley shuffles and angles her head to the left.

Violet grimaces a little. "He's over there."

I follow her line of vision to see Chase standing a few feet away with his back facing us. Standing in front of him, just concealed from view by his body, is a petite girl. Her black braids are barely visible beside his bicep, but I'd know that loud laughter anywhere. I don't realize I'm craning to get a view of her before my palm almost slips out from underneath me and I readjust myself with a squeak.

Leonie Campbell has enviably clear skin and a pretty smile, which is on full display as she chatters to Chase. It's clear that she's talking a mile a minute, but he seems to be enjoying it. I feel a strange ache in my chest, watching them. Leonie is making him laugh quite a lot. Surely, she can't be *that* funny.

My eyebrows furrow slightly. I wish I could hear what she's saying.

"Are you alright there, Erika?" Violet asks, recapturing my attention. When I finally rip my gaze away from Chase and his friend, I see that she's watching me with interest. If her amusement wasn't recognizable already in her voice, it's written clearly across her smirk.

"I'm fine," I defend, folding my hands in my lap. "I just really like her T-shirt."

Alec cocks his head. "I never took you as a fan of *The Last Airbender*."

"Are you kidding?" I scoff. "I love that movie."

"It's a TV show, Erika."

"Of course, it is." I nod. "But it's very filmic. The camera angles are so cinematic."

Miko groans and buries her face in her hands. "Erika, honey, it's an animation."

I open my mouth and I'm about to spout another round of spontaneous bullshit when Joe shakes his head at me. His grin is wide and goofy, and without the need for words, it tells me exactly how little they believe me. My next excuse is stolen from my lips. Instead, I make a noise of complaint and glare down at my unfinished sandwich.

"That's it," Miko soothes, placing a hand on my back. "No need to dig any deeper."

"Who's digging?" Chase's velvety voice sounds from my right, shortly before he slips into the free seat beside me. He smells like cologne and something oddly sweet, and it draws my burning face out of hiding. I smile sheepishly at him. He steals one of my sandwiches and begins to chew.

"Erika is thinking about getting into agriculture," Miko says seriously.

Chase frowns in amused confusion, his pecan eyes alight as they turn to me. "Well, I suppose pigs do belong in a farming environment."

My embarrassment instantly forgotten, I swat him on the shoulder.

"Now, now, Chase," Miko says, lazily stretching her arms behind her and yawning. "Hogs don't like it when you mistake them for pigs. It makes them mad."

"Not you too!" I groan. "Why is everyone picking on me today?"

"It might have something to do with your sandwich choice," Chase contributes helpfully, chewing through his stolen triangle with a slightly wrinkled nose. He swallows loudly, then shakes his head. "Turkey salad on brown bread just *begs* to be picked on."

"You're still eating it."

"I'm saving you the pain, gorgeous."

I roll my eyes and begin to eat my own picked-at triangle. A moment of silence lulls past before Dylan decides to break it.

"I didn't know you and Leonie were friends, Chase," he says conversationally. His eyes flit to mine for half a second before they land on the idiot beside me, eyebrows raised.

"Yeah," Chase says with his mouth full. "Her friend wants a second date with me, Leonie was the messenger. We know each other from history class."

"What was the result?" Alec asks.

Chase shoots Alec a blank look. "I said to let her down easy."

"Ouch."

"Don't worry," I pipe up. "She'll realize that she dodged a bullet soon enough."

Chase bumps me lightly, his mouth too full of stolen bread to spout an insult.

"What about you, Erika?" Riley asks sweetly, popping a fry into her mouth. "How do you know Ellis Jackey? Because he hasn't stopped staring at you since we arrived here."

Chase audibly swallows the last of his sandwich.

"Oh, El is one of Dylan's friends," I say dismissively, poking at a fallen piece of lettuce on my tray. Ellis is sitting at one of the tables to our left, with some of the other football boys. I noticed him when I walked into the cafeteria, but we don't tend to speak much outside of class. He joins track sometimes.

I finally take a glimpse around the table, and, to my horror, the others have all twisted around in their seats to assess the handsome linebacker, only a few tables away. I gasp and flap, my words slurring together in my haste. "No, no! Don't stare at him all at once!"

"I think we've caught his attention," Violet confirms, chewing a fry that she delicately lifted from Riley's plate, and continuing to stare blatantly.

"His whole table are getting up. I think they're leaving," Miko reports.

"They're going to come past us to get to the door," Riley says, nodding.

"Guys!" I hiss.

I know exactly when the football boys are approaching because, suddenly, the girls are twisting around in their seats again and attempting to act inconspicuous. I dare a glimpse over my shoulder. The group are weaving their way through the tables to the exit. The football tucked under Jack's arm tells me that they're probably headed for the field. Closest to us, on the right-hand side of the group of boys, is Ellis. He smiles at me, outstretching a tanned arm to flick my braid playfully as he walks past.

"Hey, Erika."

"Hi," I say, with an uncomfortable smile.

Ellis's hazel eyes shift away to focus on the cafeteria exit and I finally release my restrained breath and turn back to the table. As soon as he's out of hearing distance, Riley leans towards me, stretching over her tray with no regard for the messy ketchup sachets.

"It's official. It's true love. He's mad about you."

"Or just mad," Chase mutters lowly.

My elbow finds his stomach and I hear an *oomph*.

"Do you like him?" Dylan asks, his eyes a little too wide and voice a little too casual for my liking. Ellis is one of his closest friends on the football team. If he really does like me then Dylan certainly knows about it and will likely report back any intel.

I shrug helplessly. "Not really."

"Ouch." Alec says for the second time in the past five minutes, clutching his chest. "Hearts are being broken left, right, and center today."

"It seems we have more than one heartbreaker in our presence after all," Joe drawls, leaning back in his seat and crossing his arms across his chest smugly. His eyes flit between Chase and me, as if shaping us up for battle. "A real *hoe*-down throwdown."

"Call me a hoe again and I will smack you with the tool namesake."

Joe gasps. "She's ruthless *and* violent."

"All the best women are," Miko chimes, sipping at a tall bottle of strawberry milk.

"Ellis does like you," Dylan admits, folding a torn-off piece of sandwich box in his fingers. "I'm pretty sure he's going to ask soon. He's just ... warming up to the idea."

"He seems like an alright guy," Alec contributes, shrugging.

Chase clears his throat beside me, instantly capturing the attention of the table. He pauses, toying with our patience, before outstretching his defined forearms in front of him to rest on the polished surface. His smirk is debonair and dangerous.

"Well," he says. "*I* think that he has the personality of a self-service checkout."

Joe snorts. Even Violet smiles.

"Are you saying Erika deserves better, Chase?" Riley

asks, raising an eyebrow. I turn to follow her gaze, unable to restrain my curiosity about what he'll say next.

Chase's smirk twitches slightly, barely visibly. He glances at me for half a second. "Actually, Riles, I was implying that's the reason they're such a perfect match."

"Dickwad," I mutter, picking up the damp piece of lettuce from the table to throw at him. "I've had phone battery that lasted longer than your relationships."

Chase captures my wrist before I can release the lettuce. His eyes, inches from my own, are buttery with playfulness, framed with expressive, dark lashes. "I'm *known* for lasting, gorgeous."

I glare into his stupidly beautiful face, disconcerted by the warmth flooding up my arm at his touch. I draw out the best card I can think of for this situation: my ace of spades.

"Oh really, *Squidge*?"

The victory instantly disappears from Chase's chiseled features.

"Squidge?" Alec echoes.

"Don't you dare," Chase warns me in a low voice. I assess the threat in his expression with smug delight and beam back at him.

"Why do you call him Squidge, Erika?" Joe asks, leaning forwards.

"Don't tell them."

"Erika, please," whines Joe.

I look at Chase. Look at Joe. Back again. "It's an inside joke."

"If you say another word—" Chase threatens.

The words tumble out of me as fast as I can manage them.

"Basically, I convinced this waitress that he had erectile problems an—aah—"

Before I can finish my sentence, two strong arms have encircled me around the hips, and I'm lifted into the air like a sack of flour and hauled over a hard shoulder. The world turns upside down and I'm dipped into momentary confusion, staring at a cotton blue back. When I finally realize my position, it's too late, and Chase has pinned my legs firmly to his chest, forcing me to struggle with the inadequacy of my abdominal muscles. Every squirm, every twist, is startlingly unsuccessful.

"No, help—" I wheeze. Chase's shoulder is digging into the soft part of my stomach, making it almost impossible to speak coherently. "I'm—ah—trying to say, h-h-he's squidgy—"

I hear Chase's voice override me, a loud announcement, as his grip on my legs tightens. "We need to go now but it's been so nice having lunch with you all."

"Help!" I cry again, twisting my torso to try and reach up. Cursed laughter begins to bubble down my throat and before I know it, I'm giggling and gasping with spurts of breathlessness. My stomach cramps with the pressure of lifting myself and I collapse back down lifelessly.

"Have fun you two," Violet calls from somewhere behind me.

"Why would I have fun?" Chase responds. "I'm just taking the trash out."

I smack a useless fist into his back. Then, with one last huff of effort, I try to push myself up again. As the world straightens into coherence once more, my arms pressed against Chase's waistband to hold my body up, I catch sight of a figure strolling through the cafeteria with enrapturing poise and power, like a lioness amid her pride.

Principal Blythe watches me with an unwavering,

unsettling smile as she weaves through the lunchtime chaos on her way to her office. Her eyes lift to Chase, then return to me. She nods.

And suddenly the urge to giggle is gone, swept back down my throat by remorse.

13

Wet and Wild

Me: Hi
Me: I have a proposition
sQuidge: Has nobody ever told you that it's naughty to text in class?
Me: I want to do something tonight
sQuidge: hmm
sQuidge: like what?
Me: Not sure yet. Are you free later?
sQuidge: I'm weighing my options
sQuidge: homework or hanging out with you? :// it's tough
Me: my homework is more thrilling than your jokes, I know that much
sQuidge: you are the type of person to be thrilled by homework
Me: What do you say then?
sQuidge: I'm in. Where are we going?
Me: Open to suggestions
sQuidge: Meet me at the pool, 7pm
sQuidge: I'm feeling a swim

Me: That's after swim practice. Won't it be locked?

Me: Chase?

sQuidge: When has that stopped us before gorgeous?

I click my phone screen off with a sigh, sliding the device into my back pocket where I can't be tempted to read the messages again. It's two minutes past seven and I'm standing outside of the locked doors to the Lindale High swimming pool, a building that Miko and I haven't set foot in since we'd hang out here to drool over the swim squad as freshman students.

Tonight, we'll both see the pool again. Only, one of us will be hiding.

My fingernails are digging so hard into my palm that when I open my fists, a line of small crescent-shaped marks split my hand like a stormy sea. It's not the first time tonight that this has happened. I lean back against the wall and splay my fingers across the brick. The tranquil dusk settling over the school grounds is deceptively pretty. It speaks nothing of the girl crouching in the bushes somewhere, or the ambush lying ahead.

I wonder if Miko is feeling as uneasy or as guilty as I am. I don't think it's possible.

"Hi, gorgeous."

A voice interrupts my anxious thoughts, and I become aware of Chase, ambling towards me with an easy smirk and a spotless white T-shirt. On his lower half, he's wearing a pair of swim shorts. The reality of swimming with him, in the bare minimum of clothes and completely alone, hits me, and a wave of anxiety crashes through my body. It was something I had completely forgotten to worry about, in the larger scale of tonight's events.

Suddenly, the black bikini under my clothes feels a little tighter.

"Have I rendered you speechless?" Chase is in front of me now, standing with his head tilted patronizingly. I can see that underneath the teasing, however, is genuine curiosity.

"No," I mutter quickly, shoving my hands into my short pockets. "I'm just nervous."

"Ah." Chase scratches his jaw. "Don't worry. We'll be careful, we won't be caught."

That's not why I'm nervous! I know we'll be caught.

Any worries are cut short as Chase takes a step forward, leaving my mind blank with surprise. He is close enough now that I can feel the warmth of his breath fan over my face, and if I wanted to, I could count every single beauty mark and freckle on his complexion. One of his hands slides up to my hip and sits in the curve, like it was meant to be there. His gaze, which had been glued to my face, finally tears away to follow the movement of his other hand, up to my hair. It winds through the curls at the side of my face.

Then he smiles slightly and pulls out my bobby pin.

"I'll need this to pick the lock," he says, brandishing the thin strip of metal in front of my face. He's biting back a smile when he turns to the door lock beside me, but the telltale laughter dances in his voice and incriminates him. He teased me on purpose.

"You're an asshole," I mutter.

He grins at the lock, continuing to twist the pin. "I know. It's so fun."

With a particularly loud click, the door unlocks and Chase swings it open. He gestures for me to enter, that particularly irritating smile still sitting proudly on his face.

Rolling my eyes and ignoring the coiling unease in my stomach, I step into the building. The pungent stench of chlorine clings to the humid air, instantly overwhelming my senses. As we walk past the seating stands—Miko's hiding place—the pool becomes finally visible: a turquoise rectangle in the center of the space, irresistibly calm. The stage for tonight's events. I swallow, and glance at the changing rooms on the right side.

"Should we—" I begin to ask, twisting around. "Oh!"

Chase's shirt is already up and over his head. He peels it from his arm and drops it, puddling cotton on the tiles. His toned chest commands no less attention in the low lighting.

"You're wearing your swimsuit under your clothes, aren't you?"

"Yes," I mumble, my voice oddly thick as I watch him kick his sneakers off.

"So, take them off, Monroe." His head cocks to the side. His eyes seem darker in this lighting, and they spark like hot coals. "Or do you want me to do it for you?"

"Very funny."

"Suit yourself."

The last thing I see is his smile before he twists, runs, and throws himself easily into the pool. Water splashes my legs and laps into the drains at the pool's perimeter. When he emerges, his hair is inky dark and dripping down his forehead. Droplets cling to his cheekbones, his septum, the swell of his bottom lip.

Have mercy.

Averting my gaze from him, I take a deep breath and undo the button of my shorts. Swiftly, like ripping off a

Band-Aid, I slide them down my legs and push them into the little pile beside his T-shirt. Without removing my long-sleeved top, I take a few running steps and cannonball into the swimming pool.

Water swells around me, invading every crevice of my body and face to greet me. When I finally pop up to the surface, it takes a few seconds for my eyes to adjust past the blurring droplets. I smooth the hair away from my face and wipe my nose. Chase is swimming a few feet away in the water, leaning back until the rippling waves of my arrival kiss his Adam's apple.

"Why did you keep your top on?" he asks, as if confused.

"I just prefer to keep it on."

Chase continues to look at me, as if he needs more explanation. I try again.

"I just . . . feel more comfortable covered up."

Chase frowns, his tongue darting out to catch a bead of water on his lip. "Okay, but you have no reason to be self-conscious, you know."

Betraying me, my eyes flit to the seating area where Miko will inevitably hide to make the recording of us. This moment feels too private, too dangerously intimate, and I almost long to see her black space buns sticking out from among the rows of empty seats.

"Thanks, I just . . ." My words stick in my throat as I look back at Chase, and I struggle to dislodge them. "My eczema is pretty bad on my arms at the moment. It's not pretty."

Chase frowns. "Erika, you're always pretty."

"No, don't say that," I say, almost whining, as I propel myself backwards through the water to put some distance between us. "I'm not trying to fish for compliments. This isn't a big thing, like, *at all*. I just don't like showing my arms when they're bad."

Chase swims closer, expertly, his arms barely breaking the skin of the water. "Gorgeous."

I shake my head, almost desperate. "You don't need to make me feel better."

"Okay, I won't."

I groan. "You still have those sympathy eyes like you want to tell me I'm pretty."

"I call you gorgeous every day," Chase says, shrugging slightly as he treads water. "It's hardly out of character for me. Will you let me see your arms?"

"I don't like how this is becoming something," I complain, gripping my elbows underwater and praying that if I hold them protectively enough, the ravaged dry skin there will heal instantly, as if chlorine ever soothed eczema. "I don't need you to compliment me or say anything at all. I mean it."

"Okay." Chase hums in consideration. I'm not sure if it's the humidity, or the chlorine getting to my head, but he looks utterly, devastatingly hot. "How about you show me, and I will promise not to say anything at all?"

I hesitate, but eventually my grip on my arms loosens and I relent. "Okay."

Without moving his eyes from mine, Chase swims closer. Close enough that our legs clash and kiss under the water as they move, like lovers and haters. Close enough that every time he moves an inch, the water ripples around both of us as if we were one. Close enough that he can reach for my wrist under the water, and I can let him.

He lifts my arm to the surface and the maroon cotton of

my top clings to my arm like a second skin. He begins to peel up my sleeve, exposing me more inch by inch, in a motion that is more furiously, searingly intimate than any make-out session I've had with a boy, ever. Slowly, the skin of my lower forearm becomes dry and split, and the urge to pull my arm back intensifies. When the entire crook of my arm is revealed, Chase releases the sleeve.

As promised, he is wordless as he examines my arm. The red, textured skin seems to burn under the heat of his gaze, but when he finally looks away to meet my eyes, the relief is only momentary. Because the burning is starting again, this time in my face. Chase holds my eyes for a few long seconds before his chin drops again and his head moves down.

I don't realize what he's doing until I feel the warm pressure of his lips on my forearm. *Oh my god.*

When he calmly pulls away, I have no words to greet him with.

"I think I really did render you speechless this time," he says quietly.

This guy is more dangerous than he looks.

"Not speechless," I manage to say. Even now, I can't let him win our battle.

Before I'm recovered enough for more words, his wicked grin returns. His hands press down on my shoulders, and I'm dunked down into the cool water, startled back into reality by the current of bubbles tickling my ears as they race to the surface. My eyes close as the water envelops me completely. I feel scarily vulnerable, yet warm and cocooned.

When I resurface, my old self resurfaces with me, and I instantly shove a wall of water towards the idiot opposite me.

Only when he's laughing, and I'm not so distracted by my own skin, do I notice the small black shape on his right collarbone. Tentatively, I reach out a finger to touch it. A crescent moon tattoo, no larger than my thumb. Chase inhales sharply.

"Clearly your skin tells a story too," I murmur, examining the wet mark. "Want to share?"

"It's just a tattoo," Chase says stiffly. "It doesn't mean anything."

"All tattoos mean something. Even if it's just that you like the moon."

Chase rolls his eyes, leaning back into the water until the top of his chest breaks through. He's pretending to be relaxed. "Fine, then I like the moon."

I swim a little closer. "Are you a werewolf?"

"Erika." Chase sighs, finally glancing at me.

"You don't have to tell me," I say earnestly. "I just don't know much about you."

Chase shakes his head slightly and splashes me half-heartedly. "You don't need to."

I feel a little disheartened, but I disguise it by splashing him again. As the water slaps his face, he shakes his face clear like a dog and then fixes me with a playful scowl. It's magical, how quickly he begins smiling when no personal questions are involved.

Whenever he isn't overwhelmed by my superior splash game and ability to generate walls of water, he's splashing back and we're chasing each other around the pool, calling out the *Jaws* theme tune and pretending to be sucked under water by a hyper-unrealistic Great White Shark.

I'm having so much fun that I can almost ignore the

camera lens pointed at us, from between two of the seats on the lower row.

Almost.

"Erika! Welcome, welcome, come on in."

Sada swings open the front door and the warm air of the house floods out to greet me on their front step. I've always found Miko's house completely comforting. Even her hallway is fresh and airy, filled with plants and reed diffusers, and studded with large bay windows that paint light all over the wooden floors. Her house is smaller than mine, but beautifully decorated. Sada is a sole trader for interior design and she's incredible. I come over for dinner quite often, but the beauty of each room never fails to impress me.

As I step inside, Sada pushes the door shut behind me. I watch her register my wet hair and spare T-shirt, but she doesn't question it. "Would you like a drink, Erika?"

"I'm okay thank you," I reply. Sada can be strict at times and she values manners, but her smile is kind, and she wears those thick woolly sweaters that make her a lot less intimidating. She wants the absolute best for her kids, and Miko has so much respect for her.

Soft padding on the stairs alerts me to my best friend's presence.

"I have good news. I've just found out that Okan is making sukiyaki," she says as she skips down the last few steps. Her hair is tied up and she's wearing black leggings and an oversized sweatshirt with llama slippers on her feet. I eye her fluffy warm toes with jealousy.

"Just the thing I need," I agree, smiling weakly. "When are we eating?"

"Five minutes," Sada replies, gesturing to the kitchen with her thumb. "I'm going to finish, and I'll be in shortly. Miko, call your brother for dinner, please."

"I will," Miko replies. She hesitates, waiting until Sada has completely left the room before she grabs my hand and begins to tug me up the wooden stairs. Her voice, despite being out of earshot now, is hushed. "How are you feeling? This is all so intense."

"I feel like a deflated balloon," I say with a grimace. When we reach the upstairs hallway, with the thick woolen carpet that always makes me sneeze, I can't help but sink back against the wall for strength. "So, reporting time. Did you manage to get the footage?"

Even to my own ears, my voice sounds bitter and defeated. Hesitantly, Miko nods.

"How much did you see?"

"I think I arrived in time for the second shark attack."

"Nothing before?"

"No," Miko says, frowning. "Why? Did something happen?"

"No, no." I peel away from the wall and examine the wet patch from my hair with disdain. "I just wanted to know how long the footage is. Can you definitely tell it's him?"

Miko nods her head tentatively, barely even a movement. Something in my chest still plummets at the news that our strategy has been successful. After everything I've done to be in this position, all the lies I've told, I'm still searching for a way out that won't bring my deceit crashing down around me.

"I guess we're set then. We've got everything we need to kick him out of school."

"I'm sorry, Erika," Miko says quietly.

I shrug lifelessly. "At least it's over."

"You have time. You can wait."

"I'm not sure how that helps anything really."

"I think..." Miko hesitates before finishing her sentence. "I think you should consider telling him everything. He might feel betrayed, but at least he'd have a warning that the principal is after him. He'd know to be careful."

The moment of consideration that lulls comfortably between us is interrupted by the sudden burst of rap music booming from Kaito's room, at the other end of the hall. In this house, with all of its thin walls and wooden floors, sound travels easily, and I can hear the enunciation of each dreadful word, feel the bass thrumming through the bottom of my feet. Miko makes a grumbling sound in her throat and turns to face her brother's door.

"Kai, turn that trash off. Dinner is ready!"

After waiting a few seconds for a response, she sighs and calls again.

Still nothing.

"Nandayo," Miko complains. "He makes me walk to his door every time."

"I'll come with you," I offer.

As she begins to walk towards her brother's room, I follow closely behind. Kai's room is left at the top of the stairs, and in all the time I've known Miko, I've only ever seen inside once. Kai has never been particularly hospitable. He tends to steer clear of human contact.

As we approach, the thump of the music becomes unbearable and Miko's expression turns into a scowl. She doesn't bother to knock as we reach his door. Twisting the handle, she throws open the door to reveal the dark interior of Kai's room.

The room is a *lot* darker than I remember it. The thick drapes are drawn, and his walls are forest green and covered in posters of bands and singers. He sits in the dark with only a small lamp lit, lying in a pile of disheveled black sheets. He bolts upright as the door splinters light onto his bed, and his expression is furious as he pauses his music.

I glance around, taken aback by what a dive he's living in amid this immaculate, exquisite house. He doesn't manage to get a word out in protest before I've noticed what is on the bedside table, closest to the door. My breath catches in my throat, and I gawp in horror.

A small, transparent plastic bag filled with green buds. Identical to the one that fell to the ground in the Admiral parking lot.

Miko's gaze follows mine and we both stare at something neither of us wants to see.

"Oh, Kai, no," Miko breathes.

14

The Lost Boys

I curse before I can stop myself. Miko has frozen stiff beside me, staring at the bag of weed on her sixteen-year-old brother's beside table. For a second, a brief blink of an eye, Kai looks scared. His eyes are dark and startled with anxiety, his lips parted as if he's going to speak, but no words come out. No explanation, no defense.

Then he looks mad.

"Get out!" He states the words so frantically that they spur Miko from her paralysis, cutting through the silence like a hot knife. His tone is equally sharp, but neither is any match for his expression. I don't think I'll ever be able to remove this image of Kai from my memory: eyes wide with panic, yet features pinched with fury. Like a threatened dog snarling in defense. "I can't believe you didn't knock—you, you—get out!"

I stumble back towards the door, but Miko stands firm. Her expression has become entirely detached. Her voice, while soft, sounds indisputably deadly.

"What are you doing, Kaito?"

"Nothing, I—" His voice fractures, revealing the core of fear and stress beneath his exterior defenses. Hurriedly, he swipes the bag from the surface and pushes it under his pillow, out of sight. "Just please shut the door, Miko. Okan can't hear this. Please."

"Erika, shut the door," Miko commands.

I click the door shut behind me and collapse my weight against it—partially for Kai's security and partially because my head is still spinning with this revelation. I knew that Kai was on the road to trouble, but I never thought that he was so far along as drug possession. I can still picture him sitting cross-legged in his Overwatch pajamas, headphones on and yelling at his friends about their PlayStation game. He still seems like a child to me.

Miko's hands are clenched into fists by her sides. "Explain. Now."

"I don't take anything, okay?" Kai pleads, leaning forward over the edge of the bed until his arms are resting on his bony knees. His hair is sticking out in all directions, disrupted by his pillow, and it makes him appear even more vulnerable. "I just protect it for my friends when they need me to. Please don't tell Okan, Miko, I'm begging you."

It doesn't look very protected out on your bedside table, I think, but all Miko says is, "How long has this been going on?"

"Only the past few weeks. A few of the older guys . . . they asked me to keep it for a few days, so their parents don't find it. That's all. I don't use it, it's theirs."

"And you agreed? What if Okan finds it?"

"Please don't tell her, Kumiko, she'll make me go and live with him. You know she will." He reaches forward to touch her hand. Even in the dim lighting of the lamp, his eyes are dejected and sincere.

Emotion breaks through Miko's impassive expression for the first time: her forehead creases in distress. Her hand is now laced tightly with her brother's. Their parents' divorce was only made official this year, after a long period of separation. Their father, whom Miko describes as a rational and unfeeling man, relocated to somewhere in Washington. Miko doesn't discuss him very often or in much detail, but it's clear that he broke Sada's heart.

It seems that he broke his son's heart too.

"She wouldn't force you," Miko says, although her voice trembles uncertainly.

"You know that she thinks I could benefit from him," Kai says quietly. "If she finds out about this, after all of the other stuff... I don't think she has enough patience left."

"Then why are you doing this?" Miko tears her hand free from his and drags it over her face. "Why do you keep doing stupid things like this if you don't want to leave? It's like you want Okan to send you away."

"I just want them to like me, Miko. They're my friends."

Her shoulders hunch as she exhales into her palms. "Goddamnit, Kaito. This isn't fair. I'm trying to hold this family together and you're making it so hard."

"I'll stop keeping their stuff for them, I swear. It was just a stupid thing I agreed to do. I won't ever bring it here again. Just please don't tell her."

Miko's hands fall back to her sides. "How do I know if I can believe you?"

"I would never hurt you," he vows.

"You'll stop looking after it for them?" Her voice is strained. "You swear?"

Kaito nods fiercely. "I swear."

Miko glances back at me. Her eyebrows are furrowed with worry. She doesn't need to speak a word because I already understand what she's asking of me.

"I won't breathe a word about this," I promise.

"Okay." After offering me a weak smile, she turns back to her brother and sighs tiredly. "This is my last straw, Kai. I won't cover for you again. Get rid of that bag."

"I will."

Sensing the finality of her words, I step aside from the door. Miko turns on her heel and pulls hard on the handle, letting the light from the hallway splinter across Kai's messy carpet. She hesitates as she reaches the doorway and looks back at her little brother.

"This house has already lost one family member. Please don't let it lose two."

I follow her out into the corridor. Kai's sullen expression and the darkness of his room are the last things I see before he shuts the door behind us, punctuating the conversation with off-white paneled wood. The second that we're alone, Miko's shoulders sink.

"Miko," I murmur, turning to my best friend. My hand is on her shoulder, and I squeeze it lightly. She looks utterly shell-shocked, but I can see the tears beginning to brim in her eyes. Soon, they will spill over.

"For God's sake," she mutters.

I pull her to my body and squeeze as tightly as I can, as if I can absorb her stress. She doesn't deserve this. She works so hard to push him in the right direction and encourage him to make the right decisions. Miko's fingers hook into my lower back painfully, and she buries her face into the crook of my neck, as if she can hear my thoughts. Although she doesn't shake with sobs, I can feel a stray tear roll over my collarbone.

"It will be okay," I murmur, stroking her hair. "It will all be okay."

She doesn't move for a while, and I don't tell her to. She remains cradled in my wet hair as I stroke her back to a slow beat until, finally, she's ready to speak.

"I need to tell Okan at some point," she whispers into my shoulder. "If this keeps getting worse, then maybe going to Washington is the best thing for him."

"He knows what's at stake now."

She pulls away from our hug, running fingers under her eyes to catch the traitorous tears. Her skin is flushed, and her mascara is slightly smudgy.

"I'm sensing you may want some time alone," I say softly. "Am I right?"

"Yeah, I think so." Miko bites her lip as she smiles. "Thank you, Erika. I mean it."

"Anything for you," I promise. "And you know I mean that too."

The crisp evening air nips at my exposed arms as I run aimlessly through the streets.

I watch every scuff of my sneakers on the concrete, unknowing of where I am or why I'm doing this, and uncaring. I'm losing light by the minute. Every gust of wind bites like a punishment, and dark clouds gather like school bullies in the dusky sky. We've been due some Oregon rain, but the timing of this seems like just another cry from the elements for me to stop jogging around like a restless idiot.

Kaito Tamura has given me no reasons to care about him. He snaps at me, ignores me, and stresses Miko consistently. Yet, beneath his attitude, he is just lost and lonely because he's experienced a brutal separation from his dad. I don't have enough bearing on Kaito's life to reassure him, but perhaps there is another boy I can protect. Perhaps the reason that Kai's situation has unsettled me so deeply is because I know that I have the facility to help someone in a similar situation. To pull them back from the edge before they make a mistake.

And I have been selfish enough not to do it.

I know I need to tell Chase about my deal with Blythe. It's the right thing to do.

I'm torn from my thoughts by a particularly zealous gust of wind that plasters my T-shirt to my body and reignites my shivers. In hindsight, it was not a great idea to run around the streets with bare legs and damp hair. I should have gone home to get changed before I started trying to clear my head. Slowing my footfall, I take my phone out of my back pocket. Only as the screen lights up do I realize how dark my surroundings have become.

9.39 p.m. I click Google Maps. I'm on ... *Halstead Avenue*. The road leading up to the cliffs, on the north side of Lindale. A forty-minute walk home, but I don't want to go there.

A feeling like relief warms through my body and I force my stiff fingers to text.

> Me: Hii, do you happen to know Chase's address?
> Riley-poly: ... Is this for a booty call
> Riley-poly: no shame!! but this gal wanna know if you're

gonna hoe
Me: the only thing I will be underneath tonight is my bedsheets. Just need to talk
Riley-poly: ahh:(
Riley-poly: Where are you? Asking Alec where Chase lives now and if not then we can come pick you up x
Me: Halstead Avenue, near the cliffs x
Riley-poly: Alec says you're right by him! He lives by the bus stop—it's called Forest View. Can you get there on your own or do you need us to come & get you?
Me: DW, I've got it, thank u! x
Riley-poly: text me when you're home safe pls <3

Sliding my phone back into my pocket, I begin to walk further up the incline of Halstead Avenue. The road winds in and out of the dense cliff forestry, as if it can't decide which it prefers. The houses here are all set well back from the street: large ivory structures hiding behind gates and long gravel driveways. I hadn't ever really thought about what kind of house that Chase would live in, but it's surprised me that it's one like this.

"Forest View," I mumble under my breath. "Forest View."

After about five minutes of walking, a set of birch gates appear on my right with a hand-painted plaque swinging from a rusty nail. Over the top of the gates, I can see a set of children's swings in the yard and an impressive, cream-colored house with a front porch. Hanging baskets swing from the edge of the roof. Anxiety rises up my throat and sits, hard and uncomfortable, in the very spot that makes it difficult to breathe.

This is it. No going back now.

Not trusting myself enough to enter the yard, I send Chase a text.

> Me: Come outside :)

A few minutes pass, and just as I'm beginning to worry that I'm in the wrong place entirely, the front door swings open. A boy in black storms out onto the porch, a human tornado. He looks completely at odds with the sweet decoration of the place: the children's toys and the pretty flowerbeds. The heavy green door slams behind him, and he thunders down the yard towards me. It's definitely Chase—I can recognize that irritated expression from yards away.

I raise my hand and I'm about to greet him when he snaps.

"What the hell are you doing here?" he asks angrily, pulling the gate open. I stumble backwards as my hand is torn from the wood. His hair is disheveled, crescents of purple beneath his eyes that weren't so apparent in the rosy hue of the pool room.

"Riley sent me your address. I—wanted to talk to you about something."

"What?" He stops a few feet away from me, his chest heaving up and down with labored breaths. He makes no move towards the car. "How did Riley know my address?"

"She didn't. Alec did."

"They shouldn't have told you." His voice is sharp.

"Right, well my apologies, I did not realize I was visiting a Mafia boss," I reply, a little bitterly. I avert my gaze to the ground, chewing my chapped lip. "I just, I really needed to see you and I thought—I don't know, I thought you'd be okay with it."

We both stand in silence for a moment.

"Cleary this was a mistake," I mumble. What is his problem? He's appeared at my house, completely unannounced and almost smashed a window. I had thought we were past this bickering phase. Shaking my head in disappointment, I begin to back away. "Never mind. I'll just go home."

Chase groans and roots his hand in his hair. "Don't."

"Forget I even came here, okay?" I call back, clasping my cold arms to my chest and twisting to face my route back down the hill.

"Wait."

I continue walking.

"Erika, will you just pause for one second?" Chase snaps behind me. "You never let me get a word in. Just give me a second!"

His attitude triggers my own temper and before I can stop myself, I'm twisting around to scowl at him. My limbs are trembling violently now, but I can't discern whether it's from annoyance, anxiety or the rain that's spitting over us. I don't care anymore. "Chase, I've had a really shitty night. I came here because I . . . I wanted to see you and talk to you about something. It's fine if you don't, I get it, but please don't try and start a fight with me."

Chase stares at me. Finally, he mutters, "You're cold."

"What?"

His words are barely audible. "You're shivering."

I glance down at my bare skin, flush with goose bumps. My voice softens. "Yeah."

Suddenly, Chase is striding towards me, tugging his loose-fitting black hoodie up and over his head as he does.

He's upon me in moments. His hair is even more disheveled than usual, and he's holding the hoodie up with outstretched arms. I instantly step back.

My words are quiet. "Chase, you don't need to—"

Before I can protest further, he's looping the material over my head. The world and the lost, imperfect boy in front of me disappear entirely for a few seconds. Instead, I'm overwhelmed by the strong, familiar smell of *him* and the warmth of the cotton where it has clung to his body.

When my head finally pulls through the material, I'm fully aware of, and embarrassed by, the dazed, sentimental expression on my face. My hands don't quite reach the wrists of the hoodie, and the hemline comes to my mid-thigh, longer than my shorts. Despite being oversized, stolen coziness instantly floods through my torso. After a few uncertain seconds, Chase finally looks at me,

"Chase—" I mumble.

"Erika." He tugs me sharply towards him by the strings of the hoodie. "Wear it."

Then, his bare arms lift up and around my shoulders and he tugs me the final few inches into his body. I sink into his chest with zero resistance, my arms winding around his lower back and my nose pressed to the thin cotton of his T-shirt. I slot into his embrace like a missing piece: my head on his collarbone, his chin propped on my hair. My shoulders sag with relief at the comfort of the sensation. All this time, desperately wandering around in the dark, and all I needed was *this*.

"I'm sorry," I mumble into his body. "I should have asked you, before I came here. I know how uncomfortable you get when it comes to your personal life."

Chase's chin moves on my hair. "You don't need to apologize. I snapped at you."

"I shouldn't have assumed you would be okay with this," I say, pulling out of the embrace just enough to look up at Chase with a weak smile. A raindrop hits my cheek and skims down like a tear.

"You're going to be ill if we don't get you home," he says, frowning at me. "The rain is getting worse. I'll get the car."

Then, as quickly as his arms arrived, they disappear again. I watch him jog back through his house gates to the driveway, clutching my arms to my body and inhaling his scent until I feel giddy. The rain is heavier: sticking my hair to my forehead and soaking into my sneakers, but it is powerless to wash my smile away.

A blue truck crawls out of the gates and parks just ahead of me on the right. Its plate is peeling slightly at the back, and there's a *Princess on Board* sticker in the back windshield.

"Get in," a voice demands through the open window.

Smiling, I jog towards the passenger side and throw open the door.

The interior is warm and smells of the yellow air freshener hanging from a string on the rear-view mirror. I slide into the seat and shut the door behind me. Chase wastes no time whatsoever in pulling away into the road before I've even clicked my seatbelt into place. His blue T-shirt is splotchy from the rain, and for the first time, I notice the design on its front.

"Is that a Build-a-Bear T-shirt?"

"Huh?" Chase glances down at himself, as his strange choice of clothing has only just dawned on him. "Oh. Um, yeah. I . . . found it at a thrift store."

"Interesting choice," I remark.

"Shut up." Chase laughs, but it sounds unnatural. He adjusts his rearview mirror. "So, anyway . . . what happened tonight? You wanted to talk to me?"

My smile disappears at the reminder. "Yeah, I did."

"Are you okay? Did someone hurt you?"

"I'm okay," I assure him, turning to look through the rivers of rain streaming down the window. "I'm just not sure how much I can say about the whole situation without betraying someone's confidence."

The road winds through the dense forestry of the cliff, down towards civilization. Every so often, I can catch the glitter of the town lights through the tangled branches ahead. There's something quite comforting about the way the trees shroud us.

"So . . ."

"Hypothetically," I begin. "A kid I know is looking after drugs for his friends. He's keeping them in his bedroom, so that they won't get into trouble."

"And I assume this kid is—"

"No, no," I interrupt. "A strictly hypothetical situation."

"Right," Chase replies, catching on. "Well . . . hypothetically, of course, it sounds like they're taking advantage of him. They aren't his real friends."

"Yeah."

We reach the bottom of the cliff, where the forestry dies away, leaving us exposed and vulnerable to the glare of the town. Chase turns onto the busier road and falls in line with the other vehicles. The red brake lights ahead distort in the growing water droplets on the wind screen.

"It's hard to know how to help him."

"Well, you could start by cutting him off from those friends."

"What?" I look back at Chase, surprised by his matter-of-fact advice.

"Cut him off," Chase repeats, his fingers wrapped loosely around the steering wheel and eyes focused on the road ahead. "From the people that are leading him astray. Support him until he finds better people. Don't punish him for it, guide him."

My breath catches.

"Hypothetically," he adds, after a second.

"You're right."

Chase smirks, undercutting his serious tone. "I'm always right."

I can't summon a witty response to Chase's brag. My head is already working overtime to unpick the mess of my thoughts. If, theoretically, we could guide Kai away from the bad decisions, to prevent him from moving away, then I see no reason why I couldn't do the same thing for Chase.

Suddenly the answer to all of my problems is staring back at me, with eyes the color of coffee beans and twice the caffeine content. If I can find a way to prove to Principal Blythe that Chase deserves to stay at school, that he can stop these irrational acts of delinquency, then maybe she won't be so insistent on his punishment. Maybe there's a way that I can help Chase, instead of sabotaging him, and still stand a chance at getting into Stanford.

Maybe both lost boys can be saved.

15

Aro-cuddle

I place a protective hand over the popcorn bowl.

"Mickey," I warn with my *I'm-serious-this-time* voice. "You can't eat it all before they actually arrive. One more piece and I'll send you out to buy more."

"Erika," Miko says, crossing her arms and imitating my nagging tone. "I saw you stuffing your face earlier, on my way back from the bathroom. It's not all me."

I glare at my best friend from the opposite side of the kitchen island.

Between us, splayed across the smooth granite surface, is a large assembly of junk food, soda cans, and skin-enhancing face masks. Miko suggested nail polish too, but I quickly decided against that. Dad hates the smell. To keep my parents happy and upstairs, out of our way, avoiding harsh odors is necessary. The food has been nibbled on, and I haven't told Miko about the other packet of popcorn hidden away in the cabinet. If she knew about it, she'd have no problem finishing the rest of the current bowl.

"No more snacking," I order, my tone stern. "For either of us. Okay?"

"Fun sponge." She sticks her tongue out at me and stalks out of the kitchen.

"Be careful," I call after her, "you're becoming saltier than the popcorn!"

Riley and Violet are both due to arrive soon for a slumber party. I thought it was about time to organize a girl-gathering, and nothing says bonding like practicing skincare while simultaneously demolishing the rest of your organs with junk food. I grab a final piece of popcorn before I follow Miko to the living room. The last one. Definitely.

Miko is standing by the bay windows staring out into our driveway. She turns around to face me, scowling and pulling at her pajama shorts to cover more of her legs.

"I forgot to shave," she grumbles. "Do you think they'll notice?"

"On a scale of small household cactus to King Kong, exactly how hairy are they?"

"Hm," she mutters, peering down and stroking a tentative hand over her knee. "I'd say we're at the fluffy woodland creature level. It's been a while."

"If they notice, just tell them you're insulating for the cold weather."

"Yes." She nods, straightening up. Her Donald Duck pajamas rise around her legs again. Now that I'm focusing, I can see the telltale downy strokes of hair on her skin. "This is why I keep you around."

I snort and collapse onto the couch. "Don't lie, you keep me around because my bedroom has good lighting for your Instagram selfies."

"Don't underestimate yourself! You also help me decide which picture to post."

"Not that you ever listen."

"Yes, *but* your opinion helps me realize why I disagree with you."

I roll my eyes but there's a smile on my face. Miko's Instagram profile is one of those flawlessly color graded, cohesive mood boards that all the real social influencers have. She must know that she doesn't need my help. I think she just wants me to feel included, because my own profile is a shabby, jumbled mixture of group pictures and bad-quality concert videos.

Just as I'm about to retort, a movement catches my eye. A small red car is pulling onto the gravel driveway in front of my house, just behind the shrubbery. Violet and Riley have arrived. I watch them climb out and I feel a tingle of anticipation in my stomach. It feels strange to be hanging around Chase's friends without him.

"Come on," I say to Miko, pushing myself up from the couch. "Our guests are here."

She's frowning. "I hope they don't like snacks."

"I think that Peter Kavinsky in the movie is so much nicer than the book version," Violet comments, crossing her feet on the coffee table and squinting at the television. Riley shakes her head vigorously; oblivious to the aloe-vera mixture threatening to drip from her face.

"I love book-Peter. He's such a realistic teenage guy."

"I think the movie realizes his biggest character flaw," I say, pointing at the screen. Peter is talking to Genevieve in the restroom, but it's considerably milder than his obsession with his ex in the books. "Like ... if a guy is that obsessed with his ex-girlfriend, is he ready to be dating again? I'm Team John, I think."

"Yeah, Team John. Peter needed to take some breathing room before he started looking at other girls," Violet agrees. Her hand drops into the bowl of popcorn on her lap and a few pieces spray out over the couch. "Honestly, someone should throw me into a romance novel. I'd call out *all* of the petty stuff that they shouldn't be dealing with."

Riley snorts. "There wouldn't be a romance left at the end of it."

Violet grunts her agreement through a mouthful of salted popcorn. "Teaching girls what they deserve is the ultimate cock-block."

"And the best kind," Miko chimes in, raising her glass of lemonade. She's sitting beside me, wrapped in a SpongeBob blanket to hide her hairy legs. She shudders and tugs it more tightly around herself. "I can't even *think* about dating at the minute. I can barely keep myself happy, let alone an idiotic male."

She glances at me, and I offer her a soft, reassuring smile.

"Is everything okay?" Violet asks. She must have noticed our moment.

"Yeah, yeah," Miko nods her head adamantly, but her gaze has dropped to the floor and she's biting her lip. "I'm fine, just troubles at home."

Riley reaches over for the remote on the coffee table, turning down the volume on *To All the Boys I've Loved Before*. It's been playing in the background for a while, but we've been chatting, and nobody has paid much attention to it. I don't know about the other girls, but I've seen it more times than I can count anyway.

"Do you want to talk about it?" Violet asks. Her dark eyes are warm and earnest. "Riley and I are pretty fabulous listeners. We have a lot of experience."

"It's true," Riley confirms. "We are the international elite of listeners."

Miko hesitates for a second or two. She may have a lot of friends, but she trusts only a close few with knowledge about her family life. Finally, she says quietly, "I'm just worried about my brother. My parents finalized their divorce recently and he's found it tough. He's acting out in all of these stupid ways... I'm scared that he'll have to go and live in Washington with my dad."

"I'm sorry, Miko." Riley's expression creases with empathy. "That sounds really stressful. How are you holding up?"

"Okay I guess," Miko says. She shrugs, as if to alleviate the pressure of her situation, but the action is sad and heavy. "Everything feels so unstable right now, and I think a massive part of that is because Kai is struggling to adjust. I just really can't stand the idea of him moving away too—I need him here."

"I'm sure this isn't going to last long," I say, reaching over to squeeze Miko's knee. I need to remind her that I'm here. "He's going through a rough patch but he's a good kid. You just need to show him that you aren't going to give up on him."

Miko twists her fingers together and she's staring at her feet. "Hopefully."

"Have you thought about a counselor?" Violet asks. Her voice is tentative and slow, as if the idea is dangerous territory, but I've made the same suggestion a few times now. Violet adjusts her position on the couch to lean towards

Miko. "Maybe talking to someone about how he's feeling would help him to feel more settled and comfortable again."

"I honestly don't know if he'd open up. He's never had many school friends or people to talk to—he's trained himself to deal with things alone."

"All you can do is show him that he's not," Riley says. "And maybe with enough persistence, he'll have the courage to listen to you."

"I'm trying my best." Miko smiles a little. "Thank you."

"What are friends for?" I say, nudging the empty bowl of popcorn with my toe. "We comfort you even though you've eaten *far* more than your share of the popcorn."

"Feelings make me hungry," Miko protests.

"Everything makes you hungry."

"Speaking of feelings..." Riley turns her head pointedly to face me, a devious smile lighting up her innocent face. "What's going on with you and Chase, Erika?"

Play dumb.

My eyes widen with surprise. "Nothing, why?"

"Don't mess with us," Violet accuses, wagging a teasing finger at me. "Literally everyone in the *room* can sense the connection there. Has anything happened or not?"

My oblivious façade crumbles. "Guys, you're reading too much into a total non-event."

"Has he said anything?" Riley leans forward in her seat, elbows rested on her knees. Her blue eyes narrow on me. "You know, about *feelings*..."

"No—"

"Aside from calling you gorgeous *constantly,* giving you his sweater, kissing your arm when you told him you hated your eczema, and the consistent flirtatious banter," Miko interrupts, counting all the things I've rashly confided in her on her fingers. "Oh, and that sensational embrace in the rain."

Riley slaps her thighs victoriously, and Violet squeaks.

"Exactly," I say dryly. "Nothing. Chase Thatcher does this with everybody—he's checked out every girl in Lindale High as if she were a library book!"

Violet grins. "If all girls are library books ... you're his pristine, $15 hardback."

"Gah," I groan, collapsing backwards into the couch and pulling a cushion against my face. My voice is muffled under the velvety fabric. "You're all wrong. We just click, that's all."

Miko leans over from her end of our couch and snatches my protection away, exposing my burning cheeks. Her expression is unimpressed. "You've got to be smarter than this if you want to go to Stanford, Erika Monroe."

The words bring an irritating rush of excitement to my stomach, and I fight to keep a straight face. I don't want to get too carried away in daydreams and theories, because the relationship I now seem to have with Chase is complicated enough as it is. If I even think about the possibility of something *more,* the hurricane of anxiety in my brain grows tenfold. I need to work on convincing Blythe that he deserves to stay, and I can't afford any more distraction if I'm going to even start on that work.

"Let's stop talking about Chase. There's nothing to report," I say, picking at a loose thread on the edge of my safety cushion. I lean forward, prepped for gossip. "Seeing as we're playing this game of confessions, I want to know what happened between Violet and Dylan."

Violet's smug smile disappears, and she flicks her lip ring with her tongue.

"Ooh," Miko enthuses. "Yes! You two went out for what—a month? And then you ended, but continued being friends? Everyone was so confused."

"They weren't the only ones," Violet says with a small, knowing smile. Riley bumps her shoulder comfortingly, in an exchange oddly similar to that between me and Miko and previously.

"You don't have to tell us if it's too personal," I contribute. "There's no pressure."

"No, no," Violet shakes her head, dark nails tapping on her knee. "I'm happy to talk."

Her gaze falls to her knees and clings there desperately. The words take a while to surface, but we wait patiently. An unspoken consensus to give her the space she needs.

"Um ... essentially, going out with Dylan ... it surfaced a lot of stuff for me. Thoughts and questions that I had about myself, that I'd buried down and didn't want to deal with. It was like ..."

She swallows. Riley places a hand on her arm.

Violet's words begin to splurge out, faster and faster, in painful relief. "It was like, I kissed him ... and an alarm was going off in my head, telling me that I have no idea what I really want, who I like, who I *am* ... I started questioning my sexuality more and more, to the point where being with him, being so distracted about who I wanted, or if I was deceiving him ... just a mess of emotions and questions constantly ... it felt wrong."

I stare at Violet in silent awe at her honesty as she struggles for the right words.

"I told him that I thought I might be bisexual, and he was really supportive. He understands that I need to be on my own while I figure this ... *me* out. I can't be in a relationship with anyone while I'm working on this—it's not fair to him for me to be so distracted, and it's not fair to me either. I want to be comfortable and safe."

She exhales sharply and looks up. "So yeah. We broke up on the romantic front, but we're still friends."

"Wow," Miko says softly, leaning forwards in her seat until the blanket is puddled around her waist. "I'm so proud of you. That must have taken so much courage."

"I think you've got real integrity—to be so true to yourself." My words pour out like liquid, smooth and confident and without the need for a moment's hesitation. I look into the dark eyes of the gorgeous, vibrant, fearless girl ahead of me. Her features, usually so poised and confident, are trembling with uncertainty. For the first time since I've known her, Violet looks scared, unsure, and wavering. Which, I decide, means that I need to help.

"I think that whoever you are," I tell her, and the tremor in my voice is genuine, "whatever color of the rainbow, you are completely and utterly loved."

Violet's eyes are glossy with tears, and when she smiles, droplets tumble down the curve of her cheeks. "Oh! Thank you both. So much."

Riley's arm loops around Violet's shoulders and she squeezes tightly, a curtain of curly auburn hair shrouding her vulnerability from view. "We're all here for you. That's what friends do."

"I'm here for you too, so please, guys, let's go back to psycho-analyzing Peter Kavinsky," Violet says, wiping the mascara rivers from underneath her eyes and grinning freely. "And *then* we can watch *Twilight* and discuss everything right and wrong with Edward Cullen and Jacob Black."

"I like that plan," Miko says, settling back into the couch.

Riley turns the volume of the movie back up, and a warm contentedness with the stinging smell of popcorn settles around us. After a few minutes, my phone vibrates on the arm of the couch, the first interruption to our newfound, peaceable comfort. I see a name flash up on screen, and instantly reach out for my device.

> sQuidge: Free tomorrow?
> Me: I'm expensive, actually

Just as I'm watching the three dots that indicate he's replying, a cushion hits me squarely in the face. The collision with my nose makes my eyes water a little, and my phone falls into my lap.

"Hey," I complain, peeling the cushion away. "What was that for?"

Violet is looking at me smugly: the culprit behind the vicious attack. "That smile you wear while you're messaging him tells me there's a lot more than *nothing* going on."

I blink in surprise. They know.

Violet cocks her head tauntingly. "Riley, do you smell smoke?"

"I think I do."

"Is it getting a bit hot in here?"

"Aside from my presence, it is pretty hot," Miko chips in.

Violet laughs. "I think that's because someone's *pants* are on fire."

Three cushions are thrown at my face in unison.

A finger prods into my shoulder.

"Wake up, Sleeping Beauty," a voice coaxes distantly.

Someone shakes my side and I cling to my pillow, twisting in my sheets to escape the distractions. *Let me sleep*.

"Erika. Wake up."

I ignore it again, and the voice sighs. If I had the energy, I'd reach up and hit them around the face for all of this noise that they're making. As far as I know, there isn't a reason I need to be awake right now. Can't they see I'm *tired*? Let Sleeping Beauty do what she does best.

"Wake up before I pour cold water on your face."

"Go away, Mom!" I grumble, curling up into the couch cushions and refusing to open my eyes.

A heavy weight plunges down on the couch beside me, denying me any space or comfort as I'm shoved forcefully into the gray cushions. "I don't know what's more concerning—your language or the fact that you think I'm your *mom*."

"You're right," I grunt. "Whoever you are, you're way more annoying."

Squinting in the morning light, I move my head the minimal amount possible to get a good view over my shoulder and curse when I see familiar brown eyes staring down at me.

"Do I need to fetch some soap to wash out that foul mouth of yours?" Chase asks, an irritating smirk playing on his lips. He's wearing a white T-shirt; I can see the collar thanks to the way his torso is curved over my shoulders. The urge to elbow him in the stomach intensifies. It's a perfect angle.

"No," I huff, turning to face the back of the couch again and closing my eyes. "But maybe put some on the floor so you can *slip-slide* the hell out of my face."

There's laughter in his tone. "Wow, you're so grumpy when you wake up."

"Wrong dwarf," I snap, pulling a cushion over my head. "I'm actually *Sleepy*. Go away."

In one fluid movement, Chase hooks a hand over my shoulder and tugs me down sharply until I'm lying flat on my back on my makeshift bed, glaring up at him. He looks far too put-together and smug for this ungodly hour, and my hand instantly flies upwards to shove him away, only for my wrist to be caught promptly in his fist. He looks down at me with playfulness. The scent of his cologne clings to the air I'm rapidly inhaling.

"Now, now, gorgeous," he murmurs. "Be nice."

"Why are you here?" I groan. "Who do I have to maim for letting you in my house?"

"Your sister actually." He glances towards the living room door quickly. "Violet and Riley are up, now, getting ready. The boys are all waiting in the kitchen. We're going to the beach."

"The beach?" I echo in disbelief. "It's the middle of the night!"

"It's 11 a.m., Erika," Chase chastises, shaking his head so his hair tousles. "Get up."

"Can't you send me a postcard?"

"No."

He releases my wrists and rises up from the couch, continuing to watch me with expectation. Releasing another groan of reluctance for good measure, I slide my bare legs free of the blankets and force my slumbering body into a standing position. Yawning and brushing the messy hair away from my eyes, I return to consciousness just in time to see Chase's eyes lingering on my pajamas.

"I know, I know," I mumble, rubbing my eyes. "I'll change."

Chase smirks. "I quite like the avocados actually. Can't they stay?"

Too tired to find a retort, I push into his arm and shove him backwards a couple of feet as I storm determinedly to the door. "You're waking up the real dinosaur. Good luck with that."

I point a thumb towards Miko, snoring contentedly on the floor mattress, before I leave the room. The remnants of last night's slumber party still clutter the coffee table—some browning avocado mixture, scattered popcorn kernels, and an assemblage of unflattering polaroid pictures—but I can't bring myself to face the mess just yet. I'll deal with it later.

As I'm nearing the stairs, I hear Miko's small scream of horror from the living room. I can't imagine her first thoughts when she opened her eyes to see Chase peering over her as she woke.

"Woah, Miko, your legs—"

Then I hear her yell. "No, no, no! Where is the SpongeBob blanket?!"

"You—you're like a *tarantula*."

"Get out now! Right now!"

Despite my morning grouchiness, I catch myself laughing.

16

Beach Please

"I hate it!" Miko snaps, frantically attempting to brush the sand from her towel with oily hands. She lifts her palms, now encrusted with a thin layer of grit, and hisses in irritation. "I hate putting on sunblock on a beach—it all just sticks and it's *impossible* to get rid of it unless you go in the sea... and then you need to reapply again!"

"Just ignore it," Violet suggests from behind us. She's stretched out on a stripy beach towel, looking infuriatingly classy in aviators and a red bathing suit. Around her, the rest of us have attached our towels like a giant patchwork picnic blanket, decorated with lounging bodies, sunblock bottles, my Polaroid camera and Riley's ginormous yellow beach-bag. She, Alec and Joe have all left already to go swimming.

"But I feel like one of those little sand crabs," Miko whines. Another flurry of sand flicks up into the air as she shakes her towel. It clings desperately onto the breeze for a few suspenseful seconds before dancing down to land on my shins.

"You're definitely not a sand crab, Aragog," Chase's voice sounds smoothly from the towel behind me. After the incident this morning with Miko's mortification over her unshaven legs, he's taken to nicknaming her *Aragog*, after the hairy tarantula in *Harry Potter*. As expected, Miko has not taken kindly to this comparison.

She scowls and throws her water bottle at him.

"Ouch," Chase complains, as it smacks violently into his elbow. He peels his arm away from his face and squints in the bright light for a few seconds, before his eyes adjust and find me, shamelessly ogling him. Then, that stupidly attractive smile. Somehow, it's even more potent when he's lying shirtless in the sun.

"Careful, gorgeous," he murmurs through his smirk. "Keep staring like that and I might think I have your heart."

"The only thing you have is an ego the size of Jupiter," I mumble, turning my chin away in an attempt at carelessness. I gaze down the pale beach towards the wink of orange light reflecting from the waves. My fingers claw into the towel I'm sitting on. He's right of course, I need to stop staring. It's awkward to be caught out.

"Are you guys ready to surf now?" Dylan asks, rolling lazily onto his side.

The urge to level the playing field sparks victoriously in my chest, eliminating any damp embarrassment.

"Sure." I turn back to Chase with the semblance of a smile.

I can make him stare, too.

In one smooth motion, I tuck my thumbs under the hemline of my T-shirt dress and lift it up and over my head, exposing the indigo bikini I'm wearing beneath. As my textured hair falls messily around my shoulders, I have the satisfaction of watching that smug smile fall from Chase's features as his attention diverts to my freshly exposed skin.

"Careful, Squidge," I say nonchalantly, reaching backwards for a bottle of sunblock. "You should probably stop staring or I might think I have your heart."

One corner of Chase's mouth tugs into a half smile and his teeth slide out to catch it before it grows. Although speechless from my teasing, his eyes are lazy and undeterred as he gazes at my face. They're the color of warm chocolate, and my stomach lurches.

No. I have the power here.

I lift up the bottle of sunblock, my gaze locked steadily with the dark-haired deviant lounging smugly on his towel. It's time for more ammunition; it's time for a wild card.

"Dylan, would you mind coming to do my back for me?"

I watch the second that my words hit their target; Chase's eyes narrow and his smile disappears. A tantalizing thrill shoots up my spine and my limbs begin to tingle. *He's jealous. He's absolutely jealous.* Dylan is wordlessly climbing over Riley's things to approach me, but Chase's eyes don't move from mine until the blond boy is sitting on my towel behind me, the sunblock in his hands.

Dylan has helped me like this at least a million times before—it means absolutely nothing to either him or me. But it definitely means something to Chase. I have to restrain a shiver of anticipation as Chase clears his throat. His eyes are glued to Dylan's hands.

"Lift your hair up," Dylan directs.

I bunch my hair at the base of my neck, and with both hands, scoop and smooth it upwards into a makeshift ponytail at the top of my head. Dylan begins to rub the cream over my lower back, his hands quick and purposeful, familiar. I scarcely notice the sensation at all because my attention is tethered to the boy opposite. I bite down on my lower lip and Chase makes an almost inaudible noise of complaint.

Violet, her aviators on her head and a smile wide on her face, leans across her towel to poke Chase in the cheek. "I think you have a little drool there, buddy."

Chase fixes her with a dark glare. "Shut up."

Violet's laughter bubbles out like champagne as she rolls backwards onto her towel again, melodic and unstoppable. "You've met your match with this one, Thatcher."

"You're damn right he has," Miko teases.

I try to bite back the smile on my face as Dylan's hands remove themselves from my skin and my hair falls once more around my sticky shoulders. I can't bring myself to look at Chase. I can't. I can't risk undermining my previous bold actions with the blush that's threatening to burst pigment across my complexion. *Did I actually just do that?*

"All done," Dylan says cheerily, gently pushing away from me and clicking the cap of the sunblock closed before tossing the bottle to the side. "Everybody ready for surfing now?"

Nodding, I follow the others and stumble up to my feet. Miko and Violet are chatting animatedly about anime shows as they lift their smaller surfboards from the heated sand and begin to stroll down the beach. Dylan follows, flicking up dust with his heels as he jogs to catch up, a strong arm looped around his surfboard. I suppose I wouldn't want to be left alone with Chase and me either, after that little performance.

I reach where my surfboard is wedged upright into the sand and take a deep breath. My smaller, rounded white board is positioned directly beside a sharper red model.

Before I can even consider my escape, I feel the warmth of Chase's torso as he steps closer to my back. His skin is mere inches from mine, so close that I can feel every vibration in the air between us. My breath becomes shallow with nervous anticipation, but he is silent as he traces a singular finger over the bridge of my shoulders. Scooping up a lock of hair and shifting it behind my neck, he finally speaks in a low, rough murmur.

"He missed a bit."

Then that one singular finger is rubbing gently at a smear of sunblock at the side of my neck. I exhale forcefully. I think if I didn't, I would forget to breathe.

"You're just unstoppable, aren't you?" I mutter. "A flirtatious force of nature."

His finger slips over my shoulder, finds a grip, and uses it to twist me around. His eyebrow is raised. "Oh, I'm the flirty one?"

"You started it."

"You finished it."

I roll my eyes but my smile bites through any attempt at nonchalance. "Hardly. You just can't resist anything with a pulse, Squidge."

Chase's hand on my shoulder loosens until it slips free completely. A curl of hair falls in front of one of his eyes, an interruption to his intense stare. "Is that your theory?"

"You see a lot of pretty girls for one date only," I say carefully, shuffling my bare feet in the sand. "So, I assume that means you're easily attracted to people, but not for long."

"Nice logic. But incorrect."

Just as I'm about to question Chase further, I become aware of shuffling sand and voices to our left. Riley, Joe, and Alec are traipsing up the beach towards us, each of them soaking wet and shivering in the stinging cool breeze. Riley smiles apologetically at us, her arms clasped tightly around her chest to seal in warmth. Her auburn hair is unusually dark when wet, hanging in two long braids either side of her head.

"Sorry, guys. Came to get our surfboards."

"Hope we weren't interrupting anything," Alec says slowly, his eyes flitting between us. Impulsively, I take a step back so that our proximity isn't so apparent.

"Oh, we definitely interrupted," Joe says cheerily, reaching for a blue surfboard jutting out of the sand. "But they can postpone their moment until after surfing, right guys?"

"Right," Chase drawls, running a hand through his hair.

"Now, now, Chase," Joe says, swinging the surfboard under his arm and fixing his best friend with a semi-serious frown. "Lose the attitude. Nobody likes a shady beach."

Riley rolls her eyes at Joe before turning back to me with a sweetly hopeful expression. "So, you two are up for catching some waves now, right?"

I glance at Chase, with curiosity gnawing at me behind my strained smile.

"Sure."

"You need to look at the angle of the wave more. See that it's angled towards the left? If you lean towards the left, you'll be able to ride it for longer."

Chase shakes his head, flicking droplets like staccato bullets across the water surface, and laughs.

"You know," he says, rubbing water free from his nose and gripping his surfboard with the other hand, "I didn't anticipate *you* giving *me* surfing advice."

"Why not?" I ask with vicious innocence, treading water softly as a gentle wave lifts my feet from the sea floor. "You didn't... actually think you were good, did you?"

Chase frowns. "If you *dare* say something like that again..."

"You'll what?" The white surfboard under my right arm lifts me over another wave, completely undeterred. My smile, too, is unwavering as I wait for a response that doesn't come. "It's okay, Chase, it's not about the winning... What do they say to losers again? Oh, that's right—it's about the *taking part*."

"I hope that you can swim as quickly as your mouth runs."

With laughter bubbling from my chest, I twist towards the incoming wave, and with both hands guiding the surfboard nose-dive into the water. The wave swells and shoves around me with tangible momentum while I carve my route to the other side. Once I pop up through the surface again, I catch a glimpse of Dylan riding the next wave. His golden hair shines in the sun, strong arms outstretched, and a line of white foam follows the slicing motion of his surfboard through the water.

"He's the best," I call back to Chase. "Look how good he is."

Chase swims up beside me, scowling as he watches Dylan remain upright on the board. "Don't think I've forgotten that you just called me bad at it."

"You're good at it," I say, focusing on Alec and Riley as

they paddle side by side. "In fact, you're all quite good at it. Do you come often?"

"The boys and I have done it since we were little. Riley and Violet are newer," Chase says with a loose shrug. Our legs collide under the water as we float. "What about you?"

I look to the side. "Chloe and I used to come on weekends. She's way better than me."

"You say that about everything, Erika."

"But," a voice gasps from our left, "I win at being the most useless."

I twist to see Miko floating up beside us on her yellow board. Her fringe is sticking flat to her forehead, her face is pale, and her hands are fisted tightly around the lip of the surfboard as if trying to punish it. She heaves another exaggerated breath.

"Why does every wave decide to drown me, Erika?"

"You're really not a beach person, are you?"

"I'm very much a land person. On a couch, preferably. With popcorn."

"Well, that makes sense. Tarantulas are land creatures," Chase inputs unhelpfully.

Miko raises her chin just enough to send him a fierce glare, before quickly abandoning that plan to press her cheek against the board and close her eyes. Chase chuckles.

"Time to go back to your natural habitat?" I suggest.

She nods horizontally. "I'll see you beach babes later."

I twist to watch Miko as she paddles back inland. The tide is lowering as the afternoon sun beats down, and the distance of swimming has decreased significantly. I note the moments when her feet hit the seabed, when her knees break the surface of the water, and when the froth swills affectionately around her ankles. It is only at that point that I can trust that she won't fall over and drown. She's worryingly uncoordinated sometimes.

As I'm adjusting the grip on my board, I catch a glimpse of a familiar dark-haired man wading through the shallows nearby. He's wearing a pair of dark sunglasses, so the only indication that he's looking out to sea is when he raises his hand in greeting. I twist around just quickly enough to see Chase gesture in response.

"Is that Seth?" I ask in surprise, turning back for a second evaluation.

"Yeah, he told me he'd be passing through."

"That's cool, can't he join us?"

Chase shakes his head. "Nah, he's busy today."

"How did you meet them all?" I ask softly, lifting my torso up to rest across the surfboard and watching him with curiosity. "Get into all of the drag car stuff?"

His answer is evasive. "It's kind of complicated. Not even really interesting."

Unwrapping one of my arms from my board, I raise a tentative finger and press it to his collarbone, where a small crescent moon marks his skin.

"Something to do with that?"

His eyes flash almost painfully at the intrusion. "Erika, I don't want to talk about it."

"That's okay," I mumble, withdrawing to my previous position. "I just feel conscious sometimes that ... you know a lot about me. Family, insecurities. I don't know anything about you; you shouted at me for just turning up at your front gate."

"I'm not ready to tell you anything yet," he says bluntly.

His legs propel his board away from me, and he stares distractedly in the direction of the others.

"I get that, I just thought—"

"Erika." His voice is low and irritated. "Just stop."

I blink. "Fine."

I watch in numbed silence as he pulls his lean body up onto the board, and without looking back, begins to paddle deeper into the waves. He's aiming for Joe and Dylan, bobbing slowly amongst the larger surf. I'm not sure it really matters where he's heading. He seems more concerned with what he wants to get away from.

"Everything okay?" Riley calls from my right, pulling her board towards me. As much as I hate to admit it, her presence doesn't quite fill the emptiness there.

"I'm getting whiplash," I say. "He's mad at me again."

Riley follows my gaze. "I can see that. Do you know why?"

"I complained that he doesn't tell me anything about his life." I wince after the words exit my mouth. It's a complaint that sounds even more petty and unnecessary aloud.

Riley's hand moves to my fist and envelopes it with a soft squeeze. "Chase likes to keep everyone at arm's length. I've known him for a while now and I'm not sure we've ever had a conversation beyond surface-level teasing or small talk."

"Really?"

She nods firmly. "Everybody has struggles, but he's one of those people in life that can cover it so easily with a laugh and a joke that you almost forget he's the same."

"His safe territory," I agree with a sigh.

"People put up walls to protect themselves from getting

hurt. It's a natural defense mechanism, and I know because I've done it myself," she confesses, smiling sadly. "Give him time, support him. When he realizes that there's no threat, he'll make it all worth it."

With the warmth of the sun on my face, salt on my lips, and a hand squeezing mine, I suddenly don't feel quite so helpless. I look sideways at Riley.

"You always know exactly the right thing to say, has anyone ever told you that?"

Her smile grows until it sparkles in her eyes. "Yeah, definitely one person."

Chase collapses down on the towel beside me, leaning back on his elbows. He's wearing a black T-shirt and shorts now, but his hair is still damp and salty. His eyes, in the tangerine sunset, are practically indulgent. "Penny for your thoughts, gorgeous?"

"You seem to be in a better mood," I comment wryly, averting my gaze back to my feet. My toes continue to rake through the soft sand in swirling patterns.

"Yeah, about that—"

"It's cool," I interrupt. I bring my knees up to my chest abruptly and wrap my arms around my body. "You don't need to say anything. I shouldn't have pressed."

"Erika," Chase groans lowly. His hand finds my forearm, and, with a soft tug, he unfastens my protective position. I almost collide into his shoulder with the momentum but manage to steady myself just in time. When I look up, his handsome face is startlingly close. His lips soft, eyes softer still. "It upset you."

"I'm not upset," I argue. "I'm just tired."

"Okay." The right-hand corner of his mouth tugs up into that delicious smile that sends tingles through my chest. "So, let me make it up to you?"

"What did you have in mind?"

"Get on." To my surprise, he stands up and twists around to show me his back. His arms are straight by his sides, ready to catch me as I jump up.

I splutter out a laugh. "Absolutely not."

"Get on my damn back, gorgeous. We're going for a walk."

"You'll drop me!"

He shakes his head, laughing. "Stop whining and get up."

Every aversion to the idea quickly dissolves into my desire to be carried by him, and with a breathless laugh, I climb to my feet and launch myself up onto his back. His arms are prepared for the impact, looping under my thighs and holding me securely to his body. My hands slot over his strong shoulders instinctively, and as I press my body to the warmth of his T-shirt, I can feel the hard planes of muscle even beneath the cotton. He quickly adjusts me.

"You need to hold tighter," he mutters. "It won't be my fault if you fall."

Rolling my eyes, I slide my hands down from where they were tentatively clasped to his shoulders and loop them just below his neck. This one movement presses me even more tightly to his body, and my head rests on his shoulder with startling proximity to the side of his face. My legs tighten around his waist, and he nods, satisfied.

"You're enjoying this too much, Squidge," I mutter, as he begins to walk.

He twists his head slightly to look up at me, just enough

that I catch a glimpse of the wicked grin that's curving his mouth. Instead of denying it, he asks, "And you aren't?"

Touché.

My noise of complaint elicits another laugh from him as we walk back down the pale sand towards the water. We've attracted our fair share of attention from the others, but I'm too content to care. The sun is warming my back deliciously.

"So, tell me," I say, resting my cheek on my shoulder as I observe the side of his face. "Is this how you treat all the girls?"

"Funnily enough, no," Chase scoffs. "I don't act like a donkey with most people."

"I think you're more of an ass than a donkey," I comment lightly. "But seriously—you haven't given one of your dates a piggyback before?"

"Do you really think that my dates entail me carrying girls around all evening?"

"No, of course not." I roll my eyes. My thumb skims over his collarbone absent-mindedly and I can't help but notice his shiver. "But I guess I pictured your first dates as being all wild and flirtatious because that's just the kind of person you are. I mean, I'm only your friend and you made a whole firework display for me."

"That was different," Chase mumbles.

"Well, what does a date with you look like then?"

Chase stops walking. Before I can comprehend what's happening, he twists his head around to look at me over his shoulder. His face is so close that our noses are almost brushing, that our breaths mingles, and I can taste caramel on the tip of my tongue. His decadent eyes are blazing hot and only inches away, and they melt away any coherent thought of mine instantaneously. *Holy shit.*

"Why?" he murmurs, cocking his head slightly. "You interested?"

I tear myself out of my reverie and force my head back, out of proximity, before I can want something stupid. Before I can *do* something stupid.

"I'm interested in how you've managed to charm the pants off so many girls," I say, as evenly as I can manage. "I want to know what your tricks are."

Chase releases a breathless laugh and faces forwards once more to continue walking along the wet sand. "I have no tricks. People just want what they can't have."

"You're saying they date you *because* they know it'll only be one date?"

He nods. "And they think that maybe they'll be the one to get the second."

"What do you actually do on the dates, then?" I ask curiously. My arms tighten around his neck again, and hesitantly, I return my head to its previous position above his shoulder. I know that it's unlikely that he'll surprise me again. That should make me feel safer, but instead, there's a stir of disappointment in my chest.

"Nothing special. Dinner, maybe. A walk around the park."

"That sounds..."

"Boring?"

"Unlike you," I correct, watching him with concern. He doesn't like to talk about himself, and I don't want to push to the extent that he's uncomfortable. Slowly, his impassive, angular features begin to crease into a frown.

"It is unlike me," he confesses quietly. "I don't want to go on these dates, Erika."

"Why do you go on them, then?" My voice is soft. A bare murmur that wouldn't be audible if I wasn't so close to his ear.

He sighs. "Because I don't want to go home."

Almost as soon as the surprise has swelled within me, understanding follows.

"So, the one date only thing—"

"—is to stop people from hurting over me," Chase finishes firmly. "Miko said it. Hearts don't break after one date. If people are going in with the expectation of it being one date only, they aren't as disappointed when it is."

I can only thank heaven that he can't see my facial expression right now, because I think he'd interpret my tenderness as pity. He goes on dates with so many people to keep himself *busy*. To keep him away from home. That's why he only goes on one date with them all. He isn't looking for a relationship, or even a fling. He's looking for an excuse to stay out of the house.

After a few seconds, I finally fathom words. "I wasn't expecting that."

"It's a bit sad, isn't it?" Chase says with a humorless chuckle. "I can only rely on my friends so much. They're busy, they have lives and work. Dating helps with those times when I can't rely on the others, but I still don't want to go home."

The urge to kiss Chase is growing stronger by the second, clawing its way up through my hammering chest and into my mouth, but I am forced to bite it back. Instead, I settle for pressing my forehead into his neck. The skin there is warm, and I close my eyes and try stupidly to convey how sorry I am through that small patch of contact.

"You can rely on me, Squidge."

Chase is silent for a few seconds, and the sounds of the beach around us remind me that as intimate as this moment feels, we are not alone. I am grateful that I didn't kiss him.

Finally, he murmurs, "Thank you, gorgeous."

"Can I ask you something? Is that..." My voice strains. "Is that the reason—"

"The reason I said yes to helping you?" Chase finishes. "Yeah, it is."

"Wow." I huff out a breath. "Huh."

He chuckles. "Yeah. So, now you know."

"I'm always here, y'know ... If you ever want to avoid another boring date."

I lift my head away from his neck, cringing at how abhorrently uncomfortable that sentence was to say. I know Chase has picked up on it too, because that playful ring has returned to his voice, and he glances back at me.

"You just don't want me to go on another date."

I roll my eyes. "You caught me."

"Do those dates make you jealous, Erika?"

I'm almost relieved at the return to our usual banter. As grateful as I am that Chase opened up to me, I'm so stiff and awkward when it comes to showing affection. This teasing, our teasing, is so comfortable that I can sink into it thoughtlessly.

"Flatter yourself much? I'm not jealous."

"Well, what are you then?"

"A Homo sapiens," I respond flatly.

"Really?" Chase stops to shift me slightly up his back,

releasing an exaggerated groan of effort. "Are you sure that you aren't something a little stockier? With a snout and a little curly tail? I mean, they call it a piggy-back for a reason..."

My mouth drops open and automatically, I slap a palm against the center of his back. It makes a harsh noise, but it wasn't hard enough to hurt him. Chase begins to laugh.

"You don't have to come up with a metaphor to call me *Babe*, Chase. I know that you're dying to."

Chase glances back at me again with that heart-stopping grin that I'm getting so ridiculously accustomed to.

"I prefer gorgeous."

17

Chemical Reaction

"Thin layer chromatography today," Mrs. Lopez announces sharply, gesturing to the whiteboard behind her. She paces between the front desks, sliding her whiteboard pen into the pocket of her lab coat. Nobody talks over her. "Sort yourself into groups and follow the task sheet. I will be surveying each group in turn for anyone who has questions."

She makes a dismissive gesture with her hand, indicating for the groups to assemble. Even then, it takes a few seconds for everyone to begin talking. It's a wonder that a woman so small can have such total command. Sighing, I grab my papers from my desk and stand up, ready to join my usual group of friends at the front and begin the experiment.

"Monroe!" a familiar voice calls over the noise. "Get over here and tutor me."

I look over to see Chase, Dylan, Joe, and Alec in the corner of the room. Joe is waving me over to their desk, his expression expectant. They've been in my chemistry class all semester, but we haven't had a group experiment since before I knew them. Now I suppose it's only right for me to go and join them. I offer an apologetic wave to the girls at the front and weave my way through the desks towards my new group.

I can't help but feel doubtful. This grade is massively important to me, especially now that I have no guaranteed place at Stanford, and, well ... I know what these boys are like.

Dylan must read the apprehension on my face as I take a seat at their desk. "Don't worry, Ricky, I'll keep them in line. We'll focus."

"Speak for yourself," Joe says. He bumps shoulders with me, grinning cheekily. A pencil is slotted behind each of his ears. "I plan on causing chaos."

I roll my eyes, reaching behind my head to tie my hair into a ponytail. "Technically, it's chaos and *Chase* that are only one letter different."

Chase is sitting across the desk from me, leaning on his forearms. I can't help but be *mildly* distracted by the freckled skin and muscle exposed from his rolled-up sleeves. When he hears me mention his name, he glances up from the worksheet and winks at me.

God.

Alec hands Dylan a pair of safety goggles. "This is to protect you against their public shows of flirtation." He raises his eyebrow pointedly at me, and I realize that he's talking about Chase and me. Our flirtation.

"Chase only flirts with the prospect of getting detention," I counter with a smile.

Joe frowns. "He flirts with me more."

Chase's eyes narrow and he straightens from his slouched position to snatch another pair of goggles from Alec's grip.

"If you all keep talking about me, I will fuse your lips together with whatever chemical I can find."

"Cyanoacrylate would work," I hum, tightening my ponytail.

The boys turn to look at me in surprise.

I release my hair and smirk. "Chemical name for Superglue."

A moment of surprised silence passes. Then, to my surprise, Joe loops a strong arm around my shoulders and kisses me firmly on the top of my head. One of the pencils that are tucked behind his ears falls to the ground with a clatter.

"She!" he declares enthusiastically. "She is going to get me that A that I need!"

"No pressure," I complain, still tucked beneath Joe's arm.

Chase discreetly shakes his head and refocuses his attention on the worksheet.

"If you want an A, I suggest you start working," Mrs. Lopez instructs from behind us, her tone critical. "You haven't even sorted your equipment out yet."

"All in good time," Joe pipes cheerily.

"And you, Thatcher," Miss Lopez pauses in her walk by the desk to place a finger on the worksheet in front of Chase. "I suggest you make that work neater or get another person to do the writing. I like to be able to read scientific tables."

Wearing that classic Lopez frown of disappointment, she wanders away.

Dylan and I separate from the table to collect the necessary items for our experiment. The teacher always lines the assorted equipment at the back of the classroom, so it's an easy task. I grab a beaker, lid, filter paper, pipette, and the plate. Dylan gathers the solvent and the analyte, and we grin at each other as we meet back at the desk. Lopez has moved on to criticize another group, so we have some breathing room again. I lay everything out neatly.

"Draw a line in pencil about half an inch from the bottom of the plate," Alec instructs. Chase leans down to do so. His mouth is pressed into a thin line and his chirpy mood seems to have disappeared.

"He doesn't like Mrs. Lopez," Dylan whispers to me.

"Yeah," I mumble, recalling our detention. "I know."

While Dylan uses the pipette to drop the analyte across the paper, I direct Chase to fill the beaker with a small amount of solvent. In this experiment, it's important not to use too much otherwise the results won't show, so I lean down to improve the accuracy of my measurement. Liquid drizzles slowly into the bottom of the beaker.

"Shii... take mushrooms!"

The sudden noise startles Chase, and the hand holding the bottle tips, releasing a glut of solvent into the bottom of the beaker. Alec raises his finger. The edge of the glass plate has sliced his fingertip, and already the blood is beginning to drip.

"You okay?" Dylan asks Alec. Alec nods but creatively curses again under his breath. Riley must be rubbing off on him, with her adorable alternatives to swear words.

Mrs. Lopez is approaching us now.

"Crap, that's way too much solvent," I tell Chase, my attention turning back to the beaker. We're over the mark by almost fifty percent.

"I can see that," he responds snappily. "Alec shocked me."

Someone is moody.

"We should get a funnel."

Chase remains sullenly silent.

"Everything okay over here?" Mrs. Lopez arrives behind me, her eyes scanning the scene before her. Alec has left to find a Band-Aid for his finger, leaving Chase, Dylan, and I staring gormlessly at her. Her eyes focus on the beaker. "Far too much solvent. You'll need to pour some back into the bottle. Funnels are in the cabinet at the back."

Chase sighs.

"Everything okay with that?" she asks sharply.

"Peachy," he mutters.

"Get back to work, please. Maybe put somebody else in charge of pouring too." She gives Chase a pointed look, and I realize that she doesn't like him very much either. Dylan and I exchange worried expressions as Chase's shoulders stiffen defensively.

"I didn't do anything wrong."

"I didn't say you did," Mrs. Lopez responds coolly. "Back to work."

As she wanders away to visit another desk, Chase bites his lip and refuses to look up from the desk. He reaches out for the beaker, but his movement is too harsh for the thin glass. The beaker tips away from his contact and lands horizontally—ethyl acetate spilling across the wooden surface. Chase curses quietly.

I don't know what to say. I just watch hopelessly.

Chase's hand flies up to the back of his hair, and he tugs at the strands with frustration. His lips are parted, breath coming hard and fast.

"Chase," Dylan begins quietly. "It's okay—"

"I need a minute."

He shoves Dylan out of his way without apology, and storms towards the exit. Mrs. Lopez calls his name repeatedly, her scathing tone cutting across the ambient noise. He ignores her. All I can do is watch in shock as he slams the classroom door behind him, escaping into the school hallway.

Holy hell, I'm never going to get this guy out of the line of expulsion.

"What just happened?" Dylan asks slowly. "He seems so freaked out."

"I don't know," I respond. My voice sounds strange—detached, almost. Before I can even process what I'm doing, my feet are following Chase's footsteps towards the classroom door. I can hear Mrs. Lopez calling me too, but I ignore her. I'll speak to her afterwards and explain. Dylan can clean up the solvent spillage. They don't need me. Chase does.

What am I doing? Why am I running after him?

I burst out into the hallway, breathless. Chase is crouched against the wall of lockers. His arms are wrapped protectively around his knees and he's glaring at the opposite wall. He doesn't look at me as he speaks.

"What are you doing?"

"I—I don't know," I respond shakily. "I came to find you."

He turns to face me, his expression cynical. "Why?"

"I thought you would want help."

My voice sounds small and vulnerable, and I realize what an idiot I must look like for chasing after him. He clearly wants to be left alone, and I know absolutely nothing about his life or why he reacted in that way. He's just going to shut me down.

Chase is staring at me, his chest rising and falling with

every labored breath. Even from his crouched position on the floor, he's intimidating, like a frightened animal that I'm trying not to spook. I'm just waiting for the cutting words that tell me to get lost.

"Why would you want to help me?"

"Because I'm your friend," I say, more confidently this time.

Chase turns back towards the opposite lockers.

I release a slow breath to calm my stuttering heart. "Look—um. I know that I don't know what you're going through, but I can tell you're hurting. I just want to help."

He shakes his head. "I'm not hurting, I'm just aggravated."

"Okay, well . . . can I try to cheer you up?"

This idea is met with a dismissive shake of the head. "I don't need you to make me feel better, Erika. I can handle this stuff on my own."

"You think I don't know that?"

"I don't know why else you'd be here." He continues to stare obstinately at the lockers, searching the scratches and blemishes in the primary yellow paint for a distraction from my presence. I can see the tendons jumping in his arm from his tensing muscles.

"Just because you *can* deal with things alone doesn't mean that you have to."

"You should go back to class," he answers stubbornly.

"No."

His gaze finally moves from the lockers, but only to glare up at the ceiling tiles in frustration. One of his arms breaks free from its embrace to tug on the back of his neck. "Can you listen to me for once? Please?"

"Why should I? You never listen to me."

"I never listen to anyone," he says with a sigh. "Just go. You'll get into trouble."

"You know I don't care about that."

He answers with another sigh, which I take as an indication of his defeat.

I approach tentatively and slide down the lockers to sit beside him, with my legs stretched out in front of me and my hands knotted in my lap. I've never seen the hallway from this angle before, and for a few moments of peaceful silence, I occupy myself by gazing around at the distorted height of the lockers and the dirt on the linoleum floor.

I sense the time to speak again.

"What's wrong, Chase?"

He glances at me and chews his bottom lip. "Nothing."

"You can trust me."

"I know."

I decide to push once more. "So, why did you get so upset?"

"I don't know," he replies, his shoulders slumping defeatedly. "I just get overwhelmed sometimes when I feel like someone is judging me. It makes me defensive."

"Really?" I mutter sarcastically. "I could never tell."

"Shut up." For a brief second, I think he's almost tempted to smile, but it doesn't last long enough for me to tell. He kicks his feet out, to mirror my position. Now, we're both staring at our sneakers, as a handy distraction from the intimacy of this moment. "I just can't take it when a teacher stands over me with that smug face and tells me how stupid I am, when I'm actually *trying* for once. It's different if I'm messing about."

I stay quiet.

"I don't like showing people the real parts of me," he continues slowly. "Y'know—when I actually want something, when I'm actually putting myself out there."

"Why not?"

"Because then something like this happens." His hands fling up to illustrate his frustration. "Someone looks at me like that, and I just want to get out of there."

"You're afraid that people won't think you're good enough," I realize quietly.

It takes him a long time to reply.

"Can I ask you something?"

"Of course."

His voice is low, urgent. "Why did you choose me to help you act out?"

I hesitate. I begin to twist my hands, fingernails digging into skin, and I notice Chase turn to watch them in my peripheral vision.

"Because I heard things," I murmur finally. I toy and twist my fingers, forcing myself not to look at the vulnerable boy beside me. "I knew that you were confident enough to help me. I wanted my family to notice me and the more I spoke to you, the more I felt like we were the same. As much as you resist it, you just want someone to see you."

Guilt sticks in my throat like tar, and I swallow hard.

"I'm not like you, Erika."

"What do you mean by that?"

"Oh, come on," he says, turning to show me his scathing, doubtful expression. "You have loads of friends, perfect grades, a full family. When your college accepts you, you'll be out of this sleeping town like a shot and the rest of us will just be left in the dust."

"Chase—"

"My life is very different."

"Is that really what you think?"

"It's what I know."

I groan and pull my hands over my face. "I know I'm lucky, I know that, but so are *you*. You're smart as hell, and you have amazing friends around you that love you—you easily have as much potential as I do, Chase."

"Potential?" Chase repeats, tasting the word as if it's bitter. "You came to me to tarnish your reputation; I think that speaks wonders of my potential."

My hands slip down from my face. I watch him, dismayed. "Do you really not see it? Do I really have to shout at you, and be shouted at, trying to tell you how amazing you are?"

He smiles, but it's not the kind of smile I was hoping for. This expression is drained of any optimism. "The minute your parents show you that support that you want, you'll go back to your perfect life, and I'll still be here, Erika."

I pull my knees up to my chest. "You think I'm just going to leave?"

"Aren't you?" he asks simply.

"No!"

"Why not?"

"I want to stick around and be there for you," I say firmly. My arms tighten around my shins, and I can feel my heart pulsing with nerves. This boy pushes me to my absolute limits. One minute I'm shouting at him, the next I'm confessing. "If you want me to."

He turns away. "You don't know anything about me."

"Try me. Maybe talking to someone might help."

"I could get a counselor for that."

Ouch. I can't help but feel a bit stung. After running out of class to see if he's okay, and risking landing my ass in detention, I thought he would at least be nice about shutting me down. At least he's being clear that he doesn't want me to badger him anymore.

"You can still talk to me about what's hurting you. I'm here for you."

He shakes his head. The final rejection.

My chest burns. I begin to climb to my feet.

"Where are you going?" he asks sharply.

"Back to class." I sound pathetic and upset, and I hate it. I hate that he can make me feel like this. My emotions are so uncontrollable around him.

Chase stands up, and with infuriating speed, positions himself to stand directly in my path. He's taller than me, not by a massive amount, but it's still enough to silence whatever smart-ass remark I was about to make. He stares down at my face. His pupils are dilated, and his cheekbones are still burning red with residual emotion.

"Are you actually getting mad at me again because I won't talk to you about my problems?" he asks in disbelief.

"No," I snap. I twist away from him, facing in the direction of the chemistry class I should be attending. "I don't know. Maybe. It's just frustrating when you care about someone, and you make an effort ... and they basically tell you that they don't need you."

"I never said that."

I turn to glower at him. "Look, if you don't, that's fine, but I'd prefer not to make an idiot of myself any longer. Okay?"

"How are you making an idiot of yourself?"

"Because I'm out here, instead of in there, where I'm supposed to be."

He steps closer. "Then why are you out here?"

I throw my arms up. "Stop playing dumb. I'm your friend and I want to support you, but you won't let me close enough to try!"

"I don't need to tell you anything," Chase says bluntly.

"No, you don't. You're right, you absolutely don't. I just thought you might want to." I pace backwards, annoyed at myself for making such a massive ordeal out of nothing. "I'm stupid for thinking that. I can see you don't want to talk, so I'm going back to class."

"Erika," he says with a groan, catching up to me. "Please stop freaking out."

"I'm not freaking out. I'm embarrassed."

"Embarrassed? How is it embarrassing?"

"Because I ran out of class after you! I embarrassed myself in front of everyone and made this big gesture and it doesn't even mean anything—"

"It does." He takes a step forward, putting his hands on my arms as if to press the words right into me. His eyes are wild, running over my face in confusion. "It does mean something. It does, Erika."

It's only now that his hands are on me that I notice how heavily I'm breathing. I try to relax, lifting my hand up slowly to peel his away. Chase watches me silently as my breathing steadies. We're standing so close that we're almost pressed together, and the urge to reach out and touch his jaw is excruciating. But it's not the time. I bite my lip in attempt to repress the urge, but the movement catches his attention. Suddenly he's looking at my lips.

Every part of me is tingling under his gaze.

"I know I'm freaking out over nothing," I whisper finally. "Please just ignore me."

Chase blinks a few times, then steps back. "No."

"Chase, I'm going to age prematurely if this argument continues."

"I trust you, Erika," he admits, visibly frustrated. "You infuriate me to no end, but I do trust you, more than anyone. I just don't talk to people about my home life, it terrifies me. I'm too ... vulnerable there."

I physically deflate. I'm acting so immaturely.

"I know. It's wrong of me to get frustrated, I'm sorry."

"I want to talk. Every time I think I'm ready to say it, it just doesn't come out."

"You don't have to tell me anything."

"Erika, will you listen to me?" He huffs, pushing himself closer to me again. Somehow his hand is now loosely wrapped around my hand, and it feels strange and warm and addictive. I never want him to let go. "I said I want to."

I stare at him and nod, not trusting myself to speak.

Chase exhales deeply, closing his eyes tight. "Come over, after school."

"What?"

He opens them. "Come over. It's easier if I show you."

"I—I have track practice tonight."

"After that, then. I can meet you at the school entrance."

"Chase, are you sure about this?" I ask uneasily. I feel like I've forced him into talking about himself now, and he's right by saying that he has no obligation to tell me anything. I want him to trust me on his own, I don't want to guilt him into it.

His hand moves from mine to dance its way up my arm, leaving a trail of tingles from the contact. My pulse begins to quicken. He traces part of my cheek with his finger, lingering at the loose curl in front of my ear. Then his hand grasps my hair bobble. He slides it out of my hair slowly, torturously, until my loose curls spill out over my shoulders.

Then, clearing his throat, he rips his hand away.

"I'm sure. I want you to see me."

I barely wait for the principal to invite me inside before I burst into the office, breathless and determined. I've been running since I left the changing rooms. Chase is waiting for me somewhere in the parking lot, but I need to get this done before I meet him. Every step from my last class has only increased my momentum; I can't afford to pause or deliberate.

"Mrs. Blythe, please may I speak to you for a minute?"

The puppet master looks over at me from where she's standing at the window. Her fingers are curled around the vertical blinds like they're harp strings, and upon recognizing me, she smiles brightly. One by one, her fingers detach from the charcoal fabric, until it's finally released. The blinds flutter back into place hurriedly. I have her full attention.

"Ah, Erika. I trust you have some results for me?"

"No," I say, breathing heavily. "I just want to talk."

Blythe, who was in the process of approaching me, falters in her steps. An accusatory frown creases her forehead. "Oh really? What might that be about?"

I don't move any further into the room. My usual seat, the

chair in front of her desk, sits familiar and unoccupied only a few feet away, but it stirs up bad memories of looking up into the intimidating eyes of a woman who knows exactly how to manipulate me. I think I'd rather face Blythe on equal ground this time.

"I've come here because I need you to give Chase another chance," I say, as steadily as I can manage. My hands are clenched into balls at my sides. "I need you to give *me* the chance to prove to you that he doesn't deserve to be expelled."

The blinds slice a shadow into the afternoon glow from the window, splaying stripes across the navy carpet. Blythe stares at me with disbelief for a few, torturous seconds. Then, slowly, she begins to smile. Her smile grows more and more until it becomes dangerous. Angling her chin towards the ceiling, she chuckles. The shadow halves her face.

"Of course. I should have known this would happen." Her hand falls down onto the desk. "I saw it in your face the last time you came here."

"You think I'm weak for allowing my emotions to disrupt this assignment."

She scoffs. "Erika, that is a ridiculous suggestion. No, I just expected you to value your future more than a boy. Clearly, I overestimated your ambition."

"I value my integrity."

Blythe looks at me with dull curiosity, tapping her fingers against the desk as if counting down every remaining second of her patience for me. "That pride will affect your ability to seize opportunities, Miss Monroe."

"This isn't pride," I say firmly. "I am standing in front of you now, at the expense of my future, and asking you to change your mind."

Her features flatten with irritation.

"I'm not stupid, I know this means that the reward is no longer on the table," I continue, as evenly as I can manage. "I just want a fair letter of recommendation, like every other student applying. I'll work hard for Stanford on my own terms. I just need you to realize that Chase isn't who you think he is, that he doesn't deserve to be punished."

"I don't appreciate having my authority challenged, Erika."

"At times, all authority needs to be challenged."

Blythe steps back and sinks down against the windowsill behind her, crushing the blinds flat against the glass pane. Her thin knuckles clamp over the wooden lip that she rests on. The room is plunged into shade. "I suggest you leave my office now."

"But—"

"Now, Erika."

I pause for another second before I move, but the cold fury in the principal's features informs me that my time and her patience are equally expired. With disappointment weighing in my chest and my gaze on the floor, I turn to exit the room.

"Please consider it," I say, before the door shuts.

The air of the reception is warm and light, an escape from the oppressive shadows of Principal Blythe's office, but it can't lift my mood. I failed. I can't believe I failed.

What am I supposed to do now?

"There you are." A smooth voice says from behind me. I twist, sick with horror, to see Chase leaning against the reception door with curiosity written in his features. "I've been looking for you, I thought we were meeting at the gates. Are you ready to go?"

"Yeah," I blurt, pushing my trembling hand into my back pocket before he can notice. I clear my throat and stretch my lips into my best attempt at a smile. "Of course."

18

Heart to Heartbreaker

Chase releases a rattled sigh as he switches the ignition off.

We're in the driveway to his house: a large, sweeping section of paving that curves around to the front door. The house hasn't changed since I last saw it, but I am a lot more blatant in my curiosity. I still cannot understand how this large, cream-colored family home with the swings in the yard belongs to Chase. There are flowerpots lining the pathway up to the door, and an old-fashioned brass knocker on the dark wood. I couldn't have imagined Chase, so private and protective, to live somewhere so... cozy.

"Your house is gorgeous," I comment softly.

"I guess." He makes no move to get out of the car.

"Are you sure about this?" I worry, unclicking my seat belt. I twist my legs to the left to face him. "I don't want to make you uncomfortable. Please don't feel pressured."

"I don't feel pressured. It's just scary."

"I'm terrified of everything," I admit sheepishly. "Sharks. Heights. The dark. Birds. Disappointing my mother. Crabs. Pick anything and I've probably had a nightmare about it."

"Crabs?" Chase glances at me amusedly. "You mean the animal or the—"

"The animal," I interrupt hastily. "I don't like the pincers. My point is, if there's anyone that you can be scared in front of, it's me. I couldn't ever judge you."

"Crabs, really?" He's grinning.

"Chase. I'm trying to have an emotional breakthrough, here."

He shows his palms in surrender, but his sparkling eyes betray his amusement. "Sorry, sorry. No judgment zone."

I glance out of the window at the unassuming house. Now that his worry has dissipated and he's been laughing, it looks more like a place that Chase would call home.

"Exactly," I say. "So, are we going inside anytime soon?"

Chase's smile weakens. "I guess we should."

I squeeze the top of his hand in encouragement and climb out of the car. The long-overdue rain has passed now, and all that remains is the glitter of wet grass and the damp, earthy scent of the countryside. Set back against the cliffs, uphill from the town, Chase's home is in the ideal location. If it wasn't for the giggles and shrieks coming from the house, it would be almost silent here.

"Exactly how many brothers and sisters do you have?"

Chase locks the car and begins to walk slowly in the direction of the front door. "That's a complicated question. Technically none."

"Step siblings?"

Chase hesitates. Finally, he shakes his head. "I have four foster siblings."

I blink. *Foster siblings*.

"Are you—"

"I'm adopted."

I stare stupidly. This had never occurred to me, not once. My curiosity about Chase's home life meant I had brainstormed a multitude of scenarios, but somehow, this never entered my head. Caught off guard, I have absolutely no idea what to say to him.

"Oh."

"Didn't expect that?"

I finally close my mouth. "No, I guess I didn't."

"My parents adopted me when I was a baby. They couldn't have kids of their own." We stop at the front step, and he chews his lip. "When I was three, they started fostering too. Kids stay here until they're able to find their own adopted families."

"That's amazing," I murmur. The giggles and shrieks have stopped now, and I can hear the tranquil whispers of the forest.

"Yeah, they're really good people."

He fumbles with the door key, and my stomach begins to churn uneasily. I have no idea how Chase feels about his family, or what to expect when I walk in. I just hope that I can make a good impression. This is such a big deal for him, and I want to prove that it was a good choice to share this part of his life with me.

Chase finally manages to click the key in the door and pushes it open.

A "welcome" doormat greets me upon entry. The floor is coffee-colored wood, scarred and marked with use, and there's a small rattan rug in front of the stairs. The walls are all painted cream with sections of exposed brick. A shoe rack sits opposite the entrance, underneath an array of hanging plants, filled with children's shoes which are spilling out onto the floor. A small pair of Scooby-Doo flip flops lies discarded nearby.

"It's so nice," I say in awe. I kick off my sneakers instantly and pad towards the left wall in my socks. It's studded with family photographs in mismatched frames.

I scan each picture in fascination, a warm realization spreading through my chest.

"Don't tell me—"

"Every child they've fostered," Chase confirms, shutting the front door behind us.

Each photo features a smiling couple, holding or standing behind a child or pair of children. Some of the pictures are taken in front of the house, others are elsewhere. Each photo is unique to each child. Their ages range from toddlers to teenagers, with different ethnicities and varying expressions. The one thing that they all have in common is the smile on their faces, and the names that are scrawled in biro in the top corner of each photograph.

Luis. Penny. Omar. Serenity. Aaliyah.

"Where are you?" I ask, turning around. Chase is watching me with a soft expression.

"Up there."

I follow his finger to see a larger photo in the top left. It's older than the others, faded with sun and age, and slightly blurry. The same smiling woman—with dark braids, brown skin, and a bright sweater—is cradling a tiny, porcelain baby. He has the dark, curious eyes of a newborn, hidden in the swathes of a crochet yellow blanket. It's the only picture on the wall without a name scrawled in the top right corner.

Something touches my hand and I look down to see fingers lacing through mine.

"Come and meet my mom," Chase murmurs, looking down at me.

I smile and nod. Inside, my heart is racing.

Chase tugs on my hand, leading me along the hallway to an open door exposing a large kitchen. The cabinets are walnut, with dark countertops scattered with pamphlets and coffee mugs. Standing beside the large stove, stirring a pan of what appears to be soup, is the woman from the pictures. She looks equally vibrant in a pair of frayed blue jeans, flip flops, and a pink bandana. There's a small blond toddler balanced on her hip.

"Mom," Chase releases my hand to sling his rucksack to the floor. "This is Erika."

She spins around in surprise, and the wooden spoon falls into the pot.

"Don't scare me like that!" she scolds, adjusting the small boy on her hip. He is sucking on a binky and staring at me with surprise. She smiles at me. "I'm Ava. It's so nice to meet you finally. I'd offer to shake your hand but..."

She lifts her palm to show me the soup splashes.

"That's okay," I say with a laugh. "It's really nice to meet you too."

"Chase told me you don't have any dietary requirements, but I'm assuming he didn't bother to ask. Is chicken pasta okay for you?"

"That sounds great."

"Fantastic." Ava turns her attention back to the pot on the stove. "Have you offered your guest a drink, Chase?"

"Not yet," Chase grumbles. "Erika, would you like a drink?"

"I'm okay, thanks."

He looks at Ava pointedly. "See? She didn't even want one."

"It's always polite to ask."

He makes a disapproving noise and leans back against the countertop. On the fridge beside him, adhered with an assortment of magnets, is a collection of children's drawings. The entire surface of the fridge is covered in colored paper and stick figures. I've only been in this house for five minutes, but it's already clear to me that Chase's parents have created such a warm and welcoming environment for their kids.

As if reading my mind, Chase finally speaks. "Where are the others?"

"Oscar was driving me up the wall, so I've settled him in front of a movie now. The girls are upstairs, and Leo is helping me cook the food, aren't you honey?" She bounces the toddler on her hip, prompting a small gargle of surprise. "Dinner is at six."

"Okay." Chase latches onto my wrist again and tugs me towards the kitchen door. "I'm going to show Erika my room."

"Keep that door open, please."

"Oh, it's not like that," I correct hurriedly. "We're just friends."

Chase continues to pull me out of the room. I glance back from the doorway just in time to see Ava laugh.

"I'm sure I'll see that through the *open* door."

Before I can respond, I'm pulled out of sight and back into the cool hallway. Chase is leading me towards the stairs, but a sudden flare of panic prompts me to rip my wrist away. His steps falter and he looks back at me in surprise.

"Your mom thinks we're boinking!" I hiss.

A slow smile emerges on his lips. "That's what you're freaking out about?"

"Yes! My mom would be following us upstairs with a rifle!"

"Well, don't," he responds simply. "She'll figure out that we aren't... *boinking*."

I nod, unsure of what else to say. As we continue upstairs, my head swerves back and forth like a tourist while I scramble to take in everything around me. This house is big, but it's full of life and crowded with interesting knick-knacks. Even the stack of books on the top step captivates me—a well-loved gardening guide, and an assortment of children's titles. When we reach the upstairs hallway, we take an immediate left. The closest door to the stairs.

"This is me," Chase murmurs, pushing it open.

The first thing that strikes is me is how cold the room is. The windows on the far side are wide open, drapes rustling in the breeze. Chase's bedroom isn't large, but the lack of clutter helps it to feel that way. His double bed, dressed in gray sheets, is pressed against the wall. There's a bedside table with a lamp, a built-in closet, and a desk with a large TV and a gaming console. I was half-expecting bikini posters and dirty laundry, so this is a surprise.

"I think I might freeze to death in here." I break the silence, clutching my arms.

Chase rolls his eyes and strides over to close the windows. His room is situated at the front of the house, above the garage, with a view of the sweeping driveway. He grabs the black hoodie hanging from the back of his desk chair and chucks it towards me. The bundle of thick cotton hits me in the chest, and its intoxicating scent follows shortly afterwards.

I raise an eyebrow.

"Looks good on you," he says simply.

I turn around and pull the hoodie over my head, hiding my emergent blush. As I pull the baggy hem down over my jeans, I spot a silver picture frame on Chase's desk. The photo inside is of a young boy with a medal around his neck and a toothy smile. His father kneels beside him proudly, a protective hand wrapped around his shoulder.

"Is that your dad?"

"Yeah." I'm conscious of Chase's warmth as he comes to stand beside me. "He still comes to every one of my games. He's really good with the kids, too, they all adore him."

"This house ... it seems really nice. Your family seem so lovely, Squidge."

"Yeah, they are," he says softly, glancing at me. "I'm very lucky."

"If you don't mind me asking ..." I watch his features carefully. "Why are you so protective of your home life? I assume not many people know about it."

"Alec, Joe, and Dylan have known since we were kids. They're the only ones," Chase confesses. I watch as a crease of stress appears between his eyebrows. "I guess, I'm scared that people would see me differently. That they wouldn't want me ... as I am."

"Anybody who doesn't want you," I murmur, "is not worth your time anyway."

"My first experience in the world was being rejected, Erika," Chase says, wincing slightly. "I might not remember it, or her, but that kind of knowledge haunts you a bit."

"I'm so sorry. I can't even begin to imagine how difficult that must be."

"Thank you," Chase says, then quickly shakes his head. "But I have a loving family, and no experience of living in limbo. Some of the kids I've met have spent most of their lives in the system, waiting for someone to help them. Desperate for everything that I have."

"Just because somebody else hurts more doesn't make your pain worth less," I remind him. I long to reach out and hug him, but I can't be sure that he would want that type of comfort. I try to pour how much I care into my words instead. "Only you can fully understand the pain of your experiences. Don't deny yourself the right to be heard."

He stares at me. Without taking his eyes from mine, he lifts my hand up from my side and presses his lips to my fingers. They're warm, and soft. My insides melt like butter.

"You really are gorgeous, you know that? Inside and out."

"Thank you." My voice sounds embarrassingly breathy.

Chase squeezes my hand. "I'm happy that you're here."

"Good." I smile. "I am too."

"Do you want some jelly?"

The boy sitting beside me, Oscar, holds out a sticky teaspoon. His fingers are coated in strawberry goo and his smile is impossibly endearing.

"I'm okay, thanks, you enjoy it," I reply, grinning.

Oscar can be no more than six years old, but his curly hair and abundance of freckles ensure that he'll be a heartbreaker one day. Aside from Leo, the shy toddler glued to Ava's side, Oscar is the youngest of Chase's foster siblings. I was surprised to find out that Saira and Eliza are both in their last years of elementary school. Somehow, I pictured all of Chase's foster siblings to be below eight years old. Then I had the harsh realization that the older a child becomes, the less likely they are to be adopted.

These girls are still waiting for their chance.

"Not everybody likes jelly as much as you do, Ozzy," Sam teases from across the table. His face is grooved with smile lines, and his hair is peppered with age. Although logic dictates that they have no genetic connection, I swear that I can recognize Chase's warm brown eyes in his face.

"Are you sure you've had enough to eat, Erika?" Ava asks, gesturing to the half-demolished apple pie in the center of the table with an encouraging smile.

"As much as I'd love more, I think I'd explode," I confess, rubbing my bloated stomach. The top button of my jeans is straining. "Thank you, though."

"Nonsense. It's nice to have someone around that doesn't complain about the food I put in front of them," Ava says, frowning pointedly at Saira. Saira grins and continues to push the dessert around her bowl with a spoon.

"Anyway," Chase begins, folding his arms over the table. "Before we go upstairs, I wanted to tell you that Alec's eighteenth birthday party is this Saturday. Is it alright if I go?"

"I don't think we have any plans," Ava responds, feeding Leo a spoonful of custard. "We might go out for dinner, but you wouldn't be interested in that anyway."

"So, is that a yes?"

"Yes, we can take you," Sam confirms. "Are you going too, Erika?"

I nod and smile as best I can through my sip of water.

"You're still going to be able to pick me up from Charlotte's house, though, right?" Eliza worries. Her black hair is pulled into a ponytail and she's wearing a faded Captain America T-shirt. This is the first time she's spoken during the meal.

"Of course. No later than 10.30 p.m., remember?"

"Okay," she agrees begrudgingly. "Thank you."

Any further conversation is interrupted by little Leo elbowing his bowl from the table. The plastic hits the floor with a loud bang, undoubtedly spilling custard all over the floor. The toddler's eyes are wide, and his bottom lip begins to tremble dangerously.

"Oh, Leo." Ava sighs, staring down at the mess.

"That's our cue to leave," Chase mutters, nudging me with his elbow.

Ignoring his comment entirely, I lift my napkin from my lap and push my chair back to stand up. "Would you like any help, Ava? Can I do anything?"

Ava looks at me with surprise, a pile of napkins already in her grasp. "Oh, no, no sweetheart! Don't worry about it, it's just a little spill."

"You two are free to head upstairs, we can handle this," Sam assures me, beginning to gather the plates. "If you need a ride home later, just give me a shout."

"That's really kind of you, thank you."

"Come on, let's go." Chase stands up from his seat and touches my arm lightly.

I barely have time to thank Ava again for dinner before his hand is back in mine and he's leading me out of the room. Behind us, tears are beginning to dribble down Leo's cheeks and Saira is rushing to gather cleaning supplies from the kitchen. I glance back doubtfully. My mom has always raised me to be the kind of girl that helps clean up after dinner, not the type to leave the second that my appetite is satisfied.

"Why were you in such a rush to get out of there?" I ask Chase as we ascend the stairs. "I feel so bad for not helping to clean up."

"Don't worry. They wouldn't let you help much anyway, you're a guest. Plus, I've earned a free pass for the amount of stuff I help them with."

We reach his bedroom and Chase makes a direct beeline for his bed. He slings himself down onto the pillows, stretching out languidly with his ankles crossed and arms folded above his head. His expression is expectant. Leaving the bedroom door ajar, I tentatively approach Chase's bed and perch myself on the edge of his mattress. I angle my torso towards him and begin to pick at a loose thread of cotton on my jeans, avoiding eye contact.

"The thing your mom said," I wonder aloud. "About how you wouldn't consider going to dinner with them. What did she mean by that?"

Chase's legs, strewn beside me on the bedcovers, seem to stiffen. "I don't spend much time at home. You already know that."

"But, why not? Your family are so lovely."

"Yeah ... they are."

I look up from my jeans just as Chase closes his eyes. After a few seconds of weighted silence, the deep grooves of stress between his eyebrows flatten out. His face visibly relaxes, and his eyes open once more.

"They're not my family because it's only temporary," he explains softly. The arms above his head shift into a more comfortable position across his stomach. "I try not to get too involved with the family dynamic, because I know they're all going to leave sooner or later."

"What do you mean?"

"I mean ..." Chase hesitates. His gaze drifts to the bedcovers. "I try to keep to myself a lot because there's no point in getting attached to a family that's never consistent."

I feel a squeezing sensation in my chest. "You mean ...?"

"I've grown up surrounded by a lot of different people," he says, glancing at me. His eyes drop back to the covers as quickly as possible. "I was attached to a lot of my foster siblings, only for them to disappear when they were adopted. No contact with me at all ... Every one of them just left my life in an instant."

Realization spreads over my body like a chill. This boy is terrified of being abandoned. I open my mouth, but before I can say anything, he's continuing.

"Before you say anything, I know, I *know* how selfish it is to say that." He speaks through a grimace. "I should be happy for them because they've found what I've been lucky enough to have for my entire life. They've found a home. I have absolutely no right to feel sorry for myself."

"It's not selfish," I interject quickly. "I can see why that hurts."

Chase's hand falls from his stomach, and his voice becomes quiet. "I just feel like I've had a lot of people leave me, Erika."

I can't resist the opportunity to grab his hand again. His skin is warm and calloused, and my fingers lace naturally through his like fitting jigsaw pieces. I squeeze his hand comfortingly. "Have you tried to make contact with any of them?"

"What's the point? They have new families, happier lives."

He looks up at me finally, but his smile is sad.

"I don't even talk to my current foster siblings anymore, you know. How awful is that?" He laughs and shakes his head. "These kids come into our house, and they need me to help them feel safe, but I reject them because I'm just too damn scared of being hurt."

"It's understandable to be scared," I murmur. "But not everybody is going to leave."

His thumb plays with mine. "Remember the first text you sent me?"

"The one where I called you desperate?"

"Yeah, that one. Although, that's not the part of the message that stuck with me." He watches our fingers interact; touching, bumping, pinching. "You said something like 'you'll find someone who sticks around'. Right at the end. It was a punch in the gut."

The cold reality of my words dawns on me, and my mouth falls open. "Oh—"

"That's why I was so moody when I saw you next."

"I'm so sorry, Chase. I had *no* idea."

"You couldn't have. Not your fault."

"It is my fault," I admit, squeezing his hand again. "And I'm so sorry that I was so judgmental when I met you. I couldn't have been more wrong in my estimations."

Chase's lips part slightly, and he stares at me with surprise, his eyebrows slightly furrowed. Suddenly, the warm hand that was entwined loosely with mine has constricted into a secure and solid grip. With a sharp tug, he pulls me towards him. I collapse onto his chest with a squeak of surprise.

Before I have time to react or adjust my position, his arms loop around my body to hold me prisoner.

Not that I'm in any rush to escape.

"What are you doing?" I laugh breathlessly, craning my neck back to look up at him. My head is resting on the top of his chest, just below the sharp line of his jaw.

"I'm hugging you," he responds simply.

"Why?"

"Because I want you to stay here."

In response, my left hand loops over his chest and I pull myself firmly to his side. His arms tighten around my back, until there is little to no space remaining between our bodies. The less space there is between us—between our lives—the better.

"Everybody leaves, eventually." He buries his face into the top of my head. I can feel his nose pressing into my hair. "I really, really don't want you to."

"Don't worry, Squidge," I mumble. "I'm like bubble gum. I stick around."

"I hope so."

Despite the gentleness of our embrace, I can hear the insistent thuds of his heartbeat beneath my ear. It's reassuring to know that I'm not the only one with a racing pulse.

"Trust me," I whisper into his T-shirt. "I'm not going anywhere."

19

Genetic Failure

The frustration of being too warm is what stirs me from my slumber.

With a groan of discomfort, I reach blindly towards the tornado of sheets twisted around my legs. I am pinned by a leg strewn lazily over mine, and it takes half a minute of dim struggling to disentangle myself. The air in Chase's bedroom is refreshingly cold, but the body pressed to my side is warm and it creates a delicious sensation of comfort. The arm underneath my neck hooks around my chest to tug me closer, and Chase's sleepy rasps of breath fan across my neck and make my skin tingle.

It feels so natural to be nestled within his arms, to smell his intoxicating scent on the pillow pressed to my nose. Nevertheless, I can't shake the feeling that something is wrong.

Why am I sleeping beside him?

The question in my mind rings as incessantly and annoyingly as a morning alarm. I begrudgingly open my eyes to examine my surroundings. The room around us is washed with dark blue shades of night. His drapes are still open and moonlight spills across the carpet. I reach across for my phone and swipe, but the brightness of my lock screen is enough to make my eyes water. It takes a minute before I can stand to see without squinting, and I am finally able to determine the numbers at the top of the screen.

12.36 a.m. That seems strangely late. I must... *Oh no.*

"Crap," I exclaim, bolting upright in bed. My drowsiness ends in an instant, and my focus sharpens upon the seven missed notifications from my mother. Three missed calls, four frantic text messages demanding to know my location. "Crap!"

"What is it?" Chase sits up, his arm still wrapped protectively around my hip. His voice is deep and thick with sleep, and he squints at the screen with confusion. "What?"

"It's past midnight," I wail, leaning into his shoulder for support. "We must have fallen asleep, and I didn't message home. My mom is going to eviscerate me."

"Okay, okay," Chase murmurs, rubbing his eye with his free hand. "Just give her a call now because she's probably worried. You can stay here tonight, it'll be fine."

My fingers are already flying on the keypad, texting sincere apologies and promises to be home within the hour. "I can't stay here tonight, I can't."

"Why not?"

"She already thinks I'm too distracted from school at the moment," I explain while checking through my hastily assembled text. "If she thinks I'm sleeping in a boy's bed too, I'll never hear the end of it. I can already smell the disappointment."

I press send on my apology text at the same moment that Chase's fingers touch my chin. With a gentle but deliberate movement, he angles my face towards him. Even in the gloomy lighting, I can see that he is watching me intently from underneath his messy bed hair. "Erika, why do you care so much about disappointing your mom?"

"Huh?" I ask stupidly, fixing my own hair. "Oh, it's not... I don't care *that* much."

"Yes, you do." His voice is soft, but insistent.

"No, I just..." I trail off and glance away uncomfortably. My phone has fallen into my lap, and I begin to twist the bedsheets between my fingers. "I just want to make her proud of me, that's all. It's not that I'm scared of her."

Chase frowns. "Why wouldn't she be proud of you?"

"Have you met my sister?" I ask, laughing in my awkwardness. "It's nearly impossible to impress *anyone* when you're standing beside Chloe Monroe. I would know, I've been doing it for almost eighteen years. I'm a bona fide expert."

"Funny," Chase remarks, squeezing my hip. "Because I think the only person that compares the pair of you is you."

"That's not true." I shake my head. My fingers are wound so tightly in the bedsheets that they're beginning to color red. "My mom adores my sister—she can do no wrong. Always good grades, awards, promotions, decisions. Mom never has to tell her to do something, Chloe just handles everything perfectly on the first try."

"And you're not that way?"

"I'm not awful," I mumble. "I'm just not the same. I mess up and I'm disorganized, and my mom loses patience with me because I don't just... *coast* through life in the same way that Chloe does. Sometimes I wonder if they picked up the wrong baby at the hospital."

"You? Disorganized?" Chase echoes incredulously. "You're

applying for Stanford, right? You juggle about fifty extracurriculars in a week and you manage to have a great social life. You seem perfectly organized from where I'm standing."

"Compared to Chloe, I'm useless," I say with a helpless shrug.

"What about your dad? You don't really mention him."

"I think he sees me," I say, after a moment's consideration. "He's quite laid-back about anything school or success-related. He just wants us to be happy, so I don't ever really feel like I'm disappointing him."

"Okay, I'll entertain this for a second." Chase laces his free hand through mine and tugs it away from the sheets. My fingers are warm, tingly, and glowing red from my anxious fidgeting. "Even if Chloe is this superhuman you describe, how exactly does that make all of your achievements any less valuable, Erika?"

"It doesn't," I say quietly. "I know that I'm not my sister, and I shouldn't compare but... just for one moment, *I* want to be the impressive daughter."

"That's why you want to get into Stanford."

"If I can get into Stanford..." I swallow loudly. "Then maybe I can prove that I don't just exist in Chloe's perfect shadow. I can excel in my own, individual way and become the type of person that would make my mom equally proud."

Chase's arm tightens around my waist and his free hand moves from mine to caress my cheek. "What about the type of person that makes *you* proud?"

"Well yeah. That too."

"That should be your main focus, gorgeous," Chase says, shaking his head. "And I'm sure that your mom is equally proud of you, regardless of where you go to college or whether you sleep over at a boy's house. How could she not be? You're incredible."

"Thank you, Squidge." I lean my head onto his shoulder.

We sit in comfortable silence for a few seconds before my phone buzzes on the crumpled bedsheets. Facing upwards in clear view, the glowing lock-screen photo of Miko and me is partially obscured by a curt text notification from my mom.

Momma Bear: Do I need to come and collect you?

Before I even have the chance to look upwards and ask Chase for his zip-code, I feel him shaking his head. His warm lips touch my forehead in a short but tender kiss. "I'll take you home, don't worry. Just let me grab my car keys."

He detangles his body from mine and slides off the bed abruptly, leaving me in a dizzy stupor. My forehead still feels warm and damp in the spot where his lips were once pressed, and there is an unmistakable squeezing sensation in my chest as a response. How can one little action put my pulse in such a frenzy? Before I can overthink the gesture too much, I climb off the bed and begin to gather my things.

The rest of the house is unlit and silent, aside from the jingle of the car keys swinging from Chase's hand. His family are all asleep, and I deliberate each one of my steps on the wooden stairs for fear of waking them. Luckily, we reach the hallway without any complaints from the floorboards. Chase turns on a small rattan lamp, flooding the house entrance with a warm yellow glow as we hurry to tie our shoes. It is as I'm tying a double knot that my gaze wanders back to the photograph wall, and I notice something I had previously missed.

"Seth," I whisper aloud in realization.

A yard below my usual eyeline is a photograph of a young teenage boy, with a cheeky smile and raven black hair. Although his jaw is sharper now and his skin is patterned with tattoos, the juvenile face in the picture unmistakably belongs to Seth Bautista. Any doubt is eliminated by the signature biro scrawl in the corner of the frame.

"He was one of my foster brothers," Chase mumbles quietly, standing up to his full height. "The only one that I actually kept in contact with."

"So that's how you two know each other."

"Yeah."

"Well," I mumble. "I'm happy that you have him."

Chase makes a humming noise of agreement. "He's family."

He opens the front door as slowly as possible, but it could never be noiseless. We both listen with bated breath for sounds of any movement from upstairs. After a few seconds confirms that his family remain undisturbed, we step out of the house into the cool night air. My nose tickles as I inhale: a telling symptom of hay fever that marks the cusp of summer.

Chase shuts the door and pushes his keys and hands deep into his jean pockets. Then, he begins to stroll down the path towards his car. His steps and voice are gentle because we aren't entirely out of earshot yet. "That's what the tattoo is, you know."

"The moon tattoo?"

Chase nods. "Seth has a matching one on his finger. I wasn't sure if you'd spotted it when we saw him at the bar last time."

"I never made the connection," I confess. It's slightly frustrating to know that the clue to Chase's tattoo was under my nose the entire time. I remember registering the small dark shape on Seth's finger. "What was the significance of a moon then?"

Chase's smile is sad, tainted by bitter nostalgia. He looks up, to where a crescent moon glows determinedly in an obsidian sky. "It's consistent, reliable, and it always comes back. It seemed pretty meaningful at the time."

"The sun comes back too," I remind him gently.

"Yeah." He looks at me, and his smile becomes earnest. "I know."

When I finally tiptoe into my front hallway at 1.12 a.m., there is light glowing through the gaps in the living room door frame. I pull a face—I had hoped that my text would have reassured my mom enough that she would go to bed. The fact that she's stayed up means that I will have to suffer the consequences of both her frustration and sleep deprivation. I remove my sneakers as slowly as I can, taking the time to untie each lace fully, but I can only postpone the inevitable for so long.

I knock softly on the living room door as I enter. "Mom?"

Mom is slumped in the center of the couch, nestled between two large cushions, with the TV remote outstretched in her right hand. A small lamp and the television are the only sources of illumination for the room. She flicks through the channels with staccato bursts of noise and color, settling on nothing but the chance to avoid looking at me.

"Mom, I'm sorry if I worried you," I say gingerly, clinging to the door frame.

She finally sighs. Her hand, with the remote, falls to her lap and randomly selects an antiques channel. She mutes the noise before we can hear much detail about the vase in question, plunging the room into a stark and uncomfortable silence. Finally, she looks at me. The gaunt lighting exaggerates the dark circles beneath her eyes.

"I assume you went to Miko's house?" she asks tiredly, folding her arms across her chest. I notice that she's already wearing her comfy red pajamas.

"No," I mumble, daring to set foot into the room. I perch uneasily on the arm of the other couch, lacing my fingers together in my lap. "Actually, I was at Chase's house."

"Chase?" Mom frowns. "You were asleep with a boy?"

"It's not like that, Mom, we're just friends."

It's the first time that label has felt like a lie.

"Is this the elusive friend who put you in detention too? No wonder you've been so distracted recently," she says, leaning her head back into the couch. "Did you manage to eat anything? There's some leftover lasagna in the fridge if you're hungry."

"I'm okay, thank you, I had dinner with his parents," I respond. "And I haven't been distracted. I'm still working really hard for Stanford."

"Are you sure about that, Erika?" Mom sighs, brushing her knees. "Because it seems to me that your social life has swallowed everything else. When was the last time you had one of your study sessions with Miko?"

"Not that long ago!"

"Long enough."

"I'm allowed to go out and spend time with friends, you know," I say defensively. "My entire life doesn't have to be devoted to getting into college or obtaining a scholarship. I work hard enough."

If only she knew just how hard I've been trying. Would that even be enough for her?

"It's about striking a balance, Erika." She stands up from the couch and pulls her dressing robe more tightly around her body. The expression on her face is weary. "I just want to make sure that you aren't losing sight of what is most important. The person you are and everything that you're aiming for. Boys and parties can come later."

I scoff. "If I have to turn myself into a robot to go to college, then I don't want it."

"That's not what I'm suggesting, and you know it," she replies sternly. "I just think you should remember that work is your priority. Your sister didn't..."

She trails off and bites her lip, but the damage is already done in those three words.

"My sister didn't what?"

"She didn't..." Mom flails her arm uncomfortably as she searches for the right words to say. I could save her a few seconds by informing her that there is no right way of phrasing this comparison, but I'm too desperate to watch her fumble over my inferiority. "She *focused*, Erika. She had ambition, she dedicated herself and she got into Oregon State. You can too."

"I am not my sister," I utter coldly. "So, stop expecting me to be."

"I don't expect you to—"

"Yes, you do," I interrupt, standing up from the couch. It may be because I am still raw from my conversation with Chase, or it could be that I'm overly tired, but irritation has invaded my common sense. My pulse is hammering as I think about the approval that I am so desperate to obtain, yet so far from achieving.

"Erika."

"Maybe, one day, you'll be able to look at me without seeing Chloe's shadow," I say quietly. "But until that day, you're going to remain sorely disappointed."

Mom watches me in stunned silence as I stalk towards the door. I refuse to stand here and be reminded of my genetic failure.

"Goodnight, Mom," I mutter as it closes behind me.

"Need any help?"

Chloe is standing in the open doorway to my bedroom, leaning against the frame with her ankles crossed. She's wearing fluffy socks and sweats, and even from meters away I can see the bloodshot tiredness in her eyes. She doesn't look like her young, chirpy self. She looks older; she looks like Mom. I smile at her and nod, turning to face my mirror again. I watch in the reflection as she pads into my room and takes a seat on my bed.

"Does this hair look good?" I ask, evaluating my reflection. My frizzy hair has been attacked with styling spray and is hanging around my face in ringlets. I release another curl that I've been coiling around the barrel of the curling iron. I don't style my hair often, so it's strange to see my wild mane look sleek and glossy. It's Alec's eighteenth birthday party tonight and I want to look... impressive.

Chloe hums. "I think you need to go a little looser. Less ringlets, more beach waves."

I hold up the curling iron.

"You can do it by yourself," Chloe grumbles, but she approaches, nevertheless. Standing behind me at my small vanity, she ignores my gaze in the mirror and begins to run her fingers through the curls to loosen them. I always longed for hair like hers, that she could neaten into braids or ballerina buns. My hair is so unruly in comparison.

"Like this." She takes the curling iron from my hand and coils a new section of hair loosely around the barrel. She holds it there for less time than I did. "See?"

I watch her face carefully. The low lighting from my desk light emphasizes her lusterless complexion and red-rimmed eyes. "Do you want to talk about it?"

Finally meeting my gaze in the mirror, Chloe shakes her head. "I'm just stressed about work. It's nothing you can help with, really."

"You're working too hard."

"I know, I know."

"Isn't your workload going to get bigger, when you get to this new place?"

"Technically, yes."

"Chloe—"

"I really don't want to talk about me," she insists. "Let's talk about you instead."

I hesitate.

"Erika, talk."

I sense not to press her on the topic. "What do you want to know?"

Chloe smiles, releasing another curl. "What are you wearing to the party?"

"I'm not sure yet, I'm very open to recommendations," I say with a smile. "Or if you were feeling particularly generous, I wouldn't object to you lending me that blue dress."

"Erika." Chloe raises an eyebrow. "I haven't even worn that dress myself yet."

"I'd be very happy to trial it for you and let you know how it performs."

She rolls her eyes. "Is Mom happy about you going to this party tonight? She told me that you two had a bit of a fight last night when you got home."

My smile disappears. "I don't care what she has to say about it. I've studied all day."

"Yeah, it sounds like you deserve a night off." She clicks the curling iron off and places it on the heat mat on my vanity. Then she fluffs my newly wavy hair around my shoulders, tugging at strands to loosen them. "All done. Looks gorgeous."

"Thanks." Quietly, I add, "I really want to look good tonight."

Chloe seems to catch my hint instantly because her eyebrows shoot up. "It's happening, isn't it? You and Chase?"

Instead of talking to her reflection this time, I twist around in my chair to stare at her. I haven't mentioned anything about Chase to her. "How do you even know about him?"

Chloe rolls her eyes, walking backwards and collapsing onto my bed. "Erika, you hardly have to be Sherlock Holmes to figure it out. The way you talk about him, the chemistry between both of you . . ."

I wait expectantly. Eventually her innocent smile collapses. "Miko told me."

"Of course."

"Come on then," Chloe enthuses, watching me with sparkling eyes. "Fill me in."

I clear my throat and try to ignore the apprehension twisting in my stomach. "I like him a lot, and I think there's a chance that he likes me too."

Chloe slaps her knees with excitement. "You must be feeling giddy right now."

"Not quite," I respond, with a shaky laugh. Standing up from my vanity, I walk over to my dresser, where my clothing options are laid out neatly. My fingers dance over the floral miniskirt. "I'm in a bit of a sticky situation. I've been keeping something from him, and I don't know how to tell him now without betraying his trust. I really don't want to lose him."

Chloe makes an empathetic humming noise and purses her lips. "A lie?"

"Yeah, a pretty big one."

"Confessing your mistake is always going to make you seem more trustworthy than trying to cover it up. He might be mad at you for a while but . . ."

"Yeah." I sigh. "A long while, I expect."

"It's Chase Thatcher, right?" Chloe asks, leaning back against my headboard and crossing her legs languidly. Her blond hair fans across my pillows, and there's a small crease between her eyebrows as she recalls. "The guy you asked me about, that time in my office? Quite tall, brown hair, smirk that makes the freshman girls giggle?"

"That's the one."

"The principal came and asked me about him a while ago," Chloe wonders aloud. "Is he in some kind of trouble? He doesn't strike me as a bad kid."

"Blythe seems to have it out for him," I reply carefully. I

reach for the skirt and top combination on my bed and position it in front of my body, inspecting myself in the mirror. The skirt looks like it could be too short for a family-friendly party. "What do you think about your new boss, actually? She seems quite ... cold and calculated."

"She works very late," Chloe points out. "She's clearly dedicated to her work. She's always carrying that damn folder. She never puts it down."

"She keeps it in a locked drawer, I think." I swap the skirt for a pair of red pants, but this combination seems too formal. "Chase mentioned that the parking lot always fills up late at night. She must stay at school until almost midnight—isn't that wild?"

"The parking lot fills up?" Chloe repeats, frowning.

"Yeah, every night at ten. No idea what that's all about."

"Yeah," Chloe mutters. "That's odd."

"Anyway," I say chirpily, turning around to brandish the red pants. "What do you think about this combination? I know it's a family party, so I want to look approachable but—"

"Also hot," Chloe finishes, nodding. "I get you."

"Exactly."

"You always look good," Chloe says pointedly. "But you can borrow my new dress and some heels. Cinderella is proof that a new pair of shoes can make your entire night."

"Thanks, Chlo. You fancy helping with my make-up too?"

Chloe's makeup always looks effortlessly amazing; she knows how to compliment her face with only a few products. Tonight, I want my eyeliner wings to soar, I want my lips to be irresistible, and I want my eyelashes as black as my soul and as long as the list of people I've thought about punching.

"Okay, but don't get used to it." My sister sits up cross-legged, with a cushion in her lap. Her foot is twitching in the way it always does when she's excited. "You're going to look great, Erika, and if he doesn't make a move then he's an idiot."

"True," I say with a laugh. "Now, get to work. I'm not paying you for chit chat."

Chloe stares blankly at me. "You're not paying me at all."

"Every minute with me is priceless, Chloe. My company is payment enough."

Chloe rolls her eyes. "Lord help Chase if he ends up dating you."

I throw an ankle boot in her direction, but she dodges it easily.

As I watch my sister leave the room to fetch the outfit, I feel a surge of appreciation. As annoying and superior as Chloe can be sometimes, she'll always have my back when I need her. That's why as soon as she's ready to talk about why she's so stressed, I'll be there with a tub of ice cream in hand, ready to have her back too.

20

Goosebumps

I stand on the front porch of the cream-colored house, clutching my arms and shivering. Chloe informed me that I should bring a jacket because "it's not summer yet," but of course, I ignored her. *It's an indoor party*, I said. *It'll be fine*, I said. And now, here I am, freezing my lady balls off while I try to remember which number Alec said his house was. I curse aloud, clutching my bare arms for warmth as I examine the russet front door for non-existent clues.

I'm pretty sure it had a nine in it. Possibly.

"It is number nineteen, you're right," Miko says, appearing beside me with a wry smile. She's dressed in a pastel yellow jumpsuit that flatters her long legs, with matching bows around each of her braids. Noticing my interest, Miko glances down at her outfit and quirks out a hip. "I look like I should be the fourth Powerpuff Girl, right?"

"You make lemon sherbet look sexy," I confirm, winking at her.

Miko rolls her eyes and leans forward to press the doorbell.

"How are you feeling today, Mickey? How's Kai?"

"Good, yeah ... He doesn't seem to have been in any trouble recently, so hopefully, okay. I think the Washington threat has finally sunk in." Miko makes her best attempt at a smile and shuffles her feet on the porch step. "It's all I've been able to think about for so long, so I don't really want to talk about it tonight. I hope that's okay."

"Of course, it's okay. No explanation needed."

"I just want to relax and have some fun without worrying about him for once," she says, shrugging loosely. "I need to focus on myself."

I bump her shoulder encouragingly. "Sounds like a plan, Batman."

Before we have a chance to talk further, the front door opens and Violet's smiling face peers out at us. "Ooh, you're here! Come on in, you two look fantastic."

Violet stands back from the door to make room for us to enter. She looks particularly fierce in a red blazer and matching lipstick; a combination with the same power and charisma as her personality. Miko squeezes her tightly before moving further into the cinnamon-scented house to greet the others. I haven't dared to look beyond Violet yet. My stomach makes a weird gurgle of nerves at the thought of seeing Chase again.

"You look hot," Violet mouths, pointing to my legs. I chuckle and hug her.

From what I can see of my surroundings, Alec's house is beautifully decorated. The couches in the living room are mauve, plush with cushions, and the wallpaper seems expensive. There's a large bouquet of roses in a vase on the hallway table, which look so immaculate that I doubt they can be real. As Violet moves to close the door, I suck in a breath and force myself to acknowledge the people standing further down the hallway.

"Erika, you look gorgeous!" Riley gushes, waddling slightly in her heels. She's wearing a green shift dress and her auburn curls tumble freely around her shoulders.

"You too! Alec is a lucky man," I say, pulling her into a hug. She smells like vanilla and hairspray. I can't help but look over her shoulder until my eyes rest on the person I've been searching for. He's standing at the entrance to the living room, wearing tight black jeans and a maroon-colored shirt. And he's staring right back at me.

Riley and I pull apart from our hug, and her expression is triumphant. "Chase totally checked you out when you walked in. The guys were all teasing him."

"I can hear you, you know," Chase calls. He crosses his arms over his chest, and the moon tattoo on his collarbone winks at me from under the loose material.

Riley glances back at him and shrugs. "Oops."

"Hey, you two are here!" Alec appears beside his girlfriend, sliding an arm around her waist naturally. He's dressed in a gray shirt, with a pink glittery party hat strapped around his head. "Welcome to Casa Alec. Can I interest you in some alcohol-free punch?"

"There are kids around so no drinking tonight," Riley explains.

Miko waves her hand dismissively. "I can get equally hyper from candy anyway."

"Skittles work for you?" Alec asks. Then he shares a smile with Riley that hints at an inside joke of some kind. "We have every color of the rainbow."

"Come on, I'll show you the buffet." Violet loops her arm

through Miko's and begins to tug her in the direction of the living room. The others begin to filter in behind them, and Dylan bumps my hip playfully as he passes.

As I take up position at the tail of the group, a hand bumps mine and alerts me to Chase's presence. He stares directly forwards and refuses to acknowledge me, but his arm continues to brush against mine as we walk. Sensations spark through my shoulder and dance down through my spine at the fleeting contact.

"Hi, gorgeous," he says finally.

I bite my lip but it's impossible to keep away my smile. I focus my attention on the eighteenth birthday bunting strung around the living room. "Hey Squidge."

He clears his throat. "You look..."

"Thank you."

"Just facts," he replies simply.

"What were you up to today?" I ask. "Your replies were slower than usual."

"Oh, I was at work—uh, working out. I was working out."

I consider pushing for information but decide against it.

Alec's living room smells like birthday cake. String lights and bright bunting are strung around the room's perimeter, children are winding through adults' legs for their game of tag, and the sound of chatter and laughter almost overpowers the music humming from the speakers. Our group huddles on the right-hand side of the room, leaving Alec's family to surround the loaded buffet table. At the center of everything, a dark-haired woman rushes around with a tray of cupcakes. Her cobalt eyes identify her as Alec's mother.

"So, what are your plans for your actual birthday tomorrow then?" Dylan asks Alec. My attention is drawn back within our circle, but I make a mental note to visit the cupcake stand later. Hopefully I'll have the opportunity to thank Alec's mom for hosting us.

"I hope that it's fairly relaxed, I don't really want a big event," Alec responds, scrunching his nose a little in distaste. "Probably just hanging out with my family and Riles. We might go to dinner or something, I'm not sure."

"Speaking of family ..." Eyes scanning the room erratically, Joe leans forward into our gathered circle. His voice is quiet and urgent. "Has everyone arrived now?"

"Yes," Alec responds slowly, his face warped with confusion. "Why?"

"No reason, no reason at all." Joe shrugs unconvincingly and leans back.

I look across at Violet to see if she can decipher Joe's odd behavior, but she shrugs cluelessly. Even Chase is frowning at him. What on earth was that all about?

"Well on that note," Miko chirps, interrupting the awkward silence. "I'm going to go and examine the buffet table. Anyone coming?"

Seemingly grateful for the change of focus, Joe nods eagerly. I watch as Miko disappears into the crowd, with Joe and Violet following shortly behind. She's wearing a wide smile as she describes her favorite Japanese candy, and her banana earrings are bouncing with the excited movements of her head. It's nice to see her like this—so carefree and animated. I want her to stay this happy forever.

Or at least just for tonight.

Although the bowl of peach-colored punch has been inoffensive to every other guest at this party, Joe has been glaring coldly at it for the past thirty seconds. The plastic cup in his hand remains almost full, and distaste lingers in his expression from his first sip.

"That bad?" I tease, drinking from my own cup. It tastes like tropical juice.

"This stuff doesn't even have grenadine in it," he complains. "Not even an *alcopop*."

"I'm pretty sure you can survive without White Claw for a night, Joe," Chase says, rolling his eyes. He is standing on my other side, closely enough that our clothing whispers together and our hands flirt. I know that he's doing that on purpose, and my anticipation for his next move only grows with each teasing touch. My stomach is flipping so often that it should consider a career in gymnastics.

"You'd be surprised," Joe mutters, completing another periodical survey of the room.

I crane my neck to follow his eyeline. "What do you keep looking at, weirdo?"

"Nothing, just people!" Joe says with a huff, placing his cup on the table. Before he can restrain his meerkat impulses, his gaze drifts around the surroundings again. Only, this time, his reaction is markedly distinctive. Flinching with surprise, he vomits a curse word under his breath and ducks his shoulders down. I jump slightly as his head pauses in line with my chest, just low enough for my shoulders to hide him from sight.

"Dude," Chase says lowly. "No. Move."

Joe ignores the demand entirely. "Get me out of here."

"Joe—"

"Chase, if you love me at all, you will remove me from this room," Joe whispers frantically. Then he glances apologetically at me. "Sorry to use you as a shield, Erika."

"No worries."

Using our bodies to conceal him from the rest of the guests, we usher Joe towards the exit door as inconspicuously as we can manage. As soon as we arrive in the hallway, he dives out of sight into the gap beside the table, almost knocking the vase of roses off balance in the process. My curiosity is eating at me, and I can't resist the chance to peer back into the living room. That's when I spot the new addition.

A girl with short black hair and clustered freckles is laughing with Riley.

"Natasha," Chase says, following my line of sight. When I turn to look at him, his face is twisted with incredulity. "Why on earth are you hiding from your girlfriend, man?"

Joe winces. "She's not technically my girlfriend anymore."

Oh.

"You two broke up?" Chase exclaims. "When?"

"The other day. It was mutual . . . but awkward, still." Joe gestures frustratedly at the front door. "Please can we have this conversation outside?"

We move our conversation outside. Alec's street is devoid of activity and the silence is almost as chilly as the breeze. Instantly, my hands wrap protectively around my upper arms as if to physically suppress my goosebumps. Unfortunately, it has little effect. By the time that Chase has closed the door behind us for privacy, I'm shivering, and my bare skin is carpeted with raised pimples.

Wordlessly, Chase pulls me back against his body and envelops my torso within his arms.

"What happened with you two?" he asks Joe over my shoulder. The warmth of Chase's chest against my back is making the temperature considerably more bearable.

"We just ... didn't talk anymore. Neither of us were putting in any effort," Joe confesses, digging his hands deep into his pockets. Although his neutral expression is well-practiced, his eyes betray his disappointment. "We decided that we're better off as friends."

"Easy to say that, less easy to put in practice," I murmur empathetically.

"Exactly. I'm not ready to see her just yet."

"Why on earth would you come here then?" Chase asks. I can feel his torso shake with a laugh of disbelief. "You didn't consider that Alec's cousin might show up?"

"Alec said that everybody had already arrived!" Joe groans.

"You're an idiot," Chase remarks. I can practically hear his eyes roll. "But ... I am sorry that it didn't work out for you. It seemed like you guys clicked so well."

"We still will. Just not right away."

"So, what's your plan now?" I question, cupping my hands around Chase's forearms to keep them wrapped around me. I don't want him to think that just because I'm no longer shivering, he is free to remove them. "Surely you can't stay out here all night."

"No." Joe chews his lip and scrutinizes the dark street. "My car is right around the corner, so I'll probably just head home now. I doubt the party will last much longer anyway."

"I'll let Alec know why you left," Chase says.

I let my hands fall from Chase's arms. "We can walk you to your car too."

"Cheers guys." Joe reaches across to ruffle my hair affectionately. "I don't even mind being the third wheel for you two. We make a pretty cute tricycle."

Chase releases me from his arms to swat Joe lightly around the back of the head. As the boys begin to laugh and play-fight, I lead the way down the driveway towards the empty street. My arms are wrapped tightly around myself again, but the blush burning my cheeks is warming me plenty. When I glance back finally, Joe has somehow managed to stoop Chase into a headlock, despite the height difference. Laughter bubbles from my lips.

"Just around that corner." Joe nods in the direction of his car, but the grin on his face disappears abruptly as he looks behind me. "Wait, hold on. There's a couple of shady guys."

Chase instantly straightens up.

Alarmed, I turn around and observe the street ahead anxiously. After a few seconds of loaded stillness, there is a movement in the shadows just beyond the halo of the streetlight. As I squint, I'm able to decipher two figures in dark hoods, standing only fifteen yards away on the street corner. The scene is oddly familiar. I watch with fascination as their shadows converge on the sidewalk, and they lean their bodies together to speak intimately.

Chase clears his throat loudly.

The guy facing in our direction looks up at the noise. From underneath the dark hollows of his hood, a pale face stares directly at us. His eyes are coal black in this lighting and his square jaw is darkened with dense stubble. I realize with a fearful pang that I recognize his face from a situation not dissimilar to this one. This is the same man who was dealing weed in the Admiral parking lot, when Chase and Seth left me alone.

Only this time, the offence of our presence is obvious. His face distorts with irritation.

Noticing his friend's reaction, the other guy turns to glance over his shoulder. I only manage to see a shock of dark hair and a familiar expression of annoyance, but a fleeting second is all I need to recognize a face that I know so well. My stomach falls to my feet with dread, and I feel my shoulders slump. *No.*

It's Kaito.

"Get out of here," Joe shouts. "We've already called the cops."

The cowards don't even deliberate for a second. Before I can release my breath, they've already darted in the opposite direction. Trying to chase Kai or shout after him would be fruitless. They're at full sprint by this point. I watch the figures grow smaller and smaller, standing hopelessly in the road. The sky is beginning to spit with rain.

I hate that this scenario is beginning to feel familiar.

I lick my lips to return some moisture to them. A sinking pit of dread churns in my stomach as the wind swipes them dry again. I no longer care about the cold. All I can think about is that I'm going to have to be the one to break the news to Miko. I'm going to have to be the one that disappoints, stresses, and hurts her. She was finally beginning to relax.

He promised.

"Erika," Chase murmurs. The concern is evident in his tone and his hand brushes my arm with notable tentativeness. "What's wrong?"

"It was Kai," I say quietly. "I don't know what he was up to, but he was up to something. He promised that he'd stop with all of this. Miko is finally focusing on herself again! I don't know how I'm supposed to tell her... He could be sent to Washington, I—"

The moment my voice breaks is the moment that his arms find me. He presses me into his body so tightly that I can almost forget that there's a world outside of this embrace. His fingers stroke my back in soothing, lazy rhythms and his lips are pressed into the top of my hair. If I close my eyes and breathe in his smell, everything else fades.

"It's okay," Chase murmurs determinedly into my hair. "We'll fix this, gorgeous."

"I can help too." Joe's chiming voice sounds muffled to my ears. "I can be pretty good at getting information."

"Yeah, we'll scout it out tomorrow," Chase continues, tracing circles over my spine. "Figure out if he's really in trouble before you tell Miko. You want to be sure."

I nod.

"We'll just make sure we have all the information we need before you do anything, okay?" Chase pulls back out of the hug to examine my face. I can only imagine how wearied I look, but I attempt a smile, nonetheless. "Joe and I will help you with this."

"Okay," I mumble. "Thank you."

His molten brown eyes watch me with unwavering tenderness. "Anytime."

My stomach begins to fizz with anticipation as I look up at him, and our silence thickens with delicious tension. That is, until Joe clears his throat.

"I'm going to head to my car now," Joe declares. "So, uh. Give me a shout with the details for tomorrow and ... have fun, I guess?"

Neither of us reply.

"Please remember that Netflix and chill is only one *d* away from Netflix and child!"

"Bye Joe," Chase replies stiffly.

We listen and wait, locked like statues in a frozen embrace, as Joe's footsteps round the corner. The sound ebbs away until all that remains is the tranquility of the empty street and the rain drizzling ceaselessly over our bodies.

"Erika." I've heard him say my name before, but never quite like this. He hooks his finger underneath my chin and directs my face up towards his. I have no choice but to obey; I am utterly helpless. My thoughts have disintegrated into unintelligible, internal screaming. No smartass comments, no capability to tease.

"Yes?" I whisper.

Rainwater clings to his lips like beading.

"I just..."

His dark eyes trail over my face leisurely, lingering on my eyes before moving down to focus on my mouth. He smells like home and his breath is warm in the misty rain. Every part of my body is hyper-conscious of him. I can feel his hands heating my hips through the thin material of my dress. Our chests touching. My pulse thrumming in my ears.

"If I tell you what to do," I whisper, "will you listen, for once?"

"That depends on what it is."

"Kiss me?"

I don't have to ask again.

I'm closing my eyes. Then it's happening.

His lips are soft and damp, and they steal any coherent thought from my brain. All I can focus on is him. The way his lips are gentle, yet urgent. The way his arm tightens around my waist, bringing me impossibly closer. Every movement he makes tells me that he's wanted to do this for as long as I have, and it is blissful. His free hand traces my wet jaw, leaving trails of heat in its wake, before rising to wind itself through my hair.

I've never been kissed like this. I've never *felt* like this during a kiss. I've sunk into him completely, instinctively. My hands are on his strong shoulders, tugging him closer, and then they trace up to the nape of his neck. I feel him shiver. I don't want this to end.

When we finally pull away, we stare at each other in surprise for a few seconds. I can't process that it's happened. His nose brushes mine, and we're both struggling for breath. My arms are flush with goosebumps again, but it's not from the breeze. I know that one of us needs to speak eventually. I know that the moment needs to end.

"Maybe you should listen to me more often," I suggest finally.

And then he smiles.

21

Kai-Spy

"I do love the smell of sexual tension in the morning."

Joe stretches his arms above his head as he yawns, and his fingers hit the ceiling of the car. He's painfully cheery today and it's obvious why.

"People like you are the reason we have middle fingers," I grumble, turning my attention back to Miko's house. We've been positioned here for almost half an hour, with no sign of movement from Kaito yet. Admittedly, this is not the most efficient plan, but no other suggestions were made. We could end up playing lookout for hours. Who's to say that Kaito is even awake yet? He could even be out of the house already.

The only silver lining to this situation is that by forcing myself to focus on Miko's front door consistently, I have a welcome excuse to avoid looking at Chase, who is sitting directly beside me. He must have told Joe about the kiss. There's no other reason that we'd be attracting so much teasing. Well, more so than usual.

"Don't worry," Joe says, placing a comforting hand on my

shoulder. He squeezes gently. "I'll stop. You can *kiss* the jokes goodbye now."

"Punny," I respond, twisting in my seat to glare at him.

"Now, now, Erika, don't *peck* my head off."

I woke up on cloud nine this morning, thinking about that kiss. I was practically giddy with desperation to see Chase again. Now I can't even look at him because Joe is making this entire situation so uncomfortable. That isn't even the toughest part. Now that I've kissed Chase once, all I can think of is how much I want to do it again. I squeeze my hands together as the images of Chase's hands in my hair flood irrepressibly through my mind.

"Okay that's it," Violet says, dropping her phone to her lap. She was a late addition to the plan, and she's spent the majority of the time texting, but I'm still grateful to have another female presence in the car. Her hand finds the back of my seat and her eyes narrow with accusation. "I've missed something, haven't I? What's happened?"

Joe gasps delightedly. He's going to take pleasure in this. "You don't know?"

"No, she doesn't," I mutter. I pull my sweater sleeves down over my hand, forcing myself to focus on that movement and not my confused friend. "Not yet."

I haven't even told Miko yet, let alone anybody else. I should have—Miko would have told me by now, had it been her. I guess the moment I shared with Chase last night just felt too private. I wanted to keep it as our little secret for a while, to shelter us from the onslaught of jibes and jabs from our friends. I knew that the first question the girls would ask is what Chase said to me about his feelings, our relationship, anything.

And . . . he didn't say much of anything.

"Well." Joe's smug voice snaps me out of my reverie. "Last night, Chase and Erika surrendered to their inner longings."

"What?" The alarm in Violet's tone is understandable.

"They kissed last night. Apparently, it was one hell of a kiss, too."

"Joe." Chase finally snaps, his eyes narrowing on his best friend. It's the first time he's spoken. The expression on his face matches his dark sweatshirt: moody. "Cut it out."

One hell of a kiss. I feel a surge of pride as I realize that Chase must have described our moment very positively. My sour expression morphs into a lazy grin. Chase glances over at me, his frown faltering for a second. Noticing my self-satisfaction, he groans and resumes staring at the door. Joe has struck a chord.

"One hell of a kiss, hey?" I brag.

"He described fireworks," Joe adds. "He said he'd never felt more alive."

"I heard that Erika could do that to a man," Violet confirms.

"He said he felt sorry for the people that will never know what it's like to kiss her."

"It really is a cruel world."

"He said that her lips are like a drug."

"Well then, he's definitely an addict."

"He said he's going to make himself a mistletoe hat."

"It'll be like Christmas every day."

"He said—"

"Okay, okay, I know how talented I am," I interrupt before Joe can make another jibe. I have now entirely neglected my duty to watch Miko's door, because Chase's glowering expression is much more interesting. "Can you even stand being this close to me, Squidge?"

"This is all very funny," Chase says sarcastically. "But haven't we got a job to do?"

I'm just happy I'm not the one being teased. I'll jump on this bandwagon if it saves me from being the butt of the jokes.

Joe shakes his head and tuts. "Erika, tell your boyfriend to loosen up a bit."

"Shut up, Joe."

"He's not my boyfriend," I reply, rolling my eyes. As soon as the words have left my mouth, I realize that I may have just said something wrong. My posture stiffens, and my hands curl around my thighs as I make every effort to avoid looking at Chase. We haven't talked about anything serious yet. He's not my boyfriend. He can't be. Right?

"Not yet," Violet says, snorting.

The conversation dies away into awkward silence, and we all resume our task of staring at the house. It's boring work, and Joe's whining and grumbling isn't making it any more enjoyable. As I'm about to classify this plan as a colossal waste of time, the front door opens. A few seconds pass, and Kai emerges. He surveys the street superficially, but his eyes gloss over the details.

He strides down the driveway, oblivious to our watching eyes.

"It's showtime boys," Violet whispers.

It takes about twenty minutes for Kaito to walk to his destination: a small, secluded playground at the edge of Lindale, where the town meets the forest.

Sheltered within a clearing of fir trees, and remarkably

unpopulated on a Sunday morning, it's the perfect location to conduct secret affairs. Kai sits alone on a swing with his hands clasped on his lap and his hood pulled up. He rocks back and forwards gently, as if to lull away his anxieties. It feels almost intrusive to watch him.

"We shouldn't be doing this," I mutter, trying to look around me without being poked in the eye by a branch. We're crouched in a line around the perimeter of the playground, disguised by a gnarled shrub. I can only imagine how strange we look to anyone behind us.

"If he's broken his promise, then Miko needs to know," Chase says quietly. "Better to scout it out and know for sure than to rush in and falsely accuse him."

"What if he saw me yesterday?"

"I'm pretty certain that he didn't," Joe reassures me.

"Shh, there's someone coming over," Violet hisses, peering over the foliage.

Sure enough, as I push back the branches to examine the scene, I notice a tall stranger approaching the swing set. Unlike Kaito, his hood is not raised to hide his face, leaving his dirty blond hair and sullen expression exposed. I realize instantaneously where I recognize his face. Although there's no trace of the blood remaining, his nose is still identifiably crooked from the impact of my foot.

"Maxi-pad," Chase whispers. "That's Max Tennyson."

"The guy you got in a fight with?" Violet asks, palms on the ground and leaning towards us so that her voice doesn't carry.

"The guy I kicked in the face for grabbing my leg," I correct smugly. "Can't really call it a fight if I floored him with one move."

Joe raises his hand for a high five and I slap it proudly, but quietly.

The two delinquents are now sitting side by side on the swings, only a few yards away. Although we're close enough to hear what they're saying in theory, the ambient noise from the playground complicates our plan. The main disadvantage of this spot is the cuts and bruises that I've accumulated just from squeezing in here. Plus, I'm terrified that there's a spider somewhere nearby. *Charlotte's Web* is like a horror movie to me.

"Can you hear what they're saying?" I murmur to Joe. I'm straining my own ears to hear them, but unfortunately there's a couple of noisier families on the opposite side of the playground who easily eclipse their murmured conversation. I'm coiled like a spring as I peer through the bush, and equally tense. Can those children stop giggling for a second? I fight the urge to march over and inform them that the see-saw isn't as hilarious as they make out.

Joe shushes my low grumbling, and I scowl. It's not my fault that he picked the worst hiding place in history, and we can't even hear their conversation.

"I think they're talking about stock," Chase whispers. His eyes don't deviate from the targets. "Could be flock, or rock, or clock, though, for all I know."

"Kai is wringing his hands together," I note. "I think he's frustrated."

"What is Max saying? I can't make anything out," Violet adds.

I force my head further between the branches in attempt to get a better view, but I can't see well from this angle. Beside me, Joe has his tilted his head uncomfortably between two bars of the perimeter fence. If Kai looks now, Joe will look like a decapitated head amongst the shrubbery. I can't help but smile at the thought.

"Max isn't really saying anything, but he doesn't look happy..." Joe chuckles, and the sound is muffled within the dense leaves. "I'd be lying if I said I wasn't enjoying this. I feel like part of Mystery Incorporated."

"That makes sense," Violet comments. "You do look like a bush monster."

I poke Joe's shoulder lightly. "Try and figure out what he's saying, Scooby-Doo."

"Okay, okay. Give me a second."

He pushes further. It's a good job that the fence bars are quite spaced out, or we could imprison him here forever. I can feel my knees aching from kneeling for too long. I'm pretty sure I'm resting on a stone. I wait impatiently, examining a small ant trotting his way across the patio a meter or so ahead of us. I bet that ant can hear their conversation.

"Kaito is saying that he doesn't want to keep the stuff anymore," Joe mutters.

I glance up at him, ant forgotten. "What do you mean?"

"He's worried about his family finding out." Pause. "Max isn't having any of it."

"What?" My voice lowers with dread. Even Violet is grimacing uneasily. What if Max hurts him? I have no understanding of the depth of trouble that Kai is in, or how to help him get out. If he's involved with real dealers ... I shiver at the prospect.

"Max just gave him a couple of little bags," Chase says softly. "Kai put them in his pocket. He's taken them."

The sinking feeling in my chest materializes through in

my body, and I slump out of my kneeling position to collapse on the ground. "So that's it then. I was right."

"That's it." Violet reaches over to squeeze my hand. "And you need to tell Miko."

"She's going to be so stressed," I whisper despairingly. "I don't understand—"

I'm interrupted by the sensation of something crawling up my bare leg.

Before I can help myself, I release a loud scream.

A giant, thick-legged spider is walking over my skin. Powered by sheer horror and adrenaline, I launch myself backwards and begin to scramble out of the bush. My hair catches on the twigs, shooting pain through my scalp as it snags, but I am uncaring. All I can focus on is getting that thing *off* me. I land in the grass, breathing heavily. The beat of my heart sounds like helicopter blades, and I wonder how it hasn't torn free from my body.

Violet and Chase are wearing panicked expressions as they scrabble out of the bush.

In the meantime, Joe is standing up. In full view of everyone.

"What's he doing?" I hiss. We are sheltered behind the bush, completely clear of anyone's view. Joe Travis, in contrast, is standing in broad daylight and full sight of everyone in the playground. Including Kai and Max.

He releases a shockingly girlish scream.

I begin to laugh.

"Help me!" Joe screams. "I just dropped my phone and I think there's a snake in the bush!"

By this point, I've figured out that he's covering for my scream, to let us escape from sight. Kaito might not recognize Joe, but if he sees me then he'll know instantly that he's been caught. He knows that I will tell Miko. Chase grabs my wrist again and with a silent nod of agreement, we begin to shuffle in the direction of the forest cover.

I struggle to contain my laughter as Joe flaps around. A woman has seized her purse and is hitting the bush madly, trying to shoo the "snake" away and cursing frantically in French. Meanwhile, the playground is in chaos. Children are wailing in horror, a mother is clutching a baby to her bosom and Joe Travis is standing at the edge of our previous hiding place, releasing repeated high-pitched screams.

He may be a goofball, but I think he just saved the day.

"This coconut latte is downright sexy," Miko announces, placing her glass back down onto the table between us. She runs a tongue over her top lip, catching the milk moustache that had been sitting there. "Freaking sexy, I tell you."

"Not as sexy as you."

"Erika, if we compared everything to me, the world would be a very ugly place."

I chuckle, watching Miko as she tears open the top of a second sugar packet. She tentatively pours half of the packet into her mug, smiling down at it like an artist admiring their work. I will never understand those odd people that can't round up to a whole teaspoon. Miko likes one and *a half* sugars in her coffee. Extra, extra hot.

I think she enjoys being problematic.

"So, what's up?" she asks.

I reach down for my bitter cappuccino. The baristas in this coffee shop always stencil out the shape of a different leaf in the chocolate powder dusted on top—it's one of the reasons that I like this place so much. Today's leaf is an oak, and the coffee is so pretty that I almost don't want to take the first sip. I do, though—it's always worth it.

Sweet Traditions Café is nestled on a street corner in town. It's no bigger than my kitchen at home, but the hanging plants, woven rugs, and cracked leather couches make the space feel magical. Miko loves it for the Instagram appeal—it's a gorgeous backdrop.

"I have something to tell you," I say uneasily, placing my glass back down.

"Okay. Shoot."

I exhale sharply and obey. "Kai is keeping weed again."

Miko stills. Although the spoon in her drink is now motionless, the liquid still swirls and rages with momentum. She looks up at me slowly. "What?"

I explain everything. The encounter last night on the dark street, the agreement to gather information and evidence, and the definitive proof that we saw at the park. By the time I'm finished talking, my mouth is parched again, and I reach for another sip of coffee. It takes me a couple of seconds to realize that Miko has no intention of responding. She's staring down at her coffee, stirring absentmindedly, although the sugar will be long dissolved by now.

"Mickey?"

"Yeah, sorry," she murmurs, dropping the spoon. She looks up and I can see the tiredness in her eyes. Suddenly my worry is growing threefold. "I just fazed out for a minute. I thought this was finally over with."

"I know. I'm so sorry."

Miko ducks her head, taking the abandoned spoon from her coffee and placing it on the table. Her voice is strained.

"I know that you had good intentions ... but the next time that you get involved in my family's problems, please have the courtesy to involve me too. Especially before all of our friends."

Her point hits me like a kick to the chest. Of *course*, that was the wrong thing to do. Why would I think that it was okay to take her issue into my own hands?

"I'm so sorry, Miko," I whisper. "I never thought about it like that."

"I forgive you. Just please don't do it again." She offers me a small, encouraging smile. "He's my brother and I deserve to know what's happening, every step of the way."

"Yes, you absolutely do."

I examine her face closely, searching for signs of distress, but Miko's features have relaxed. Guilt festers in my stomach. Hurting her feelings is the worst regret in the world.

I reach back down for my coffee, purely for the sake of holding it. I cradle it in my hands as a form of support, and the warmth radiates through my palms. There's something so reassuring about a hot mug.

"I love you. I'm here for you, Miko."

"I know that," she says, nodding. "I'll have to speak to Okan about it later."

"What do you think she'll do?"

"Scream at him," Miko admits, looking abashedly to the window. "Yell at him about how disappointed she is. She'll tell him that he needs to go and live with Dad, and he'll fight that tooth and nail. Everything will be horrible." Miko squints her eyes shut with discomfort.

"I'm so sorry." My voice is hoarse.

"Yes." Miko clears her throat and angles her face upwards, still unable to look me directly in the eye. "But it's the decision he made. He will have to suffer the consequences."

"Kai knows you love him, and that you'll do anything to help him." I reach forward to clasp my best friend's hand. "You're such a good sister, Miko. You're an angel."

Miko's eyes gloss with tears.

"I hope so," she says brokenly.

"Come here," I murmur.

I hurriedly place my mug back down to the table and extend my arms to my best friend. Miko sniffs and stands up to move onto my couch, cuddling up beside me. She loops her legs up onto the cushions and places her face into my collarbone, hidden from the view of the window. My arms automatically wrap around her shoulders. I can feel the damp patch growing on my T-shirt and her shallow breaths.

"Let it all out, shh."

Miko releases a hiccupping sob, and then the dam opens. She clutches me tightly as she cries, and I let her sob all over my T-shirt while I press kisses to her forehead. I can't imagine what she's going through, I really can't, but my chest hurts to watch her like this.

"You're so selfless," I murmur into her hair. "The kindest person I know."

"I know he's a nightmare, but I really don't want him to move away."

"Of course, you don't."

I hold her for another minute while she collects herself and steadies her breathing. When she pulls back, she sniffs and looks down. There's a black pool of moisture beneath her eyes, tinted with mascara. She runs her fingers underneath to catch it, only to smudge some further up towards her eyebrow. I lick my thumb quickly and dab it onto her face to catch the last, reluctant black smear. Good as new.

Miko cracks a weak smile. "You're such a good friend."

"I don't feel like it. I'm so sorry, Miko," I say softly. "Is there anything I can do to help the situation? Anything at all. You just say the words."

Miko takes a deep breath, leaning back into the cushions on the couch and brushing her hair from her face. A few stray strands stick to the tears on her cheeks. "I can take it from here. This will be good for him. I know I don't seem like it but I'm a big, brave girl."

"I know you are. You should've seen the spider that was on my leg earlier. It was huge, and it had legs hairier than yours," I tease. "I wasn't brave at all."

"Oh, no."

Miko's face suddenly crumples, and my teasing tone disappears instantly. Clearly, I misjudged the atmosphere.

"What's up, Miko? What's wrong?"

She slaps her hand onto the arm of the sofa, frustrated.

"My latte is going to be cold," she whines.

I stare at her in utter surprise. Her lips quirk into a small smile.

"Fancy getting me another?"

22

The Right Name

The intercom crackles with static as it reverberates through the school grounds.

"Erika Monroe, proceed to the principal's office immediately."

I shut my locker door slowly. There was something uncanny about that message. Brian's upbeat and animated voice was unusually robotic, and he didn't say please. He always says please. I turn to scrutinize my surroundings, to see if anybody else noticed the change in tone. A couple of girls across the hallway are watching me with curiosity, but their heads turn sheepishly to the wall when I stare back.

Nobody else seems to be paying attention. Maybe I'm just being overly paranoid.

Wrestling with my illogical unease, I sling my bag over my shoulder and begin to trudge in the direction of the principal's office. The thought of another confrontation with Blythe has soured my mood and filled me with apprehension. I have no idea what excuse I will fabricate this time to divert her misguided attack on Chase, and I don't have time to come up with one in the duration of this walk. No choice remains but to woman up and tell Blythe how twisted her objective is.

As I'm nearing the reception, while other students are filtering away to their classes, I realize why the intercom message felt so unnatural. It wasn't the tone, or the lack of manners.

For the first time in three and a half years, Brian said my name right.

I'm analyzing the potential significance of this detail when I notice Miko standing just outside of the reception. She's staring at me. Her arms are hanging limply by her sides and her face is crumpled with stress and despair. Immediately, my pace quickens.

"Miko?" I say hurriedly. "What's wrong?"

"I tried to stop him." She glances frantically at the reception door. "He must have overheard us talking about the video. I... he took my phone, Erika, I don't..."

Icy dread engulfs my body in an instant.

"What video?" My voice is a raw whisper.

Miko watches me helplessly. Her lips struggle to shape the right words—excuses, explanations—but her voice can't follow through. My breath is stuck in my throat, aching like a boiled candy that I've swallowed too quickly. I want to demand that she tell me that this is a prank, a lie, a big wind-up. But her silence has never been so tangible. The reception door opens, and Brian leans out with a somber expression. His tie is crooked.

"Erika, you're needed in the office now."

I nod faintly.

As I turn to enter the air-conditioned reception, Miko's hand grazes the back of my arm. I don't turn around. The churn of disconcertment in my stomach has intensified into nausea. I'm trembling but it has little to do with the temperature of the room. The door to the principal's office seems to tower over me with novel height. I wonder if this will be the last time that I ever see it.

With numb hands, I push it open.

Principal Blythe is nestled comfortably in her leather chair, one leg crossed neatly over the other. Her auburn hair is pinned into an elegant updo, emphasizing the sharp features of her face. Fully loaded gray eyes detect my presence, and she straightens her posture for attack. In the seat opposite her, with his hands fisted around the wooden arms of his chair, is a brunette boy. He twists around to see me, and my worst fears are confirmed.

Chase Thatcher is positioned in her firing line.

Any remaining hope I have dissolves in the acidic taste on my tongue.

"Take a seat, Erika. We've been waiting for you."

I collapse into the chair beside Chase, and my bag falls to the ground with a clunk. The nauseous feeling has climbed up to my chest. My heart squeezes agonizingly when I consider that in the following conversation, he will discover my betrayal. He will hurt.

"Erika?" Chase leans sideways. His voice is a nervous mumble. "What's going on?"

The pain in my chest intensifies. I am forced to glare at the wall to my left and blink rapidly to keep my stinging tears at bay. I can't possibly articulate an answer that would encompass how sorry I am, how much I care about him and how big my mistake was. So, instead, I remain silent. Chase moves back into his previous position.

"I'll answer your question, shall I?" Blythe says, leaning forwards eagerly. She rests her elbows on the desk and laces her fingers together in front of her pursed lips. "An anonymous student came to me this morning to submit footage of you both in the swimming pool after hours. A building that is locked every day after swim practice."

She pauses to assess us both in turn, her eyebrow arched in an expression of distaste. "As I'm sure you already know, breaking and entering school property is strictly prohibited. I'm immensely disappointed in both of you for being so irresponsible."

I risk a sideways glance at Chase. His body has slumped into the stiff chair and his face is painted with bewilderment. I want to reach out, but I know that if I move my hands from their knotted grip on my sweater, they will betray me by quivering.

Blythe's voice is frosty. "Would either of you care to give me an explanation?"

"No," I choke out. "No explanation. It was a mistake, and we are so sorry."

I sense Chase looking at me. It takes all my energy to avoid looking back.

"How did the person obtain the footage?" he says finally, turning his attention back to the principal. My cheek feels cold without the warmth of his gaze. I release a slow, shaky breath. "Surely that means that they were in the building after hours, too?"

Blythe shakes her head, and a stray piece of hair falls from her perfect chignon. She corrects it immediately. "The individual who came to me didn't film the footage. They found a memory stick, which had been discarded in the library."

My wandering gaze settles upon a navy USB stick, resting smugly atop a pile of sticky notes. For something so small, it will have a devastating impact.

"Right," Chase mutters.

I thank my lucky stars that Miko is safe, and that Kai protected her. I wouldn't be able to cope with the guilt of knowing that my selfish motivations dragged two of my favorite people into hot water. I haven't yet figured out how I'm going to cope with just one. The prospect of Miko getting in trouble for trying to support me is just too much to bear.

"Do you have anything else you want to say?"

"It was a stupid thing to do. It won't happen again," Chase professes.

"Okay." Blythe drops her hands from their poised position and places them flat on the table. "As punishment for your behavior, the school board and I have made the decision to suspend you from Lindale High for the remaining duration of this week. You must leave the school grounds immediately after this meeting. Do not return until Monday morning."

My right leg begins to quiver uncontrollably.

I don't quite know how to interpret the vehemence of my reaction to the news that we have escaped expulsion. Part of me is relieved. Despite the intent behind that video, Chase's prospects haven't been entirely sabotaged. He can still come to school on Monday—work hard, see his friends, and plan his future. Another part of me is crushed. A suspension is still a permanent mark on his record and a punishment he doesn't deserve to suffer. This will always be on my conscience. This is entirely my fault.

Chase is watching my shaking leg.

"Consider this suspension as a warning," Blythe continues. "If something like this happens again, I will have no choice but to consider expulsion."

Her words drip with command. Kaito may not have provided evidence extreme enough for the school board to agree to expel Chase, but with one more strike, he is hers. Undoubtedly, she'll manipulate some naïve, ambitious student into doing the work for her, just as easily as she did with me. Laughter of sheer disbelief bubbles up my throat.

Could this woman be any more calculating? Any more unscrupulous?

Her eyes narrow. "Something funny, Erika?"

"No," I say, sobering up quickly. "Painful, actually."

The principal pushes her chair back and promptly stands. Her face stretches into a smile so thin that it's practically transparent, revealing the malice hiding beneath. "Unless you have any urgent questions, I think that it's time that you both left my office and begin your week of suspension. We will meet again on Monday morning before you start classes."

Chase and I collect our belongings and rise from our seats. He manages to escape this suffocating room before Blythe addresses us again, but I am less lucky.

"Oh, and Erika?"

I feel my skin prickle with goosebumps. I stop and clear my throat before I turn around, but it has little effect on the obstinate lump of anxiety clinging there. "Yeah?"

Principal Blythe is leaning over her chair and gathering papers on her desk. Her smile is vindictive as she studies me. "I won't be needing your help anymore. Thank you."

I know what those words mean.

Too overwhelmed to form a response, I turn and stumble out of the office. In the bright light of the reception, I close my eyes and sink back against the nearest wall. My breathing is strained, and my hands are tingling. I squeeze my rucksack in my arms like a lifeline. A presence appears in front of me.

"What's going on?" Chase asks in a quiet, yet firm tone.

I don't want to open my eyes, but eventually, I have to.

He's standing only a few feet away. His hair is unusually messy, tugged in various directions, and his expression is tender with confusion. The sight of his frown almost breaks my heart. He deserves to know the truth, and he deserves to be aware. I can't make the same mistake that I did with Miko—protecting her by keeping her in the dark. This is perhaps the only remaining control I have over the mess which I created.

This is the right thing to do; it always was.

"I heard what she said," Chase says. "She said you were helping her."

Brian isn't at his desk. We're alone in the room.

Swallowing the bile rising up my throat, I focus my attention on the bewitching brown eyes of the boy standing in front of me. My dad always taught me that if you want to apologize to somebody, you should look them in the eye and speak from your chest.

"Before I tell you everything," I answer finally. "I want you to know that I care about you so much. I have been selfish and dishonest, and I am unbelievably sorry for that."

"What are you talking about?"

Deep breath ... one, two, three. Bite the bullet.

"Blythe wants to expel you," I confess, suffocating my rucksack in my arms. "She came to me at the beginning of the semester and told me about all the trouble that you've been in. She promised that she could get me a scholarship for Stanford if ... if I would provide evidence suitable for your expulsion. She blackmailed me."

"She ... she, what?" Disoriented, Chase shakes his head repeatedly. "What?"

"I realized pretty quickly that I couldn't do it to you." The words, once so difficult to formulate, are now free flowing. A psychological dam has been demolished, and all the guilt and the deception I've been holding in for over a month pours out in a torrential flood. "But she manipulated and threatened me. My plan was to convince her that you didn't deserve expulsion ... but all of the Kai stuff got in the way, and then—"

"Wait," Chase interrupts, lifting a hand. "You mean to tell me that this entire time that we've been hanging out, you've been trying to get me expelled?"

"Not the entire time." I can hear my panic escalate in my own voice, and I step closer to him. "I couldn't do it. I was trying to change her mind about you."

Chase stumbles backwards. His expression is twisted with revulsion, and it cuts through me like a hot knife through butter. "Does that mean the video is yours?"

"Miko was in the swimming stands," I confirm quietly. I can feel the shame weighing on me physically—slumping my shoulders and pushing me into the shrunken posture of humiliation. "I planned the video, but I never intended for it to get into Blythe's hands. I never even got close to sending it, Chase."

"Because it incriminates you?" Chase laughs bitterly. His hands fly up to his face and cup protectively over his eyes. "I can't believe this. I can't. I can't believe *you*."

"No, because I didn't want you to be expelled!"

"Why does this woman want to expel me anyway?" Chase asks incredulously, flinging his hands back down again. His cheeks are red and flushed. "I don't understand! I'm a straight A student, I work a part-time job most weekends, and I don't get into trouble unless it's for talking in class. I'm not exactly a daredevil!"

"I ... what?" I frown. "No, no. She said that you were a vandal ... you kept drugs and were prone to violent outbursts. She said that you were a scar on the school's reputation."

"She *what*?"

I stumble over my words. "She, um. She said that you were a delinquent."

Chase's lip curls into a sneer. He laces his fingers through the front of his hair and tugs. "You know me pretty well by now, Erika. Does that match my description?"

"Um, well ..." I hesitate as I consider my impression of Chase. "What about the graffiti? Breaking into the pool? Taking me to a dodgy bar across town?"

"I only did all of those things because I thought that was what you wanted from me!"

"No," I argue. "No way. Why would you do that?"

"Because—I don't know," Chase exclaims, throwing his arms out. "Because I was sick of tedious dates and killing time by walking around the park? Because it was nice to do something exciting for once? And hey—maybe even because a little part of me wanted to impress you."

I shake my head.

"Yes, Erika!"

As much as I try to resist the harrowing realization, it seeps through me like a chill. Chase may go to the shady side of town and circulate with drag racers and tough cookies, but he never partakes in the events. I haven't seen him touch drugs; I've only seen him receive detention once and his grades are always immaculate. He vandalized Blythe's car, but Joe gave him the paints ... Blythe's deceit dissolves more with each memory, until I'm left with the stinging realization that the image I had of Chase was entirely fabricated.

"So, you're not a delinquent," I admit finally. "But why would she be so desperate to expel you if it wasn't for your behavior? She didn't even know you."

"Probably because she knows that I've seen the shady stuff she gets up to," Chase replies, with a hostile shrug. "You know, the host of visitors that fill up the parking lot late at night? That was going on even before the semester started."

"No." My statement is weak. "No. No way."

"There's no other explanation, Erika. I'm not a bad kid."

"No, no, it can't be to do with that."

"Yes, Erika. This woman has got a personal vendetta against me, and she used you as her pawn. And the worst part is that you *believed* her."

I can hear the hurt in his voice. Guilt strangles me. "I—"

"So, you're just like everybody else," Chase continues, his

voice quietening. His eyes are glossy with unshed tears. Any excuses I have disintegrate under the heat of his glare. "You had one look at me, and you knew that I was dispensable. Easy to get rid of. You decided that I was worth expelling before you even met me."

"Chase—"

"I told you about my family." His voice cracks. "I showed you stuff that I don't show to anybody. How could you stand there and let me spill my hardest truths while knowing that you were exploiting me?"

He looks down at the floor.

"I'm so sorry." My voice trembles. "I'm so sorry. I was so wrong, Chase."

"I wish you hadn't lied to me," Chase says thickly. "That's the worst part. It takes me a lot to trust, and I trusted you. I don't let anyone see me, but you did."

"You still can trust me," I plead. My eyes are prickling with tears, and I have to fight to restrain my sob. "I was trying to stop this from happening. I wanted to protect you."

Chase shakes his head adamantly. "You're not the person that I thought you were."

These words are the most agonizing yet. The warm tears spill onto my cheeks and my sob is loud and desperate.

"I'm not going anywhere, remember? I'm still here and I still care about you."

"Okay."

For a split second, I feel a spark of hope. However, it is quickly extinguished when he tightens his grip on his rucksack strap. His lips are pressed into a firm line.

"I guess I'll be the one to go this time, then. Goodbye, Erika."

He brushes past my arm on his way to the door. The contact is brutally familiar.

I don't see him leave the room because my vision is too blurred with tears, but I hear the door click shut. It feels like the last punctuation mark at the end of a heartbreaking novel. Then, the only sounds remaining are the mechanical whir of the air conditioning fan and the high-pitched gasps and whimpers of my own making.

"Can I get you a Kleenex?"

I look up to see Brian lingering in the reception doorway. I didn't hear him enter. He's wearing his usual crumpled jeans alongside a panicked expression that I'd probably find funny if not for the circumstances. He points awkwardly at the blue box of Kleenex on his desk. Wiping away my tears roughly with the back of my hand, I release a hollow laugh.

"I think I'd need the whole box, but thank you."

"Take as many as you need," he says, waving his hand dismissively. He attempts a smile, but it's all teeth. "I'm supposed to tell you to leave the school grounds immediately, but your friend is waiting outside for you. I'll turn a blind eye for a couple of minutes."

"Thanks, Brian," I mumble. As I stand up from the chair, my limbs ache and complain as if I've been sitting for hours upon end, instead of a measly ten minutes.

"Don't mention it."

He squeezes my shoulder sympathetically as I walk past him. Slinging my rucksack onto my back, I leave the reception to greet my awaiting best friend.

She is leaning against the wall beside the door, one leg

folded up and her lip between her teeth. When she notices me, her foot drops to the ground.

"Erika," she rushes out. "There you are. I was so worried—"

"Please just don't," I interrupt. My voice is tired, and I don't have the energy to raise my volume. "I just can't listen to it right now. I want to go home."

Miko leans back. "Listen to what?"

"Anything." I look over at the exit doors. "Explanations, consolation, apologies."

"Apologies?" she echoes. "What do I have to apologize for?"

"I don't know, you tell me." I move to brush past her, but she steps into my path. Her berry-colored Doc Martens split into a wide, unwavering stance.

"Why are you mad at me, Erika?"

I can feel my irritation upsurging. I sidestep her and try to move towards the exit again, but she blocks me again.

"Miko, I can't have this conversation right now."

"Just tell me," she demands.

"No."

"Tell me."

"You're really going to make me talk about this now?"

"Yes, I want to know," Miko snaps.

"Fine!" I explode, propelling myself away from her. "You want to talk? It happened on your watch, Miko! He got into *your* phone."

"Yes, Erika, he got into my phone." She speaks through gritted teeth. "He clearly already knew that the video existed, so he stole my phone, and he knew my passcode."

"Okay." I shrug.

"Okay, so what about it?"

"Okay so you're telling me that you were completely powerless to stop him?" I say scathingly, wrinkling my nose. "You couldn't have sent me a warning text or anything?"

"Erika, you're missing the part where I said he *took* my phone. I still don't have it—I was waiting outside of the damn reception for you so that I could warn you!"

"And what about the other thing?"

"What about the other thing?" she asks indignantly.

"Were you really powerless to stop him?"

For a split moment, Miko hesitates. That moment is enough for my vexation to increase tenfold. I step towards her, my voice laced with accusation.

"Or did you let him walk all over you again?"

"Erika," she says in a low, warning voice. Her hands are knotted into fists by her side.

"You need to tell him to grow up, Miko!" I say, stepping closer still. "He knows exactly what he's doing, but by treating him like a kid all the time, you're just enabling him to act like one! It's no wonder he doesn't listen to you!"

My best friend glares at me with rage in her eyes, but her lips remain pressed tightly together. Her weapon is silence, and it is the most effective tool in her disposal. Without her fiery rebuttal, my insult hangs in the air uncomfortably. An unjustified attack. In seconds, most of my anger has dissipated. Without the haze of red coloring my thoughts, I can see the situation clearly, and the guilt sets in.

My best friend stands in front of me, her chest heaving up and down with effort. She knew that I was lashing out at her because I was hurting, but she chose to stay and take the brunt of it. She remained standing there, despite all I said.

"Miko," I whisper. "I'm s—"

"Go home, Erika."

With bowed shoulders, she turns on her heel and walks away.

I feel the familiar dry burn of oncoming tears, and I wonder how it's possible that I have any left to cry. Miko's retreat is unbearable to watch. The concoction of guilt, anxiety, and regret churns and gurgles in my stomach like poison. I have poisoned myself with the way that I have acted, the manner in which I have treated the people I care most about. I know that I need to leave school before I'm escorted out, but I can't stand the thought of staggering home alone.

Before I'm even conscious of my intent, I begin walking towards Chloe's office.

My walk is slow and disjointed, but it prevents me from thinking too much. I'm lucky that first class has already begun, because if people saw me like this, they'd likely think I was under the influence. I can already picture the concerned stares, the muffled laughter.

By the time I reach Chloe's door, I don't have the self-control or patience to knock. I throw my entire body weight into the wood, expecting it to swing open as it usually does. However, the door holds firm. The only sign that I've pushed it at all is the rattle of a lock.

It's locked? Where is she?

Confused, I stand on my tiptoes to peer through the glass panel at the top of the door. The office is gloomy with shadow; the blinds are still drawn. Did she not come into work this morning? Her desk, usually cluttered with homely knick-knacks and coffee mugs, is clear aside from a large cardboard box. Where is she? Why is she not here?

I sink back onto the heels of my feet. Why, at the time that I need her the most, has my sister left me alone too? Barely suppressing the wave of emotion threatening to overwhelm me, I turn in the direction of the school exit.

I clutch my aching arm and begin the long and lonely journey home.

23

Call Me Out

The whispering outside of my bedroom door is my first indication that my parents are home.

I hit the space bar on my laptop to pause my Netflix show and listen. My mother's erratic whispers are the easiest to decipher. I can hear odd words like "hell" and "irresponsible" and "trespassing": enough to piece together that Blythe has told her everything. At least that saves me a job. Meanwhile, Dad is making soothing, humming noises in a futile attempt to calm her down. He should know by now that when my mom is truly furious, she wields the detonative force of a nuclear bomb. No survivors remain.

Three soft knocks at my bedroom door. Then, it is pushed open slowly and my dad appears in the doorway, cradling a coffee mug. He's wearing his after-work clothing: a pair of faded blue jeans and his thick, fluffy socks. His T-shirt is pink, with an animated pug on the chest pocket. He assesses me with kind eyes, but his sigh reveals his disappointment.

"What the hell happened, kid?"

He hands me the mug of coffee, and I thank him with a

smile. Then, pushing away a pile of clothes at the foot of my bed, he takes a seat. My room was reasonably clean this morning, but sad people are always messy. There are clothes, chocolate wrappers, and Kleenexes surrounding me in my cocoon of bedsheets, but I can't bring myself to care about that.

I take a sip of the hot coffee. It eases my sore throat slightly.

"I wouldn't know where to start," I confess.

"Okay, okay." Dad grimaces, rubbing his temples to alleviate his stress. I can tell he's disappointed in me, and it hurts. "Well, your mom wants to talk to you about it. She ... uh ..."

"Wants to pulverize me?" I finish.

"Not far off." He cracks a wonky smile, then reaches across to squeeze my foot through the thick comforter. "She wants the best for you, just remember that."

"I know."

"Good. I'll leave you two to talk." Dad brushes down his knees and stands up from the bed. He attempts a stern expression, but it never really looks right with his friendly face. "And Erika? I know I'm not good at the discipline thing, but don't do that again. You know so much better."

I thought that my emotions had almost numbed by this point, but I was mistaken. Unable to summon words, I answer him by nodding. It seems to satisfy him, and he leaves the room without another word. Although my father rarely gets mad at me, his disappointment feels infinitely worse. After placing my coffee mug on my bedside table, I bury myself further under the blankets.

"Erika?"

Mom's greeting is sour. I hear the sound of the drapes opening; rings scraping against the chrome rail. Then, after a few seconds of peace, a hand is peeling my safeguard blankets away. The late afternoon light attacks my eyes and I shrink backwards, my arm flying over my face protectively. "Come on, get out from under there. I want to talk to you."

"You don't have to say anything," I mumble. "I *know*."

"No, you don't know." A weight sinks onto the foot of my bed and I lift my arm away from my eyes to see my mom glowering at me. She's still wearing her navy blazer and shirt from work, but her blond hair is messily escaping from the claw clip at the back of her head. "I don't know what's been going on with you recently, Erika. The detention and lack of focus is one thing, but breaking into school property? What the hell were you thinking?"

"I was thinking of all the ways that I could best disappoint you," I respond sarcastically. Then, I lift a finger and mime an epiphany. "Ah wait, I forgot! I don't even have to try."

"No, Erika. You're not allowed to get snarky with me this time," Mom warns. "You completely crossed the line."

"I know I messed up!" I say frustratedly, smacking my hand down on the comforter. "I am painfully aware. You can save yourself the time and energy of this conversation, Mom, because you cannot possibly make me feel worse about myself than I already do."

"What could you possibly want to break into the pool for anyway? This doesn't sound like you, Erika, I don't see how you could be so careless."

"I don't know! We were messing about, Mom."

"Messing about? What about Stanford?" she demands.

I wince at the mention of Stanford. Thus far, I have

successfully avoided thinking about how this suspension will affect my college résumé. It's been easy to remain preoccupied by my shattered relationships with my two best friends, but this predicament is glaring at me, and I can't ignore it forever. Without Blythe's assistance, or even her respect, my chances of being accepted to my dream college have slimmed considerably. Yet it feels selfish to be worrying about that, in the wake of everything that I've done.

I can't be sure that I even deserve a place there anymore.

"Okay, point proven," I mutter. "Clearly you *can* make me feel worse about myself."

"Don't make me out to be a villain, Erika." Mom's voice turns steely, and her fingers clench the bedsheets. "It's time you wake up and start holding yourself accountable. If you want to go to Stanford—with a scholarship, no less—you cannot afford to make stupid and reckless mistakes like this."

I can feel my anger mounting dangerously. My emotions have been bubbling and boiling in me throughout my hours of solitude. It's only a matter of time until they erupt.

"I'm sorry I can't be perfect," I snap.

"I don't expect you to be perfect, Erika, I expect you to be *sensible*. Respectful. Responsible!"

"You bestowed all of those genes on your other daughter, I'm afraid."

"Chloe has nothing to do with this," Mom cries in disbelief. "You can't keep bringing up your sister every time I dare to give you any criticism!"

"Why can't I? You never criticize her!"

"She didn't break into school property," Mom finishes bluntly. "This conversation is about you, Erika. I'm not holding you to Chloe's standard, I'm holding you to your own."

"I'm so tired." My voice breaks on the last word. I lean forwards until my torso is bowed to the blankets, and my fingers scratch painfully over my scalp. "I'm so *tired* of being the problematic daughter. The pressure of following her example and living up to your expectation is exhausting. It matters so much to me that I end up hurting the people I care about, for nothing!"

"Erika, listen."

"No." I groan loudly. "No, I won't listen. I know what I've done. I don't need you to tell me how bad it is, or how disappointed you are, because I already know. Even when I'm working my ass off, I fail to be as smart, as kind, and as accomplished as Chloe. She would never be suspended, but I was. And I'm sorry that I was, and that I've failed you, but please *spare me* the agony of telling me."

"It's not—"

"I don't need you to remind me that I'm a disappointment."

"Erika." Mom sounds lost. "It's not like that."

I lift my head up just enough to show her my eyes, saturated with unshed tears.

"You will never see me outside of her shadow. I was destined to disappoint you."

My tirade seems to render my mom speechless.

She stares at me with utter bewilderment. While I do feel guilty for my outburst, my words were raw with truth. I don't think I can handle any more criticism from her, no matter how warranted it might be. She takes about a minute to collect herself. It is only when her breathing has returned to its regular rate, and her features have softened, that she speaks.

"Is that really what you think?"

"Yes," I admit, sighing.

"Erika." She reaches out to tug my hands away from my hair, where they had been pulling at my roots. Her voice is gentle but insistent. "You are not in her shadow, and you never have been. You are right that I am proud of the woman that Chloe is, and all that she has achieved—"

My head begins to sink back down, but Mom catches my chin before I can look away.

"However." She stresses the word clearly. "That does not make me any less proud of you. I am lucky to have raised two beautiful, strong, and unique girls—*both* of whom have their moments of stupidity. Your differences from Chloe do not mean that I value or love you any less. They never have."

I close my eyes.

"I am proud of you every single day, Erika," she continues. "I push you so hard because I know how intelligent and ambitious you are; I just want to ensure that you live up to your own expectations. Not to mine."

Hesitantly, I open my eyes.

"I am disappointed that you got a suspension," Mom confesses, raising her eyebrows to furnish her point. "But that has nothing to do with Chloe. I know how much Stanford means to you, and I would hate to see you ruin your hard work with impulsive decisions like that one."

I nod. She takes my hands in hers and squeezes them comfortingly.

"My love for you has never been conditional on your academic achievements, and it never will be. I don't care which school you get into, or if you even go to college at all, so long as I know that you tried your best and stayed true to yourself."

"Okay," I mumble.

Relief spreads like a warm shower over my spine, loosening my taut muscles and coaxing away the knots of stress. I feel lighter, and I can breathe more deeply. A weight is gone, a weight both physical and psychological that I have been carrying for months. Years, even. The weight of my mother's expectations, my sister's success, and my own impossibly high standards for myself. It is beyond freeing to release those shackles.

"Can I ask you a question?" Mom asks gently. Upon my nod, she laces my fingers through her own. "When have I made you feel that I compared you to Chloe?"

"Um." I pause cautiously before I speak. "Little things, I guess. You praise her much more ... but then, she does more things that are worthy of praise. You show off her achievements to your friends, you ask her for advice before you ask for mine. If I'm ever struggling with work or sport, you'll always recommend that she helps me because she's so good at everything."

Mom listens with a pained expression.

"It's hard not to make comparisons when she's so naturally gifted," I correct hastily. "Even when we were little, she coasted through life so easily. I thought the world of her ... but it meant that I started thinking badly about myself."

Chase's words come back to me, hurting all the more now for the tenderness they carried then: *the only person that compares the pair of you is you.*

"Most of this comes from my own insecurity, rather than you," I concede.

Mom leans forward to press a tender kiss to my forehead. "I'm sorry for ever allowing you to feel like you didn't matter as much. You mean the world to me, Erika."

"You mean the world to me too, Mom."

She releases my hands and outstretches her arms instead.

Without hesitation, I sink into her cozy, familiar embrace. My arms wrap around her back tightly and my head lands on her chest, just high enough that she can rest her cheek on my hair. She smells like the perfume Chloe and I picked out for her birthday. Squeezing me tightly, she rocks us back and forth slowly and I am lulled into that nostalgic sense of peace which only my mother can provide.

I missed her so much.

After a few minutes of comfortable silence, a question springs to mind.

"By the way," I say into her shirt. "Where has Chloe been? I looked for her at school today, but her office was empty. I really needed her."

"She didn't tell you?" Mom asks. The hint of surprise in her tone is enough to make me pull back from her arms. She's frowning. "Chloe took the day off today because she needed a break, so she's out with some old friends. She's been really unhappy with her work recently . . . She's decided to hand in her notice."

"What? She's quitting?"

Mom nods. "She's planning to do it sometime this week. Turned down that promotion opportunity too. She's overwhelmed, I think."

Reeling from this new information, I sink back into Mom's arms. I knew that Chloe had been a little stressed with work recently, but I didn't realize it was so pressing.

Why wouldn't she talk to me about it? I tell her absolutely everything.

Then it hits me. Maybe that is exactly the problem. The sickening twist of guilt returns to my stomach—a sensation that's becoming horribly familiar. I think back to all my recent conversations with Chloe. Every single one has been about me.

I release a guttural noise and hide my face in Mom's shirt. I have been so selfish, so wrapped up in my own agendas and relationships, that I've neglected to check in with my sister. I have taken her support and her reliability for granted, without ever paying her the same kindness. When was the last time I asked her anything about her life, besides obligatory small talk questions about her day?

When was the last time I made it clear that she could talk to me about anything?

"I'm a horrible sister," I confess aloud. "I had no idea."

"You're not a horrible sister," Mom says, stroking my hair comfortingly. "Just give her a hug when she gets home. I think she probably needs one."

I nod.

"What do you say we go downstairs and order some pizza? I'm craving pepperoni."

"That might make me feel a little better," I admit hoarsely. "Especially if we get nachos on the side."

"Hmm." Mom considers my proposal. "We can decide that after we've discussed the terms for your house arrest—how about that?"

"That seems fair." I speak through a yawn. My persistent emotional breakdowns have really taken it out of me. "I love you lots, Mom. Thank you."

"I love you too, sweetheart."

She kisses my hair, and I can tell that she means it.

I'm lounging on the couch in my avocado pajamas, picking through the last scraps of my nachos, when I hear the front door open.

Mom looks across at me knowingly. She's been teasing me for my restlessness and impatience ever since she informed me that Chloe was on her way home. Waiting for my sister's arrival has been painful, and now that I can finally hear her kicking her shoes off in the hallway, I spring up from the couch with newfound energy. My nacho box sits abandoned on the cushion, dangerously close to my father's grabbing hand, but I am beyond caring.

"Chloe."

I stand in the living room doorway, watching my sister wobble off-balance as she struggles to unclasp one of her heeled sandals. Her hair is frizzy around her shoulders, and she's wearing smudgy eyeliner and a mini skirt I haven't seen her wear since she was my age. I'd forgotten what Chloe looked like when she lets her hair down. She's gorgeous.

"Hey," she greets, kicking away her sandal and standing up. "How are—uh, um, oh."

Unable to restrain myself any longer, I attack her with my hug. My arms loop around her neck, I squeeze myself tightly to her body and press my cheek against her collarbone. This is perhaps the only time that I won't be envious of how much taller she is. After a few seconds of rigid surprise, her arms wind slowly around my back, and she squeezes.

"Everything okay?" she murmurs. Even now, she's still looking out for me.

"I'm really sorry to hear about your job," I say. She stiffens as she registers my words. "And I'm really sorry that I haven't been there for you. I will do better, I promise."

"You don't have to apologize. I know how much you've had on your plate." Chloe makes a humming noise of endearment, then hastily adds, "But thank you."

I pull back from our embrace. "Do you want to talk about it? We have pizza."

"You guys got pizza without me?"

Grabbing her hand impatiently, I lead her into the living room. Mom and Dad are still lounging on the couches, watching a documentary about war on the history channel. The string lights are glowing, and the room smells like garlic and grease. The last box remains open on the coffee table, stained with oil and strewn with crumbs. As Chloe and I take our seats, Dad leans forward to scoop up the last slice of pepperoni.

"Dad," I say sharply. "The last slices were for Chloe!"

He freezes instantly, but it's too late. His teeth have already sunk into the melted cheese. After a guilty pause, he swallows his bite and offers Chloe a sheepish smile.

"Oops."

"It's alright," Chloe says, rolling her eyes.

"And you ate the rest of my nachos," I complain, poking at the empty tray.

Dad winces. "Oops."

It's at that moment that a phone begins to vibrate somewhere beneath me. My nachos temporarily forgotten, I twist and begin digging amongst the throws. When I finally pull out my cell from the crack at the side of the couch, I am surprised to see Miko's face fill the lock screen. Instantly, my pulse accelerates. Hurrying my apologies, I scramble out of the living room and into the private hallway.

She's calling me. *Why is she calling me?* I pace back and forth worriedly.

My voice shakes when I press the phone to my ear.

"Hello?"

"Hey," Miko greets curtly.

"Hi."

A second of hesitation. Then: "I'm calling to check if you're okay."

My heart warms with her concern, and I have to bite my lip to stop my smile from growing. I don't want to get my hopes up, I know that she is probably still hurting because of me. I have a lot of apologizing to do before I can feel satisfied with our friendship again.

"I've been better," I admit. "Thank you for asking, though. Are you okay?"

"Not in top form." She pauses again, this time for a few seconds. There's a shuffling sound on her end of the line. "I wanted to let you know that I'm ready to hear your apology."

"You are?"

I can't help it anymore: hope surges within me.

"I know you were just lashing out, but what you said really sucked, Erika."

"I know it did. I'm so sorry, Miko," I murmur, pressing the phone more closely to my ear. "I really didn't mean any of it, I was just looking for anybody else to blame but myself. I didn't want to take accountability. That was really unfair of me."

"It was unfair." Miko hums in agreement. "You know better than anyone that I haven't changed my passcode in years. Most of Lindale High knows how to get into my phone at this point."

"You should maybe think about changing it now," I suggest tentatively.

"Probably."

"I really am sorry, Miko," I profess. "You're my best

friend in the world and you didn't deserve to be spoken to in that way. I know you were trying to support me."

"I suppose I can forgive you," she says finally. "Don't do it again, though."

"Never," I vow. "Do you want to come over? We're about to order more pizza."

"Ooh," Miko says with interest. "Popcorn too?"

"I can make that happen."

"I'll be over in five."

"See you then."

Grinning with relief, I remove the phone from my ear and hang up. I feel so much lighter with the knowledge that I have repaired my relationships with my sister and best friend. Although I am still racked with guilt for what I have done to Chase, things feel a little less hopeless with Miko and Chloe by my side. They are always, unfailingly there to support me, and I will never take that for granted again.

I move to stand in the living room doorway.

"We're ordering more pizza, are we?" Mom asks amusedly, her eyebrow raised.

"We are," I confirm happily. "We have company coming over, too. Does that violate the terms of my house arrest?"

Mom waves her hand dismissively. "I'll let it slide, just this once."

Filled with gratitude and love, I resume my position on the couch and cuddle up to my mother's side. As the ad break begins to play in the background, I close my eyes and picture the boy with dark curly hair and a moon tattoo. The boy that I betrayed.

As much as a belly full of pizza and a house filled with family has lifted my mood, I won't be able to rest until I've apologized for everything that I did. Regardless of whether I lose Chase or not, I need him to hear that I will never forgive myself for breaking his trust and acting so selfishly. Hurting him has been the biggest mistake of my life.

This is the moment I realize I'm in love with him.

24

Saving Kai

I never thought it was possible to miss being at school, but it is only the Wednesday of my week of suspension, and I am already going stir-crazy.

I've watched the pilot episodes of four separate television series. I've reorganized the spice rack according to social media aesthetic, and I've baked and iced some unsightly chocolate cupcakes. I decorated them with edible One Direction stickers I found in the cabinet, but I purposefully avoided checking the use-by date.

I am in the process of licking the icing from my third cupcake and watching a documentary about an octopus when the doorbell rings. I glance at the clock on the living room mantlepiece. 2.34 p.m. Too early to be one of my working family members.

I haul myself up from the couch, shrouded in a crochet blanket, and trudge into the hallway. Without bothering to check through the peephole, I swing open the front door and open my mouth to begin dismissing whichever salesman or campaigner has dared to interrupt my tedious afternoon. But I never get the opportunity to speak.

Miko flings herself into my arms, but by the time I've recovered enough from my shock to return the hug, she's already pulling away. She's too panicked to stay still, yet she doesn't brush my hands away quickly enough to hide the fact that she's trembling.

"It's Kai," she explains before I need to ask. "He called me. Erika, he skipped school. He's really drunk and—and he's with a load of weird guys in some *bar*."

Her voice cracks on the last word, and her head falls forward onto my shoulder.

"I have no idea where he is," she wails. "I'm re-really freaking out."

"Shh, it's okay. We'll find him," I say, with more determination than I feel. I snake one arm around her shoulders, while my free hand strokes her hair rhythmically. Adrenaline accelerates my pulse until I can hear my blood thrumming in my ears. "Did he say anything about where he is? The bar's name or location?"

Miko pulls back to shake her head. "He only said that he'd passed a post office. I've called again but he's not picking up. I—I'm panicking, Erika. He could barely speak."

"I think I know where it is," I say. My voice is thick with dread.

Miko inhales sharply at the first sign of hope. "You do?"

"Yes," I say after a moment's hesitation. "But you aren't going to like it. Do you remember when I told you about that shady bar that Chase took me to—the Admiral? The one with the drag cars? There's a post office only a few streets away."

"Okay." Miko nods adamantly, wiping away her tears. "Okay."

I lift my thumb to my mouth to chew on my nail. My mom told me that I wasn't allowed to leave the house, as one of the conditions of my punishment. But this is an emergency. I can't let Miko go to that place alone. I watch my best friend shake with nerves, and any resolve I had to stay here dissipates. My thumb nail breaks in my mouth.

"I'll come with you," I say hastily, before I can change my mind. I pull my torn nail away from my teeth and shove my hand into my back pocket. "We'll find him, Miko."

Overcome by gratitude, Miko grabs my face and plants a firm kiss on my cheek.

"I love you so damn much. Thank you, Erika."

I shed my blanket in the hallway and slip on my sneakers as rapidly as I can manage. I don't even get the chance to change before we're climbing into Miko's car and speeding away from my house, my documentary, and my half-eaten cupcake.

Miko switches off the ignition, but neither of us move to get out of the car.

Our momentum has been lost. We sit in silence, staring at the decaying bar through the protection of a windshield. Our determination to save Kai faltered the second that we were confronted with the realities of our situation. We don't know the kind of people that are in there with him. Nobody knows where we are. I'm still wearing my icing-stained sweatpants. And our idea is to—what? Storm in there, steal the kid, and escape the bad guys?

Sounds like the disastrously bad plan in every spy movie I've ever watched.

"Why would Kai come to the Admiral?" Miko whispers. Her fingers touch the door handle tentatively, toying with the prospect of opening it.

I can't answer her question, so instead, I lean across to squeeze her free hand. Her face is pale, and she's staring forwards at the assemblage of men protecting the bar's entrance. They're sitting at picnic tables and drinking merrily, oblivious to our presence, but it's an intimidating obstacle for a couple of girls, nonetheless.

"Let's get this done," I urge. "But we need to stick together. Stay close."

"Yes." She nods. "Okay."

Without further delay, we leave the protection of the car and begin walking through the parking lot, towards the front steps of the Admiral. The building looms over us like an oppressive storm cloud, and soon, we will encounter its turbulence. The men at their tables do not address us, but I can feel them watching as we pass. This place feels anything but welcoming.

I try to swallow, but my mouth is devoid of moisture.

Music is playing; soft jazz music. Its source is a tiny speaker at the far side of the room; I can only hear it because there aren't many people in here. Cigarette smoke lingers in the air and makes my eyes sting as I scan the room for Kai. The bartender, a man with greasy hair and sullen face, is polishing his surface with a rag. A woman sits on the stool in front of him. I recognize her lipstick smile—the waitress that offered to serve me alcohol.

As I twist to examine the left side of the bar, my view is immediately interrupted by the proximity of a familiar, strong torso. I inhale sharply. His fresh, masculine scent has an indisputable effect on my body: my knees weaken, and my shoulders sink with relief. It's him. I tilt my chin upwards slowly until I'm staring into the pecan eyes of Chase Thatcher.

God, I've missed you.

"What are you doing here?" he demands, glancing behind me at Miko. "It's not safe."

I remain unable to summon words, so I'm grateful to hear Miko's response.

"My brother is somewhere in this craphole, and I need to bring him home," she says determinedly, appearing at my side. Although her voice is fierce, her forehead is still creased with worry. "He's so drunk that he's barely conscious. Have you seen him anywhere?"

Chase shakes his head. "I've only just arrived."

"Why are you here?" I hear myself ask.

Chase looks back down at me. I didn't realize how ridiculously accustomed I have become to seeing him smile, laugh, and smirk. His detached expression cuts through me like a blunt blade, and I recoil before I can tell myself that he has every right to hate me.

"Giving someone a ride," he answers curtly.

I take sudden interest in the floorboards beneath us.

"Excuse me," I hear him say. I look up again to watch him address the seated waitress bluntly. "We're looking for a kid named Kai. Have you seen him?"

"The cute one," she responds, laughing. She crosses her legs. "He's in the back."

"Thanks." Chase shoves a hand into his pocket, and strides towards a door on the far-right wall of the bar. The menacing, metal grin of a car grill hangs on the wall above the entrance to the back room. I reach for Miko's hand, but quickly regret that decision when her tight grip begins to cut off the circulation to my fingers.

The back room is darker, lit by a large, dingy lamp and a small window. The walls are lined with shelves of cardboard boxes and bottles of liquor, and in the center of the room is a table. Three guys are sitting around it, and only two of them look up as I enter the room. Kai is resting in the middle, with his hands and arms flat on the table and his eyes closed. The others are playing a card game.

"He's here," I murmur as Miko follows me into the room.

"Who the hell are you?" the man closest to me asks. He's staring at us with raised eyebrows, as if he can't believe our audacity to interrupt. It's only upon noticing his crooked nose that I recognize him as Max—the guy that I kicked. The dark lighting and purple shadows beneath his eyes age him far beyond his teenage years.

"We are taking him home, is what we are," Miko responds firmly. She pushes past me, and steps behind his chair to reach her brother. Kai shows no sign of consciousness as she shakes him and the hollow feeling in my chest begins to grow.

"Easy there, sweet." The older guy pushes his chair back against the shelf, cutting off Miko's route back to the doorway. He touches her arm and smiles, but there's something about the way he bares his teeth that is unsettling. "Our good friend Kai, here, is joining us for a few drinks. Harmless fun, really. I don't think he's ready to leave yet."

Chase steps forwards. "He's leaving. Now."

The man lazily rolls his head to the side to assess Chase. Max has stilled. There's no soft jazz in this back room, nothing to soften the silence. The only sound is Miko's ragged breathing as she continues to shake her brother. I can see her desperation in the way her fingers are digging into his shoulder blades. He looks so young, shrunken over the table.

"And who are you?" the man asks finally, his voice dangerously soft.

"Kai's real friend." Chase's shoulders are tight with stress, but he isn't backing away. He's just brash enough to stand up to these creeps. "Now, personally, when I see my friend lying unconscious on the table, I think that they might have had enough *harmless fun*."

Kai grunts, and I realize with relief that Miko has managed to wake him. His eyes are glazed and slow as he registers the scene around him. The labored flops of his movements make it obvious he'll struggle to walk. I feel a surge of emotion as I watch him clasp Miko's hand. He's scared. Kaito is scared.

The frustration and urge to protect him hits me solidly in the chest, spurring me into movement. I take the free route along the wall and begin to help Miko bring Kai to his feet. Together, we support him under his arms and lift his body from the chair. The kid is surprisingly heavy. I have to kick his feet a few times to remind him that we need his help. Eventually, he catches on. We edge along the wall, while the two bullies watch in silence.

"We're leaving now," Chase announces bitterly. "Enjoy your game."

The door swings open before we even have a chance to approach it. A tall, raven-haired guy strolls in, rifling through a wad of cash in his hands. His arms are crowded with black ink tattoos, but it's the small crescent moon on his finger that catches my attention. I look up at his face with horror.

There's no way. It couldn't be.

"Is the kid still here? I need him to—" Seth stops speaking abruptly as he looks up from the money and realizes the number of people in the room. He notices Chase first, and his lips part with absent excuses, before recognizing me and the slumped boy propped on my arm. He recovers from his shock quickly, plastering on his signature charming smile. "Well, isn't this a party? I didn't know you guys were here."

Chase ignores Seth's attempts at casual concealment. His voice is low and laced with threat. "Tell me this isn't what I think it is, Seth."

"What do you mean?" Seth asks unconcernedly, shoving the cash into his back pocket. "Kai is a friend of mine. Aren't you, Kai?"

Kai releases a low, groaning noise. His head collapses onto Miko's shoulder.

"He's a kid," Chase spits. His hands have clenched into fists at his side, and his shoulders are squaring primitively. "What the hell are you thinking?"

"He doesn't do much," Seth says, lifting his hands in surrender. "He helps me to look after the gear sometimes. It's not like I'm asking him to deal or anything."

"You're screwing up his entire life," Miko hisses. "He's sixteen! Look at him!"

Seth casts a cursory glance in Kai's direction, his lip curled with distaste. Any attempt at charm has now fallen cleanly from his expression, revealing the callous, unsympathetic attitude beneath. It is terrifying to realize the artifice of such a likeable persona. "It's not my fault that he can't handle his drink. Take him home if you want."

"I can't believe you," Chase fumes. "I knew you got up to some shady stuff every now and again but dragging in sophomore kids? What the hell is wrong with you, Seth?"

"I needed help and he was there."

"You mean he was easy to manipulate," I correct sharply. The ache of Kai's weight on my shoulder is beginning to spread across my back. It's becoming difficult to hold him up. I notice the drool seeping from the side of Kai's mouth, and I'm instilled with panic again. "Miko, let's get Kaito out of here. He might need a doctor."

Miko's expression is torn between fury and dismay. She glares intensely at Seth, then switches to behold her brother's inanimate face again. Begrudgingly, she nods.

"Let's go," I usher. But she's not quite finished.

"I dare you to come near my brother again," she hisses at Seth. Her delicate features twist with a hostility that I have never seen her wear. Despite her frog necklace and fluffy sweater, she has managed to become alarmingly intimidating. "No, really, I dare you. I will have you arrested before you can even breathe his name."

Seth's neutral expression doesn't flinch. Instead, he reaches out to Chase.

"You should stay here. We need to talk about this."

"Don't touch me." Chase rips his hand away just in time to avoid Seth's grip. His pupils are dilated, and his cheeks are flushed with anger. "This is beyond ... beyond screwed up. I can't believe you would do this, Seth. Who the hell are you?"

"Chase."

"Get out of the way before I put my fist in your face," Chase mutters darkly.

Seth sighs, and side-steps away from the door to open our exit route. Chase makes a point of slamming his shoulder against Seth as he passes back into the quiet bar. I wonder if their relationship will ever be the same after this. If Seth's charm was convincing enough to fool even his foster brother, God only knows the type of manipulation he is capable of.

Miko and I begin to drag the barely conscious Kai out of the room. I wasn't planning on saying anything else, but as we pass Seth and I catch another glimpse of the moon tattoo on his finger, I cannot resist the impulse.

"Come near Kaito, or any other sixteen-year-old kid, again and I'll kick you so hard that your tiny balls pop out of your eye sockets."

I embellish my threat with a sweet smile.

Seth doesn't manage to craft a response.

The trudge through the bar is slow and torturous, but as we step into the fresh air outside, the relief of Kai's safety makes it all worth it. Wordlessly, Chase takes Kaito from us and supports his weight on the walk through the parking lot. The sight of him helping Kai, despite everything that has happened, makes my heart squeeze with longing. He assists Kai into the backseat with equal parts strength and gentleness.

"Thank you for all of your help," Miko says earnestly, as Chase stands up again. "I can't even begin to tell you how much I appreciate it."

"It's no trouble." Chase clears his throat uncomfortably, and glances briefly at me. "I'll probably head home now, but if you need any help with anything, just holler."

"Thank you," she repeats.

"I'll—uh—see you both around, I guess." With an awkward nod, Chase spins on his heels and begins to stride away. My heart aches a little more fiercely with every step he takes.

"Why didn't you say anything?" Miko asks.

"Because he doesn't want anything to do with me." I manage to swallow the pain and force a smile. This isn't the time to feel sorry for myself. "Come on, let's get Kai home safely."

I recognize the unhealthy pallor of Kai's face through the window. I slide into the passenger seat and look back at him, curled up against the faux-leather upholstery. As much as it's horrible to see him so unwell, I'm grateful that he's safe with us now. His eyes are open, which is already a significant improvement to five minutes ago.

"Erika?" he mumbles.

Surprise colors my tone. "Yeah?"

"I'm really sorry for sending in that video," Kai confesses, clutching his stomach and wincing with discomfort. "You didn't deserve it. I was just angry."

Oh.

"Thank you for helping me get home. Even though I've messed everything up."

"It's okay," I reply softly. "Everybody makes mistakes. You're safe now."

With a tired smile, Miko starts the ignition. Turning back around, I nestle into my seat and watch gratefully as the Admiral disappears in the rear-view mirrors for the final time.

"She did *what?*"

Chloe is standing on the opposite side of the clearance

rack. Her hands are frozen on the pink sweater that she just complimented, and she is staring at me with astonishment.

"She asked me to help her expel him," I repeat, shuffling through the rack of sale items. A mohair sweater sparks with static under my fingertips. "She wanted me to provide evidence that would give her the excuse to expel him. That's how Kai found the video."

"Why did you say yes?" Chloe asks incredulously.

"Because she told me that she could get me a scholarship for Stanford." I look down at the clothes, shamefully avoiding Chloe's scrutiny. "At the time, that seemed like the most important thing. I thought it would be simple, but ... it quickly became complicated."

My uplifting, casual shopping trip with Chloe has taken a deeper turn than anticipated. While Chloe persuaded Mom to allow me out of the house for a few hours, it was agreed with the intent that it would distract me from my regret. Instead, our light-hearted conversation has quickly escalated into a full breakdown of the previous month's events.

I had thought that describing each of my mistakes would be painful and triggering, but it's actually a relief to tell someone about them. The moral dilemmas that have burdened me for so long now fly freely in open air.

"I can't believe you didn't tell me this before." Dazed and disbelieving, Chloe resumes her inspection of the pink sweater. She's wearing lipstick today. As her lips purse with dismay, she almost looks like a doll. "You should have talked to me about it."

"I made the decision to help Blythe, knowing that it was a selfish thing to do," I confess. "You're always so kind and selfless. I guess I didn't tell you because it would become clear how wrong my choice was."

"I guess that makes sense." She lifts a hanger from the rail, then places it back almost as abruptly. "But I still don't understand. Why is Blythe so desperate to expel Chase that she resorted to bribing a student?"

"I'm not really sure." Abandoning my search for jeans, I move around the rail to stand beside Chloe. She already has three items slung over her arm. "Chase thinks it's a personal vendetta, because he's spotted her shady activities at the school every night."

Her head swivels quickly. "Does she know that he's observed her, then?"

"I don't know. I never got the chance to ask."

Chloe turns back to the rail, biting her lip pensively.

"It would make sense," she says, after a moment's deliberation. "She came to you on the first day of school, so she must have already known him somehow. Either a professional or personal grudge ... either way, she's very corrupt."

"It's worrying," I agree. Reaching out my hand, I stroke the pile of sale clothes that has assembled on Chloe's forearm. "Are you buying these things?"

"Oh." Chloe looks down in surprise. "No. I was playing that game where I pretend that I have the money to afford buying everything I want."

"And you picked this?" My nose wrinkles as I pluck a fluffy purple cardigan from the top of her arm. "I'm not sure I'd buy this even if I had all the money in the world."

"It's cute!" she defends, tugging it back from my hand. She strokes the lavender atrocity affectionately, before placing it back on the rack. "I shouldn't buy it, though. I need to save my money until I get another job."

I touch her empty arm. "Any thoughts on what you want to do yet? Mom mentioned that you turned down your friend's offer."

"Yeah, it's not for me. I'm not sure what I want anymore," she admits. We begin to walk in the direction of the store exit, and her gaze flits around the displayed clothing distractedly. "I was always so confident that I knew what would make me happy. What my future would look like. That logic failed me and that leaves me with nothing. No plans, no ambitions, no ideas."

I watch her with alarm. Seeing my expression, her eyes widen with panic.

"It's not as depressing as it sounds, I promise!" she corrects hurriedly. "It's quite nice to know that I can restart and do whatever I want to do with my life. Almost ... freeing."

We walk out of the store and back into the cool, airy mall environment. It's Thursday evening, so there aren't as many people cluttering the space as there would be on a weekend. Although neither of us has purchased anything in the three stores we have visited, it's been quite therapeutic to window-shop and browse sale racks with my sister.

"I'm happy you feel that way," I chime. "The possibilities are endless. I'm sure a million and one companies will be jumping at the chance to employ Chloe Monroe."

"Here's hoping," she says with a laugh. "We'll see next week."

As I'm about to press the conversation deeper into Chloe's hopes and plans, I spot a brightly colored store window on the right. My next question is instantly forgotten. My steps alter instinctively, until I'm standing and staring into the charming window display of the *Build-a-Bear* workshop. Positioned on a swing-set, beside a pink teddy bear in a floral dress, is my little badass bear. His quiff and leather jacket mark him as the same bear I forced Chase to take a photo with, all that time ago. The polaroid is still on my pinboard at home.

"You want to go in?" Chloe asks from behind my shoulder.

My reply is soft and faintly hopeful.

"I think I have an idea."

25

Bear-y Sorry

After a week of insightful reflection and unparalleled boredom, my arrival at school on Monday morning is a welcome return to normality.

I watch out of the passenger-side window as chattering and jostling teenagers stream through the gates, coloring the gray school grounds with vibrancy and laughter. Despite my nerves, it's comforting to know that I will soon be flowing through the school halls with them. As I'm searching for a familiar face, a red Volvo pulls into the parking space beside us and rudely obscures my view of the entrance.

The leather squeaks in complaint as I twist back around in my seat.

Chloe's hand falls from its grip on the steering wheel, and she smiles reassuringly. "Don't worry. I'll walk in with you."

"Thank you," I mumble gratefully.

We leave the car together and I cling closely to her side as we stroll up the path towards the doors. I quickly realize that nobody is staring or speculating about my absence in the way that I feared they would, and I am relieved to melt anonymously into the swarm. *All I need to do is get through today without any trouble or attention.*

Then I spot the police car, which is parked beside the school shed.

"Cops?" I stop in my tracks, confused. "What on earth?"

It seems I'm not the only one to notice the strange visitors in our parking lot. As I look around me with new awareness, it becomes clear why I have not been subjected to the curiosity and gossip that I expected. A student suspension pales in comparison to the hot gossip of a potential crime. Student conversations are buzzing with possibilities.

"Erika," Chloe says slowly. "I might have something to tell you."

"Yeah, what?"

Before she can respond, I am distracted again by the sight of two cops exiting the school building. Both are dressed in signature navy uniform, cradling large cardboard boxes in their arms. Students clear intuitively from their path. It is only as they stride past Chloe and I that I notice the unmistakable purple ring-binder balancing on top of one of the piles.

Principal Blythe's binder.

"What the hell is going on?" I wonder aloud, watching the cops walk away.

Chloe clutches my shoulder and swings my body around to face her. Any protest I might make is immediately silenced by the urgent expression she's wearing. Her lips are pursed, and her eyes bore down into mine with frightening intensity.

"I spoke to someone on the school board last week," Chloe confesses. Her hand is squeezing my collarbone incessantly, and I can't tell if it's supposed to be for my comfort or her own. "I told them everything that you told me. Blythe is now under investigation for money laundering and bribery."

It takes me a few seconds to process her words. When I have finally summoned the mental energy to respond, all I can articulate are odd syllables.

"I . . . you, um—what?"

"It'll be a long process before they have the evidence needed to make an arrest or charge her," Chloe continues, grimacing. "You and Chase will probably need to speak to all kinds of people about your experience. They will have questions; they may be intrusive—"

"Chloe, what?"

"In the meantime, you'll have a cover principal."

"Slow down, slow down," I say with a huff, pulling back from her grip to examine her face carefully. There's no trace of deceit in her features. "You're telling me you did this?"

"Before I left my job," Chloe confirms, wincing. "I know you probably didn't want me to get involved, but that woman abused her authority and bribed you! Plus, the parking lot thing is very suspicious. It was my responsibility to tell someone about what happened."

"And she's gone?" I echo in disbelief. I look over at the principal's office, as if the closed gray blinds will reveal all truths. "She's not our principal anymore?"

Chloe shakes her head fiercely. "She's no longer trusted in that position. I'm not sure who is due to replace her, but they will be a significant improvement."

"So, you . . ."

"Went behind your back?" Chloe finishes nervously. "Yes."

"Wow." I take a step back, blinking furiously. "I ... um ... wow."

"Please don't be mad."

"Oh, I'm not mad," I correct. "Just shocked ... Money-laundering, really?"

Chloe surveys our surroundings quickly to ensure that our conversation isn't being overheard. "Apparently there's been some anomalies in the school accounts."

"God." My laugh is breathless. "Oh my god."

"I'm sorry." Chloe groans. "I didn't know that they were searching her office today or I would have warned you. I just didn't want to overwhelm you on your first day back."

"Don't apologize." I press a hand to my forehead. The skin is flushed with warmth. "I just can't believe you did this. That this is actually happening."

"You forgive me?"

"I ... thank you." Incredulous laughter bubbles from my chest as I consider that I will never have to see Principal Blythe's vindictive face again. Light with gratitude and relief, I throw my arms around my sister and squeeze her tightly. "Thank you for always looking after me, even when I don't ask you to. You're the best sister in the world."

Her arms squeeze me almost as tightly. "I will always look after you, Erika."

With my nose pressed into her frizzy hair, I watch over her shoulder as the cop car crawls away from the school parking lot. Maybe there really can be a return to normality.

"It's him," Riley reports, glancing back at us. "He's coming."

The surge of anticipation freezes me to the spot.

"Are you sure it's him?" I ask nervously. "I'm sure there's

a lot of brunette boys with trust issues and a tattoo. Try, like... every teen fiction story, ever? There's a strong possibility it isn't Chase. Also, have you visited an optometrist lately? I—"

Riley interrupts my tangent. "Definitely him."

As I begin to fabricate my next excuse, Miko addresses me.

"Erika, this is not the time for panic," she urges. Placing both hands on my shoulder blades, she pushes me towards the corner of the hallway: the position with the best viewpoint of Chase's locker. "Now, get your pretty ass to your vantage point *pronto*."

"This was a bad idea," I mutter. "This was such a bad idea."

"Why?" Riley is standing just behind my shoulder now, and her voice is low and laced with challenge. "He's never going to forgive you if you don't try to apologize. This is a sweet gesture. It's a good starting point."

"He's going to think it's stupid."

"He's going to see that you're *trying*."

"You're both going to miss it if you don't look now," Miko hisses, craning her neck to peek around into the bustling school corridor. "He's at his locker."

Battling my flight impulse, I move towards the edge of the corner we've been hiding behind. It takes me a few seconds to locate his face amongst the lunchtime chaos, but once I do, I couldn't possibly focus on anything else if I tried. My breath clings stubbornly in my throat as I watch him laugh with Alec. Somehow, despite the universally-unflattering, fluorescent lighting in our high school, he looks radiant.

"Erika, stop checking him out," Miko says, batting my arm.

"It's hard not to!"

Chase is opening his locker door. My stomach lurches.

Too late to take the gesture back now: he's already staring at it with a faint frown. My vision is glued to him as he pulls the badass bear from his locker for closer inspection. His hands smooth over the fluffy quiff, adjust the leather jacket and straighten the *"Bear-y Sorry"* card tied to the right paw. Shaking his head lightly, he places the bear back into his locker.

Without opening the card.

The metal lockers make a clanging noise as I fall back into them, away from the corner and my view of Chase. I close my eyes, but the image of him rejecting my gesture replays on a loop in my mind. It hurts more than I thought it would have. I wasn't expecting miracles, but I confess that I believed he would at least read the card. That bear harks back to one of my favorite memories. Maybe our relationship isn't salvageable after all.

"Erika?" Miko asks cautiously.

I respond without opening my eyes. "He didn't read it."

"I know." She squeezes my forearm. "But you can try again, right?"

Despite my crushed optimism, I know that she's right. I need to find another way to get through to him. While he may never forgive me—and that is his right—he needs to hear how much I regret my deceit. The more I consider my *Bear-y Sorry* gesture, the more apparent it becomes that I cowered out of facing him. If I was him, I wouldn't have accepted that corny, low-effort apology either. After all that I have put him through, the very least he deserves is for me to confront my own actions head-on.

With a newfound resolve, I open my eyes.

"I think you need to speak to him in person," Riley suggests, clearly operating on a similar line of thought. "As sweet as the gesture was, it wasn't direct enough. He needs to see the apology in your eyes."

Look him in the eye and speak from your heart. A gem of wisdom from my dad. He may act silly and tell stupid jokes, but his advice is remarkably astute.

I need to come up with a new plan.

Evening is my favorite time of the day to run.

The warmth of the day has drained from the air, the streets are tranquil, and the sky is just dusky enough that the lights strung along the main street have flickered into activity. I can afford to wear running shorts instead of leggings without fear of being too cold. I can observe amber windows as I pass, like freeze frames from an old movie, and speculate about the family sitting around the table to eat. These are the perfect conditions for clearing my head. Today, more than ever, I relish them.

"Erika," Dylan calls from shortly behind me. "Can we have a break for a minute?"

Interrupted just as I hit my rhythm.

Reluctantly, I slow my footfall until I reach a natural stop. There's a familiar burn in my calf muscles, and my chest is rising and falling at rapid speed. It's been a long time since I've enjoyed a run so much. Hands on my hips, I turn around to wait for Dylan, who is strolling sluggishly towards me. His hand clutches his chest, and his expression is bemused.

"Did you have an extra spoonful of sugar on your cornflakes this morning?" he teases, laughing breathlessly. "I could barely keep up with you."

"I was on house arrest for a week," I reply, grinning. "Lots of energy to burn off."

"You're telling me. I think you left Usain Bolt in the dust, back there."

I fall into step beside him. While I was prepared to keep running for a while longer, my muscles are relieved to sink into a lazy, languorous walk. As I attempt to regain control of my breathing, my gaze wanders around our surroundings. The houses are well-kept and equal in size, with matching square yards. This area feels strangely familiar.

"My knee is killing me," Dylan confesses. "I think I pushed it too hard today."

"Oh no." I twist around in alarm. "Is that my fault?"

"Of course not. I wanted to keep up with you."

"Even still." I observe his slight limp and wonder how I hadn't noticed it before. "When you get home, put some ice on it to reduce any swelling. Try some stretches, too. It's better to keep it moving than to let it seize up."

Dylan seems surprised by my advice. "Okay. I can do that."

"You might need to steer clear from running for a while, too. At least, for as long as it's still hurting. You don't want to exacerbate it if it's a strain injury."

"Noted, Doctor Erika." The humor in his voice is evident.

"Hey," I protest. "I'm trying to help."

"And I appreciate it," he amends hastily. "In fact, I could picture you as a doctor. Osteopathy, or physiotherapy or something. It would suit you."

I shrug my shoulders half-heartedly. "Maybe."

"I know, I know. Heart set on Stanford."

"Where are we?" I interrupt distractedly, pausing in my

step. The house on the corner of the road has caught my attention, but I can't identify what makes it any different from any others on the terrace. Perhaps I came here for a house party one time? Or maybe I know someone who lives here? I strain to remember but come up blank.

"I'm not sure," Dylan says, stopping beside me. "This street isn't on our usual route."

Finally, it clicks.

The paved driveway. The shrub. This is the street corner where Chase and I hid, after we fled the diner without paying. This is the driveway where we caught our breath and laughed with the exhilaration of escaping Principal Blythe. Standing here now, staring at the empty sidewalk where I once felt so alive, highlights his absence to a whole new degree. I miss laughing with him, chastising him, charming him.

"Erika?" Dylan asks. "What's wrong?"

I had almost forgotten he was here.

"I was here with Chase," I answer, gesturing at the street corner. "That time we ran away from the diner. We came here."

"Ah."

"Yeah." My smile is feeble. "I'm not sure we'll ever be like that again."

"You will, Erika," Dylan insists. He bumps my shoulder—that comforting gesture guy friends use when they're too awkward to offer you a hug. "You won't lose him because you won't let that happen. Even he knows that."

"He doesn't want to talk to me. How do you apologize to someone who doesn't even want to be near you?" I shake my head. "I don't have the first clue how to reach out to him."

"Then just go with something simple. Invite him to talk—just the two of you."

"You think he'd do that?" I tear my eyes away from the street corner, to look at Dylan. My voice drips with disbelief.

"I think if he's ready to accept your apology, he would probably prefer something with no pretenses," Dylan explains, pushing his hands into his pockets and leaning against the nearest lamp. "No gestures, or gifts or peer pressure. Just you."

"You're right," I say, after a moment.

"I'm always right, remember?"

I reach out to ruffle his sweaty hair; a sure-fire way to erase that smug expression forming on his face. "Maybe just this once. Thanks, Dyl." He scowls and begins to adjust his fringe.

While my companion is occupied with fixing his hair, I contemplate my options. If the best way to apologize to Chase is to invite him for a conversation, then I need to choose somewhere private, inoffensive, and unbiased. A middle ground. Having the conversation at school would be too pressured, with the potential for eavesdroppers. It's wrong to ask him to come to me, and there's not a chance I could expect to visit his house again.

My gaze settles upon the lonely street corner.

Just like that, my next idea begins to formulate.

A vanilla milkshake and a Pepsi, without ice, are arranged on the polished metal table.

I made sure to choose the same booth as last time—even the same side. If the tool of nostalgia lies freely at my disposal, then I may as well make use of it, and the diner seems to agree. The same neon pink signs glow on the wall, all the more striking now for their contrast to the darkness outside. Even Gemma, the server we traumatized, is working tonight. She's cleaning tables so I haven't spoken to her yet, but I have faith that she'll recognize me.

Everything has aligned to set the scene for the perfect apology. Now, all that remains is for me to execute my part perfectly.

That, and for the guy to actually show up.

I texted Chase about forty minutes ago to invite him, but I have yet to receive a reply. There's a high probability that he will never show up, and I will continue sitting here for another hour, counting pity-glances from the waiting staff. I suppose I've risked it all by buying two drinks, instead of just the one. Sue me, I'm optimistic. Despite the logical part of my brain insisting that he has no obligation to come, I stubbornly believe that he will.

I find myself staring down at a fry on the patterned floor, recalling how we crouched under the table to hide from Blythe. The way he pulled my hood up, and tucked my hair behind my ears, when he knew I was scared. The way his voice sounded when he called me gorgeous. My eyes squeeze shut with longing, and I reach for the first sip of my milkshake.

I look up just in time to see Chase walk into the diner.

He's wearing an oversized, navy crewneck and a troubled expression. He looks gorgeous without even trying, and I instantly kick myself for not changing out of my sweaty running clothes before I came here. Hopefully, I don't smell. I wait self-consciously as his head swivels around, searching the tables, until our eyes inevitably meet.

It's like a drug hit, accelerating my pulse tenfold.

It takes a few seconds for Chase to begin approaching the booth. As he nears, he clears his throat and averts his eyes to the patterned tiles on the floor. I contemplate the possibility that he's as nervous as I am, but swiftly dismiss it. There's not a chance in hell.

He slides into the seat opposite, just as he did the last time we were here, and my heart lurches. This is the closest I've been to him in over a week, yet somehow, we have never felt so far apart. He's inspecting everything in the room besides me, and I am confronting the likelihood that this will be the last conversation we ever have. I can barely stomach the thought of saying goodbye. A painful silence ensues.

"Hi," I greet finally.

26

To be Continued

I've broken the silence but there is little sense of relief. The word hangs in the air between us, weighed down by expectation. Chase reaches for his Pepsi and sips from the edge. Even as he places the drink back down, he continues to cradle the glass between his hands.

"Hi," he mutters eventually.

Our silence resumes for a few seconds longer.

"Thanks for the drink."

"It's okay." My fingernails drum on the table, a desperate attempt to fill the gaps in our splintered conversation. "Thank you for meeting with me. I wasn't sure if you'd come."

"I wasn't either," Chase says, leaning back against the red pleather seat with a sigh. For the first time since sitting down, he dares a glance in my direction. It only lasts a fraction of a second, because he can't stand the eye contact. The rejection when he turns away, while small, aches ferociously. Have I hurt him so badly that he won't even look at me?

"Do you want me to talk?" I ask quietly.

He hesitates. "I don't know, Erika."

"I suppose that's better than a no."

"I wouldn't count your lucky stars just yet." He gazes out of the window at the poorly lit parking lot, stroking the base of his glass absentmindedly. I know that he's regretting his decision to show up. I scramble to find words that might convince him to stay.

"I really miss you," I confess. If I squeeze my eyes shut while I say it, it's less intimidating to admit aloud. "This week has felt like a lifetime."

More hesitation. "I miss you too, Erika, but you know that isn't enough."

"What do you mean?"

"I mean you messed up," he answers bluntly. He looks at me properly now, but it isn't the tender moment that I've been craving. His expression is cold, detached—lips pressed into a grim line. "You threw me under the bus, and you lied to me the entire time. Missing you is not a good enough reason to place my trust in you again."

I shut my eyes again briefly. This time because they are stinging with tears.

"I can't begin to understand how badly my actions hurt you," I say, once I have recovered enough to keep the tremor from my voice. "But if you believe anything that comes out of my mouth today, please believe this. Breaking your trust, after you worked so hard to give it to me, was the biggest mistake that I have ever made."

"I trusted you more than anybody, Erika. More than Joe, even."

"I know," I say thickly. "And I'm so, so sorry for what I did."

His exhale is shaky. He begins to play with the rim of his glass, and we return to our silence. I watch his toying fingers and wonder if this is how it's going to be for the entire duration of our meeting. I think I'd rather hear him shout, scream, and cry than ignore my existence completely. At least I would still mean something to him, in a warped way. At least I would have confirmation that he hasn't given up on me entirely.

As if listening to my thoughts, Chase speaks again. Uncertainty laces his voice.

"You seem to think... that the worst part was the fact that you agreed to help Blythe to expel me." He pauses. Takes the straw and spins it around the glass, once. "You're wrong about that. You didn't know me then, so you didn't owe me anything."

Sensing the direction of his speech, I bite the inside of my cheek hard.

"The worst part is the way that you decided to keep it from me. You let me tell you everything... but even as my friend, you didn't believe that I deserved the same."

I know that if I attempt to speak, my voice will break into a sob. I am determined not to cry in front of him, because that will just detract from the focus of this conversation. His feelings, his pain. This is not the time to feel sorry for myself.

"I just don't understand why you wouldn't tell me," he continues, shaking his head with bewilderment. "I could have looked past it if you'd told me early on."

"Does that mean you can't look past it now?" My whisper is raw with emotion.

Chase doesn't reply.

"I don't have an adequate excuse," I say defeatedly. My

hands are shaking, so I move them from the table to place them flat on my thighs. "I thought that if I could change Blythe's mind, you would never have to find out about my involvement. I was trying to protect you... but mainly, I was trying to protect myself. I was scared to lose you."

My voice wobbles dangerously. I take a deep breath.

"I have learned a lot recently, about why I shouldn't just handle everything on my own," I admit. "Partially, because I'm awful at creating solutions. But mainly because it's unfair to withhold the truth from people, no matter how ugly it might be. I've been trying to control situations that didn't only affect me, and that was selfish."

"It was selfish," Chase agrees quietly.

"I was so focused on this vision of going to Stanford that I forgot about the type of person I want to be when I get there."

A sip from my now-melted milkshake soothes my dry mouth, but only momentarily. My mother's words echo at the forefront of my mind, bearing a gravity and relevance that she couldn't possibly have understood at the time. *I don't care which school you get into ... so long as I know you tried your best and stayed true to yourself.*

"I understand if you can't trust me again," I say, smiling bleakly. "But I want to thank you for the time that you did. Getting to know you, being around your friends and family, hanging out every day... the last month has made me ridiculously happy."

"Erika..."

"The word sorry will never encompass how much I regret hurting you."

I can't restrain it any longer: my vision is blurring. I stare determinedly at the scuff marks on the metal table and pray that he can't see the tears that have fallen onto my bare thighs. My pulse is thrumming painfully in my ears from the effort it's taking to hold myself together. Perhaps that explains why I didn't hear him shift in his seat. And why, when my chin raises from my chest, Chase is leaning over the table with anguish in his eyes.

The kindliness I see almost sets me off again.

"Are you crying?" he whispers.

"No," I choke out. "This isn't about me."

He sighs. "Erika, this is about *us*."

Within a matter of seconds, he moves from his side of the booth to mine.

Closing the distance between us, he enfolds me in his arms with a tenderness that crumbles the last of my façade. The tears that I've fought so hard to contain stream tirelessly down my face, soaking the shoulder of his sweatshirt. Hugging him feels like coming home after an awful day at school. Like a hot shower after you've been walking in the rain. Like taking off those jeans that are too tight and deciding you don't need them.

It feels like pure, unfettered relief.

"I am so sorry." My voice is muffled in his shoulder. "I am so, so sorry, Chase."

"I know," he mumbles, kissing the top of my hair.

"Really?" I pull back from his arms just enough to get a view of his face. There is not a chance that I am leaving his arms before he forcibly removes me. His eyes are glassy with unshed tears, his head is cocked slightly to the left, and the smile he wears is stained with sadness. It's a heart-breaking expression.

"Please don't lie to me again," he whispers.

"I would never. I could never."

His hands lift from my back, to cradle my face. It is the only possible place that they could relocate to without me voicing a complaint. The salt from my tears is itching my cheeks, but he wipes the sensation away with his thumbs.

"Then I forgive you."

His words flood through my body like a medicine, relaxing every stressed muscle.

"I missed you," I say. "I missed you stupid, unbelievable amounts."

"I missed you too, gorgeous."

I know that if the Erika from a month ago could see me now, she'd question how on earth we came to be staring with gooey eyes at the arrogant asshole in every girl's contact list. If only she had an inkling of how selfless he would turn out to be. How sensitive, how charming, how funny. How much he would enliven the most mundane activities, uplift our spirit, and show us how to be brave. If only she had half a clue of what this boy would mean to us by now. Then she could have given me a heads-up.

Although I'm not sure anything could prepare me for loving him this much.

"Can we play that game again?" I murmur.

"What game?"

"The one where I tell you what to do ... and you listen."

His gaze flits down to my lips. I don't have to tell him this time.

Our lips join with a vigor that even I couldn't anticipate. The same ecstatic thrill I felt outside of Alec's party shimmers through every nerve.

The kiss is firmer, more heated than last time. Chase's

free hand cradles my jaw, the pads of his fingers warm on my cheek. The other fists in the bottom of my T-shirt. His lips move confidently, telling me how much he's missed me without the need for words. I nestle in his chest, my hands rooted on his shoulders, as our pain ebbs away and is replaced by pleasure. My heartbeat dances erratically, and I'm so happy that I could dance with it.

The sound of a tray hitting the floor. Then, a squeak of surprise.

Our lips tear away from each other, leaving us breathless. Gemma is standing at the edge of our booth, with her palm pressed tightly over her eyes.

"I'm so sorry," she says hastily, bending down to collect the tray from the floor one-handed. "I didn't mean to interrupt. I'll come back."

"It's okay." I pull away from Chase sheepishly, adjusting my top.

She removes the hand from her eyes as she straightens up. It's obvious at which point she recognizes us—her eyes widen, and her mouth falls open in blatant surprise.

"Hi Gemma," Chase greets.

"Oh." She fumbles with the tray. "Oh—um, hi."

"Nice to see you again. You'll be happy to know we worked through my issues."

"Mostly," I correct. "I'd say we're at the level of overcooked pasta now."

"That's uh—great." Gemma shifts uncomfortably. "I'm just going to go and grab something from the kitchen. I'll send someone over to take your order, okay?"

"Bye Gemma," Chase says, waving as the poor girl hurries away.

I swat him on the shoulder. His eyes sparkle with amusement and his lips are pink and tugged up into that infuriating smile that I pretend to hate.

"So," he says. "To be continued? I don't know about you, but I'm hungry."

"Starving," I agree, grinning.

I don't think I've ever felt lighter than in this moment.

One hour—and two cheeseburgers—later, Chase and I are slumped languidly in our booth.

My back is pressed against the wall; my feet propped up on the seat ahead of me. Chase is similarly sprawled, rubbing his stomach and intermittently complaining about the sickliness of the chocolate cake he consumed. We have adopted a new kind of lazy confidence, as if we own the place. Gemma is too intimidated to collect our assemblage of dirty plates and glasses, so they clutter the table between us like trophies.

"Next confession," I say, playing with the straw in my blueberry lemonade. Ice rattles against the glass. "Never have I ever had a part-time job."

Chase rolls his eyes and reaches for his drink. "Very clever."

"You mentioned it while we were arguing." I watch his Adam's apple unabashedly, as he swallows some of his Pepsi. "Since when? You never said anything about getting a job."

"This is a confessions game, gorgeous," Chase reminds me. "You don't get free rein to ask all of these other questions too."

Fishy. Why won't he tell me about it?

"You're being very suspicious, Squidge," I remark.

He ignores my probing. "Never have I ever had a vacation romance."

His attempt to divert the topic is obvious, and I can't help but wonder why he's being so guarded around this topic. Nevertheless, I decide to drop it. I am hardly in a position to criticize him for not trusting me with information. My curiosity is quickly forgotten when I raise my straw to my mouth, and I'm rewarded by his reaction. His eyebrows shoot upwards, and he watches impatiently as I drink.

He thinks I met someone over spring break. I have him on tenterhooks.

"Sixth grade," I explain, after the world's biggest gulp. "He was British, and he complimented my strawberry beach towel. We dated for a whole three days."

Chase relaxes in his seat. "Wow. Should I be jealous?"

"Definitely."

"I didn't realize I had any competition." His head cocks a fraction to the left, and the glint in his eye is daring. I had almost forgotten how much of a flirt this boy is.

"Maybe you don't," I say, shrugging one shoulder in an attempt to seem blasé. In reality, the tension is making my pulse accelerate alarmingly. "Never have I ever fallen out with a sibling."

We both drink this time.

"You mean Seth, right?"

"Yeah." Chase's teasing smile has been replaced by a pensive frown. Swinging his legs down from the seat, he readjusts his position to rest his forearms on the table. "We had a pretty big fight after that whole scenario with Kai. I still can't believe he was capable of messing with a sixteen-year-old kid like that."

"He better stay clear," I say bluntly.

"He will, I think." Chase sighs and begins to toy with his

fingers. His crewneck shifts a fraction, and the corner of his crescent moon tattoo winks at me from under the fabric. "I know it doesn't excuse his behavior, but Seth is a complicated guy. He came into the system a lot later on than I did. I was about twelve or thirteen when he moved in."

"So, he remembers his birth parents, then?"

"Unfortunately."

I pull my knees up to my chest and wrap my arms around my shins. It's getting late and the cold has caught up with me. "Do you think you two will stay close?"

"I'll see how it goes," Chase admits. His eyes dart up to mine, assessing my reaction to his reveal. "He's promised that he's going to change, and I want to see if it sticks. I'm just not ready to give up on him yet."

"That's understandable," I encourage. "He's your brother, after all."

"The closest I have to one."

"What about your other foster siblings? Have you ever fallen out with any of them?"

"No, I never really got close enough to disagree with them on anything," Chase replies. He lifts his glass from the table and swigs the final remnants of Pepsi. "I've been trying to talk to them more, now. During my suspension, I helped out with Leo a lot. Watched some animated movies with Oscar. It's not much, but it's a start."

"Really?" My excitement is evident. "You're talking to them more?"

"I'm trying to," Chase corrects sheepishly, placing his empty glass down.

"That's amazing." I reach across the table to squeeze his hand. "I'm so proud of you."

Chase ducks his head shyly, but not before I catch a glimpse of his smile.

"Thanks, gorgeous."

"What have your parents said about it?"

"Mom's pretty delighted," he admits. "I went out to dinner with them last Saturday, for the first time in ages. I won back some points, after the suspension. The fact that the principal has been accused of abusing her power helps too, obviously."

"Of course."

"I think... well, I mean, I know..."

"Know what?"

"I'm pretty certain that I have you to thank for all of this, Erika." Chase tangles our fingers together. His voice is gentle, yet urgent. "I know that it was messy and didn't go the way I expected, but you really did teach me how to open up to people. I didn't realize how closed off I had become before I knew you."

"No," I answer, shaking my head adamantly. "This has got nothing to do with me. You did this on your own. This is all you, Chase."

I watch his smile grow as he contemplates that maybe— just maybe—I'm right.

My mom swings open the front door before we've even reached it.

"Finally!" she exclaims, stepping back to allow us into the house. Her face is flushed with excitement. "How long does the journey from school take? I've been waiting for ages!"

"We went to get iced coffee after I picked them up," Chloe informs her, stepping into the house first and pecking Mom on the cheek as she does so. "Just felt like a nice day for it."

Mom hums a half-hearted response; she's already been distracted by Miko. She beams as Miko kicks off her sneakers on the welcome mat. "How are you today, Mickey? I love those earrings—are they new?"

"Um, I'm good thanks," Miko answers, shooting me a bewildered glance. She touches the cherry earrings hanging from her lobes, as if to remember which wacky pair she's wearing today. "Oh no, I made these a few years ago, I think."

"She's worn them a million times," Chloe mumbles.

Thankfully, Mom doesn't hear.

I step into the house last, clicking the door shut behind me and dropping my rucksack to the floor. Today has been my first normal school day in such a long time. I didn't have to battle a manipulative principal or navigate my spiraling moral compass, and I felt strangely grateful for the mundane worries about my upcoming calculus test. In the canteen, I sat amongst my group of friends and flirted with Chase. While it was nothing special or eventful, I don't think I've ever enjoyed my lunch so much.

I saw Kaito today, too. He was depositing his notebooks into his locker, and chatting with his gangly friend, Lewis. The boy we recruited to fight Chase, that time.

I almost didn't recognize Kai because he was smiling at me.

Even after such a good day, it's still nice to arrive home. The house smells like sandalwood and light floods through the windows. The air-conditioning unit is whirring quietly—a reminder that summer is almost here. Mom wraps an arm around my shoulders, tugging me through the hallway before I've even had the chance to slip off my sandals.

She always makes me take them off in the hallway.

"Mom?" I question, mildly alarmed. "I have my shoes on."

"Get them off, get them off quickly!"

Surprised by her urgency, I step on the heel of each shoe and slide them off while I walk. She continues to pull me towards the kitchen, and I abandon them in the hallway.

"What's happening?"

Mom purses her lips and doesn't reply. She guides me through the door into the kitchen, where an envelope has been propped up meaningfully against the fruit bowl.

"Is that . . . ?"

"It came in the mail today." Mom clasps her hands together. "Your first letter from Stanford!"

27

Birthday Bear

The red logo of Stanford, embellished with a tree, disappears as I fold the letter back together and return it to the kitchen countertop. The left side of my face is tingling with the sensation of being watched. Sure enough, when I glance to the side, three expectant faces eagerly await my reaction. I hurry to construct a convincing smile.

"It's just to thank me for applying," I say dismissively.

"Let's see," Mom enthuses, snatching the paper. She unfolds the letter rapidly, and her pupils flash from side to side as she scans the serif text. By the time that she reaches the final line, the smile on her face has widened significantly. She places the letter back down with a flourish. "Well? How do you feel? You must be so excited!"

"It's just a letter confirming receipt of application, Mom," I reply with an uneasy laugh. "It's not like I'm actually in yet."

"Still," Chloe insists, sliding into one of the opposite bar stools. She's holding a can of lemonade, which opens with a hiss. "It's your first correspondence about college!"

"I guess."

"You don't seem particularly happy about this," Miko observes. She moves around the counter to stand beside Chloe, resting her elbows on the bar and cupping her chin in her hands. She's assessing me with the same analytical expression she wears every time she gives me a present, and she's trying to decipher whether or not I like it.

"I didn't think it was a particularly big deal," I say. I sense the mismanagement of my words as soon as I've spoken, and hurry to correct my mistake. "I mean, if I get a letter of confirmation, that's when I jump for joy, right?"

Chloe and Mom are exchanging worried glances.

"Well, yeah but ..." Chloe mumbles.

"You don't feel at all buzzed about Stanford ... becoming a reality?" Mom asks.

"Sure, it's cool but ... it's not an acceptance."

"Why did you pick that college, Erika?" Miko asks, reaching across the marble counter to squeeze my hand encouragingly. "This isn't a trick question. I'm just curious."

"Because I'm, uh ... good at chemistry and I like running?" I realize that I sound unassured, even to my own ears, but I put it down to being interrogated about my life choices. "Stanford has a really good reputation for both. It's the obvious choice, and it would be an amazing to achievement to get in."

"What do you think about the campus?" Chloe asks curiously.

"It looks pretty in the pictures online."

"Okay. What's your favorite thing about Stanford?"

"I mean ..." I glance around unsurely. "Moving to California would be exciting."

Chloe quirks an eyebrow. "Is that it?"

I stumble over my words. "Um—well, I..."

"What about student life? Which college event are you most excited by?"

"I don't know," I defend, stepping backwards. My hand tears free from Miko's clutch. Three faces watch with me with equal concern, and it seems that whichever way I look, I'm being placed under a microscope and judged for my inadequate answers. "I haven't really thought much about it. What's with the third degree?"

"She's right, girls, stop it," Mom scolds, glaring pointedly at Chloe.

"My palms are sweating," I complain, rubbing my hands over my jeans.

"We're just trying to figure out if it is the right place for you," Miko says gently. "Because a Stanford admin is going to ask you what you like about their college, in your interview. And your current answers aren't very... convincing."

"I just haven't done much research yet," I protest. "I will do before my interview!"

"Erika... these are the questions you should already know the answers to. They should be the reasons you applied in the first place."

I don't know how to respond. I feel utterly overwhelmed.

"I think what they're trying to say, honey," Mom explains cautiously, "is that maybe there's a possibility you like the *idea* of Stanford—particularly the idea of being accepted or winning a scholarship—more than the place itself. Is that something you've considered at all?"

Miko nods in agreement. "Maybe it was more about wanting to prove that you *could* get in than actually going there."

"Why are you saying this?" I take another step backwards.

"We're not trying to scare you. Just consider it for a second," Chloe says.

Images of Stanford flash through my brain, but they blur and disappear before I can grasp them, like a television when the channel keeps changing. If this is my dream college, why don't I have a clear vision of my life when I get there?

And why have I not noticed this missing piece until now?

Despite the deep-seated compulsion to argue against their theory, despite years of study riveted on this one ambition, I can't seem to shake the sinking feeling in my stomach that insists they're right. As I filter through my reasons for choosing Stanford, I'm able to recognize them for what they are: vague, insubstantial, impassionate. When was the last time I felt inclined to research Stanford life? Or became so excited that I started making a ranking of my favorite dorm accommodation?

Truthfully, I don't remember ever doing that.

Maybe I never really wanted to go there. Maybe I've closed off my other options too soon. Maybe my goal was never about the college itself, but about being recognized for my achievements. I contemplate how excited I feel to attend Stanford next fall. Then I think about how Chloe reacted on the day that she received her first mail from Oregon State.

The way that she slid and danced around the kitchen tiles in her socks.

"Oh," I choke out. "Oh, God."

Mom reaches out to tug me to her side. She squeezes her arm around my shoulders and kisses me lovingly on the temple. "You don't need to decide anything right now, you still have time for other applications. It's just something to consider."

I nod faintly. "Lots to think about. Lots to decide."

"Lots of choice," Chloe corrects me, smiling as she takes a sip of her lemonade.

Choice is a much less intimidating word than decision. As I practice using more positive terminology in my mind, it becomes a little easier to process this sudden swing of doubt. Choice isn't scary—choice is freeing.

The feeling Chloe was describing last week makes so much sense to me now. Although my vision for my future is blurry, there is a sense of freedom in being untethered from one goal. I can decide a new path. Any path. Maybe I won't end up at Stanford, after all. Maybe that college does not reflect who I am. Maybe I will consider other places.

As I look around at the three most supportive women in my life, the prospect of discovering a different Erika becomes significantly less daunting. And for the first moment since opening that white envelope, I feel a spark of excitement.

"So," Joe addresses the group, "do we all understand the plan?"

"There's really not that much to grasp," Alec answers, chuckling. A giant birthday boy badge is attached to the lapel of his jacket. "I'm the birthday boy, you're my party guests. We make bears, we eat cake, we embarrass Chase."

The seven of us are gathered in a circle, standing just along from the Build-a-Bear store in the mall. It turns out that the job Chase was always so secretive about is actually as a store assistant in the children's store. Now that I look back on my clues—namely the employee T-shirt he was wearing when he gave me a lift home one time—I can't believe that I didn't piece it together sooner. Joe hasn't revealed the methods behind his discovery but somehow, I doubt he was told directly.

We did our research one lunchtime, and discovered that Chase is responsible for sales, assisting customers, and ... running the birthday bear parties. Naturally, Joe decided to book one for Alec's eighteenth birthday. Chase will most likely be helping to orchestrate the party, but he has no idea that his friends will be the ones attending it.

This is going to be so much fun.

"Let's file in then, troops," Violet declares.

"Here we go," I mumble to Dylan as we follow the others inside.

Lines of stuffed bear faces, unique and neatly arranged on blue shelves, watch cheerily as we enter the store. Alec and Joe stand at the head of the group as the ringleaders of our operation. An assistant is approaching with an apprehensive smile on her face. Her stomach swells under her primary blue apron. I doubt that they are used to hosting parties for a group of seniors here. I hope our arrival doesn't stress the pregnant lady out too much.

"Birthday party for Brian?" she asks nervously. Her face is sweet and round, and her hair is tucked under a blue cap with the store logo embroidered on the front.

"That's me," Alec announces proudly. The fake name was his idea.

"Happy birthday, Brian!" she greets warmly. "My name is Courtney, and I will be your party leader for today. Are all of the guests present?"

I can hear the others answering her, but I've tuned out the

introductory message now and I am helplessly scanning the store, searching for a boy with dark eyes and a flushed face. I wonder where he is, and if he already knows that we're here. I can't wait for him to see this.

"I'll be back in just a minute," Courtney announces. Riley is helping her take the cake to a room at the back of the store. I'm glad that Riley volunteered to carry it because it feels so wrong to ask a pregnant woman to carry *anything*, regardless of its weight. My eyes lazily glaze over the lines of teddy bears, but the one I bought last week still owns my heart.

"What the...?"

I look up at the sound of a familiar voice. Chase is standing a few feet away with a gormless expression on his face. I reach for my Polaroid camera and discreetly take a snap. Joe and Alec are cackling with laughter. Even I can't restrain my grin as I admire his blue store T-shirt and baseball cap. He looks so endearing in his uniform.

"What are you guys doing here?" Chase groans.

"Surprise!" Joe cheers, attacking him into a hug.

Joe's shoulders are shaking with laughter and Chase clutches him back dazedly. His gaze hops around the group, registering everybody present, until it finally lands on me. I am standing at the back, with a guilty hand flapping the Polaroid photo up and down to dry. Chase's mouth curves into a smile for a split second, but his attention is quickly stolen by Joe when the baseball cap is removed from his head.

Joe pulls the hat over his hair. "This party is going to be fun."

"I can't believe you're doing this to me," Chase says, snatching it back.

We stifle our giggles as Courtney and Riley return. If Courtney figures out that the purpose of this party is to prank Chase, I doubt she'd let him continue helping. She explains the schedule of the party and then leads us over to the workstations. Our first step is to choose the animal or bear skin we want to stuff. We gather in a crescent shape around the selection, inspecting the creepy skins of future teddy bears and rabbits.

Miko picks up a gray mouse.

"I shall call her Miko mouse," she announces, holding it up to her face.

"Very clever," I compliment.

A tan-colored teddy is sitting on the shelf below, with woolen fur and a slightly lopsided smile. As I lean down to select my bear, I notice Chase standing just ahead, talking to Alec and Riley. That vivid blue shirt clings to his shoulders and loosens at the small of his back, where his spine curves inwards. I straighten up in no rush.

"Could you be any more obvious?" Miko teases.

I scowl. "Shut up."

Dylan's dimpled grin informs me that he overheard Miko's comment. As he leans forward to pick a stone-colored bear, he playfully bumps against my shoulder. "You are very blatant. What's going on with you two, now?"

"What do you mean?"

"I mean, are you guys official yet?" he presses. Upon my lack of response, he continues. "Because if not, then it's only a matter of time."

"I agree," Miko adds.

"Are you waiting for him to make a move?"

"I don't like these questions," I grumble.

"I think Erika should make the first move," Miko says, a little too loudly. I reach across and smack her on the arm, hushing like a librarian.

"I completely agree."

"Shut up, both of you. He's right there!"

Fortunately for me, Courtney interrupts any further conversation between us when she addresses the group again. While Miko and Dylan may be confined to silence, the announcement of our next workstation doesn't wipe the smug smiles from their faces.

Neither does the next, or the one after that. In fact, their relentless teasing continues throughout the stuffing, stitching, and fluffing stages of our bear creation. By the time that we are nearing the costume section, I'm about ready to tear my teddy bear's head off.

"I'm not going to ask him out!" I snap.

Miko, with her eyes focused on something over my shoulder, chokes out a laugh. Abruptly, she turns around and begins to examine a lime green rockstar outfit for her mouse. Dylan, who had been approaching us with an armful of miniature costumes, pivots promptly on his heel and walks back in the direction from which he came.

Their body language tells me everything that I need to know. Embarrassment floods through my body before I've even heard his voice, but I don't have to wait long.

"Ask who out, gorgeous?"

I can't even say that I'm surprised that Chase heard my declaration. With the amount that Dylan and Miko have been teasing, and their excessive volume, it was an inevitability.

"You, you dumb oaf," I complain, turning around to face him.

"Woah." Chase's eyebrows shoot upwards at my boldness. He raises his palms in surrender. "What have I done? You don't think I'm worth asking out?"

I sigh. "Haven't you got a job to do?"

"Why, is there something that I can help you with today?" He taps his name badge matter-of-factly. "I'd be happy to assist you, Erika."

Turning back to the display of fur accessories, I struggle to conceal my blush.

Chase slides in beside me at the workshop table, leaning back on his palms. His lips are curled into a small smile and his dark eyes flash over my face. I've been waiting to speak to him for a long time. Now that he's finally next to me I can't help but feel an anticipatory tingle in my chest. The fluttery sensation of my self-control fleeing the scene.

"I don't think so, but nice customer service," I compliment, my eyes fixed solely on the teddy bear in my hands. I dare not look over at him again in case the butterflies return.

"Thank you, I appreciate that. So, why not?"

I grab a hairbrush and begin to comb through my teddy bear's fur for the umpteenth time. Nobody is paying attention to us. "Why not what?"

"Ask me out," Chase challenges. "What's wrong with me?"

"You know..." I clear my throat.

Change the topic.

"Actually, I think I do need some assistance."

"Right. Of course."

"I'm a little undecided on how to dress my bear," I improvise, finally looking up at Chase. His eyes are focused on mine and the eye-contact makes a direct hit to the butterfly cavern in my chest, just as I anticipated it would. I hold my perfectly fluffed teddy bear up to show him. "What do you think? A cowgirl? Astronaut? Maybe a president bear?"

Chase clicks his tongue. "Well, we found a Chase bear. Maybe you should make an Erika bear. Recreate yourself."

I was not expecting that answer. "Me?"

"Yup."

Chase plucks the bear from my unexpecting hands and begins to back away towards the dressing station, where the clothes and accessories are located. Violet, Miko, and Dylan have all reached this station already and they look up in surprise at our approach. A mischievous smirk is plastered on his face, and I follow him with suspicion.

"What are you doing?"

"Helping you," he responds innocently. He reaches the dressing station and instantly leans forward to grab a white lab jacket from the occupation outfits. He quickly tucks the teddy's paws through the sleeves and attaches the front of the coat together using the Velcro. "This is because you're really smart, and you're going to work in science one day."

I nod along, far too taken aback to coin a witty response.

He reaches for a little stuffed coffee-cup accessory and attaches it to the bear's paw. "This is because I still owe you that mocha that I spilled down your arm."

He remembers.

"These," he says, reaching for a pair of glittery black sunglasses and tucking them over the bear's snout, "are because you proved yourself to be kind of a badass."

"Very sweet," I remark dryly. There's sarcasm laden in my tone but it's exceedingly obvious that I'm touched by his display. Chase grins as he tucks the teddy bear into my awaiting hands—dressed in a stupid lab coat and sunglasses.

"One last thing," he instructs. I watch as he leans down to collect a pink, sequined heart from one of the displays. He hooks it to the left paw of my bear, before taking a step back to admire his creation. Finally, his buttery brown eyes meet mine.

"A heart?"

"Yes."

"What's that one for?" I whisper.

He smiles slightly. "Because I love you."

He . . . what?

"Yes, you heard correctly."

"Really?" The elation swelling inside of me cannot possibly be contained. It erupts onto my lips, floods warmth into my cheeks and curls my fingers tightly around my teddy bear namesake. "Really? You mean it?"

"You think I'm having you on?" Chase teases.

"I love you too," I say earnestly. "I love you, Squidge."

I barely have time to process the beauty of Chase's smile before our lips unite with mutual exaltation. The teddy bear is forgotten, crushed between our chests as Chase's arms wind around my lower back and tug me impossibly closer. He kisses me with equal tenderness and fervor, fingers digging into my lower back, as if he's trying to imprint this moment in my memory, in my skin forever.

When we pull away, I can still feel the tingle of his peppermint chewing gum on my lips. I love that he is beginning to taste familiar.

He removes a hand from my back and slides it between our bodies to squeeze the pink sequin heart, attached to my teddy bear's paw. His voice is a husky, delicious murmur.

"This is yours. Keep it safe, please."

"I will," I vow. I hope that he can tell how much I mean it.

At the sound of Joe Travis whooping with joy, we step back from our intimate bubble.

Joe has his hands clasped to the back of his head, his elbows high above his shoulders, as he stares at us with the glee of a child on Christmas morning. Miko is wearing a wickedly smug grin, Dylan is laughing, and Violet has her thumbs raised approvingly. Even Alec and Riley have noticed, all the way from the fluffing station. They observe like proud parents: her back is pressed to his chest, and I could swear she seems teary.

Then again, that could just be the bright store lighting.

"Bold kiss for a children's store, dude," Alec calls.

Chase laughs unashamedly.

"So, I take it that you two are official now?" Dylan presses, his eyebrows wiggling in that annoying expression he uses when he knows that he is right.

I look up at the boy beside me. "I'd say he's off the waiting list."

Chase winks.

"So, who won in the end?" Joe asks. His arms fall from his head, and he gestures between us with enthusiasm. "You know, that flirting war you two were having?"

"Definitely me," I say.

Chase shrugs. I don't think he really cares about losing.

"Good choice," Riley commends. "I'm really happy for you guys, but, um..."

"...Courtney doesn't seem so happy," Violet finishes, twisting around to gesture at the grumpy store assistant behind us. Courtney is somehow managing to help two children to stuff their bears, all whilst sending a disapproving glare in our direction. "I think that the kissing might have been *slightly* above the PG rating. Especially with the tots running around."

"Oops," Chase replies, sounding remarkably unapologetic. Removing the baseball cap from his head, he positions it over my hair proudly and tucks my hair behind my ear. "Oh well. It's not like I haven't been in trouble before."

"I promise it wasn't intentional this time," I tease.

In response, he flicks the peak of my cap.

"What do you say we get out of here then?" Alec asks, releasing Riley and rubbing his hands along the side of her arms affectionately. "Take our teddy bears and go back to that pizza place we liked, to celebrate the new couple?"

"I finish work in ..." Chase slides his phone out of his pocket. "Fifteen minutes."

"By the time we all checkout, it'll be five," Miko points out.

"What do you say, gorgeous?" Chase looks down at me, with that captivating half-smile I love so much. His hand laces through mine. "Shall I sneak out of work a few minutes early? Fancy being bad with me, one last time?"

He already knew my answer.

Acknowledgements

This book has been in progress since I was fifteen years old, and we have both grown considerably since that wobbly first draft. It is with the support and encouragement of some incredible people that I have lovingly (and stubbornly) persevered through countless rewrites and plot overhauls to create the story that I always knew it had the potential to be.

I wouldn't be anywhere without my wonderful agent, Joanna Swainson, and the lovely team at Hardman & Swainson agency. Thank you for championing my creative voice for so many years. For not only believing in my potential but offering the insight and push I needed to help me pursue it.

I have been so lucky to work with an editor as energetic and astute as Clem Flanagan. Your input and editorial suggestions have been so valuable, and it's been a joy to collaborate with you on this project. A massive thanks to the team at Black & White Publishing for working so tirelessly to turn my rosy daydreams into a reality.

To my family, friends and boyfriend: I am forever grateful that you continue to listen to my ramblings and messy ideas, and cheer on every single one of my successes.

Finally, I want to give a colossal thank you to my readers, both new and old. Your support, kind messages and loyalty have had a monumental effect on me. You are the reason I can write books, and I will never be able to express how indebted I am to you for that gift.

Lauren Price was born in Coventry in 1999 and recalls spending her childhood with her nose in a book or creating short stories. In her teens she posted her writing on the online platform Wattpad and quickly gained a devoted fanbase for her playful voice and quirky, unorthodox titles. She is a true believer in the unique meet-cute! Lauren can usually be found crying at dog videos, furiously noting to-do lists, or on a train to visit her university friends. She recently graduated from Lancaster – an English Literature degree, of course – and intends to pursue a graduate career in writing.

If you'd like to follow her on socials, she can be found with the username @laurenpwrites.